On The Trail Of King Richard III

L. M. Ollie

Taheke

ON THE TRAIL OF KING RICHARD III

This edition published 1998
by Taheke Press
30 Riverlea Road
Whenuapai, New Zealand
Email: taheke@iconz.co.nz

ISBN 0-473-05234-2

Printed in New Zealand by Wright and Carman (NZ) Limited, Wellington

KING RICHARD III

1452-1485

By courtesy of the National Portrait Gallery, London.

Acknowledgements

My first debt of gratitude must go to History, that great work of convoluted non-fiction where truth often wears a disguise and falsehoods abound.

To the numerous scholars over the years who have contributed substantially to our knowledge of King Richard III and the age in which he lived. I wish to express my thanks and admiration to all those individuals, both professional and amature, who have sought, and continue to seek to learn and publish the truth. From them I have drawn my sources, and my inspiration.

To the Richard III Society and its members, many of whom infused me with a deep sense of caring for this strange and enigmatic man.

L. M. Ollie
April, 1998

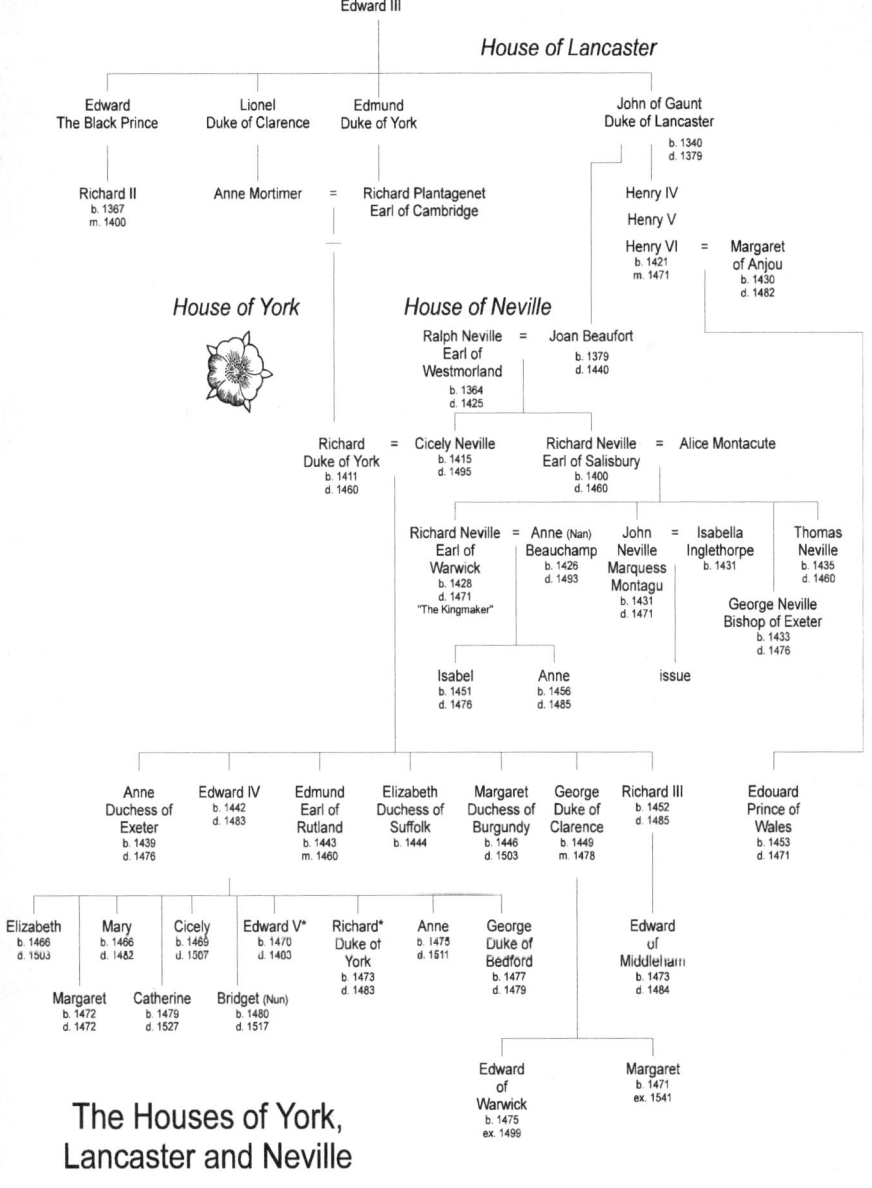

The Houses of York, Lancaster and Neville

* "Princes in the Tower"

© L. M. Ollie 1996 - 1998

Disclaimer

Although this work is fiction, special care has been taken to preserve historical accuracy within the bounds of the storyline which is, of itself, a product of the author's imagination. Any resemblance to actual persons or events in modern time is strictly coincidental.

□ Edinburgh
° Berwick

° Middleham

Preston °   ° York
                             ° Pontefract

                  ° Nottingham

Ludlow °   Bosworth °   ° Leicester
              ° Warwick
Littledean °   ° Tewkesbury   ° Fotheringhay

                              ° St. Albans
            Windsor °   □ London

On the Trail of
King Richard III

© L. M. Ollie 1996

Dedication

To my beloved daughter Alicia
a symbol of the hope we all must sustain.

August 22nd,1485
The Field of Redemore, England

King Richard:

> *Up with my tent! here I will lie tonight;*
> *But where to-morrow?*

Shakespeare -
The Tragedy of King Richard the Third
[Act V, Scene 3]

He stood just outside the King's pavilion and watched as the first pale glimmer of dawn encroached upon the landscape, eclipsing the terrors that beset the night. Around him the camp stirred listlessly. A mummer here and there, a stifled cry, shouts half heard, carried on a freshening wind, screaming of watchfulness and smelling of the primeval fear so long associated with impending death. His coal-black eyes surveyed the scene with infinite care, missing nothing, but none dared meet his gaze nor turn in his direction.

"Long has it been so." He mused, turning the thought over and over in his mind, delighting in the knowledge of the terror he evoked in the minds and hearts of the ignorant, the superstitious and the unwary. He was pleased, for was that not his intention, was that not his reason for being? And soon, yes very soon, he would be free of this, free to hunt anew and glory in chaos and the hopelessness of all mankind.

King Richard, third of that name of the House of Plantagenet, lay like a man newly racked, his skin deathly pale, his body frail beyond endurance. His face betrayed the knowledge of a sleepless night and his eyes had fear in them.

"The Dragon is on the move my lord. 'Tis time."

"The priest, where is he?"

"Gone Sire, with neither the holy blood nor the wafers to say the Mass or ease thy soul in the coming trial. No matter. Steel shall be thy strong right arm, thy armour a shield against this bastard Welsh pretender. Come my lord, I shall help thee make ready."

He turned from him then, and in a voice beyond mortal hearing, whispered - "Time to fight Plantagenet. Time to die."

Present Day
Toronto, Canada

Duchess of York:
> *My husband lost his life to get the crown,*
> *And often up and down my sons were toss'd,*
> *For me to joy and weep their gain and loss…*
> *Make war upon themselves; brother to brother,*
> *Blood to blood, self against self:*

Shakespeare -
The Tragedy of King Richard the Third
[Act II, Scene 4]

Who's carrying your bag Gail?"

"Damn it, don't scare me like that."

"I scared you?" Laura chuckled as she unfolded herself and pushed away from the frame of the bedroom door where she had been standing for the past few minutes, watching unnoticed, as Gail finished her packing. "What's in there?" she said, marvelling at close range Gail's massive suitcase while at the same time ignoring the chaos around her.

"Maybe the list would be shorter if I told you what isn't in there. Have you brought the itinerary?"

"Yes, and don't change the subject." Laura growled goodnaturedly as she fought for space on what was left of Gail's bed. "Look, there's no way you're going to be able to handle this monster. Some of the hotels in the UK have diabolical staircases meaning multiple, narrow, steep, uneven, shallow and most of the time poorly lit, so you'll be lucky if all you break is a leg. Do yourself a favour, find another, smaller bag."

"I got it on sale, a great buy and I love the colours so don't start." Finding just enough room on the bed, diagonally across from Laura, Gail lowered the lid of the suitcase to provide a natural table top. "Did you manage to get the tickets?"

Laura smiled wickedly. "Actors on rollerskates pretending to be trains?"

"*Starlight Express.* Come on, did you get them?"

"Best in the house."

"Yes," Gail exclaimed, adding two thumbs up for emphasis. "Okay, I'm ready. Let's hear what you've got planned since you've insisted upon keeping the itinerary a secret."

Laura hesitated for a moment, seeming to gather her strength as well as her thoughts. "I've set a theme for this trip, bearing in mind, of course, your request to see the grotesque, the macabre, the haunted and the downright disgusting." Gail chuckled. "A specific historical era and a particular individual."

"Yeah," Gail said, suddenly wary, "who?"

"The last Plantagenet, Richard, Duke of Gloucester, later King Richard III – born 1452, died 1485."

"You mean old hunchback, murdered-his-nephews-in-the-tower thus forfeiting the Uncle of the Year Award, Richard III? The, 'a horse, a horse, my kingdom for a horse' Richard III?"

"The same," Laura replied, offering up her most diabolical smile. "Okay smarty, so you know your Shakespeare but, do you know your history?"

She reached inside her jacket pocket then placed a full-colour, postcard-sized picture on top of the suitcase directly in front of Gail. "Here's a copy of his portrait by an unknown artist."

Gail picked up the picture and studied it closely, her head to one side, her brow knotted.

Laura watched her carefully. "I can't remember when I first became intrigued by him. Perhaps it was after reading Josephine Tey's novelette *The Daughter of Time.* The hero of that piece found it hard to believe that this face belongs to one of history's most notorious murderers. I guess I have the same problem."

"So, this is what he looked like. I agree, it's a nice face, but look, even in our time there've been mass murderers with faces like angels. What is it you hear? 'Such a nice boy, quiet, never in any sort of trouble.' Yeah, right, and unbeknown to everyone, all unsuspecting, he's torturing and murdering all over the place, burying the bodies after snacking on the choices bits. Sorry, looks are skin deep, but evil? Right to the bone baby." She dropped the picture in such a way that it landed with the face staring straight up at Laura.

Almost hesitantly she picked it up. Was Gail right? The face had a strained, almost anxious look about it, as if he were in pain. Why, and what sort of pain?

"Well, interested Gail? Feel like making a comparison between the Shakespearean version of the facts and what has been written in recent times by noted historians? After all, Shakespeare did such a good job that his side of the story became the accepted classroom history text for hundreds of years."

Laura knew that Gail would not, could not, resist such a challenge. She knew her Shakespeare, and the Bard was practically sacrosanct. Would she admit that his play was a piece of historical fiction written during Tudor times to please a Tudor Queen? Would he bend the truth to the breaking point just to see his work performed? Did he malign Good King Richard just to make a buck? Laura started to laugh and promptly slipped off the bed.

"You're getting weirder and weirder, do you know that?" Gail said as she surveyed her sister-in-law sprawled on the floor. "Come on downstairs, nut case. There's a fresh pot of coffee waiting." Gail was halfway across the room when she shot back over her shoulder. "Now I know why you were so interested in knowing if I'd studied Shakespeare's *Richard III* in school, and whether or not I understood it, cheeky bitch."

Laura chuckled. "Well, did you?" Slowly she rose, brushing imaginary dust bunnies from her jean jacket before making her way around the bed, carefully avoiding bits of clothing, magazines, an umbrella.

"As a matter of fact, I rented Olivier's *Richard III* from the video store about a month ago. Still get goose bumps just thinking about it. Scary stuff. He was a monster, and the worst part was that he was so charming too. Are you saying that Shakespeare had it all wrong?" Gail had stopped at the top of the stairs to wait for Laura.

"Oh no, Richard was charming all right." Laura caught up and together they made their way down the broad, carpeted staircase. "There are thousands of people right now all around the world who agree with that. It's the monster part that's causing all the problem and on that score, there's plenty of debate. You wouldn't believe the number of books written about him. There's a Richard III Society too. Lots of people belong. They're called Ricardians, and their aim is to basically rewrite history."

"Why?" Gail shrugged, "the guy's been dead for what, 500 years?"

"That's what I mean. Why? I'm talking about a lot of intelligent, professional people here who care deeply about this man's reputation. Anyhow, I think it'll be fun to follow the trail as it were, visit the places associated with him, and hopefully meet some Ricardians and find out the truth. Well, what do you think?"

"This is going to be a fun trip isn't it? I mean, lots of shopping, theatre and such?"

Laura frowned. "Of course. Why, what's the problem?"

"Nothing." Gail said as she moved away. "I'll get the coffee."

"Right, that's it." Laura announced as she finished going over the itinerary. "A copy for you so you can show Wayne and the girls, and, I guess you might as well have this old road atlas. It's out of date so I had a new one sent." She sighed as she gathered her notes together. "I warn you, the driving is going to be hell on wheels.

Sorry, but you did say you wanted to see as much of England as possible, so I …"

Laura was interrupted at this point when the doorbell rang. Gail hurried off then returned with a pizza delivery box and, with a flourish, dropped it on the table. "Ordered this early this morning for noon delivery. Roger warned me you were coming over so I ordered the pizza, bought a bottle of claret, trashed my bedroom and I might add, read up a little on the Kings and Queens. It was a toss-up between Mary Queen of Scots and Richard. I couldn't see us doing Mary all the way from London, so that left Richard. You've mentioned him before you know and I must admit, it's an interesting story. Who knows, maybe we'll end up joining the Richard III Society."

"I doubt if we quality."

"Why not?"

"Well, for one thing I read somewhere that most of the members are female, left-handed and librarians, which rules us out, on two counts anyway. And, you have to believe that Richard was a good guy and frankly I don't think he was, even after discounting all the Tudor propaganda."

"What do you think he was?"

"I'm not sure yet," Laura said with a shrug. "Perhaps he was no better or worse than his contemporaries. With the childhood he had, maybe he could best be described as justifiably certifiable."

"You mean he was nuts?"

Laura chuckled. "Maybe. Certainly something was wrong somewhere."

"Wait a minute while I get organized then you can tell me all about his childhood while we have lunch."

Gail disappeared into the kitchen, leaving Laura to settle into the breakfast room next door. The patio doors were open to the warmth of yet another beautiful August summer morning. It was a lovely room with its profusion of plants and dried flower arrangements, but Laura also liked it because it was the only room in which Gail allowed smoking.

"Right, I think I've got everything," Gail announced as she prepared the table.

"Are you sure you want to hear this?"

"Come on, maybe we can get some clues from those early, formative years. Tell me."

"Okay," Laura said with a sigh, "but the truth is he had one hell of a childhood."

Slowly, methodically, Laura eased Gail back through time more than five hundred years to an age of unspeakable violence, sudden death, treachery and deceit. Richard was born on October 2nd, 1452, the last surviving son of Richard, Duke of York and Cicely Neville. He had three older brothers. Edward was ten years old, Edmund was nine and George was four when Richard was born. There were sisters too. With the exception of Richard, all the children seemed to have inherited their mother's fair good looks and excellent constitution. Richard resembled his father - slender, dark haired and short of stature. He may well have been a sickly child. Although certainly not the deformed monster of Tudor propaganda, he lacked the sheer physical presence of his brothers, especially Edward, who epitomised the physical ideal of kinglike majesty.

The Wars of the Roses, in the midst of which Richard was born, involved two competing royal Houses - York and Lancaster. The prize was the throne of England and absolute power. The King, Henry VI, was mentally ill. His wife, Margaret of Anjou, was a rapacious woman whose ruling passion was her young son Edouard who was one year younger than Richard. A power struggle between the forces of the Duke of York and the Royalists was inevitable. When Richard's father reached for the golden prize, it was too late. In December, 1460, at the Battle of Wakefield, Richard lost his father, an uncle and his brother Edmund. Queen Margaret ordered that their heads be struck off and displayed atop Micklegate Bar in York.

The 'Story', as it came to be called, unfolded further as various characters leapt from the pages of history to succeed or fail on the whim of chance. Richard's exile in Burgundy, his brother Edward's successful bid for the throne when Queen Margaret overplayed her hand and lost the support of the people. The bloody Battle of Towton where 28,000 men perished, crippling the powerbase of the House of Lancaster. The coronation of a new king - Edward IV - June , 1461. From penniless exile, Richard now stood third in line of succession to the English throne. He was not yet nine years of age.

King Edward was a popular monarch who readily won the hearts of his subjects. Young Richard basked in the reflected glory of his brother's reign and adored him as he adored his mentor and namesake, Richard Neville, Earl of Warwick, known as the *Kingmaker*. Warwick, however, was not content just to make a king, he was determined to rule him as well and this Edward refused to allow. Hostilities increased when Edward secretly married Elizabeth Wydville, a commoner and widow five years older than him. A known Lancastrian, she had been a maid of honour to Queen Margaret. The court was appalled. Greedy, ambitious and arrogant, Elizabeth also had a large family, all of whom King Edward would be expected to provide for as befitting the dignity of the Queen's relatives. The elevation of the Wydville clan to positions of rank well beyond their humble origins caused considerable friction at court, ultimately leading to pro and anti-Wydville factions.

For nearly four years Richard escaped the wranglings of court life high in the moorlands at Middleham in Yorkshire. Under the watchful eye of the Earl of Warwick, Richard learned martial arts and courtly manners as well as receiving a conventional education. They were to be the happiest years of his life.

In February, 1469, just sixteen years of age, Richard, now entitled Duke of Gloucester, presided at a commission in Salisbury set up to try two alleged traitors - Thomas Hungerford and Henry Courtenay - both of whom were subsequently found guilty and executed. King Edward's determination to keep his youngest brother at his side and to involve him more and more in the administration of raw power had a sinister side. Trouble was brewing and treason rode the winds.

Sickened by the power and influence of the Wydvilles and by Edward's adulterous and excessive lifestyle, Warwick was bent on overthrowing the king he had created and placing on the throne instead his son-in-law George, Duke of Clarence, Richard's only other surviving brother. At the battle of Edgecote in June, 1469, Warwick's forces captured and executed Elizabeth Wydville's father and brother, John. King Edward was captured a few days later and taken first to Warwick Castle then to Middleham. Richard's whereabouts at this time are unknown.

Unable to govern with Edward still alive, and yet unwilling to see to his death, Warwick had no option but to release the young King after a few weeks captivity. Encouraged by the Queen to avenge the death of her father and brother, Warwick and Clarence were branded traitors. By this time Richard was old enough to bring an army of his own to bear, but not quick enough and Warwick and Clarence were able to escape to France.

In desperation Warwick negotiated an arrangement with Margaret of Anjou. In exchange for the return of all his properties, Warwick promised to support the Lancastrian cause, restore Henry VI to the throne of England and defeat Edward with a combined army of Lancastrian, Neville and French forces. As a token of his good faith, he offered his younger daughter Anne in marriage to the Queen's son, Edouard. George Clarence's dream of a crown vanished and worse, he realised that there would be no place in a Lancastrian realm for a son of York.

Warwick succeeded beyond his wildest dreams despite the fact that Edward, Richard, the Queen's brother Anthony (Earl Rivers) and William, Lord Hastings were able to take ship for the Low Lands. For the second time, Richard was to know the bitterness of defeat and exile. He was not quite eighteen.

On the 2nd of November, 1470, Elizabeth Wydville gave birth to a son within the sanctuary of Westminster Abbey. With the knowledge of a healthy male heir after a succession of daughters, Edward was inspired to reclaim his throne and put an end to the House of Lancaster - forever. With help from Charles, Duke of Burgundy, Edward set sail for England with a fleet of fourteen ships and a small army. Caught off guard, Warwick was at Coventry when news of Edward's triumphant arrival in London reached him. Disillusioned by Warwick, George Clarence defected and the three brothers were reunited.

At the Battle of Barnet, the forces of the Earl of Warwick were defeated. Warwick and his brother Montague were slain, their bodies publicly displayed at St. Paul's. French forces landed at Weymouth, and although Margaret of Anjou was initially disheartened to hear the news of Warwick's death, she was determined to raise a new army in Wales and Lancashire. Heavy rains, however, hampered her journey north so by the time she reached Tewkesbury, her army was too exhausted to continue.

The battle that followed was nasty and decisive. Richard's forces played a major role in the ultimate defeat of the enemy, many of whom died on the 'Bloody Meadows'. Young Edouard was slain on the field although it has been suggested by many, including Shakespeare, that he was captured then murdered by Edward, aided by his two brothers. What is known is that those Lancastrians who sought sanctuary within Tewkesbury Abbey were dragged out, given a hasty trial then executed in the marketplace. A few days later Margaret of Anjou was captured and handed over to Edward who displayed her like a prize of war during his triumphal procession through the streets of London.

With the son dead, it was the father's turn. On the morning of the 22nd of May, 1471, Henry VI was found dead in the Wakefield Tower. Although the official cause of death was reported as 'pure displeasure and melancholy', the chronicler John Warkworth wrote the following: -

'And the same night that King Edward came to London, King Henry, being inward in prison in the Tower of London, was put to death, the 21st of May, on a Tuesday night, between eleven and twelve of the clock, being then at the Tower the Duke of Gloucester, brother to King Edward, and many others; and on the morrow he was chested and brought to Paul's, and his face was open that every man might see him; and in his lying he bled on the pavement there; and afterward at the Black Friars was brought, and there he bled new and fresh; and from thence he was carried to Chertsey Abbey in a boat, and buried there in our Lady Chapel.'

"So," Gail mused, her head tilted to one side, "Richard did murder the old King, just like Shakespeare said he did."

"Looks like it." Laura replied with a shrug. "Chalk one up under the heading 'regicide' Gail." She smiled thinly.

"What's that?"

"A king killer."

"Nice one."

"Well, you asked about Richard's early years and, there it is. Fair to say isn't it, that late in the evening of May 21st, 1471, not yet nineteen years old, Richard Plantagenet, Duke of Gloucester became a major force in his own right. He had learned some powerful lessons on the road to adulthood, many from individuals whose ruthlessness was as uncompromising as it was heartless. A product of his age, we can tut tut all we want, but unless we're prepared to put ourselves in his shoes and see the world as he saw it, none of us can pass judgement. Richard Gloucester lived in a violent age, rent with civil war, treachery and sudden death. Twice he was exiled, declared a traitor and stripped of wealth and power. His father, brother and an uncle were brutally slain, their bodies defiled. He had seen Edward betrayed by his own brother George and by Warwick, a man Richard had looked up to and admired almost as a father. In the final frame Richard walked from the Tower of London with the blood of a dead king on his hands, as cold and ruthless as all the rest. Political Realism expressed in its most lethal form."

"Is it too late to do Mary Queen of Scots instead?"

"I'm going after this man Gail, and before I'm done, I'll have some answers to quite a few questions. One thing I do know already though, he was a thoroughly not nice proposition." Slowly she began to gather her material together.

When she looked up, Gail was gnawing at her lower lip, her concern obvious. "What do you mean by 'go after'?"

"You'll see." Laura said with casual ease.

"Leave her alone Gail." Wayne said, as he tried unsuccessfully to suppressed a yawn."

"I'm worried about her. Roger says she's practically obsessed with this man. She's not eating. I bet you she's lost ten, fifteen pounds since you last saw her."

"So what. Laura's tall and slim and you're neither. Sometimes I think you're jealous of her."

"That's not fair." Gail huffed. "If anything, she's jealous of me. You know she loves the girls. If she would just stop and even consider the idea of starting a family, then maybe everything would be okay again." Tears came to her eyes. "I know Roger's not happy."

"I've told you before, it's none of your business." Wayne warned.

"Roger says that … "

"Roger says, Roger says. That's the problem, isn't it? Both of you, nattering at her all the time. Let her be. Losing her parents like that and no family to turn to, I would think that you, of all people would be more supportive of her."

"I am, but … "

"No buts. Laura's paying for this trip, so why don't you just enjoy it. If she's got an interest in this king, whoever he is, I think that's great. At least she's getting out of herself."

"This king is a nasty piece of work." Gail growled as she tugged the duvet up to her chin.

"From what I remember of the English monarchy, none of the kings were very nice and a few of the queens too." Wayne chuckled. "Look on the bright side. Maybe next year she'll switch to Egyptian history and you'll finally get to see the Nile."

"Maybe you're right, but I can't shake the feeling that she has something in mind, something … I don't know. There's been some strange people at her parent's cottage this summer. Roger says they're wackos."

"Roger would." Wayne said as another yawn erupted. "I'm tired. I've had a busy day and, from the sounds of it, so have you. Go, have a great time and don't worry about me, the girls or anything else for that matter."

Gail chuckled. "No doubt you and Roger have things planned. I hope you two behave yourselves."

"Didn't Roger tell you? He's planning a business trip. I wish my firm had such exotic locales." He stared at Gail fixedly. "As I said, give Laura a break."

"And what's that suppose to mean?"

"I think you know exactly what it means."

Day 1
London, England

This blessed plot, this earth, this realm, this England,
This nurse, this teeming womb of royal kings,

Shakespeare -
The Tragedy of King Richard the Second
[Act II, Scene 1]

"Breakfast is coming." Laura whispered as she slipped into her seat.

Gail pushed her blanket back, stretched effusively and yawned. "Where did you go?"

"To the back of the plane. I found two empty crew seats."

"I hope you didn't try to sneak a cigarette. I've heard that passengers who do get handed a parachute."

"I'm patched."

"You're what?"

"Nicotine patches - I'm on the drip feed." Laura smiled wickedly. "What to try one? Guaranteed to be a blast for a nonsmoker."

Gail fixed Laura with her best 'we are not amused' look, then went to work trying to extricate her carry-on bag from under the seat in front. Laura turned in her seat far enough to allow Gail to pass and join the small queue forming at the rear of the plane. Before she moved on however, she leaned over and whispered in Laura's ear. "Actually, I'm proud of you. You've held up very well, with or without aid."

"It ministers, it does not gratify." Laura growled.

Gail patted her shoulder. "Poor monkey."

The Boeing 747 descended rapidly through a thin bank of cloud, corrected its course, then levelled out, cruising effortlessly at 150 knots as it prepared for final approach into one of the world's busiest airports - London Heathrow. Securely belted in their seats, some passengers' eager anticipation erupted into conversation while others checked then re-checked documentation or sat staring out the window, perhaps seeing the lush green of the English countryside for the first time.

Earlier, after a Continental breakfast, Laura and Gail had busied themselves filling in their arrival forms. The usual name, address, nationality, but Gail came to a screeching halt on the line marked 'Occupation'. "What do you think I should put down? I hate *housewife* and there's not enough room to put cleaner, school committee member, Halloween costume maker, cook, closet organizer, orphan sock finder …"

"Put down 'Lifestyle Co-ordinator'."

"Lifestyle Co-ordinator - I like that. One of yours?"

Laura nodded as she slid her completed form inside her Passport. Ruefully she had written 'Company Director'. A grandiose title, but the truth was that her little company had not proven as successful as she had hoped. Warned by those in the know, she was learning the hard way that being paid for 'services rendered' - computer training - was a hopeless task. She had boarded the aircraft with only a portion of the receivables paid, or ever likely to be.

Still childless after ten years of marriage, Laura's relationship with her husband had deteriorated rapidly over the past few months. The trip, it was hoped, would provide a breathing space for both of them; a chance to review options; an opportunity to think things through. Laura idly tapped the arm of her seat with her fingertips as she thought of her husband, Roger, who was, perhaps at that very moment, sleeping with another woman - a divorcee with a young son. Oh yes, Laura knew what was happening and she also knew that Gail had been instrumental in introducing this woman to her brother. It only remained now for Laura to choose just the right moment, when Gail was sufficiently off guard to … Laura smiled inwardly. *"Plenty of time yet. Let her enjoy herself - for awhile at least."*

Laura threaded her way between mounds of luggage, skirting tightly formed knots of hotel guests clutching tattered itineraries, their voices raised in anxious anticipation of the day's events. With a heavy sigh she dropped into the soft leather sofa beside Gail. "Bad news, I'm afraid. Our room won't be ready for at least two hours."

Gail groaned. "An eight hour flight, a delayed departure, it's ten in the morning but it feels like midnight and I want - I need - a shower." She groaned again, louder this time.

"Buck up old thing, at least we're here. London lies at our feet, waiting, so let's do it. We've got Westminister Abbey, Madam Tussauds, Herrods, London Dungeons, Covent Garden, Piccadilly. Buckingham Palace and the Royal Mews are just across the road."

"Madam Tussauds first." Gail said, suddenly excited.

"You got it."

"Well, what do you think?" Gail asked as she proudly held up a souvenir photo of herself, taken with a waxen Arnold Schwarzenegger."

"Very nice." Laura said as she luxuriated in the roomy interior of an English taxi.

"I'm going to take it out of its frame and tell Wayne that I met Arnold, we had lunch together and …"

"You'd lie to your husband?" Laura was scandalised.

Gail shrugged. "He wouldn't believe me anyhow. Nothing exciting ever happens to me."

Laura smiled wickedly as she turned towards the window. "Maybe we can change that." She whispered under her breath.

By the time they arrived back at their hotel it was nearly two o'clock. Laura watched, fascinated as Gail tried to wrestle monster bag onto her bed. "Do you want some help?"

"No, just stay there smoking that damn cigarette and watch me get a hernia." Gail said from the floor where she had positioned herself in the hope that she might be able to push the case upwards.

Laura relented and between the two of them they managed to get it onto the bed. Laura retrieved her cigarette from the ashtray. "Tell me when you're finished with it. For God's sake, don't push it off the bed or it'll end up in the lounge downstairs." Laura had to raise her voice at the end as Gail entered the bathroom, determined to take a quick shower. "Don't be long. Next stop, Westminister Abbey, resting place of kings and queens."

Gail stuck her head around the corner. "Is Richard buried there?"

"His wife Anne is, but no one knows where he's buried, if indeed, he's buried at all."

"That's strange isn't it?"

Laura considered the question. "There's a lot about Richard Plantagenet which is singular in the extreme."

"Why didn't you want to stand beside him at Madam Tussauds so I could take your picture?"

"I'm not a complete tourist you know. Come on, hurry up."

"Well, what did you think of Westminster?" Laura said over top of her wine glass. They had chosen their hotel restaurant for dinner, partly because it offered an 'Early Bird Dinner Special' plus, they were both extremely tired now and the knowledge that their beds were so close, appealed.

"Beautiful, but honestly, you tell the most disgusting stories. Where do you get all that stuff from anyway?"

"What stuff? You mean about Mary Queen of Scots' execution being botched?" Laura chuckled.

"And Elizabeth the First blowing out her coffin because she

hadn't been embalmed properly. Cromwell being dug up, the body hung at Tyburn before being decapitated." Gail shook her head in disbelief.

"Henry VII has a nice tomb though, don't you think? I especially liked the angels sitting on the lid making sure he can't get out."

Gail took a couple of sips of her wine. "Well, brat child, if you insist upon relating your disgusting anecdotes and we're planning to visit the Tower tomorrow, you had better tell me more of the Story. Last I heard Richard was wiping his blade on his pants and his brother was trying on crowns."

"My notes are upstairs." Laura said weakly.

"That's okay, I'll wait."

"Thanks a lot." Laura pushed her chair back. She was assisted by a member of the staff. Explaining the need to get something from her room, she made her apologies and left.

By the time she returned, Gail had finished her wine and had ordered another. Their meals had not yet arrived. Assisted back into her seat, she glared at Gail. "And what did your last slave die from?"

"Never mind. Have you seen the dessert trolley?" Gail's eyes fairly danced with delight.

"Not interested." Laura said with a shrug of indifference as she sorted through her notes. In all the years that Laura had known Gail, there was one constant - desserts. Gail had a passion for them, for anything sweet. Oh, Laura could, upon occasion, be tempted with a piece of chocolate, but Gail? Laura figured it would be only a matter of time before the trolley, ladened with pies, cream tarts, custard, trifle, death-by-chocolate cake, would find its way to Gail's side totally unaided.

"You need a sweet now and then to keep your strength up,"

Laura had heard this argument before. "I don't want to keep my strength up and even if I did, I'd opt for a nice B and B, not a sticky cake."

"You drink too much." Gail huffed.

"Perhaps, but by the time I've finished with this you'll probably need a stiff drink too. Ready?"

"Ready."

"With King Henry out of the way, things began to settle down. The House of Lancaster had been virtually wiped out, with a few notable exceptions, and everyone was looking forward to stable government and an end to civil war. The second half of Edward's reign may have begun as Shakespeare suggested at the end of his play - Henry VI, Part 3 - with Edward's final speech.

And now what rests but that we spend the time
With stately triumphs, mirthful comic shows,
Such as befit the pleasure of the court?
Sound, drums and trumpets! farewell, sour annoy!
For here, I hope, begins our lasting joy.

"Translated, it means 'let's party'. There have been many and various descriptions of King Edward IV, but one thing they all have in common is that he was a picture of a perfect king in his youth but as time wore on, his excessive nature began to affect his health and judgement. He was seen frequently outside 'All You Can Eat Dessert Bars' and showed up at Council meetings with sticky fingers."

Laura started to laugh and was kicked by Gail under the table. Just then their dinners arrived, carried by a bemused waiter who had no doubt seen this little performance. Laura rearranged the table, allowing room for her meal and her notes. Years of study had given her the unique ability to read, converse and eat, all at the same time.

Hardly stopping to admire their beautifully presented plates, they began, and except for the odd exclamation regarding the excellence of the meal, they ate in silence. Laura gave up first, unable to finish her plate. "Shall I continue?" She said, drawing her notes closer and her plate away.

"Yes, please." Gail said, not looking up.

"Not to put too fine a point on it, Eddie began to overindulge himself, not only with food and wine, but with women too, so that he became fat, lazy and lecherous in the extreme. A lesson to us all." Laura cleared her throat suggestively, took a sip of wine and then continued. "His Queen must have turned a blind eye to all this, perhaps seeing advantages in his adultery and its attendant guilt to press him for more and more favours for her family.

"Richard was no doubt eager to get out of London and away from court. He may have disapproved of his brother's lifestyle, but he couldn't have done so too strenuously since it would appear that he had a least one mistress and was supporting two bastard children - John and Katherine."

Gail looked up, shocked. "Naughty boy."

"Mistresses, illegitimate children, no big deal in those days or any days for that matter." Laura shrugged. "Anyhow, since Edward was content to rest on his laurels, enjoying a good time at court, Richard took upon himself the task of securing the realm in his brother's name. I'm not going into all the grants, titles and land transfers with which Edward rewarded those faithful to him. Suffice to say that Richard was amply rewarded by his brother, especially in the north.

"Before leaving London to take up permanent residence in Yorkshire, he asked Anne Neville - Warwick's daughter - to marry him. She consented, which shouldn't come as a surprise considering her situation. Her father was a grade-A traitor and she had been married, or at least betrothed, to the late and unlamented Edouard Lancaster, Prince of Wales. Richard was no fool. By marrying Anne, he would inherit all the rights to Warwick's northern holdings and, he hoped, a share of the Beauchamp estates which Warwick had inherited through his wife. Anne would also provide him with necessary introductions to the clan-like northern families. Although in all likelihood King Edward didn't approve of the match and perhaps foresaw some difficulties with brother George, he finally gave his consent.

"In July, 1471 Richard headed north with his own household and retainers and took up residence at Middleham, which must have pleased him no end. He was also granted the former Neville lordships of Sheriff Hutton and Penrith and the whole of Warwick's holdings in Yorkshire and Cumberland. Not a bad start for a kid not quite nineteen years old."

"This kid had already murdered someone." Gail huffed. "That's a start too."

Laura shrugged. "Hey, he only did what he had to do."

"Yeah, sure. Continue."

"Thank you. By the autumn of 1471, Richard was back in London on urgent family business. George - and I should use his title - Duke of Clarence, was dead set against Richard's marriage to Anne, his sister-in-law. Ever the dog in the manger, George insisted that all of the Beauchamp lands were his and went so far apparently as to have Anne hidden in an inn in London to keep her out of Richard's hands. Richard's spy network soon found her and she was taken to St. Martin's to await the King's pleasure.

"Although King Edward was capable of extreme anger - a hallmark of the Plantagenets I might add - he was generally the type of man who tried to make all the people happy all the time. The brothers argued back and forth in private until finally the case was handed over to an official hearing. A temporary arrangement was sorted out but the wrangle between the two Dukes was to continue for some time.

"Anne and Richard were cousins as well as in-laws and a papal dispensation should have been sought prior to their union, but this formality was overlooked and they were married, in July I think, 1472. Richard's son Edward was born in December, 1473, at Middleham."

"He had a son? I didn't know that." Gail was genuinely surprised.

"You see, the Bard missed that. Didn't even mention it."

"Just the best reason going for murdering the Princes though, isn't it?" Gail said, smiling maliciously. "A clean succession - thanks Dad."

"I see, so you like Shakespeare's version better? Usurp the throne and kill the kids just for fun? Don't bother mentioning the fact that Richard was a family man."

"Will just used poetic licence, that's all."

"Oh well, that's all right then." Laura replied derisively. "We wouldn't want historical fact to get in the way of a good story line, now would we? Shall I continue?"

"Sure."

"While her estates were being argued over, the widowed Countess of Warwick remained in sanctuary at Beaulieu Abbey. In June 1473, Richard had her brought to Middleham to be with her daughter prior to the birth of young Edward. Speculation on Richard's reasons for having her under his roof range from 'isn't he the nicest boy' to 'that will shut the old bag up'. Apparently, she had been writing to anyone of importance complaining about the unfair treatment she had received regarding her estates. She had every right to complain. Apparently she had been stripped of her inheritance by her two darling son-in-laws. Actions which were technically illegal, by the way, so the boys circumvented the law by having her declared legally dead. Nice trick, eh?"

"Could they do that?" Gail asked, surprised.

"They were royal dukes. What do you think?"

"You mean they got away with it because of who they were? That's not fair."

Laura chuckled. "Fair, yes well, I think if you check down through history you'll find that the law, despite every effort, tends to bend a little under pressure." She paused for a sip of wine.

"Anyhow, after his success with his mother-in-law, Richard put the screws on another widow, the dowager-countess Elizabeth Howard. She was the mother of the Earl of Oxford, one of the last surviving Lancastrian supporters and menace at large. Richard was granted the lands of her rebel son but the lady had considerable holdings in her own right which Richard wanted as well. He took her into custody, ostensibly to prevent her from helping her son's cause and then terrorized her into surrendering her inheritance to him despite the fact that he had absolutely no right to it. He didn't use physical force or anything. The tactic he used was to suggest that she come up for a visit to Middleham, a journey which, because of her age, the distance and the fact that it was winter, would most certainly have killed her."

"That's terrible!"

"Terrible or not, it worked a treat and he got away with it. King Edward obviously turned a blind eye despite the fact that he knew that what his brother was doing was unlawful. Actually, many estates were carved up by George and Richard without regard for the feelings of others." Laura caught their waiter's eye. "Want another glass of wine Gail?"

"Sure, why not?"

Laura smiled. "Not worried about drinking too much tonight?"

"No husband, no kids, get on with the Story."

"Whatever you say, ma'am. Now, where was I? Okay, in 1476 - Richard would be twenty four by then - the remains of his father and brother Edmund were taken from their resting place at Pontefract and reburied with solemn ceremony at Fotheringhay. It was probably the last time that Edward, George and Richard were together on reasonably friendly terms.

"You see, George's wife Isabel died shortly afterwards and the following January his sister Margaret's husband Charles, Duke of Burgundy was killed at the battle of Nancy. Margaret had no children, but Charles left an heiress, Mary, his only child from a previous marriage. What a wonderful idea. Why not marry George and Mary? Margaret was all for the idea and so was George since Mary, besides being one wealthy lady and desirable, was also the granddaughter of John of Gaunt and thus had a very nice claim to the English throne. King Edward vetoed the idea. The Queen must have really pulled George's chain when she suggested her brother Anthony, Lord Rivers as a possible bridegroom instead, but again Edward declined.

"Actually, George had been a pain for some time. Having his ambitions thwarted yet again must have sent him over the edge. He began to bad mouth King Edward, spreading rumours that he was a bastard and therefore an unlawful king. George's hatred of the Queen boiled over early in 1477. Apparently, Isabel had a servant named Ankarette Twynho, a respectable widow of good family. When the Duchess died, Ankarette entered the Queen's service. On the 14th of April, George had Ankarette arrested and imprisoned at Warwick Castle. She was accused of complicity with the Queen to poison the Duchess of Clarence. There was a trial of sorts, but everyone was so afraid of George that they did what he wanted them to do, which was to convict the lady. The poor woman was found guilty and immediately executed, along with a John Thoresby, who was convicted of poisoning the Duchess's baby.

"The King retaliated. In May, Doctor John Stacey and Thomas Burdett - a member of George's household - were both found guilty of complicity to murder the King by witchcraft. Georgie didn't get the hint. He continued to carry on irresponsibly and may even have been involved in a minor rebellion against the King. He continued to press his poison story, openly accusing the Queen of murdering his wife and refusing to either eat or drink at Court. The Queen was more than insulted. She firmly believed that George was a major danger to the safety of her sons." Laura chuckled. "Astute lady was our Liz - right family, wrong brother."

Gail delivered a withering glance but said nothing.

"Anyhow, she began to press King Edward hard and finally, when George interrupted a session of council at Westminster, publicly denouncing the King's justice regarding Stacey and Burdett, Eddie finally snapped.

"George was arrested and sent to the Tower. In January 1478 he was tried for *'heinous unnatural and loathly treason'*. Treason by a brother was highly unusual and George had done so at least twice. King Edward could ill afford to forgive George yet again. For the safety of the realm and his throne, he declared his brother guilty of the crime of treason against the crown. Such a verdict, by the way, carried with it an automatic death sentence. George died in the Tower on February 19, 1478, drowned, it is believed, in a vat of malmsey wine."

Gail had finished her meal by then. Satisfied and not yet ready for dessert, she leaned back comfortably in her chair. "Shakespeare has Richard as one of the prime movers behind George's death. He saw George as an obstacle to his own ambitions. True?"

Laura shrugged. "Certainly Richard profited nicely from George's death in terms of titles and properties, so frankly, I can't see him shedding too many tears.

Anyhow, he stayed well clear of the court, partly because he was disgusted by the King's excesses. I wouldn't call Richard a prude exactly, but by all accounts King Edward went well beyond the bounds of decency, seducing married women and carrying on in a very undignified manner. The King was not alone in all this either. The Queen's family, notably her two sons from her first marriage and one of her brothers, were just as involved in this scandalous behaviour. Another participant was Lord Hastings who introduced King Edward to Mistress Jane Shore, who very quickly became the king's favourite mistress.

"King Edward left the north of England in Richard's capable hands. Everything which he asked for was granted him, so by degrees Richard became the most powerful man in the country and he began to flex that power, gathering to him men whose loyalty would be to him first and the King second. Not a difficult task really since many regarded the royal affinity as mainly Wydville-based. Most of Richard's supporters were Northerners who had a natural dislike and mistrust of anyone south of the Trent. A dangerous imbalance of power was generated which would ultimately lead to disaster.

Laura paused, suddenly saddened. "And disaster did strike on the 9th of April, 1483. At just forty years of age, King Edward died. Richard was in the north and did not attend his brother's funeral and as far as I'm concerned, the Story stops there. What happened next is best discussed when we're at the Tower of London where we'll have the benefit of atmosphere to augment the tale."

"What?' You can't stop now." Gail said in surprise.

"Yes I can." Laura said indignantly. "What I've talked about so far is pretty dry old history. He did this, she was that, but I'm determined to go slowly and methodically through the time from King Edward's death in April 1483 until King Richard's death in August 1485. The Tower of London was where it all started, and so shall we. You, my dear sister-in-law, shall have to wait." With that final, emphatic statement, Laura closed her notebook.

"Does this mean it's dessert time?"

"Go for it."

After a interval of nearly catatonic indecision and two mind changes, Gail finally chose the Black Forest Cake slathered with extra whipped cream and freshly cut chocolate curls. Just as the waiter was about to place the dish in front of Gail, Laura asked if it might be possible to adjourn to the lounge. Promising to follow with Gail's dessert and coffee, he escorted them into the lounge. Laura selected a small alcove away from the bustle of the dining area and spread herself out across the small, pale pink leather sofa. Gail sunk into the matching wing chair. It was almost 7:30 pm.

Laura watched as Gail tackled her dessert, musing on the truth of the saying that some people eat to live and others live to eat. The waiter brought a large pot of coffee.

"Drink that and you won't sleep tonight." Gail warned.

"Nothing but nothing is going to keep me awake, thank you."

"Please continue with the Story. I'm not tired yet and I so enjoy it. I want to be up to speed before the Tower tomorrow."

Laura sighed. "Okay, but straight to bed afterwards."

"Right, Mum." Gail said in a high pitched voice.

Laura rolled her eyes, picked up her notes again, turned to a new section and began. "The reason why Richard didn't attend the funeral was because he didn't know his brother was dead."

"You mean no one told him?"

"Exactly, and I'll you why in a minute. In his will, King Edward named Richard sole protector of his children and the realm. This implied that Richard would govern the kingdom while the young King Edward V was a minor and that both boys would be his responsibility. It shows you the measure of trust that Edward placed in his brother."

"He'll be sorry." Gail said in a voice heavy with prophecy.

"He wasn't sorry, he was dead. Shuffled off the mortal coil he did, leaving one hell of a mess behind. A Protectorate was unacceptable to the Queen who reasoned that if her son was crowned immediately, then she and her family could rule in his name. Richard Gloucester, as we both know, had other ideas.

"Young Edward was at Ludlow Castle where he maintained a household as befitting the Prince of Wales. On the 14th of April his uncle and governor Anthony Wydville, Earl Rivers, told the boy of his father's death. The Queen immediately made arrangements for his safe conduct to London, originally planning to send a sizeable army to escort him. Lord Hastings, sensing trouble, insisted on only a small force which the Queen finally agreed on.

"Lord Hastings was in London at the time of the King's death and had attended Council meetings. It soon became obvious to him that the Wydvilles planned to exclude Richard from any voice in government. Hastings hated the Wydvilles with a passion and the feeling was mutual. When he realized that they had intentionally not told Richard of his brother's death, Hastings sent word to him, giving him the bad news and suggesting that he make haste to secure his position as Protector. He suggested too, that he should take young Edward into his protection and authority before the boy reached London.

"Richard must have received Hastings letter with alarm. Young Edward had been raised and tutored by his mother's family, and Richard must have realized that a Wydville-dominated Council, ruling on behalf of a child-king, would be a disaster for him and the country. He had to act immediately or risk the possible loss of all his wealth and power. He may well have believed too, that his political and personal survival depended upon swift and decisive action.

"He arrived in York around the 21st of April with a sizeable retinue of Northerners, all dressed in deepest black. He attended a funeral mass for the dead king and then swore an oath of fealty to the young King Edward V. From York he moved rapidly south to Nottingham where he met with an agent of the Duke of Buckingham.

"Now, Henry Stafford, second Duke of Buckingham was one of the foremost peers of the realm with impeccable bloodlines. His loyalty lay historically with the House of Lancaster, but since he was only six when Edward IV took the throne, he was too young to appreciate the significance. While still a minor, he was put into the care of Elizabeth Wydville, an arrangement he hated since he viewed the Queen and her family as upstarts. At eleven he was forced to marry the Queen's sister, Katherine Wydville. Buckingham was about two years younger than Richard, I think, which would mean he would be in his late twenties at this time and I might add, the father of a healthy young son despite the fact that he supposedly loathed his wife. Interesting character, Buckingham.

"Anyhow, Richard sent him an urgent note soliciting his help and support. For Buckingham it was an ideal opportunity to not only crush the hated Wydvilles, but once Richard was helped into power, Buckingham felt sure he could successfully lay claim to estates he felt were his by right. Buckingham agreed to meet Richard at Northampton.

"Richard then wrote to the young king asking what route was being planned for his journey to London. He suggested that it would be really nice if Edward could join him and the Duke of Buckingham at Northampton and together they could enter London in triumph. What a great idea."

Gail chuckled.

"Earl Rivers, the Queen's brother, was either politically naive, unaware of the danger or just plain stupid, because he agreed. I don't know what his problem was, but after learning of the King's death, Rivers stayed on at Ludlow for several more days before setting out for London. Richard made good use of the delay to position himself on the board.

"Just as Edward entered Northampton, his half-brother Sir Richard Grey arrived from London. Obviously more politically astute then the uncle, Grey promptly escorting the boy fourteen miles south to Stony Stratford before returning with Rivers and a small detachment of men. Richard and Buckingham arrived, only to find that all they had in their net was Grey and Rivers. It was too late in the day to do anything, so the Dukes invited Rivers to join them for dinner. Rivers may well have told Richard and Buckingham everything about what the Queen had planned, the rulings in Council, the fact that Richard would be denied all power. It is doubtful if this was news to Richard. His spy network had been working overtime. Rivers went happily to bed, only to wake up, locked in his room under heavy guard.

"Early the next morning both dukes set out for Stony Stratford with Grey in tow. The young King was unaware of Rivers' arrest and greeted his two uncles joyously. Richard greeted his young sovereign with all the usual show of respect, giving no hint whatsoever of his true intentions. If Richard was the dissembler he was said to have been, he must have put on a very convincing performance. Gradually however, he began to pry Edward free of his retinue, suggesting that the young king was surrounded by men of dubious moral character, low bred and even went so far as to accuse them of trying to deprive him of the office of Protector which had been conferred on him by the late King. Richard even hinted at plots to murder him and finally broke the news of Rivers' arrest to the young King. Edward was stunned. He defended his uncle, but Richard remained firm, insisting that he, and only he, knew what was best for the young king and for England.

"When Grey tried to intervene, a quarrel ensued and Richard had Grey arrested along with Sir Thomas Vaughan who was the King's Treasurer and close companion and Sir Richard Haute, a distant relation and loyal friend. The arrests were probably made in Edward's presence. Bereft of those closest to him, Edward stood helpless now as Richard dismissed the 2000 men of the royal retinue."

"I'm surprised that he was able to do that." Gail said.

"I agree. Richard hadn't been officially declared Protector, so technically speaking, everything he had done so far was illegal, acts of tyranny if you like, but let's face it, if you were a soldier assigned to accompany the young king and someone as powerful as the Duke of Gloucester told you to shove off home, what would you do?"

"Shove off home." Gail said, nodding her head.

"Right, and quickly too, I bet. Richard and Buckingham then returned to Northampton with the king and their prisoners firmly in hand. I doubt if Edward was allowed to see Rivers. Richard spent the rest of the day writing to the Council and the Lord Mayor of London explaining the situation, and assuring them that the young king was now in good hands, rescued as it were from the very jaws of perdition.

"It would be interesting to know what Edward thought. Chances are that he was more then a little apprehensive. He didn't know his Uncle of Gloucester very well, and what he did know had been told to him by the Wydvilles. Certainly Richard's actions lately would hardly have endeared him to the boy.

"When the news reached London, there was pandemonium. The Queen, with the help of her son Dorset, fled to sanctuary at Westminister after first dividing up the royal treasure. Now Edward IV had dabbled in the lowly business of trade and had acquired a tidy little fortune. In fact, he was one of the few kings who died solvent; downright rich actually. Naturally, the Queen had her daughters with her and her other son, Richard, Duke of York. She took over the Abbot's house and apparently did some damage while moving in all her personal affects. I bet the Abbot was super pleased. Archbishop Rotherham of York arrived soon after the Queen entered sanctuary and gave her the Great Seal of England, which he held as Lord Chancellor.

"People milled about the streets of London, talking, speculating and some even went so far as to don armour, rallying to the Queen's cause. Mancini wrote that there was *current in the capital a sinister rumour that the Duke had brought his nephew not under his care but into his power, so as to gain the crown for himself*. This is all rumour of course, but the news of the Queen's flight into sanctuary would have been sufficient fuel to spark controversy and unease amongst the citizenry.

"On the 2nd of May Richard had his prisoners sent north, probably to Pontefract. He received a letter from Hastings that day too, telling him about the reaction in London, the Queen's move into sanctuary and Rotherham's unwise surrender of the Great Seal into the Queen's hands. Richard immediately wrote to Council, ordering Rotherham's dismissal as Lord Chancellor. He then wrote to Thomas Bourgchier, Archbishop of Canterbury, asking him to secure the Great Seal and ensure that the treasure was safe. When Richard found out that it had been taken by the Queen and Company, the proverbial really hit the fan." She chuckled.

"And," Gail added, "I don't suppose he was too pleased when

he learned of the Queen's decision to seek sanctuary either."

"No, he wasn't at all pleased. He had been working overtime, assuring everyone that things were just fine, and then she pulls a stunt like that. It's tantamount to saying that she feared for her life and the lives of her children."

"Didn't she?" Gail said.

"Didn't she what?"

"Come on Laura, she must have been afraid of Richard, otherwise why do such a thing?"

"I think she was afraid of her own unpopularity and of Richard's power. She was prepared to fight him, but only from the safety of blessed sanctuary."

"Could he have done her an injury - physically I mean?"

"No!" Laura said, indignant at first. "Well, not openly. There were laws against that sort of thing, even in those days. The worst he could have done was to lock her away somewhere, and of course, take the kids. That's why she decided to take the initiative, and I might add, the treasure.

"Anyhow, Richard wasted no more time. On the morning of May 3rd, Richard and Buckingham escorted Edward out of Northampton on the road to London.

"The two Dukes rode on either side of Edward during the procession into the city, proceeding to St. Paul's, where the young king was installed temporarily in the Palace of the Bishop of London. Richard then summoned all the magnates and citizens to pay homage to their young sovereign which was done with great joy and relief. Hastings especially was super pleased that all had gone well and no one had been hurt. I guess he didn't bother asking Richard where Rivers, Grey, Vaughan and Haute were.

"With all that out of the way, Richard posted guards about the King's person, then retired to Baynard Castle. He shuffled the Council a bit, got rid of individuals whom he knew were either hostile or of no value to him, until he had a hard core of men he felt sure he could trust. The first order of business at this new

Council concerned a proper residence for Edward since the Bishop's Place was old and unsuitable. Various places were suggested, but it was Buckingham who first put forward the idea of the Tower. Council agreed, and so Edward was moved there sometime before the 19th of May."

"I do not like the Tower, of any place. Isn't that what Edward said when he heard the news?" Gail asked.

"Well, that's what Shakespeare suggested he said, but in fact, the Tower had not yet acquired its sinister reputation; the Tudor's did that."

"But, Henry VI and George, Duke of Clarence both died there, so young Edward must have been at least a little apprehensive about going there." Gail was sticking firmly to the point. "And, considering the way he had already been treated, he might have been downright scared."

"Perhaps, but he didn't have any choice in the matter anyway. Historical precedence would demand that sooner or later he would have to stay at the Tower prior to his coronation. Besides, he wasn't kept in some dark, dank tower or something. South of the White Tower, in what was called the 'Royal Ward', there were a number of massive wooden structures, a banqueting hall, privy chambers, an audience chamber and royal bedrooms. It was quite sumptuous really. I'll show you what I mean tomorrow. The night before his coronation however, he would be expected to stay in the White Tower, praying all night in the Chapel, but other than that, he had the run of the royal apartments."

"Where he would be watched day and night."

"Where he would be carefully watched day and night." Laura said, emphasising the word 'carefully'. She paused then and lit a cigarette.

"So, you admit that Richard had the boy under close guard?"

"Absolutely. Some would suggest that Richard was just making sure that the boy didn't hurt himself; have an accident or something."

"Sure," Gail said with more than a hint of sarcasm. "Come

on Laura, Richard kept a close watch on that child because he had no intentions of ever letting him out, not alive anyway. He probably hoped that he would have an accident - a fatal one."

"Now Gail, you're jumping to conclusions. There's absolutely no evidence up to now to suggest that Richard had any designs on the boy or his throne. In fact, after he was proclaimed 'Protector and Defender of the Realm' on the 10th of May, Richard encouraged the Council to set a date for Edward's coronation - the 24th of June to be exact.

"Richard's role of Protector got off to a bumpy start though when Council began to ask questions about Rivers, Grey, Vaughan and Haute. Richard wanted Council to draw up warrants accusing them of complicity to murder, calling them traitors. The Council more or less refused since there was absolutely no evidence to support Richard's claims, plus since at the time Richard had not yet been officially declared Protector, the 'Stony Stratford Four' could not be accused of treason. Richard was encouraged to release them, but of course he wouldn't - and didn't - do that. Almost from the start he was being challenged, and when Council went on to suggest that Richard ought to do something to improve the Queen's condition, he must have gone ballistic."

Gail chuckled.

"Well," Laura said, smiling, "Richard probably knew by then that the Queen had spirited away the royal treasure and here was Council suggesting that he should do something in consideration of the Queen's *good dignity and safety*'. Obviously Council didn't consider her a threat although her continued presence in sanctuary was becoming an administrative embarrassment. Richard wanted to see her out, transferred if possible to a lovely nunnery somewhere - like in Yorkshire for instance.

"Eventually Richard appointed a committee of lords, headed by Buckingham and the Archbishop of Canterbury, to go and reason with the Queen. No luck. All Richard could do publicly to alleviate her condition was to encourage people to visit her and many did, for a while. That was probably a mistake. Elizabeth Wydville was an experienced manipulator, capable of extreme charm and ruthlessly ambitious for herself and her family. Believe me, she was still dangerous. But Richard had to put up with it in the end when it became obvious that she wasn't leaving. As much as Richard might have wanted to pull her out by force, he dare not do that and risk the Church's wrath. No doubt he posted spies who kept him informed of all the comings and goings.

"I've often wondered just how much the Queen told her children. Elizabeth of York was seventeen and the youngest, Bridget was three years old and, of course the second son Richard, Duke of York. It must have been extremely difficult for the young Elizabeth who should have been at court having a lovely time, not stuck in an abbey with her overbearing and aloof mother. If the Queen tried to poison her children's minds against Richard, she wasn't entirely successful, as we shall soon see.

"And that, my dear, is it for tonight." She closed her notebook with a resounding thud. "The Tower of London awaits our arrival on the morrow."

Day 2
Tower of London - Covent Garden

Prince: *I do not like the Tower, of any place:*
Did Julius Caesar build that place, my lord?

Buckingham: *He did, my gracious lord, begin that place,*
Which, since, succeeding ages have re-edified.

Shakespeare -
The Tragedy of King Richard the Third
[Act III, Scene 1]

Laura casually flipped through the *Official Guidebook to the Tower of London*, which she purchased along with their tickets. "Ready for this Gail?"

"Sure. Bleak looking though, isn't it?"

"It's a fortress and a prison. I don't think it was meant to be pretty. Come on, let's hurry and catch the next tour."

"Good morning ladies and gentleman, children. I am a Yeoman Warder. One of thirty-eight Yeoman Warders who guard this Tower and call it home. I will be conducting you on a brief introductory tour of Her Majesty's Tower of London. Sometimes referred to as a *Beefeater*, I must tell you that I am not that fond of beef, and in fact, had a nice leg of lamb for my dinner last night!" Several members of the tour chuckled.

"On your right is the Middle Tower which guards the entrance area outside the moat and the outer ward, which has a total of six towers and two bastions and abuts the Thames wharf to the south. Beneath you is the dry moat. At one time it was filled with water, and I use that term loosely. It was, in fact, a giant cesspool which stunk to high heaven. It did, however, provided an excellent deterrent for those individuals who, for various reasons, wished not to use the usual entrance ways." More laughter.

"To the left of you is the Byward Tower, the gate house of the outer ward. Originally this Tower was fitted with a wooden drawbridge which could be drawn up in times of trouble. As you walk through, take note of the portcullis. The wooden gallery which you see above was constructed in the early part of the 16th century."

Taking the lead, he drew his audience along the causeway and through the archway between the two turrets which together form the Byward Tower. Just beyond he halted, waiting patiently for everyone to come through. "We are now between the inner and outer walls. The inner wall is forty feet high and there are thirteen towers built into it. The first tower you will notice is the Bell Tower, one of the oldest and most secure of all the towers. At various times it has been a prison for such notable individuals as Princes Elizabeth, who later became Queen Elizabeth I, Sir Thomas More, Bishop John Fisher and the Duke of Monmouth. Begun by King Richard I - the Lionheart - it has been called by various names over the years, the Belfry Tower, the Curfew Tower and the Red Tower. Because of its proximity to the River Thames, it is built on a base of solid masonry five metres above the original river level. The tower itself is eighteen metres high and contains two floors.

"As we approach Traitors' Gate ladies and gentlemen, let me remind you that you have entered the Tower of London voluntarily and will be leaving, no doubt, in a few hours. The same may not be said of many of the individuals who came through, under Traitors' Gate and climbed those stairs.

"The Lady Princess Elizabeth was conducted to the Tower through this gate on Palm Sunday, 1554. She was a young girl of twenty years, but despite her youth, she was a strong-willed young woman. Climbing up a few steps, she promptly sat down in the pouring rain and refused to go further, insisting that she was not a traitor and did not deserve this fate. It took a considerable amount of coaxing before she finally allowed herself to be escorted to her lodgings in the Bell Tower. To get there she would have had to pass beneath the Bloody Tower behind you.

"Originally called the Garden Tower, it received its more ominous name in Tudor times because of its association with the two Princes, the sons of King Edward IV who, legend has it, were murdered in this tower by order of their uncle, Richard, Duke of Gloucester, later King Richard III. The Bloody Tower houses a fully functioning portcullis which weighs two ton. Before a windlass and pulley system was installed in 1848, thirty men were required to raise and lower it. There were originally two such gates installed in the inner and outer gateway. Unlike the other towers here, the Bloody Tower is square and serves as the gateway into the inner ward. It has had its share of famous prisoners as well, including Sir Walter Raleigh, Sir Thomas Overbury, Archbishop Thomas Cranmer and the infamous Judge George Jeffreys.

"To the right is the Wakefield Tower which housed the Crown Jewels until 1967. Its most famous prisoner was King Henry VI who died there in 1471 under mysterious circumstances. The bridge above connects St. Thomas's Tower to the upper floor of the Wakefield Tower. Now, if you will follow me, we shall go through the entrance way here - note the portcullis above - and you will receive your first clear view of the White Tower."

The cobblestones beneath the Bloody Tower were hard and uneven and Laura was grateful that they both had worn sensible shoes. The land rose dramatically then as the great central Keep came into view.

"Construction on the Tower of London was begun by William the Conqueror shortly after his victory at the Battle of Hastings. For those who do not remember their history, that was in 1066.

The White Tower was the first structure built. It is 90 feet high and measures 118 feet by 107 feet. It received its name during the reign of King Henry III when he ordered the exterior whitewashed prior to the arrival of his bride, Eleanor of Provence in 1236. For most of its 900 year history, it had been the tallest building in London.

"Ladies and Gentlemen, I will leave you now to wander about the Tower grounds at your leisure. Take particular care with the Tower ravens please. They are a carnivorous bird with a keen appetite for fingers, so beware!" He did his utmost to sound suitably foreboding. Several tourist did laugh however, probably because they had not as yet seen a raven, nor had an opportunity to appreciate it's size and evil demeanour.

"The ravens have been in evidence at the Tower since its inception so they feel they have a right to be here and are, in fact, encouraged to do so, since legend has it that without the ravens, the Tower will fall and the kingdom with it. It is just a legend of course, but just to make sure, the birds' wings are clipped but, I might add again for your safety, not their beaks nor their talons. Should you have any questions, please ask and I shall endeavour to answer them for you."

A middle aged man next to Gail whispered to his wife out of the corner of his mouth. "Martha! Ask the man where William the Conqueror put the toilets."

Laura eased herself down onto a wooden bench, lit a cigarette and watched as Gail turned full circle, taking in a much as she could but, as yet, not understanding very much of it. "Well, where do you want to start?"

"It's bigger than I thought."

"Eighteen acres I think, with more history per square inch than anywhere else in England. If you want to see inside the Bloody Tower, we best do it now before this place gets too crowded."

"The two Princes, I thought they were smothered or

something so how did it get the name 'Bloody Tower'?" Gail asked as they hurried along.

"That name came later. During their time it was called the Garden Tower because it looked out over the Constable's garden. If the two boys were murdered there, and it's doubtful, they certainly didn't meet a bloody end. Typical Tudor propaganda. The same nonsense that gives Richard a withered arm, hump on his back all that rubbish. I, for one, find it very hard to believe that Richard would have housed the boys there. It's just too close to the exit plus, if it took thirty men to handle a two ton portcullis, it wouldn't be what I would call secure. Anyhow, must pay my respects to Sir Walter, patron saint of smokers." Laura grinned wickedly as they took their place in line.

Sir Walter Raleigh's prison had been faithfully recreated, furnished at it may have been in his day and included a portrait of the man himself. The fireplace was certainly large enough to have heated the room and included a bread-oven on the right-hand side. A few of the original floor tiles attested to the palatial accommodation offered to prisoners of rank.

"Where to now?" Gail whispered as she relinguished her place to the press of tourists behind them.

"The Wakefield Tower."

"Isn't that where King Henry VI was murdered?"

"Yes." Laura replied gleefully.

"Right," Gail snapped, "and afterwards we can go and have scones and jam."

Laura turned on Gail in a flash. "What's wrong?"

"Knowing what I know about Henry's death, I think this is going to be a sad experience, that's all."

"After everything you've heard, I'm surprised. But, you don't have to go. I'll meet you back here in half an hour." Laura began to turn away.

"No, I want to go." Gail said hurriedly as she clutched Laura's arm.

"Good, because I'd hate you to miss seeing one of the oldest parts of the Tower."

Together they walked down towards the gate under the Bloody Tower, through it and across to the stairs leading up to St. Thomas's Tower on the right-hand side of Traitors' Gate.

They wandered through the two rooms, the first stripped of its wall coverings to reveal the construction techniques used so long ago. The second room, however, was decorated as it might have been when this portion of the Tower comprised part of the royal apartments.

Having viewed the tower from every angle, they stood poised at the entrance to the bridge which connects St. Thomas's Tower to the Wakefield Tower. Without saying a word but giving each other looks which spoke volumes, they proceeded across to the magnificent vaulted beauty of the Wakefield Tower.

Here too attempts had been made to restore the tower to its original medieval appearance. There were several striking features including a replica of a throne, resting on a raised dais. Painted gold with a fleur-de-lis pattern, it seemed a little out of place but, Laura reasoned, perhaps it is was not beyond the realm of possibility that King Henry did have something like this in his prison. Two stone lions lay in front of the chair as foot rests, but no amount of decoration could make the chair comfortable to sit upon. Two huge wrought iron candelabras, ablaze with real candles stood on either side of the throne, while above, a massive iron ring held numerous slots in which small electric bulbs burned where once candles would have been placed.

But the most arresting feature was the chapel. Beautifully decorated with a tile floor and stained glass window, it was small but lovely. A brightly painted wooden screen either side of the small entrance way separated the chapel from the octagonally shaped room, so Laura was required to bend forward to read the plaque set into the floor in front of the altar - *By tradition Henry VI died here May 21, 1471*. Laura read this aloud but when she turned,

Gail was nowhere to be seen. Wandering around a bit, Laura found her sitting on a stone seat in one of the recesses, gazing out the window.

"Have you noticed anything unusual?" Gail said as she turned to look at Laura.

Laura frowned. "What do you mean?" It was obvious that Gail was uneasy.

"We're the only people in this room and have been for several minutes. Don't you think that's rather odd?" Gail rose then and walked past Laura to the centre of the room and stopped, staring at the chapel. Laura joined her and the two of them stood in silence while the sounds of the outside world seemed to drift away, leaving them cocooned in a realm of imagination.

"Do you know what a misericord is?" Laura asked in a whisper. Gail shook her head.

"The name is derived from the Latin, misereri - to pity, and cor - heart. To show pity, compassion or mercy. It's a dagger, a very special dagger made of the finest steel, encrusted with gems and worked all over with Christian symbols. It was long, slender and extremely deadly. During the Crusades, each knight carried his own blade, but not for use in battle. Hidden away on his person, the misericord was only revealed long enough for it to be blessed by a priest during the Mass which always preceded any encounter with the infidel. Should a knight be badly wounded in battle, his misericord would be used by his companion to deliver the coup de grace rather than allow him to fall into enemy hands. It was, if you like, a form of consecrated murder, blessed and sanctioned by the Church."

Gail stared at Laura, her face a mask of horror and fascination. "Go on," she said in a hushed whisper.

Laura took a deep breath. "It's my belief that Richard Gloucester committed ritualistic murder here, in this room, using a single, deadly dagger - a misericord - cunningly crafted into the shape of the cross so as to ensure the thrust and sanctify the wound."

"Oh my God." Gail said, catching her breath.

Suddenly, and without warning, the spell was shattered as two rambunctious boys entered the room, stopped and shouted in unison. "Cool."

Laura and Gail moved back towards the window recess. They sat quietly, watching the boys as they explored the room, but by the time their parents joined them, the children had seen enough and were on their way again, out and down the vice, leaving their parents behind. With just a cursory glance about them, they too hurried from the room. As their footsteps and muttered conversation faded, Laura, Gail and Henry's prison were once more enveloped in silence.

Gail rose quietly and wandered off a few feet before turning, to face Laura. "Even knowing all the reasons why, Richard still shouldn't have done it. And, if you think he's going to get off lightly because he might have killed Henry using some sort of religious ceremony or something, you're wrong. It's still murder."

"All right," Laura said, turning in her seat slightly to look out of the window. "Then let's forget the misericord idea and go with the version universally accepted for nearly 500 years - Shakespeare, Henry VI, Part III. Or, how about some twisted Shakespeare? Richard came into the room - this room - 'Hi Henry old bean, I've got good news and bad news. First the bad news, your son Edouard, is dead. I killed him. The good news? You're going to join him'."

"Will you stop." Gail said, feigning shock but at the same time trying hard to suppress a grin. "King Henry was a nice man."

"Right," Laura said, "he was a great guy but a terrible king. Richard didn't kill him because he was a nice person you know. Put yourself in Richard's shoes. It was Henry's government, notably Queen Margaret and her Lancastrian supporters, who killed Richard's father, brother Edmund and his mother's brother. Richard would never forget the indignities done to the bodies. The heads were cut off and displayed at York, his father's decorated with a paper crown for heaven's sake. I think Richard's love for his father was motivation enough to do the deed. He probably would have loved to have done Margaret of Anjou a major injury too, but of course, that sort of thing wasn't done in those days. Perhaps it's just a coincidence, but did you know that Richard's father died on Wakefield Green and his brother on Wakefield Bridge? Henry died here in the Wakefield Tower. Talk about revenge! It makes you wonder if Richard was aware of the significance of the name 'Wakefield'.

"Richard had a duty to perform and he did it. I'm not suggesting for a moment that he enjoyed it, but in the final analysis it wasn't a case of 'will I or won't I', he had no choice. The strength of his brother's reign depended upon the wholehearted support of everyone and once the son was dead, there was no point in keeping the father alive. I think too, that Richard probably despised Henry for allowing the monarchy to degenerate to such an extent that the country was being run by the Queen and her minions. Henry's preoccupation with the ethereal while his kingdom went to hell in a handcart would have only angered someone of Richard's temperament who saw power as a living force, to be wielded, not wasted."

They sat quietly then while a steady stream of tourists arrived, looked around briefly and proceeded on. Finally, gathering her things together, Laura stood up. "Ready to go?"

"Yes, I guess so."

They exited one at a time down the spiral staircase, or vice, to the lower level then outside to the pathway which led from the gate of the Bloody Tower back up the incline to the White Tower. The walk was not only slightly steep but they were hedged in on both sides by walls, the one on the right now in ruins.

"I know you feel sorry for Henry but look, he was well taken care of while he was here, and I don't think he chaffed one bit against his lost of freedom. He had every comfort, which is more than can be said for most of the prisoners kept here."

Turning towards a small patch of lawn just in front of the

Chapel Royal of St. Peter ad Vincula, Laura pointed. "There's the spot where three queens died. Two were King Henry VIII's wives, and the third was a tiny, frightened girl of sixteen. More victims were to follow for various reasons, but mostly to do with the 'King's Displeasure'. The Chapel there became a yawning pit into which were thrown the remains of many otherwise decent human beings who dared to defy the Tudor regime. Between 1540 and 1640, more people were tortured here then at any other time. That's the Tudor age, not Plantagenet."

Gail was drawn to the spot where a simple plaque marked the site of the scaffold.

"Very few people were executed here." Laura continued. "Most died on Tower Hill, which was more public and a lot more entertaining for the masses. Five women did died here though."

"Tell me about them." Gail said, her voice low and sad.

Laura began to tell Gail, in horrific detail, the deaths of Anne Boleyn, Catherine Howard, Lady Rochford and Jane Grey. She left the best to last. "Margaret of Clarence, Countess of Salisbury, was executed in 1541. Margaret was the daughter of our very own George, Duke of Clarence - Richard's niece. She was an old lady in her seventies by then but that didn't stop Henry VIII. Why he felt that it was necessary to execute an old woman is beyond me, but as usual, it had something to do with treason. She didn't make it easy for him though. Apparently she refused to put her head on the block since that was what traitors did, so the poor executioner ended up hacking at her neck and shoulders before the decapitation was finally accomplished."

Gail fixed Laura with a steady gaze.

Laura smiled wickedly in return. "See, Richard wasn't that bad. At least he didn't go around butchering old ladies. Hey, don't blame me, I'm just telling the story."

"Where do you get all this stuff?" Gail asked in mock disgust.

"It's a hobby." Laura said with a shrug. "You have to admit it's interesting though. Not the usual cut and dried - excuse the pun - material we studied in our history books."

"You know what you're doing, don't you? All this talk of the Tudors is suppose to soften me up for what Richard did here. Well, it's not working. I want to hear about the Princes. Come on."

Laura watched as Gail walked resolutely towards a rank of benches resting in shadows on the west side of the White Tower. She hesitated briefly before joining her. "Don't you want to see more of the Tower first? I know, let's see the Chapel and have a quick tour through the White Tower, which is filled with armour mostly, then we can go and have lunch. Over lunch we can get back to the Story. Okay?"

Gail eyed Laura briefly then agreed. Together they walked the short distance from the site of the scaffold to the Chapel Royal of St. Peter ad Vincula.

As Laura approached the door, she rummaged in her bag for her notes regarding the Chapel and its 'inhabitants'. "Before we go in, can I read something here about the Chapel which, I think puts this particular building in context with its surroundings and with other churches we'll see during our travels? This is what Lord Macaulay in his 'History of England' wrote:

'In truth there is no sadder spot on earth than this little cemetery. Death is associated, not, as in Westminster and St. Paul's, with genius and virture, with public veneration and with imperishable renown; not, as in our humblest churches and churchyards, with everything that is most enduring in social and domestic charities; but with whatever is darkest in human nature and in human destiny; with the savage triumph of implacable enemies, with the inconstancy, the ingratitude, the cowardice of friends, with all the miseries of fallen greatness and of blighted fame.'

Laura sighed. "And yet, for all that, it's a very pretty place, especially since it has been restored to something like its original glory."

Inside, the Chapel was indeed magnificent. The sunlight poured through the latticed windows and fell on simple pews of English oak. As Laura and Gail were confronted by the wonders of the interior with its wealth of memorials, it became instantly obvious to them that this was a special place, yet they were alone. The west door, which had closed behind them, cut off all sounds of the outside world and as the two of them stood transfixed, utter silence descended.

Laura was staring at a brass plaque which named, in order of internment, the most notable individuals buried in the Chapel when she realized that Gail had moved elsewhere. Laura was loathed to break the silence and disturb the almost mystical spell with which the Chapel held her, so in a very low whisper she said, "You know, it's strange that no one else has come in. You don't suppose that maybe we shouldn't be in here?"

"Well, we aren't going to touch anything but just in case, we'd better hurry and see as much as we can. Where are the queens buried?"

"At the altar, I think."

"How many people are buried here do you suppose?"

"Somewhere between fifteen hundred and two thousand."

"What?" Gail practically shouted in surprise.

"Remember, the Tower was home to a lot of people over hundreds of years. The Yeoman Warders and their families, the blacksmiths, the zoo keepers, the workers and their families in the mint and the armouries. The list goes on and on. When a new floor was laid in the last century, it was discovered that there was no more room and that some of the more recent internments were barely two feet below the surface. Queen Victoria was informed, and in accordance with her wishes, many of the bones in the nave were placed in new coffins and reburied in the crypt. With new bodies going down all the time, many of the older coffins had been broken and their contents scattered. It must have been quite a mess."

Before Gail could respond, the door to the outside opened slowly and a Yeoman Warden appeared. "I am sorry ladies, but the Chapel is only open to visitors at specific times. I must ask you both to please follow me out through this door, immediately."

He wasn't angry. In fact he was very polite, but there was a slight hint of exasperation in his voice. He was waiting for them just beyond. Simultaneously they both offered their sincere apologies and then hurried on their way towards the White Tower, with Gail in the lead. They were almost around the northeast corner before Gail stopped and took a deep breath of relief.

Laura chuckled. "What did you think he was going to do, chop off our heads?"

"Well, you never know. *Tourists found Headless - Illegal Chapel Invasion Suspected.*" Gail spread both arms wide, imagining the evening news report in vivid colour.

"Get a grip," Laura said, smiling broadly, "he let us go, didn't he?"

"Yes, but this is the Tower of London and we're still inside it. He has our full description and when we try to leave, well … " Gail drew her index finger across her throat, making a gurgling sound."

Laura laughed. "I hate to rain on your parade sis but, according to the guidebook, the last person to die by the axe was Lord Lovat in seventeen forty-something. Chances are in this day and age, they'll just put you up against a wall and shoot you. A lot less messy too, although perhaps not nearly as entertaining."

"Ha-ha."

"Come on, I'll buy you a nice cup of coffee to help settle your nerves. There's a place close by, I think."

Despite its diminutive size, the kiosk which butted up against the inner portion of the south wall offered an excellent selection of both hot and cold drinks, flavoured coffees and desserts. Wooden benches, set within the recess of the wall, offered them an excellent vantage point from which to view the White Tower. A perfect spot, it would seem, to discuss the horrific events which culminated in Richard's ascension to the English throne.

Laura set her coffee cup aside while extracting the notes from her bag. Glancing at them briefly, she looked up, straight at Gail. "Before we can talk about the two boys, we have to discuss Richard's seizure of the throne. We left the Story with all the principal characters in London, young Edward housed in the Tower, the Queen and her remaining children in sanctuary at Westminster. Right, hold on, because we're about to hit some rough water." Laura took a deep breath and began.

"When Richard was proclaimed Protector on the 10th of May, he was riding a wave of popularity. He was the most powerful noble in the realm and commanded the respect of his peers. Everyone was looking forward to the reign of Edward V, with Richard continuing to act as advisor in Council. In actual fact, as Mancini states, *'he set his thoughts on removing, or at least undermining, everything that might stand in the way of his mastering the throne.'*

"Richard had two powerful Wydvilles - Rivers and Grey - safely tucked away. Next on the list was Sir Edward Wydville, who commanded the fleet. On Richard's insistence, Council denounced Wydville as an enemy of the state and ordered the fleet to return to port while at the same time issuing a reward for his capture, dead or alive. The fleet did return, minus two ships, one carrying Sir Edward, and a portion of the royal treasure I might add, to France."

"And that money was used to finance Henry Tudor's invasion, right?" Gail said.

"Right. By this time I think Richard was getting pissed off, because he seized the estates of Rivers, Grey, Dorset and lesser members of the Wydville family and proceeded to redistribute the property amongst his supporters. This was highly illegal, but then again, it would appear that Richard wasn't particularly bothered by legal niceties. This redistribution of Wydville wealth was meant to ensure absolute loyalty from those closest to him, and men such as Buckingham, Northumberland and Howard benefited handsomely. Although Hastings continued to serve as Lord Chamberlain of

England and Governor of Calais, he didn't receive anything like the goodies that Buckingham received. It seems obvious therefore, that Richard realized that Hastings would not support him in a bid for the throne since he had made it abundantly clear on several occasions that his loyalty lay with Edward V, the son and heir of his good friend and former king, Edward IV. It soon became apparent to Richard that Hastings was now an obstacle to his ambitions and would have to be removed." Laura cleared her throat suggestively.

"Hastings," Gail muttered, "I almost forgot. Okay Laura, this is one death which I insist Richard take the blame for. Shakespeare couldn't have been that far off the mark."

"He wasn't." Laura said. "In fact, Shakespeare's version of the dramatic arrest and execution of Lord Hastings is both compelling and horrible, and historically speaking, fairly accurate I think. This was Richard's kill, no question." Laura paused, took a sip of her coffee, then continued.

"Here are the facts. Richard called a meeting of Council for the morning of the 13th of June - a Friday by the way - summoning Buckingham, Hastings, Bishop John Morton, Stanley, Rotherham, Lord Howard, and his son Thomas to the White Tower. Shortly after nine Richard arrived, all smiles and good humour. As the story goes, he requested some strawberries from Bishop Morton's garden then left the room, leaving the others to carry on with business. He returned to the Council chamber one and a half hours later a changed man."

"One and a half hours?" Gail was surprised. "What was he doing all that time?"

"Screwing up his courage, I guess. I doubt if he really wanted to do Hastings an injury, but being the Political Realist he was, he had no choice. By now even the most moderate of historians agree that he was going for the throne. And time was running out. This was the 13th and Edward's coronation was set for the 22nd, moved forward two days by Richard earlier.

"What happened inside the Council chamber is pure

speculation, but it's certain that Richard denounced Hastings as a traitor. He even went so far as to accuse Morton, Rotherham and Stanley of plotting with the Queen and Mistress Shore against him and his position as Protector. Actually, only plots against a king can be called treason, but again, Richard chose to ignore that fact. When he banged on the table, the room was filled with armed guards who had obviously anticipated the signal. Hastings, Stanley, Rotherham, and Morton were arrested on the spot. It is said that Richard told Hastings that he had better see a priest at once and confess his sins, because he wasn't going to dine until he knew his head was off - lovely thought. Certainly Hastings had very little time to prepare himself, perhaps minutes, as he was dragged from the White Tower outside to the Green next to the chapel and executed, probably with a sword. There was no time to get a proper block so a piece of building timber lying nearby was used. The really tragic part is that young Edward may have seen the execution, since parts of the royal apartments overlooked the Green and all the commotion might well have attracted his attention.

Gail sighed. "You know, I'm beginning to think that Richard was not a very nice man."

"You've had enough then?" Laura said, sensing Gail's unease.

"No, I want to hear it all. Let me get two more coffees." She jumped up. "Want a slice of carrot cake? It looked delicious."

"Sure, after what we have been talking about, a slice of something seems appropriate."

Gail groaned. "Sick, very sick."

When she returned a few minutes later, she arranged their snack between them, then settled down expectantly.

"Okay?" Laura questioned. "Stop me though if you don't want to hear any more. But remember, try to keep everything in perspective."

Gail just nodded her head as she concentrated on opening her little parcel of cake.

"With all opposition in Council either dead or imprisoned

and the rest scared witless, Richard turned to the next order of business. Securing the younger prince, nine year old Richard, Duke of York, who was still in sanctuary with his mother. When Council met on the 16th, Richard made it clear that the boys should be together, that Edward missed his brother's company and that it was improper to crown the King without his brother being there. Naturally, Council agreed. Archbishop Bourgchier was detailed to speak with the Queen, assuring her of the Protector's good office and loving regard. The fact that the Abbey was surrounded by Richard's men was not lost on anyone either. The Archbishop, fearful that sanctuary would be violated by force of arms, appealed to the Queen to see reason. He knew that Richard wanted the child out of sanctuary come hell or high water, so he employed every method of persuasion possible, promising anything rather then risk going back to Richard empty handed. Against all her basic instincts, the Queen was finally persuaded, entrusting the boy into the Archbishop's care with the understanding that he would be returned to his mother immediately after the coronation.

"Needless to say, young Richard was handed over to his uncle who promptly escorted him to the Tower, where he was reunited with his brother. For a short time the two boys were happy together, but Richard soon ordered them moved into more isolated apartments where they could be carefully monitored.

"Now, one small piece of business yet. George, Duke of Clarence's son - Edward, Earl of Warwick - just eight years old but a possible threat to Richard's plans. Although barred from succession by reason of his father's attainder in 1478, Richard knew that such decrees could be overturned by parliament. The boy's claim to the throne was technically stronger then his if push came to shove, so to avoid possible embarrassment, Richard had the child put into the custody of his wife Anne, where he was kept neatly out of sight.

"Time to take stock. All direct heirs to the throne were in his power; execution warrants were on their way north; Hastings was no more; the Council was terrified and likely to do exactly what it was told; and troops of Northerners would soon be arriving. So far, so good, except the date for the coronation. June 22nd, days away now, and the city was rapidly filling with people intent upon attending the coronation and the opening of Parliament. Time to act.

"On the 17th of June, Richard cancelled the Parliament scheduled for after the coronation and then cancelled the coronation altogether, or rather postponed it indefinitely which is practically the same thing. Between the news of the cancellations and the fact that troops were not far away, London exploded with rumour and speculation.

"June 22nd - Edward's coronation day - but instead Richard had Doctor Ralph Shaa, the brother of the Mayor of London, read a proclamation which basically stated that, since King Edward IV was a bastard, conceived in adultery, his sons were unfit to claim the throne. Doctor Shaa went on to suggest that since Richard, Duke of Gloucester and Protector of the Realm was 'the undoubted son' of York, his claim to the throne was legitimate and in the best interest of England."

"Oh boy," Gail said, shaking her head, "I hope Richard's mother didn't hear that."

"She heard, all right. She was in London for the coronation of her grandson after all. To say that she was furious with Richard would be putting it mildly. According to Vergil she *being falsely accused of adultery, complained afterwards in sundry places to right many noble men, whereof some yet live, of that great injury which her son Richard had done her*. This was a pretty disgusting trick on Richard's part. It shows you the extent of his ambition in that he was willing to publicly slander his own mother to obtain the crown. To add insult to injury, the Duchess of York was famed for her piety and had actually become a Benedictine nun. She may well have contacted her youngest son and made her displeasure known, because Richard quickly abandoned that tack for another.

"Basically, Richard put forward the notion that his brother Edward's marriage to Elizabeth Wydville was invalid, since Edward had precontracted a marriage with a Lady Eleanor Butler prior to Elizabeth coming on the scene. Such a promise of marriage was considered binding on both parties, and if true, Edward's subsequent marriage would indeed be considered invalid, and the issue of such a marriage would be considered bastards. Robert Stillington, Bishop of Bath and Wells, apparently broke this news to Richard at a very opportune moment and naturally, Richard ran with it although there appears to be absolutely no truth to the story. Certainly such an important issue should have been considered before a suitably constituted ecclesiastical court. Richard did not order such a court, probably because he knew that there was insufficient proof. The Lady Butler had conveniently died years before, so Stillington remained the only source of the story and most people chose not to believe him, suspecting his motives.

"It soon became apparent to Richard that the precontract story would not of itself do the trick, so he drove the nail deeper. On the 23rd of June, the Duke of Buckingham addressed the Mayor, aldermen and chief citizens of London on Richard's behalf. Buckingham's strategy was multifaceted. He started out by attacking Edward IV's government and the major role played by the upstart Wydvilles He then went on to suggest that, not only was Edward's marriage invalid based on the knowledge of a precontract with the Lady Butler, but his subsequent marriage to Elizabeth Wydville was itself invalid on three counts. First of all, the King had been bewitched, seduced into marriage without the consent of the Lords of the realm. Secondly, the marriage took place in secret without the banns being proclaimed as required and thirdly, the ceremony took place in a private chamber, not in the Church. No doubt Buckingham threw in Elizabeth's low degree of birth, too. Based on all this, he stated, the King and Elizabeth Wydville had lived in sin and adultery against all the laws of the Kingdom and the Church, and therefore the children of such a relationship must be declared bastards and barred from any claim to the throne.

"Reminding the commons that George, Duke of Clarence's attainder precluded his son from any title, Buckingham concluded that at the present time no certain and incorrupt blood of the lineage of Richard, Duke of York was to be found, except in the person of Richard, Duke of Gloucester. Pressing the point, Buckingham went on to describe Richard's history of good government in the north, his blameless morals, which I might add, seemed to be a sticking point with Richard. It's all reminiscent of modern politics in a way, isn't it? Having delivered his speech, Buckingham withdrew and left them to ponder the situation.

"All the talk in the world mattered little when the Council reviewed the situation. Fear and self-preservation were first and foremost in their minds. Coupled with the knowledge that a government ruled by a child would be a disaster, many opted for Richard in the hope at least that he would provide the strong, central government everyone had wished for for so long. The Council voted unanimously to offer the crown to Richard, declaring the throne majestic vacant and Richard's for the taking, which technically speaking, throws the concept of usurpation out the window." Laura shrugged. "If anything, it was more a coup d'etat.

"On the 26th of June, all the Lords gathered at Baynard's Castle and formally offered the crown to Richard who, after feigning some initial reluctance, agreed. By way of a postscript, the day before Richard was publicly declared king, Rivers, Grey and Vaughan at least, were beheaded at Pontefract."

Gail groaned. She watched abstractly as Laura packed her notes away, then suddenly realized what she was doing. "You can't stop now. What about the two boys? The Princes in the Tower?"

"That's a topic I'm easing into very carefully." She finished the last of her coffee then lit a cigarette, leaned back and regarded Gail evenly. "It's difficult to talk about the princes anyhow, since it's not 100 percent certain that the two skeletons found in 1674 are the remains of Edward and Richard, although the evidence is pretty conclusive."

Gail reeled back in her seat and stared at Laura in open surprise. "Skeletons - what skeletons?"

"In 1674, two skeletons were found in a very unlikely place. The Chapel of St. John the Evangelist in the White Tower was, at one time, connected to the royal apartments by an external tower. It was made for the exclusive use of the ruling monarch and family. By 1674, this building was in such a shocking state that King Charles II decided to remove it. The foundations of the tower, estimated to be about twenty feet square, went very deep. It was during excavations, at a depth of ten feet, that a wooden wardrobe chest was discovered. Inside were found the skeletons of two small individuals - children. It was said that the taller of the two skeletons lay on its back while the smaller one lay face down on top. It was immediately assumed that they were the remains of Edward V and his younger brother Richard, Duke of York. What better place to bury them in secret then beneath stairs meant for the private use of royalty?

"Fragments of velvet were found with the bones too, which strongly suggests that the remains were indeed the children of King Edward IV, since only individuals of such high rank were allowed to wear velvet under the restrictive laws of the land, plus velvet was imported then and very expensive. Between say 1400 and 1674, there were no prisoners unaccounted for in the Tower other then the two princes, so it's reasonably safe to assume that these two small, slender skeletons were the remains of Edward V and his brother, Richard."

Laura paused then and looked directly at Gail. "Not much fun, is it, when you're dealing with children? Hastings and all the rest, adult games played by the nobility, one against the other, like a chess match. I very much doubt if the common people of England could have cared less if men like Rivers, Hastings, etcetera were weeded out now and again, but the murder of innocent children, that is quite another matter. Infanticide has never been accepted by any civilized society, then or now.

"The bones were eventually placed in a white marble coffin and interred by order of King Charles II at Westminster Abbey. In 1933, the tomb was opened and the remains examined. The teeth were used to determine age at time of death. The results were consistent with children who died between the ages of twelve to thirteen years and nine to eleven years of age.

"Assuming the older skeleton was in fact Edward V, he was definitely not a happy camper. Examination of the skull revealed that the child probably suffered from osteomyelitis which is an infection of the bone tissue. Both sides of his lower jaw were badly infected, indicating that he suffered from swollen and inflamed gums, which would have caused considerable pain. Chances are then, he was not in very good health and was probably miserable most of the time. Could this be the reason why he was hidden away in Ludlow, so far away from court? The disease would remain chronic without treatment so it's likely that Edward V would not have ruled very well or, for very long. If the true state of his health was known, would it be reason enough to block his assumption to the throne? Did Richard learn the truth at Stony Stratford and decide then that Edward was unfit to rule?

"If young Edward was in poor health, it puts a whole new complexion on the issue. The various paintings which show the two boys as angelic may be a far cry from the truth. Edward, at least, was probably what we would call a spoiled brat, raised to the purple in a Wydville controlled environment. The younger boy was still in his mother's keeping, which again would be predominately Wydville. Remember too, Richard didn't know either of them well. We aren't taking about a uncle/nephew scenario with Richard playing with them, bouncing them on his knee if you will. Richard had spent most of the past ten years in the north while the boys were growing up. He saw them maybe twice, and that's all."

"So, what are you saying?"

"I'm saying that Richard may well have felt nothing for the

boys, and that's significant. When you're dealing with murder you have to ask yourself the same question Cicero did - 'Cui bono?' - who profits? Not even the most diehard Ricardian will deny that Richard would profit the most if both boys died by whatever means. Until conclusive evidence to the contrary is revealed, we have to put Richard at the top of the list of suspects."

"Where he belongs." Gail snapped.

"Perhaps." Laura sighed. "Anyhow, sorry to put you through all this, but when we go in there," she nodded towards the White Tower, "it's best to know a few facts. If you're ready, let's go."

Again, they made their way through the gate under the Bloody Tower, although this time Gail stopped to admire the portcullis and the massive wooden and iron reinforced doors. She paused too, to look back towards the Thames and Traitors' Gate. What thoughts raced through the minds of those unfortunate individuals as they walked through this gateway - prisoners? Gail went back over a few names; Anne Boleyn, Catherine Howard, Sir Thomas More, Princess Elizabeth. Then, Gail's mind caught on young Richard, Duke of York, running ahead of all the adults in his eagerness to see his older brother who had been proclaimed King Edward V. And, another Richard who left here a Duke and returned a King.

"Just a minute, I want to check something." Laura continued on to the northwest corner of the White Tower, looked east briefly before turning back. "There's just a small queue waiting to see the Crown Jewels. If you want to have a look, I think we should go now."

"Good idea," Gail said.

As they slid into line, Laura whispered to Gail. "Most of the royal treasure was broken up and sold by Cromwell during the Commonwealth so there are very few pieces dating from before the mid-17th century. To keep in step with the Story, only one piece, the gold Anointing Spoon may have been seen by Richard during his coronation, but since pearls were added to it by William and Mary in 16-something-or-other, it's no longer original. The other piece to watch out for is the Imperial State Crown which contains two magnificent stones. Edward the Confessor's sapphire and an uncut balas ruby which, legend says, Richard wore in his crown, well coronet, at Bosworth." Laura smiled as she nudged Gail. "One thing is certain, Richard had good taste. The jewelled coronet was worth a fortune, and he wore it atop a gilded helmet. Reason enough for someone to knock his block off, I would think."

By the time they exited the magnificent display, they were both in a state of shock. "Beats a trip to Tiffany's." Laura said, blowing her cheeks out in wonder and delight. Gail laughed as she fell in step beside Laura and together they followed the path that ran along the eastern side of the great central Keep towards the wooden steps leading upwards to the first floor of the famous White Tower.

As she climbed, Laura flipped through her volume of notes. On the landing just outside the entranceway she paused, then pulled Gail to one side. Turning to face the river, she produced a rumpled sheet of paper on which she had drawn a sketch of the placement of the various buildings as they might have appeared 500 years before. "Before we go in, have a look at this. All this open, grassy area between the White Tower and the walls, was once the Royal Ward. The entrance was via the Coldharbour Gate just around the corner on the west side of the White Tower. All that's left of it are a couple of stone circles in the grass. Where we're standing now was the site of the building beneath which the skeletons were found."

Gail studied the sketch in amazement. She had no idea that there were so many buildings contained in such a relatively small space. "So, Richard lived here?"

"I doubt it. Before he became king he rented the house of a

wealthy merchant - Crosby House. The hall portion still exists by the way. He also stayed at Baynard Castle, the ancestral home further along the Thames although his mother was usually in residence there so it wasn't an ideal location for intrigue. Once king of course, he could sleep wherever he wanted to, and he probably did." She smiled suggestively. "Come on, let's see inside."

Within, the White Tower contained a wondrous collection of armour and weapons displayed in glass cases. Laura was most impressed by the display of armour for horses, and stood a long while admiring a life-size reconstruction of a warhorse dressed in full armour, carrying a knight also suitably attired for war and accompanied by infantry dressed in leather and chain mail.

"What do you do if something like that comes charging down at you?" Laura said, looking up at the massive horse with its glittering head armour and chest plate.

"Get out of its way, I suppose."

"And beyond the reach of the mace or sword too, I bet. You know, something like this would work a treat on flat, dry ground but if that horse hit a bog or had to jump over a wall or something, all that armour would be worse than useless. No wonder so many knights were captured or died horrific deaths on the battlefield."

Finishing their tour at the northeast corner, they proceeded up to the second floor, taking care on the narrow, tapered steps.

"This spiral stair or vice is the biggest and goes from the top to the bottom of the tower complex." Laura said halfway up. "For security reasons it was placed on the other side of the entrance way to prevent the bad guys from getting upstairs easily. This is also the only tower that is round."

Arriving on the second floor level, Laura was at great pains to remind Gail that originally there was no floor above. The ceiling of the royal apartments rose through two levels in a grand Romanesque style, with a mural gallery encircling the outer walls at the level of the present third floor.

The vice brought them into what was called the 'Great

Chamber'. Turning to her left Laura guided Gail a few steps along the eastern wall and then halted before a small closet cut into the wall in an 'L' shape. "We are in the private royal apartments and this is a garderobe."

"A what?" Gail asked peering in.

"The toilet - the loo." Laura started to laugh. "Just like we learned in school, out and down the side of the tower. But, at least you had some privacy. It was somebody's job to keep the system flushed with fresh water regularly. Or, here they may have used chamber pots which would be emptied by servants. I didn't research medieval plumbing, I'm afraid. Anyhow, the only fireplace on this floor is here, midway along the eastern wall, so this must have been the living area which makes sense since the Chapel is there, on the other side. This chamber would be divided and subdivided into smaller, private areas by wooden partitions and screens. This is where I think the Princes were kept, for some of the time anyhow. Their sister, Elizabeth - Henry VII's queen - died here in 1503, on her birthday which is kind of sad." Laura sighed. It was hard to imagine with all the military hardware on display.

Laura was pleased then to pass through the archway into the Chapel of St. John the Evangelist. Gail was immediately captivated by its simple beauty. They stood for a while admiring one of the oldest and finest specimens of early Norman architecture still in existence. Unlike the rest of the White Tower, the Chapel escaped the addition of the upper floor, so they were able to imagine the concept of the lofty ceiling and mural gallery which once graced the other chambers. Though small by any standards, the Chapel conveyed a sense of strength and grace. Its twelve massive, circular stone pillars separated the space into two side aisles with the body of the fane rising to a vaulted ceiling.

"This place has so much history." Laura whispered. "Throughout the Middle Ages it was the chapel used by the sovereign when at the Tower, and it was here too that those chosen to be Knights of the Bath kept their all night vigil before being knighted by the king prior to his coronation. Now, I have something really interesting to show you."

Leaving the Chapel through another doorway in the southwest corner, Laura positioned herself at the top of a spiral staircase . "The external tower I mentioned stood just outside here. This vice spiralled down to the first floor but didn't open onto that floor like it does now, but either continued down to ground level through the external tower or, more likely, there was a set of regular stairs within that tower which took you the rest of the way to the ground. It was under those stairs at a depth of ten feet that the chest containing the two skeletons was found."

"Okay." Gail said, trying to understand what Laura was getting at.

"You know how far we are from the Bloody Tower. If the two skeletons were indeed the remains of the two Princes, then it would be quite a trick to get those bodies from way over on the outside of the Palace Ward, through Coldharbour, to their final resting place. What I am suggesting is that the Princes were killed on this floor, probably in the royal apartments next to the Chapel. Their bodies were then taken along the same route we came, out the door here and down. The chances of being seen were virtually nil, if the entrances into this external tower were watched, and the view from the Great Hall obscured by a screen or something. If it was done late at night, there wouldn't have been a problem.

"Unless," Gail said, turning to face Laura, "the Princes were confined in the Bloody . . . I mean, Garden Tower, then escorted across the Green and, as you said through the Gate late at night, then murdered on the ground floor of this external tower."

"Possible, but surely someone would have seen them and their escort. Over 300 people lived here at that time,"

"That depends," Gail said, warming to the idea, "suppose the boys were told that they were going to see their mother secretly in the Tower Chapel. They would have to be very quiet, perhaps wear cloaks to disguise themselves and then, once inside the external tower, before they had a chance to climb the stairs, they were murdered. Everything would be prepared in advance, even the wardrobe chest would be there, waiting for them, the grave under the stairway dug. That way, no bodies needed to be carried anywhere. They walked to their deaths."

"And the hair at the back of my neck is standing up. Gail, you just might have hit on a very distinct possibility."

"Now tell me, did Richard order the murders?"

Laura turned away and walked slowly back towards the Chapel. Gail watched her every movement but stayed where she was, waiting. Time seemed to stand still as Laura stood with her back to Gail, deep in thought.

"Richard ordered the executions of five men to gain the throne. He was tired, sick to death himself with the struggle and the need. He had something in mind for the boys, but I can't believe it was murder."

"You're not convincing me." Gail said, turning her head to the side, biting at her lower lip as she gazed at Laura intently.

"That's probably because I haven't convinced myself. Let's see the rest of the Tower. We can discuss the Princes later, if you don't mind, when we can focus our complete attention. We're running short of time if we want to see the basement here and the Beauchamp Tower."

Gail thought for a moment, then agreed, but as Laura moved past her towards the Great Hall, Gail took her arm and whispered, "I want to know tonight, over dinner, who killed them or else I'll jump all over your bed until you do."

"But, I thought you were going to tell me." Laura said laughing. "As I said, I'll give you all the information possible, but you're going to solve the case. This is the Great Hall by the way." She said, as she moved along, looking to the left and right. Gail let go of her in exasperation. "There's no fireplace here so there must have been a central hearth or a series of braziers perhaps, but the loos are up here at the end. Two of them - no waiting. And, there's another halfway up the vice in the northwest tower. This Hall was where all the entertainment took place and was probably the site of the Council meeting which ended so abruptly with Hastings' departure. Richard may have watched the execution from here."

Laura waited for Gail to catch up before moving towards the vice. As Laura began to descend, Gail hesitated. "I guess you don't want to bother with the upper floor?"

"Not today." Laura said, stopping on the stair to smile up at Gail before she turned abruptly and made her way down into the dungeons of the White Tower.

She stood back and watched as Gail issued from the vice. "Sorry I can't come up with skeletons hanging about or prisoners chained to the walls, moaning for water."

"Doesn't look much like a dungeon to me." Gail huffed as she regarded the freshly whitewashed walls and modern electric lighting.

"From what I've been able to find out, the real nastiness was carried out in a subterranean crypt beneath the sub-crypt of the Chapel." Laura led the way through the first compartment of the Tower on the eastern side, heading south towards an archway which led into the crypt, now largely featureless except for the massive barrel-vaulted ceiling. Laura stood on a wooden floor which strongly suggested a level below since elsewhere the floor was flagstone. The infamous subterranean torture chamber lay, Laura reasoned, beneath her feet. She shivered.

"This is how Father John Gerard described his experience when he was tortured in 1597. He was led down into the torture chamber through subterranean passages lighted by candles. *'It was a place of immense extent and in it were arranged divers sorts of racks, and other instruments of torture. Some of these they displayed before me, and told me that I should have to taste them. They then led me to a great upright beam or pillar of wood, which was one of the supports of this vast crypt.'* Anyhow, it certainly sounds like this place."

"What happened to him?"

"He was strung up for a while, suspended in iron gauntlets by his wrists. Apparently he was a fairly heavy man and tall too, so they had to dig away the earth from beneath his feet to ensure that the full weight of his body was brought to bear. He must have suffered terribly but steadfastly refused to reveal any information. He managed to escape eventually.'

"Actually, the rack was the most commonly use instrument of torture, although after the wreck of the Spanish Armada in 1588, the Tower acquired an almost inexhaustible supply of manacles, which became popular. Then there was the *peine forte et dure*, or pressing to death, although it wasn't actually considered a torture device."

"Excuse me, being pressed to death wasn't a form of torture?"

"Well, no, not exactly. The *peine forte et dure* was the only device recognized by common law. It wasn't used as a means of torture, more a means of quasi-judicial murder, or from the victim's perspective, suicide."

"Oh well, that's all right then. And here I thought maybe someone was going to get hurt or something."

Laura couldn't help but laugh. "The idea, you see, was that the estate of a man who died under torture could still pass to his heirs, whereas if he was put on trial and subsequently convicted or signed a confession and was then executed, everything would pass to the Crown. It was preferred over starvation since it was quicker and considered more humane."

Gail grimaced.

"If you don't like that, there's always the 'Cell of Little Ease' or Oubliette as it was called. It was a dungeon so small that it was impossible to either stand upright or lie down. It did little to improve posture, believe me."

Gail made a sound like a shiver, crossed her arms and backed out of the room. "Did any women suffer here?"

"Yes, one I know of, during the reign of Henry VIII, but you don't want to know."

"Come on, tell me."

Laura paused a moment, sighed, then proceeded. "Okay, I will because her story needs to be told. She was a very brave lady, not famous or anything, but she died a horrible death rather than betray others. Anne Askew was her name and her crime was her belief in the new Protestantism. We have to remember that even though King Henry VIII replaced the Pope as head of the new Church of England, he was still in every sense of the word a Roman Catholic. Anne's beliefs were heretical and it would seem that she tried to influence Henry's last wife, Catherine Parr. Anne was racked so savagely while they were trying to force her to name her fellow sectarians, that she was unable to walk and had to be carried, strapped to a chair, to be burned at the stake in Smithfield."

Laura wandered off a few paces to allow the enormanity of such a crime sink in. A hush fell. No one disturbed them. Finally she turned and faced Gail. "If we decide between us that Richard ordered the murder of the two boys then that's fine, but if so, he did it for all the right motives. Self-preservation, for the good of strong government, for his wife and young son. He did it because he hated the Wydvilles and what they represented. He did it because he couldn't stand by and see the throne of England ruled by such upstart commoners who had no idea of majesty. Against his supposed crimes, we have men like Henry VIII, who tortured, maimed and murdered to satisfy a lust for power. Not one or two, but dozens - perhaps hundreds. Here were housed instruments of infinite and unspeakable terror, a legacy from his father which he passed on to his son and then his daughters, Bloody Mary and Elizabeth.

"There you go again," Gail growled, "trying to absolve Richard of his crimes by suggesting that future kings were even more barbaric. But, you're forgetting one very important thing."

"What's that?"

"He killed children."

"There's no proof. And besides, even if he did, they were very dangerous children."

"But children nevertheless."

Gail moved away then to explore further, leaving Laura behind in deep and troubled thought. After a few minutes, Laura caught up with her on the western side just as she threw a coin into a well.

"I'm sorry." Laura sighed. "You're right, I'm going to have to keep everything in perspective. But, I don't believe he killed those kids."

Gail turned then and faced Laura straight on. "Don't you?"

Laura stretched out, luxuriating in the simple comfort of being able to sit and relax. Covent Garden spilled out around her so she people watched for a while through half-closed lids, blissfully unaware of Gail's mild agitation. Suddenly she turned, focusing her attention. "Haven't you had enough?"

"No. Come on, you promised. We left the Story with Richard being proclaimed king, right? What happened then?"

Staring at Gail briefly, Laura sighed and proceeded to extract her notes from her bag. She was tired, but now that Gail had actually seen the Tower, had developed a sense of the place, it was time to finish it. It took her a few minutes to find her place while Gail waited, a portrait of patience as she idly sipped her wine. Finally Laura began.

"Although Richard's reign technically began on the 26th of June, it wasn't until July 6th that the actual coronation took place and what an event it was. Under the circumstances you'd think he would have opted for a small, private ceremony, but it was one of the most splendid of all mediaeval coronations, right down to the cloth of gold and a mantle of purple trimmed with ermine."

"Well, I guess he felt he had to look the part." Gail shrug.

"He looked the part all right, but the Londoners weren't buying. Despite the magnificent display and the large number of nobles assembled, the atmosphere was ripe with tension and resentment.

No one was about to say very much though with the Duke of Northumberland's troops just outside the gates and the city dotted with men in Richard's livery. Actually, poor old Dickie started his reign at a decided disadvantage. Not only were the circumstances a subject of gossip and dissatisfaction, but quite frankly, he didn't look like a king, at least compared to his brother. Edward IV was a big man, fair of face with chestnut coloured hair, a regal bearing and a winning smile. He was totally charming and made a habit of stopping and chatting with the common folk who adored him and forgave him everything. Richard had none of those qualities. We know even today how important looks are for any public figure, particularly a politician. To win hearts and minds for that matter, you had to have charisma. I think Richard had it, but at a personal level, one on one, but I doubt if he was able to project himself sufficiently well to deflect the fear, suspicion and downright hatred which surrounded him. He may have seen himself as the sole legitimate heir of the House of York and the throne of England, but what did others see?

"After the ceremony in Westminster Abbey, a huge banquet was set out in Westminster Hall. It lasted five and half hours, if you can believe it. Archbishop Bourgchier anointed and crowned Richard King of England, but he didn't attend the party afterwards. Makes you wonder what thoughts raced through his mind as he placed the crown on Richard's head? All the promises he made to Elizabeth Wydville regarding the safety of the two Princes. He must have been sick with worry, knowing the boys were so closely guarded in the Tower.

"There were a few other absentees at the banquet too. Richard's mother, for starters and Buckingham's wife, Katherine Wydville, who was ordered by her husband to stay at home."

"I don't suppose Elizabeth Wydville even received an invitation."

"No, she was off the guest list too. A day or two after the coronation, Richard and Anne went to Greenwich Palace and then on to Windsor. The northern troops were sent home, much to the relief of the Londoners and life resumed its normal pace or at least appeared to. Rumours regarding the fate of the two Princes persisted, however. Shortly after Richard left the city to begin his grand tour of the country, the boys ceased to be seen altogether."

"He killed them before he left London?

Raising a warning finger, Laura paused. "Remember, no one knows for sure what happened to the Princes. Many sources have suggested that Richard had the boys murdered before he left London. Shakespeare wrote it that way, but there is evidence enough to suggest that they were still alive then. For one thing, More states that a fellow by the name of Miles Forrest was assigned to the two Princes shortly after Richard's departure. Forrest was a Northerner, had a criminal record and was totally loyal to Richard."

"Oh, oh." Gail said ominously.

Laura looked up and smiled.

With her chin resting in both palms and her body leaning slightly forward, Gail was all attention. Laura just hoped she was listening carefully because this was one version which, although plausible, left Laura decidedly uneasy.

Just as Laura was about to begin, their meals arrived. Rearranging her note book, Laura continued between mouthfuls. "On the 17th of July, Richard appointed Sir Robert Brackenbury, Constable of the Tower with the specific task of seeing to the safekeeping of the two boys. Brackenbury was also totally loyal to Richard. He had been Treasurer of the Household in the North, working his way into Richard's confidence after years of service. He was apparently considered to be an honourable man, although he also seemed incapable of seeing anything wrong in his royal master, and in fact, died with Richard at Bosworth. Brackenbury took his job seriously, no doubt realizing the potential risk posed by the two young Princes."

"What do you mean?"

"Well, Richard must have realized that attempts would be made to free the boys, spirit them away to the Continent perhaps. They were a focal point for rebellion and Richard could ill afford to allow Tower security to be a casual affair. Short of ensuring that they were closely watched and surrounded by men of proven loyalty to him, Richard seemed content to let matters rest. The boys might have lived if their mother hadn't stirred up trouble, plotting against Richard and inciting rebellion. In a sense, she sealed their fate."

"Do you really think Richard would have let the boys live out their days in the Tower? Not much of a life?"

"I don't think he actively sought their death. Keeping them out of public view as he did, he probably subscribed to the belief that, out of sight was out of mind, and hoped that his good government would eventually persuade those against him that he made the better king after all. Seems reasonable to me, but as I said, Liz Wydville just couldn't leave it alone.

"In late July, while at Minster Lovell, Richard was informed of a plot to evacuate the Princesses from Sanctuary and send them overseas in the belief that, with the female line safely out of reach, Richard would think twice about doing away with his nephews. Reasoning that if a marriage could be arranged for the oldest daughter - Elizabeth of York - to a suitable prince willing to fight to regain his wife's inheritance and naturally a throne too, Elizabeth Wydville would find herself back in power."

"It's almost as if she thought her sons were already dead," Gail said sadly.

"Perhaps. They were certainly held so securely in the Tower that they might as well have been. It would have been not only a waste of time, but dangerous too, to have attempted to rescue them, so she may well have supposed them lost.

"Anyhow, Richard sent a note to John Russell, now acting as Lord Chancellor, basically instructing him to look into the matter of the 'Sanctuary Plot' and if necessary, arrest any conspirators. Russell was only partially successful since the rebels fled abroad and Elizabeth and her daughters remained safely out of reach in sanctuary.

"As Richard continued his progress north, he must have had time to think. When he reached Gloucester he sent for a John Green, another trusted retainer, and gave him specific orders, sending Green, according to More's account, *'unto Sir Robert Brackenbury, Constable of the Tower, with a letter and credence that the same Sir Robert should in any wise put the two children to death'.*"

"No," Gail said firmly, "I can't imagine Richard would be stupid enough to write a letter. Hope the weather's nice, oh, and P.S., please murder the two boys for me. That just doesn't make sense."

Laura smiled indulgently. "The letter would be carefully worded and Green would carry 'credence', perhaps something personal of Richard's, like a ring or something that Brackenbury would recognise. Green would advise Brackenbury of Richard's intentions verbally, nothing written. Anyhow, Brackenbury refused to do the job and Green was forced to return to Richard having failed in his mission.

"The Duke of Buckingham was with Richard in Gloucester at this time. Sir Thomas More suggests that Richard told Buckingham of his decision to do away with the Princes and that Buckingham was appalled. He had helped Richard to gain the throne, but the murder of the boys was going too far. Anyhow, they had a dreadful argument. Pleading urgent family business, Buckingham quit Richard's presence and returned to his holdings in the Welsh Marshes.

"Richard continued his journey north, arriving at Warwick Castle on about the 8th of August. Green met him there and told him of Brackenbury's refusal. Richard should have been furious but instead, More paints a picture of him sitting on the loo muttering, *'Whom shall a man trust? Those that I have brought up myself fail me, and at my commandment will do nothing for me'.* Shades of King Henry II's 'will no one rid me of this turbulent priest'?

"A page heard all this and suggested that Sir James Tyrell might be just the man Richard was looking for. Tyrell was one of Richard's confidential servants. He had escorted Richard's mother-in-law to Middleham way back in 1473, had been knighted after the Battle of Tewkesbury and acted as Archbishop Rotherham's jailer in June. Currently he was Richard's Knight of the Body, which meant that he slept outside the bedroom door to ensure that his master was not disturbed. Totally trusted by Richard, he was still just a dog's body and he knew it. More suggests that Tyrell was jealous of Ratcliffe and Catesby, two relative new comers who were enjoying rewards which he felt he deserved. Tyrell craved advancement, revenge on his rivals, a special place just for him at Richard's side, and who knows, the keys to the executive washroom and a parking spot close to the door."

Gail's head shot up.

Laura began to laugh. "Sorry, thought I'd throw that in for comic relief."

"Get on with it." Gail huffed.

Laura took a sip of wine before continuing. "September 8th had been selected for the investiture of Richard's son, Edward of Middleham, as Prince of Wales. According to both More and Vergil, Tyrell was sent to London to collect the necessary robes and wall-hangings for the ceremony to be held in York. A perfect cover-up, if you will excuse the pun, for Tyrell's true intentions in London.

"More's account of events suggests that Tyrell rode to London in company with a John Dighton who was Tyrell's own *'horsekeeper, a big, broad, strong knave'*. More also states that Tyrell carried a note from the King to Brackenbury, *'by which he was commanded to deliver to Sir James all the keys to the Tower for one night, to the end he might there accomplish the King's pleasure'*. This Brackenbury did, no doubt aware of Tyrell's intentions, but powerless to stop him.

More's account of the death of the two Princes is graphically detailed, which to me suggests that his tendency to poetic license exceeded his grasp of reality. But, here it is. Tyrell engaged Forrest and Dighton to help him. Around midnight, his two accomplices *'came into the chamber and suddenly lapped them up among the clothes, so bewrapped them hard into their mouths, that within a while smothered and stifled, their breath failing, they gave up to God their innocent souls into the joys of Heaven, leaving to their tormentors their bodies dead in the bed. Which, after that, and after long lying still, to be thoroughly dead, they laid their bodies naked out upon the bed and fetched Sir James to see them'."*

Gail uttered a low groan as she leaned back in her seat, her eyes averted as she slowly shook her head. Laura watched her, concerned. This was old news to Laura. She had read a great deal on the subject, both fact and fiction, but for Gail, this account was her first real introduction into the realm of actual possibility. She was not dealing with a Shakespearean play here, but a concerted stab at historical fact. She sat quietly, head bowed, obviously thinking things through. Laura waited. Finally, she raised her head while at the same time drawing both hands close to the edge of the table, forming them into two tight fists.

"Tell me something," she said, staring at Laura, "if, for the sake of argument, Elizabeth of York had been taken from sanctuary to Europe and married to Henry Tudor, would Richard have considered it a disaster? If the two boys were alive in the Tower, it seems to me that they would be more of a threat to Tudor than Richard. I mean, I doubt if Tudor would be interested in fighting for his bride if he had to hand over the rewards of his victory to Elizabeth's brother, Edward. It doesn't make sense. Besides, you said that Richard was experienced in the field of battle so he would have welcomed the chance to prove his valour in hand to hand combat and win the throne officially." She shrugged. "Why kill the boys?"

Laura smiled. "And that, my dear, is the logic behind the pro-Richard camp, and, on the surface, it makes a lot of sense. The redoubtable More not only decided that Richard was some kind of monster, but he also assumed that he was incredibly stupid, which he was definitely not. In his haste to lay the blame at Richard's feet, he produced a morality play with holes in it big enough to run a double decker bus through.

"Elizabeth of York was the female heir to the throne. For Tudor to marry her, she would first have to be declared legitimate, and in doing so, both her brothers would regain their claim to the throne in preference to her. It would be in Richard's best interest to ensure that both boys remained in excellent health, but naturally, closely guarded as I said before. Closely guarded and bastardized, that was the way Richard wanted it. Tudor, on the other hand, would only succeed if those boys where declared legitimate and dead."

Gail smiled as she rubbed her hands in glee. "I knew Richard didn't kill his nephews." She was positively expansive now, having helped prove Richard instantly innocent of the crime.

Laura was bewildered. "Excuse me just a minute. Are you forgetting the ruthlessness of the man? What about Hastings, Vaughan, Rivers? If Richard could murder without trial, then don't you think that at least he was a force to be reckoned with? Why are you so sure that he didn't kill the Princes?"

"I'm not," Gail said, "but, I hate the idea of someone like More, years after Richard's death, going around saying with impunity, and no doubt Tudor support, that Richard was a child killer, a deformed monster, etcetera. It isn't fair and besides, logic has determined for us that Richard was an unlikely candidate. I remember studying Henry VII in school. He was a cold, calculating man. He ruled with an iron hand, unloved and unloving. Wasn't he the one that instituted the court of the 'Star Chamber' - political terror wrapped in a cloak of legalese?"

"All right," Laura said, taking a different tack. "Who did kill the boys?"

Gail smiled wickedly. "I don't know for sure, but I think you're about to tell me."

They were on their main course by then. Their waiter expertly removing dishes in such a manner that their conversation went totally uninterrupted They ate in silence for awhile, each savouring the food and the chance to think through what had been discussed so far. When Gail looked up, Laura was sitting there with chin in hand, elbow resting on the table, staring vaguely in the direction of Gail's plate. She had given up on her salad, and had in fact, moved it aside, allowing more room for her notes. Helping herself to a bread stick, she took a bite then waved it in the air.

"Okay, so let's assume that Richard left London with the knowledge that the two Princes were safely tucked away in the Tower under close guard. They were apparently seen afterwards, playing in the Lieutenant's garden. Let's assume also that Richard had decided to put off whatever plans he may have had for them until he returned to London in a couple of months or so, after he had secured the realm and won over the hearts of the people. Declared bastards, they were no threat to him and rescue or escape was impossible."

Placing her right hand on top of her notes, fingers spread, she continued. "What we need to find is someone else with a good motive for wanting to murder the two Princes. Note I said murder, as in 'cause a scandal'. A murder so foul and inhuman that it would make otherwise loyal, trustworthy men switch their allegiance. A deed so nasty that it could be spoken of only in hushed whispers behind closed doors. Rumours and whispers sufficient to rock the very foundations of a kingdom and destroy a monarchy.

"We would need someone positively evil, unnaturally cruel and malicious and," she added, tapping her first finger on her notes for emphasis, "extraordinarily ambitious. A gamesman capable of running with the hare or the hounds, and able to wait, bide his time, then strike at the appropriate moment. Someone eloquent and, most of all, capable of telling the 'big lie' and getting away with it. He should be handsome and charming too, so as to draw others in easily, like a spider might a fly."

Laura paused, reached into her bag, extracted a cigarette and lit it, while Gail watched her every move, knife and fork poised, the remainder of her meal momentarily forgotten. Leaning back, Laura prepared to enjoy her cigarette, seemingly oblivious to Gail as she idly watch a couple pass by on their way out of the restaurant. The cigarette was more than half finished before Gail could stand it no longer.

"Who?" Gail said, leaning forward.

"Come on Gail, there aren't that many characters on the stage. Who must it be? Who would have the personal power, the opportunity, the trust, all the things necessary to get close to those boys? I'll give you a clue. He killed for his own ambition, not another's."

Laura watched dispassionately as Gail shifted through the possibilities. "Buckingham." She said triumphantly.

Laura smiled and nodded, "Henry Stafford, second Duke of Buckingham." Then her face clouded. "You know, he was a strange man. The more I read about him, the less I like him. Arrogant and vain, he was unpopular at court during King Edward's reign and stayed more or less in the background until recent events. It was Buckingham who saw to Hastings execution; Richard wasn't even there.

"Richard left on his tour around the 10th of July, but Brackenbury wasn't appointed Constable of the Tower until the 17th, so who was in charge in between? On the 15th, Buckingham was made Lord High Constable of England, which meant that he was responsible for all the fortifications and defences of the realm. All the strongholds came under his jurisdiction, including the Tower of London.

"Now John, Lord Howard, was also very ambitious. He apparently wanted the title of Duke of Norfolk, which just happened to belong to young Richard, Duke of York. It seems obvious that he hoped to regain his hereditary rights through Richard once he was on the throne. John Howard was a powerful man politically, but hot-tempered, violent and cruel by nature. A most curious entry appears in his household books on May 21st, 1483. It has to do with six men working for three days, three beds, sacks of lime, nails and lengths of timber.

"There may be absolutely no connection whatsoever with the Princes, but let's try a scenario. Suppose those men were busy doing something else besides making three cheap beds and whitewashing walls, which the entry suggests. Suppose that Buckingham approached Howard in that week after Richard left London and told him that Richard wanted the boys dead at the first opportunity. Howard had received his reward from Richard on the 28th of June and was now not only Duke of Norfolk, but also hereditary Earl Marshall of England. As I said, the title of Duke still technically belonged to the younger Prince and was not really up for grabs, unless …

"Unlike Richard, perhaps Howard felt that it wasn't enough to just lock the boys away, so when Buckingham approached him, he was eager to help, thinking he was doing Richard a favour as well as following orders. Besides, he had fought long and hard to achieve his new title and he wasn't about to let a bastardised brat of a ten year old spoil things for him.

"There's no firm evidence that Buckingham accompanied Richard on the royal progress. In fact, his name is conspicuously absent from the list of guests present at a dinner in the King's honour at Magdalen College, Oxford."

"So, you're saying Buckingham stayed on in London?"

"Yes, but for the life of me I can't understand why Richard would allow a loose cannon like Buckingham out of his sight, and then to appoint him Constable of England? There's got to be something wrong here. Despite all his recent service to Richard, Buckingham was a closet Lancastrian. His grandfather had died fighting against the House of York at Northampton during the summer of 1460, for heaven's sake. Royal blood flowed thick in Buckingham's veins too, and he had ambition enough for half a dozen men, plus a strong young male heir.

"Remember, Brackenbury didn't come on the scene until the 17th. Buckingham was appointed High Constable on the 15th.

It's my contention that, with or without Howard's help, Buckingham arranged the death of the two boys sometime between the 15th and 17th of July, probably late at night and perhaps as you've suggested. He didn't join up with Richard in Gloucester until the 29th, and that was when they had the argument. Anti-Richard types suggest it was because Richard told Buckingham that he was thinking of murdering the boys, or had already murdered them. It could just as well have been the other way around."

"Richard would have been furious," Gail said, shaking her head.

"That would be the understatement of the week, but what could he do? The deed had been done, and by his most trusted adviser, friend and confidant. Frankly I think Buckingham had the whole thing planned right from the start, just after King Edward died. Become Richard's friend, help destroy the Wydvilles, put Richard on the throne, discredit him by murdering the Princes, and then, when he left Richard in a huff, he began to plot against him, which culminated in open rebellion later that year. When he arrived at his estates in Wales, guess who was there?"

"Mrs. Buckingham?"

Laura laughed. "John Morton, Bishop of Ely. Remember, he was one of the men arrested in Council when Hastings was accused of treason? He became a prisoner under the care of Buckingham. He even asked to be Morton's jailer which, in itself, is suggestive. Now, Morton was a nasty bit of work. Sly, secretive, a lover of intrigue, he hated Richard with a passion. Soon Buckingham and Morton were busy scheming together. I doubt if Buckingham told Morton the truth about the Princes. Besides, Morton would want to believe that Richard murdered them because that was just what was needed to undermine Richard, both as a man and a king. Morton must have rubbed his hands in glee. There's no doubt that Morton masterminded the events that followed. Poor Buckingham ended up being dragged along when Morton made it clear that he would support Henry Tudor and not him in a bid for the throne.

Buckingham was faced with a dilemma then. His claim to the throne was much stronger than Henry's, but without support - and he couldn't expect much after his recent attachment to Richard - he didn't have a hope. Perhaps, he reasoned, once Richard was gotten rid of, he could step forward, show his pedigree, and bump Henry off, literally and figuratively."

Gail chuckled.

"Well, you'd have to be smoking funny cigarettes to believe that a man like Buckingham would've been happy putting Elizabeth Wydville's daughter on the throne, or Tudor. Tudor's branch of the royal tree was on the wrong side of the blanket, to put it politely, so I can't imagine Buckingham accepting such a sow's ear as king.

Anyhow, Morton and Buckingham made their way to London and had a wee chat with Henry Tudor's mother, Margaret Beaufort. A deal was struck. Buckingham would help put Henry on the throne, Henry would marry Elizabeth of York, and everyone would live happily ever after. In the meantime, rumours were circulated that the two boys had been murdered by order of their uncle. Everyone assumed that that was Richard, of course, although Buckingham was their uncle too. Neat, aye?"

"And when did Elizabeth Wydville find out and who told her?"

"I would imagine that job fell to Margaret Beaufort. Again, the good news, bad news scenario. 'First the bad news. Your sons are dead, Richard killed them, but the good news is that your daughter will marry my son and be a Queen.

"Well," Laura said, leaning back in her chair and lighting another cigarette, "how did you like that story?"

"I feel sorry for Elizabeth Wydville."

"Don't." Laura said flatly. "She had her chance and she blew it. So many people hated her and her cool aloofness, her counterfeit regal bearing. Buckingham did. He hated her so much that killing her sons would have been easy for him. He might even have enjoyed it."

"You make him sound like a monster."

"He was. Do you know what Richard said of Buckingham when he heard of his defection? He called him *'the most untrue creature living'.*"

Gail turned her wine glass around and around, thinking. "Why didn't Richard denounce Buckingham. Why didn't he let the whole world know up front that it was Buckingham who murdered the Princes?"

"Well, at first I doubt if Richard believed him, and that was probably why he sent Green down to London. Green returned with the horrible truth that the boys were missing, but no one knew what happened to them or where they were, alive or dead. Brackenbury may have delayed telling Richard in the hope of finding the boys before anyone knew. Can you imagine his panic when he took office only to find his two charges missing? And I think that's important. The boys were **missing**. The idea of murder probably never enter anyone's head. Children don't get murdered!"

"But," Gail said, "everyone believed that Richard did murder them."

"Shakespeare, More, how pleased they would be, because now we have a true morality play. Richard's draconian treatment of everyone from his own mother-in-law way back in his early twenties, right through to Hastings' execution without trial - all the birds were coming home to roost. He had dared and succeeded at the most unlawful, disgusting and frankly, bloody crimes. As a result, he was universally feared and even hated. Everything he had ever done was for his own gain, even where the Church was concerned. Kill two young boys? If it meant that he could feel more secure on the throne - sure. That people believed that he was capable of such a crime - most certainly. Like his long dead brother, George, Richard became the instrument of his own destruction. Whether or not he murdered the Princes in the Tower became academic. The fact that most people **believed** he did was all that was important. And, no one knew better than Buckingham just how vulnerable Richard was in that regard.

Laura sighed as she pushed her notes aside. "Anyhow, we'll have lots of time to talk about this during our travels. Enough. At the risk of being told I drink too much, I think I'll have a nice glass of port."

Smiling broadly at Gail, she signalled their waiter. Gail recovered just in time to add a dish of spumoni ice cream to the order before the waiter hurried away.

Day 3

Windsor - Minster Lovell - Littledean - Tewkesbury

Elizabeth: *Ay me! I see the ruin of my house.*
The tiger now hath seized the gentle hind;
Insulting tyranny begins to jet
Upon the innocent and aweless throne:
Welcome destruction, death and massacre!
I see, as in a map, the end of all.

Shakespeare -
The Tragedy of King Richard the Third
[Act II, Scene 4]

Gail stood, hands on hips and watched as Laura rummage through the trunk of their rental car. "What are you doing?"

Laura straightened, then smiled triumphantly as she waved a dog-eared *Official Guide to Windsor Castle* as well as a brochure entitled *The Romance of St. George's Chapel.*

"You carried those all this way?"

"Well, they cost money and since I already had them in my library, I figured I'd save a couple of pounds anyway." She shrugged. "Besides, they're not very old. I don't suppose too much has changed. Certainly Saint George's Chapel will be the same. I haven't heard of any bodies being added, subtracted - or moved about, have you?" The question was strictly rhetorical.

"Now, let's see. Ah yes, good old William the Conqueror. He started building Windsor as part of a chain of defensive castles up and down the country. The White Tower, part of the Tower of

London was one, and there were others. A ring of nine, each twenty miles from the other and not more than a day's march away should there be trouble. The booklet goes on about all the various changes and additions made to the castle over the years. Okay, here we are - Henry VIII's Gate, circa 1511. Let's go."

Laura walked across the road quickly with Gail trailing in her wake. Both came to a halt just in front of the imposing towered gateway. Laura pointed to the panel above the arch. "Henry's coat of arms, the Tudor rose and the pomegranate, symbol of his first wife Catherine of Aragon. Amazing he didn't have that part removed after he dumped her." She huffed. Laura didn't like Henry VIII very much, and sometimes it showed.

Henry's Gate had become the official exit in recent times, so they were forced to climb the gradual slope up Castle Hill where they purchased their tickets near the entrance at St. George's Gate. Once inside the Middle Ward, they found themselves in a courtyard area with the Chapel to their left, hidden by trees while the bulk of the Round Tower loomed above them on the right, its height exaggerated by the earthen mound upon which it stood

Their progress was gently down hill now as they moved from the Middle to the Lower Ward and their first clear view of the St. George's Chapel.

Gail stepped away from Laura and turned around and around, admiring the beauty. When she glanced back at Laura, she found her staring at the Chapel with a pensive look on her face.

"There's King Edward IV's monument. Pity he didn't live long enough to see it completed." Gail turned then to concentrate on the Chapel which she had heard so much about. "The Tudors finished it. Richard may have undertaken some work, but there's no record, beyond the reburial of Henry VI of course." Laura paused, biting at her lower lip. "Hastings is buried here."

"Then, in a sense, this is Richard's monument too." Gail said, matter-of-factly.

Laura smiled thinly. "Yes, I suppose it is. Come on, I'll

introduce you to a few of the principal characters."

As they entered through the small porch on the south side, they found themselves in the nave. Momentarily taken aback by the sheer beauty around them, they stood together in awed silence.

"This way." Laura whispered as she turned to the right, walking as quietly as she could along the aisle towards the choir. Just south of the high altar, she stopped. "King Henry VI." She stood with her head bowed slightly as Gail positioned herself beside her. "I have to read to you what another brochure I have at home said.

'In the story of the chapels within St. George's the reputed brutality of King Richard III has recurred. There is one thing, however, for which he is remembered at Windsor with gratitude. The removal of the body of King Henry VI from Chertsey to St. George's'."

"Reputed brutality - that's a bit strong." Gail protested.

"Well, that's what it said." Laura shrugged. "Poor old Henry. Well, at least he has a tomb and despite attempts to divert pilgrims by moving the body here, they continued to come in droves."

"You know," Gail mused, "it must have been embarrassing for Richard. Pilgrims coming here to pray at the tomb of someone he murdered."

"Embarrassing, yes, and worse. That's why I believe that if, and I mean if, he killed the Princes, he was determined that no bodies would be found. They were meant to disappear and so they did for two hundred years." Laura sighed. As much as she wanted to give Richard the proverbial benefit of the doubt, there were times when it was very difficult to do so.

Laura moved then across the choir, behind the high altar to the northeast corner, where a stark, black marble slab was set into the stone wall. Written in letters of solid brass - Edward IIIJ - King Edward IV.

"Sorry it's so modern." Laura said briskly. "I don't think Eddie would be too pleased with this. He left specific instructions on what he wanted long before he died. Even his coat of arms which hung here was stolen by Oliver Cromwell's crowd. When repairs were being made in . . . yes, here it is, 1789, the coffins of Edward and his queen were found and naturally opened. Ned was measured at six foot four. Can you imagine?"

Gail frowned. "I thought everyone was short in those days."

"Not always." Laura replied flatly. "King Edward III was well over six feet tall and he died in 1377. Height was more a function of nutrition, I think, as was longevity. Henry VIII certainly had enough to eat, and it showed."

Gail's frown increased.

"I know what you're thinking. All those little doors, right?" Gail nodded. "They were made short to disadvantage anyone going in or out." Laura chuckled. "You see, if you were a good guy, no problem but if you weren't, all that stooping and ducking meant that you'd likely be taken out before you had a chance to straighten up, let alone get your sword out."

Gail nodded abstractly. Her gaze had shifted to a chapel near by. Beautifully decorated with medieval paintings and brightly coloured scrollwork, it was in sharp contrast to anything else yet seen.

"Lord Hastings." Laura said evenly as she walked behind Gail the short distance which separated the remains of two who had been friends and exiles together. "The guidebook states categorically that Richard III had him executed."

Laura sighed as she ran her fingers along the delicately carved stone. "The tomb suits him. He was quite a flamboyant man in life, well liked and respected. A short life, but he enjoyed it to the full I gather." She paused. "You know, no matter how hard I try, I can't understand Richard's motives in executing him. The poor man had absolutely no opportunity to refute the charges against him. There was no trial and no evidence was ever produced to justify the charges of witchcraft and treason. Maybe all those Ricardians who think that King Richard was such a great guy should come and stand where we are now."

"Maybe Richard reasoned that it was a necessary evil." Gail suggested.

"Yeah, it was evil all right but, was it necessary? That's what I'm having trouble with." Laura growled. "I mean, if Richard believed Hastings was a danger, he could have had him imprisoned upcountry, not hacked to death." Her fingers fell away. "Ready to continue?"

"Sure," Gail whispered as she too stepped back.

Slowly they walked west, down the aisle towards the Rutland Chapel. They could hear whispered conversations some distance away, but they still felt as if they had St. George's all to themselves. "There's one more tomb here which relates directly to the Story. Someone else Richard had executed." Laura paused, disappointed. The chapel was closed

Gail came to rest beside Laura. "Not another one?" She choked.

"And his brother-in-law, too." Laura leafed through the guidebook again. "I was afraid of this. This chapel isn't usually open to the public, but there are two pictures in the book here. Sir Thomas St. Leger was married to Richard's sister, Anne. She was Duchess of Exeter, but had obtained a divorce to marry her lover, Thomas. St. Leger was one of the traitors captured by Richard during Buckingham's rebellion of 1483. He was executed at Exeter which, when you think about it, is an interesting coincidence. Apparently he was a closet Wydville who hoped to marry his daughter to the Marquess of Dorset. He got some sort of trial I guess, before Richard had his head lopped off. Fortunately, Anne had died in 1476 so Richard was spared the task of explaining to his sister why her husband wasn't coming home for dinner." Laura chuckled, though Gail seemed less then amused.

Slowly Laura turned away. "Just along here is the Urswick Chapel. Christopher Urswick was a confidential agent and confessor to Margaret Beaufort - Henry VII's mother. He encouraged a Sir Reginald Bray to spend lavishly on St. George's. Bray's tomb is across the nave so we will get to him soon. Although Urswick is described as pious and humble, he was also a spy and a carrier of messages between Margaret and her son during Richard's reign. Both Christopher and Sir Reginald negotiated the marriage of Henry Tudor to Richard's niece, Elizabeth of York."

Their circuit of St. George's was almost complete now as they turned east again, past the entrance porch, to the Bray Chapel. "Sir Reginald Bray was a servant of Margaret Beaufort, and later on a favoured and trusted minister of her son. During the rebellion of 1483, Bray was heavily involved in the recruitment of men to Buckingham's cause. When he died in 1503, the nave where we're standing now was barely above ground level. He added considerably to the construction, so we can thank him for that.

"Now, just along here is the Oliver King Chapel. Oliver found himself in a spot of bother when Richard came on the scene. As secretary to young Edward V, he was imprisoned on the 11th of June, 1483, two days before Hastings's death."

Suddenly she frowned. "Do you know, I have my suspicions about Bray, Urswick and King. They did what they thought was right, but they insidiously undermined Richard's reign, turning away from him when he could have used their help and support. Why do I get the feeling that something's wrong here?" She sighed. "Jeez, I hate history sometimes."

Surprised, Gail was momentarily caught off guard. "What's wrong?"

"I don't know. It's like hearing a sour note played in the middle of a song. I mean, well, look at the size of this chapel. The money Bray was able to will towards the building of this place. Urswick's unreserved loyalty to Margaret Beaufort. These were common men and yet all three of them are buried here in the Hall of Kings at considerable expense. Why, and where did the money come from?"

Gail thought for a moment. "Well, I guess they were rewarded by Tudor after he became king. You know, services rendered and all that."

"Yes, for services rendered, but what kind of services?"

Quickly she changed the subject. "Let's go and dance atop Henry VIII, shall we?" She said, her manner suddenly upbeat and mischievous as she propelled Gail towards the centre of the choir.

"Exactly why don't you like him?"

"Why?" Laura paused to consider the question carefully. "Well, the Tudor years are always described in such glowing terms, but the truth is that much of the wealth that Henry needed to sustain his exorbitant lifestyle came as a result of the destruction of the monasteries. We'll see them, or the ruins anyhow, of some of the most beautiful buildings ever constructed. This man had them pulled down, took their treasures, destroyed tombs - Thomas Becket's for instance - and used the redistribution of the church's wealth to buy followers, toadies and sycophants. He had already run through his father's considerable fortune amassed at the expense of others.

"Personally, he was thoroughly disgusting. All this talk about Richard being a hunchback. Give me a break. Henry degenerated into an obese monster, prematurely senile and stinking from an ulcerated leg. He contracted syphilis as a young man and no doubt infected all his wives and mistresses. His daughter Mary died of congenital syphilis as did his son, young Edward VI. How Elizabeth missed it I can't guess; maybe she didn't. At least she had the smarts not to sleep with anyone, assuming of course that she was indeed the 'Virgin Queen'. Henry's physical and moral degeneration was summed up by a contemporary writer. *He changed from a young man of great promise into a violent, brutal and ill-balanced tyrant.* Ill-balanced, meaning crazy.

"Even when I was a kid I was appalled by this man and sickened by his treatment of women. Do you know, when his first wife Catherine of Aragon died in 1530, Henry dressed in bright yellow and ordered a Thanksgiving Mass followed by feasting, dancing and jousting? What a charmer!"

Laura turned to Gail, who had been listening intently while staring down at the jet black memorial stone with its plain, stark lettering. "Many still consider him a great king you know."

"Oh, don't get me wrong, he was a great king in so many ways, but he could have been better, so much better than he was."

Laura paused as a middle-aged couple arrived. Gail and Laura moved away, but not before they heard the woman remark with pride that she knew this king at least and oh, wasn't it a pity he didn't have the fine tomb his father had at Westminster Abbey.

"There, you see." Laura swung around then, looking after them as they made their way towards the nave. "Henry VIII is popular because he's know. Everyone recognizes his face. All those souvenirs with his picture on them? Ugh! If it wasn't for the fact that his parents were buried there and it was the site of his own coronation, Henry would probably have destroyed Westminister Abbey too."

Laura looked straight into Gail's eyes. "You're right, I don't like this bastard and I never will." She signed. "Enough. Although it pains me to say it, we've got to go."

"Yes, I think we'd better before you start to pop buttons or something." Taking her sister-in-law gently by the arm, Gail propelled her towards the door. "Say goodbye Henry."

Laura just growled, then brightened as she remembered something. "Oh, remind me by the way, to tell you about porphyria, the mental illness which has been in the royal family since Mary Queen of Scots.

"Sure." Gail chuckled as she lead the way out, towards Henry's Gate.

"All right, what mental illness?" Gail asked as Laura settled the car into fifth gear.

"Porphyria."

"Honestly Laura, where do you get this stuff?"

"I wrote it down here in the margin of the guidebook, knowing

I was bringing it. What, do you think I can remember all of this? Research is one thing, my memory is quite another. Porphyria is a rare, and I might add, hereditary mutation of the instructions regarding the manufacture of red blood pigment. Got it written down here see? Anyhow, one of the symptoms is episodes of lunacy, and you pee purple."

"What?" Gail shouted. Although Laura was not one to tell out and out lies, she did have a tenancy to exaggerate sometimes and Gail felt sure that this was one such occasion.

"James I's urine was a dark purple colour. Maybe that's why people thought the royal family were blue bloods." Laura started to laugh, but Gail's face remained a thundercloud which only served to amuse Laura more. "It's true, honest. James once described his urine as resembling rich Alicante wine. Frankly mine's more like a Riesling. Great trick at a party if you run a little low I guess, go around topping up glasses." One look at Gail and Laura burst into renewed laughter.

"You don't believe me but, it's true, every word. It's called the *Royal Malady*. Poor old King George III had his first bout of porphyria in early 1764, when he was twenty-six. During his second attack in 1789, he was totally deranged for four months. The disease has been traced back in the royal family to Mary Queen of Scots and forward to Queen Victoria. After that, no one's saying."

Gail stared at Laura, a bemused look on her face. "You're not pulling my leg?"

"Promise, the absolute truth."

Her smile however was a little bit too broad, her assurance too quick for Gail. Letting it go, she decided to follow her own independent line of inquiry.

Nearly an hour later, Laura pulled into the parking lot of the Old Swan Inn, Minster Lovell. Although it was obvious that the inn had been expanded over the years, the front portion was certainly in existence 500 years ago. Together they entered via the small porch into a full-blown pub atmosphere. Two massive stone fireplaces were in evidence while straight ahead could be seen the tail end of a long bar. From there the interior increased in size dramatically with wings, hallways and rooms beyond and to either side. The luncheon menu was handed to them by a young girl at the back of the bar. She came by a few minutes later and took their order, leaving them to wander around before settling in at a window table.

"I thought about staying here," Laura said, "but it was fully booked."

"Oh well, we can't do it all. Old though, isn't it? Now, where are the loos?"

A few minutes later Gail returned. "I see what you mean when you said this place was fully booked. There must be an agricultural show on or something. I just passed a group of women in the lobby, all of them wearing badges with a picture of a pig. Farmers I guess." She shrugged.

For a moment Laura's face was a complete blank. "A picture of a pig?"

"Yes," Gail said nonchalantly. "all the same - a white pig."

Laura studied Gail for a moment then began to laugh. "I think you've just had an encounter of the first kind with Ricardians. Richard's emblem was the white boar."

"You didn't tell me that."

"Sorry, I guess it just slipped my mind."

"What kind of an emblem is that - a pig?"

"A boar." Laura corrected.

"Pig, boar, whatever. Why didn't he go for something like a unicorn or a bear, or how about a bird even. You said he liked falconry. A pig - jeez."

"When cornered, isn't it true that a boar is perhaps the most dangerous animal there is?" Laura smiled, her excitement obvious. "Well, well Ricardians about. Good. Chances are they're going to the Hall, so let's hurry through lunch and catch up with them."

They bolted down their sandwiches and were on their way in record time. Within minutes they encountered a coach, empty now and parked on the side of the lane leading into the Hall. Abandoning the car at that point, they too walked in.

In ruins now, Minster Lovell was once the principle residence of the Lovell family. Built in the first half of the 15th century by William, 7th Baron Lovell of Tichmarsh as a manor house, it became crown property after William's grandson, Francis Viscount Lovell's attainder following the battle of Bosworth. Set beside the Windrush River, the buildings were arranged around three sides of a large quadrangle while the fourth side, which faced the river, had a buttressed wall in which was placed a door leading to a river landing. Unlike a castle, Lovell Hall was never intended to withstand an assault.

Laura and Gail purchased their entry tickets at the gateway. Dispersed amid the ruins they could clearly see at least two dozen women wandering around, many with guidebooks in hand. Laura purchased one and fairly dived into the details of the Hall while Gail led the way.

Gazing at the remains of the once magnificent manor house, Gail was having difficulty understanding what she was seeing. "Didn't you say something about a skeleton being found here somewhere?" She said after a few minutes wait, hoping the Laura would voluntarily surface from the book.

"Oh, sorry Gail, I was just getting to that part. Someone was thinking when this guidebook was printed. There's a reconstruction of what the place probably looked like in the 15th century. Here it is." Laura opened the guidebook wide to page seventeen, then turned it sideways for Gail to see. "Notice anything strange?"

"Like what?" Gail said.

"There's no reference to a chapel. That, my dear, is decidedly unusual." Laura paused to light a cigarette.

"Thank God, I finally found someone who smokes."

From nowhere, it seemed, appeared a girl, perhaps twenty-five years of age, slender, dressed in a pair of faded jeans, light blue silk shirt rolled at the sleeves and Doc Marten boots. She was of average build with light brown hair cut short. Laura detected a slight accent, possibly American.

"Not one smoker. A whole bus load and no one smokes."

Laura turned her full attention on this new arrival and smiled broadly. She had her first Ricardian. She still had her cigarette package in her hand, so she offered one.

"No thanks, don't like menthols. I've got my own here, somewhere." As she searched through her bag, she added. "I don't have a light. I even asked the driver. No matches, no lighters. If the bus had broken down we couldn't even build a bloody fire to keep warm. Ah, here we go - thanks." She lit the cigarette with Laura's lighter, took a deep drag, then handed it back smiling. "That's great, thanks again. I'm Rachael. You two can't be part of the R-Three trip or I would have noticed you. I bet I'm at least thirty-five years younger then anyone else on that damn bus. Don't get me wrong, there are some really nice ladies on this trip, but beyond the Society, we don't have a whole lot in common, if you know what I mean."

"I'm Laura, and this is my sister-in-law Gail. We're travelling around England for a couple of weeks."

"Lucky you." Rachael oozed. "So, why did you decide to come here?" As casual as her manner seemed, there was a slight edge to her question.

"We heard about the skeleton of a man found walled up here." Laura said casually.

"Yeah, it's an interesting story but some people think that's all it is - a story. I thought maybe you two might be members of the Richard III Society."

Gail cleared her throat and began to trace patterns in the grass with the tip of her boot, keeping her head down, her eyes averted. The gesture was not lost on Rachael.

"So, what's the deal?"

"Well," Laura said, beginning slowly, "we do have an interest in King Richard and …"

Gail cleared her throat again, louder this time.

"Gail, will you stop!"

Gail couldn't stand it any longer. "Laura's been studying Richard for months. She has enough notes to pave half of London and she's been dying to meet up with someone in the know so she can talk about him. She can't make up her mind, though, whether he should wear a black hat or a white hat."

Rachael chuckled. "So … what? You're afraid that if you talked to a Ricardian you'd only get the good King Richard story? Hey, there are lots of members who believe that he wasn't exactly sweetness and light, but I guess most everyone agrees that he wasn't as bad as Tudor propaganda made him out to be either."

"Do you think he murdered the Princes?" Gail asked pointedly.

"Wow, you sure don't take prisoners do you?" Rachael said in open surprise. Glancing at Laura and receiving nothing more then an apologetic shrug, Rachael considered the question carefully before she answered. "No, I don't think he did. When he left London they were still alive. Closely guarded sure, but alive and seen playing in the garden. I admit that Richard had the best reason going for getting rid of them, but they were equally in the way of other people's ambitions too."

Glancing at her watch then, Rachael continued. "The bus leaves in forty-five minutes. Let's walk over and see the church. It's in excellent shape, although much changed inside since Richard prayed there. If you've seen some of the beautifully decorated churches on the Continent with their brightly painted statues, decorative walls, mosaic floors and gold everywhere, then you can imagine what this church might have looked like in its heyday, before the damn puritans turned everything, including the people, into shades of grey."

Rachael led the way back through the entranceway, along the cemetery wall and into the churchyard. As they passed a group of rose bushes, Laura noted that they were either white or pale pink. No blood red Lancaster roses to be seen anywhere. As they entered the church through the side porch, Rachael leapt forward to check the notice board. "Still there!" She crowed triumphantly, then pointed. Right near the top and pinned security, well beyond the reach of even the tallest individual, was a postcard with the famous portrait of Richardvs III Ang Rex.

"I wonder who did that, and how?" Laura said.

"I did, about two year's ago I guess. The how? Stephen, my husband, is ever so tall. He can't understand my fascination with Dickie here. Sometimes I swear he gets jealous. But, he has a hobby too - antique cars." Rachael made a face. "So, I do my thing now and again, and he does his. At least I don't come home with my hands all covered in grease."

"Do you think he looked like that?" Gail asked, nodding at the picture.

"Frankly no. In fact, every time they do a reprint I swear to God he looks better and better, don't you Dickie?" Smiling up at the picture, she caught Laura's bemused look out of the corner of her eye.

Laura turned away and began to wander around the church. Rachael and Gail soon caught up with her as she stood beside a tomb, beautifully crafted with brightly painted shields around the side and, on top, a full length effigy of a knight in armour.

"The skeleton you mentioned Laura." Rachael said as she gently touched the cold stone tomb. "It was believed to be Richard's friend Francis Lovell. As you probably know, he escaped Bosworth field and made his way to Flanders. Two years later he returned to take part in a conspiracy probably hatched by John de la Pole, Earl of Lincoln - Richard's nephew and named heir."

Laura nodded.

"You know the story then?" Rachael asked.

"I don't." Gail asserted.

"And neither do I." Laura added. "My notes stopped with

Richard's death, more or less."

"Well," Rachael said, "it seems that there was a priest at Oxford - Richard Symonds - who had in his care a bright young fellow by the name of Lambert Simnel. He had been well educated and taught courtly manners. Symonds, Lovell and de la Pole decided between them to pass the kid off as the younger of the two princes - Richard, Duke of York. Young Simnel was carefully coached and prepared, but by the time King Henry VII heard of the conspiracy, Simnel was no longer pretending to be York but the Earl of Warwick - George, Duke of Clarence's son. Old Henry knew that was wrong because Warwick was locked in the Tower. He hauled him out, paraded him around for all to see then tucked him safely away again.

"The whole thing looked like a ploy by de la Pole to topple Henry and then claim the throne for himself, but it didn't work. Henry's forces massacred de la Pole's army at the Battle of Stoke in July, 1487. Simnel was captured, de la Pole was killed in battle and again Lovell escaped the field.

"What happened to Lovell then is unknown. Some say he drowned trying to cross the Trent after the battle, but the other story goes that he came back to Minster Lovell Hall and hid in a vault or cellar, trusting a servant to keep his whereabouts a secret and provide him with food, etcetera until the heat was off and he could escape again to Europe. Something went wrong. In 1708, while laying a chimney, workman came across the skeleton of a man, seated at a table, with pen, paper and books laid before him. No one knows for sure who he was or even where the remains were buried. This is the tomb of Francis's grandfather, William Lovell.

"The Hall actually has rather a sinister reputation if you care to believe the Legend of the Mistletoe Bough. Do you know it? No? Just a minute, I think I've got a copy here somewhere."

She began to dig again within the darkened recesses of her oversized bag. "Right, last one, but that's okay. It's an interesting story anyhow, whether or not you believe it." She handed the page to Gail. "I'd better go. Are you two planning to be at Bosworth Field this Sunday for the anniversary festivities?"

"Yes," Laura acknowledged, "in a place nearby called Dadlington. Are you going?"

"Wouldn't miss it for the world," Rachael said as she moved towards the door. "Dadlington. Sleeping with the enemy, eh? How about I see you both at about four, outside the booze tent. I'll find you. You can buy me a drink. Hey, maybe we can get together Sunday night and raise hell. Bye for now." With a wave she was gone out the door. It closed behind her with a dull thud which sent echoes through the old church.

"Well, she's quite a character." Gail said smiling. "Chances are she'll have a few Ricardians with her, so you'd better do your homework before then." She gave Laura a dig in the ribs with her finger before she added in a whisper. "They'll probably be recruiting new members too. Now that you're out of the closet you can … "

"Thanks to you and your big mouth."

"You're not angry at me, so quit pretending. You wanted to meet Ricardians and so you have. I like Rachael. She reminds me a little of you, so you both should either get along really well or kill each other. Should be interesting." She laughed, high pitched and forced, just like the Wicked Witch of the West.

They exited the church and wandered around the cemetery briefly before Gail found a bench near the gate. She settled herself down and began to read what Rachael had given her. "It's a poem," she shouted to Laura, who continued to pace restlessly, stopping frequently as if to monitor the air and her position in relationship to the church.

"Read it, if it's not too long," Laura said from behind a vaulted tombstone.

"Okay, here goes. It's by Thomas Hayness Bayly." She settled back in her seat and began.

THE MISTLETOE BOUGH

The mistletoe hung in the castle hall,
The holly branch shone on the old oak wall;
And the baron's retainers were blithe and gay,
And keeping their Christmas holiday.
The baron beheld with a father's pride
His beautiful child, young Lovell's bride;
While she with her bright eyes seem'd to be
The star of the goodly company.

"I'm weary of dancing now;" she cried;
"Here tarry a moment - I'll hide - I'll hide!
And, Lovell, be sure thou'rt first to trace
The clue to my secret lurking place."
Away she ran - and her friends began
Each tower to search, and each nook to scan;
And young Lovell cried, "Oh where does thou hide?
I'm lonesome without thee, my own dear bride."

They sought her that night! And they sought her next day!
And they sought her in vain when a week pass'd away!
In the highest - the lowest - the loneliest spot,
Young Lovell sought wildly - but found her not.
And years flew by, and their grief at last
Was told as a sorrowful tale long past;
And when Lovell appeared, the children cried,
"See! the old man weeps for his fairy bride."

At length an oak chest, that had long laid hid,
Was found in the castle - they raised the lid -
And a skeleton form lay mouldering there,
In the bridal wreath of that lady fair!
Oh! sad was her fate! - in sportive jest
She hid from her lord in the old oak chest.
It closed with a spring! - and, dreadful doom,
The bride lay clasp'd in her living tomb!

"Wow! I see what Rachael meant by the sinister reputation of the Hall. Once captured, it holds to the death, and beyond."

"Yes," Laura said, "there's something strange about this place. Come on, we've got to go. If you think this place is spooky, wait 'til you see Littledean."

Gail noticed that Laura seemed vaguely disturbed, her lips tight, her body rigid behind the wheel as she drove almost due west towards the Severn River and the Forest of Dean.

"You're not angry at me because of Rachael, are you?" Gail asked, her tone peevish.

"I'm not angry with you. Mildly annoyed maybe, but not angry. Besides, everything turned out okay. I'm certainly looking forward to seeing Rachael again and meeting other Ricardians too, of course."

Gail looked straight at Laura, studying her.

"What?" Laura said as she met Gail's gaze briefly.

Gail smiled, cleared her throat then turned to look out her side window.

"All right, all right, so maybe I've got some concerns." Laura said finally. "These people - the Ricardians - are well, strange. I've said that before. Did you see Rachael talking to the picture in the church? It's going to be difficult to have an objective conversation with people who are so myopic about this guy.

"Giving Richard the benefit of the doubt is one thing, but from what I've read, there are lots of Ricardians out there who have endowed him with saint-like qualities and others whose fanaticism borders on adoration."

Laura shook her head as she slipped the car into fourth gear. "This is the same guy who had his erstwhile friend and fellow exile, Hastings, dragged down that vice at the Tower and beheaded. No trial, maybe no priest either - chop! And what about King Henry? I'll tell Rachael about my misericord idea, but that doesn't change the fact that Richard killed an unarmed man in cold blood. Besides, most Ricardians, from what I've learned, refuse to believe that Richard had anything to do with Henry's death. Nineteen was much too young for such a deed. Give me a break."

She paused then, considering. "You know, I bet if all the Ricardians got together and managed to will Richard back to life, none of them would like what they'd see. He had dark gray eyes for one thing. He was described as 'hard visaged', which means he didn't smile a lot. There wasn't much in his life to smile about. One look deep into that face, those eyes. No saint there but a cold blooded, ruthless, power-hungry psychotic who cloaked himself in public sufficiently well to fool the masses, but not well enough to inspire loyalty or trust in those really close to him.

"As King, power clung to him and moved with him, leaving a vacuum in its wake. He was betrayed at the end of his reign just as he was betrayed at the beginning. Lovell managed to escape the battlefield at Bosworth. If he had been at Richard's side in that final melee, he should have suffered the same fate as Richard but he didn't because he wasn't there. He abandoned him too - a form of betrayal. Why? I just hope Rachael will be objective enough to answer questions like that."

Smiling at Gail, Laura added. "You've been ever so patient with me. Sorry to go on and on. You're right, I'm going to have to study before the weekend. I've bought all those books but I haven't had a chance to read any of them yet."

"You'll do fine." Gail said confidently

Laura cut the car's engine, then slowly turned towards Gail. "You said you wanted to see a haunted house? Welcome to Littledean Hall."

"Have you been here before?" Gail asked as she tried, and failed, to get a glimpse of the house through the trees.

"Nope. All I've heard is that walking through it is a quote - spine-chilling experience - unquote. So, either it's haunted or it has defective air conditioning. Let's find out, shall we?"

Gail went in search of the custodian, leaving Laura to inspect the house from the outside. The present Littledean Hall was built in 1612. A fine example of the Jacobean style, it's beautifully positioned high above the Severn River with magnificent views seen from carefully tended grounds, dotted with massive oaks, centuries old.

"I'm not getting any vibes." Laura said when Gail returned.

"Most of the action's on the inside." Gail whispered menacingly.

When she tried to hand Laura the information leaflet, she refused. "Your show Gail."

They entered the ground floor of the house through the front door which stood open as if in anticipation of their arrival. Gail began to read the information sheet while Laura wandered around, admiring the furniture and wall coverings, waiting.

"No air conditioning, Laura." Gail announced, her enthusiasm obvious. "Spine-chilling equals haunted and, according to this," Gail waved the leaflet, "standing room only for the spectral set."

Laura turned, hands on hips. "Good." She smiled broadly.

Gail continued, referencing the leaflet occasionally. "A family by the name of Pyrke owned the Hall for like 250 years. They had a black servant who, it is said, murdered young Master Charles Pyrke because Pryke had impregnated the fellow's sister. It's this servant who haunts the place. There's a painting over the mantlepiece showing both Charles and the servant as young boys."

Laura and Gail hurried into the drawing room to admire the picture. "It says here," Gail said, "that this picture is a reproduction done in 1982 because the original kept falling off the wall even when a strong chain was used. The ghost of this servant has been seen in several places in the house, even during daylight hours. Gosh, I thought ghosts only came out at midnight."

"Eastern or Central time?" Laura muttered under her breath.

"Bloodstains!" Gail said, as she finished reading the next section.

She turned from the portrait and led Laura across to the other side of the house and into the dining room. Just inside the doorway and to the left on the floorboards was a patch of darker wood. To both Laura and Gail, it felt dry to the touch but, the leaflet suggested that no amount of scrubbing or even planing could wash away the bloodstains left by Colonel Congreve and Captain Wigmore, both royalist and both shot to death by Roundheads in 1644.

"Better watch out, because this room is also haunted by a monk. He has been seen walking from here to the library where there was a priest's hole leading to a tunnel from the basement to the Grange of Flexley Abbey. It was a quarter of a mile long. Whow! The Grange is haunted too, with noises, shadows and a frightening white mist. Better and better." Gail was enjoying herself.

"Ready to go upstairs, Laura?" Gail called out, but when she looked up, Laura wasn't there. "Laura!"

"I'm here," Laura shouted from the base of the stairs. Gail quickly joined her. "I think what you're really looking for is up there."

"Don't go wandering off without me, damn it." Gail growled as Laura started up the stairs. When the reached the upper floor, Gail continued, but not before she gave Laura strict instructions about staying close to her. Laura just smiled indulgently.

"Okay," Gail said, her tone upbeat as she surfaced from the leaflet, "there are two bedrooms at the end of the hall, but only one is haunted. Your assignment, Miss Laura, should you choose to accept it, is to determine which room, the blue or the red, is indeed overrun by the nether world. You can take all the time you wish, or dare."

"All right, what do you suggest I do?" Laura said, content for the time being at least to humour Gail, although if things got out of hand, she was prepared to pull the plug on Gail's little experiment with the ethereal plane.

"Just go into each room, open your mind and let it happened. Ghosts are always trying to communicate with the living. Maybe you can find out how they died for instance."

Gail led Laura down the hallway but stopped short at the corner. The hallway continued another few feet before ending at the entranceway to two bedrooms; one in pale blue shades, the other bright red.

Laura surveyed the two rooms from the hallway. "I don't know about ghosts, but I'd have nightmares sleeping in the red room."

"Never mind the colour." Gail urged. "Close your eyes if you have to. In fact, it's a good idea if you do close your eyes so you can concentrate better. Come on, what are you afraid of?"

"Amateur hour." Laura muttered under her breath as she walked into the Red Room. She closed her eyes, concentrated, did all the things her coach suggested, but nothing - not a ripple.

"Why do you think ghosts would be willing to expend all their available resources just to tell me about how they died?"

"It has to do with energy." Gail said sagely. "Dying is such a traumatic event that it produces massive doses of ectoplasm or something, which mediums can pick up on. Come on, try harder. You're not concentrating enough."

"So, this is the room then. Well, all I can say is, if dying was the most exciting event in a ghost's life, then it must be a boring ghost. I want one who can communicate all sorts of exciting things, not just how they died."

A few minutes more then Laura gave up, joining Gail in the hallway once more. "Sorry, no one at home."

"Okay, try the Blue Room."

With a resigned sigh Laura walked in, promising to concentrate and let her natural life force flow as Gail had suggested. As she crossed to the middle of the room, she suddenly felt extremely cold as an invisible web of dread descended over her, invading her very soul with thoughts of hate and fear, mixed. She either saw or felt sudden, violent movement all around her, screams of anguish, then, perhaps worst of all, the sound of a woman crying.

She eased out of the room, her heart pounding, hurting her chest and constricting her breathing. Her face was chalk white as she leaded against the hallway wall, breathing deeply, her eyes closed.

Gail began massaging her arms vigorously. "Goddamn it Gail, don't touch me!" Laura growled as she stared down at a blister rapidly forming on the back of her left hand.

"What's that?".

"Some of your bloody ectoplasm, or whatever you called it."

"Does it hurt?"

"Yes, it does, as a matter of fact. Shit, I hate it when this happens." Suddenly she smiled wickedly. "I think it's fair to say that the Blue Room is occupied - totally."

"Tell me what you saw or heard?" Gail asked, keeping her voice as even as possible.

"I don't know. A fight or something, death, a woman crying. A sense of fear, sadness, it was all jumbled up. What happened in there?"

"According to this," Gail said, consulting the information sheet, "the Blue Room is so haunted that no one has slept in it for years. Besides a terrible atmosphere, clashing swords can be heard. The story goes that two brothers fought over a lady, maybe that's who you heard crying, and both men were killed in the duel."

"Oh great, so I had to pick up on that. Why not a nice love story, a passionate night on the bed in there. True love, the warmth of a life spent together down through the years."

"That's not the way ghosts work." Gail said with a shrug.

"Is that right?" Laura backed away. "Your turn."

Cautious at first, Gail slowly made her way into the room and stood where Laura had been moments before. Nothing. Try as she might, she was unable to elicit any vibrations whatsoever.

After several minutes, she exited the room with some relief. "I guess you got it all."

"Thanks for letting me go first." Laura smiled maliciously.

"That's because I knew you'd succeed. You have an extra

sense. That's probably why this whole Richard III thing is bothering you so much. Laura, you may have lived a previous life, or lives even. For all we know you could have been … " Gail's voice trailed off as Laura moved away from the wall towards her.

"Shut up, Gail." Laura warned. "I've had enough, let's go."

Once outside the house, Laura breathed the cool scented air. They walked side by side through the gardens before exploring the ruins of the Roman temple on the grounds, said to be dedicated to Sabrina, Goddess of the Severn. Finally, Gail broke the silence. "I knew you were psychic."

"Oh Gail, please." Laura said as she walked ahead.

"Remember when that big house was for sale on the mountain, and for a lark we decided to attend the open house? Remember the studio above the garage and how you refused to even go near it? You practically bolted out of the house at the end. Well, ages later I found out that the owner shot himself to death in that studio.

"You're the only person I know who can make a Oujui board work, though you won't do it now, not since that night you played with my mother and scared her so bad. Mum won't tell me what happened - said she never would either. You're no fun at cards because half the time you know what's about to be played."

Exasperated, Gail ran around in front of Laura, forcing her to stop. "I've been thinking about what you said before, about the Ricardians."

"What about them?"

"About willing the spirit of Richard back to life. If enough people could … "

Laura laughed, the sound derisive and brittle. "I was speaking metaphorically. You're a nice Catholic girl. You don't believe in ghosts, and neither does your brother." She tried to sidestep around Gail.

"Well, I believe in them now."

"Because of this?" Laura indicated her hand. "You've got to do better than that."

"Damn it Laura, I want to help. You've got a chance of a lifetime and you know it. Stop this BS and accept the fact that you're different, that you probably always have been different. Where did the misericord idea come from? You've seen that instrument Laura, I know you have. You called Richard a psychotic, and you meant it, but I bet not one of those books you've bought calls him that. I think you know more about this man then you're even aware of, and I think too, that Bosworth Field holds a strong attraction. Like a moth to a flame, you're powerless to resist and yet you fear it, fear what you might find there."

Laura stared at Gail, taking in every feature of her face. "You know precisely nothing about what you're talking about. Furthermore, you're neither emotionally nor physically equipped for the task. What you propose is not a exercise for amateurs, so I warn you now, if I decide to do just as you've suggested, then you'd better be prepared for what happens and believe me, it'll be one hell of a lot worse than what was encountered here. Do you understand me?"

Gail nodded, suddenly fearful.

Laura smiled thinly. "Come on, relax. Congratulate yourself on your intuitive skills and let it go at that." She looked down at her hand. The blister had settled into a blood-red welt the size of a quarter. "Let's go. I've got some burn cream somewhere in my bag. If I don't get something on this soon, it will turn septic."

As Laura turned away, Gail gripped her arm tightly. "What do you mean 'a lot worse'?"

Laura's eyes traced the horizon, a cut and bleeding outline of trees against a sky grown dull, bruised pale yellow by a storm approaching from the southeast. "I would think that the answer is obvious." She said casually as she turned. "It has to do with invocation."

Gail frowned.

"Prayers to invoke God's blessing yes, but also, I suspect, ritual incantation, sufficiently powerful to ..." She paused. "Trust me

Gail, that's all I can say right now."

" But Laura, I … "

"We had better get going. There's a storm coming. If you don't mind, I'd rather be in Tewkesbury when it hits."

The weather began to deteriorate rapidly as they retraced their route north. The afternoon air grew progressively colder, while a stiff wind rose, bearing with it the scent of rain. By the time they reached Tewkesbury, the clouds had gathered, low and threatening.

"We've got confirmed reservations Gail, so leave everything until later. Let's go and see an abbey." Laura leap from the car, turned abruptly and was confronted by the massive Norman tower which dominates the town.

It was cool outside but even cooler within. There were very few visitors. They wandered around, briefly inspecting the various tombs and monuments, but it was obvious that Laura was looking for something specific. Behind the high altar, at the most eastern end of the church, she found a small iron grill set into the flagstone floor. Below, shrouded in darkness was a crypt.

"This is where Richard's brother, George, Duke of Clarence is buried beside his wife Isabel." Laura said as she gazed down into the nothingness, disappointed.

"And here's a picture of what it looks like," Gail added as she moved to one side then nodded towards a colour photograph tacked to the wall. Laura quickly joined her.

The crypt or tomb was unadorned, the ceiling vaulted, while the floor appeared to be earthen. But what was most interesting was the alcove at one end, sealed by a glass panel. Behind the panel could be clearly seen a pile of bones and two skulls. If this was indeed George Clarence's burial place, and the printed sign next to the photograph said it was, it looked as through his remains had been disturbed several times, as were Isabel's. Laura was both fascinated and appalled.

"You were expecting a marble tomb?" Gail asked casually.

"Well, you'd think someone in the family could have come up with something. I mean, there was lots of time for forgiveness, if not from Edward then at least from Richard. Despite George's rotten behaviour he was, after all, their brother."

"Sibling rivalry, that's what it was. Besides," Gail added, "Richard probably had other things to spend his money on besides building a tomb for a brother who had died a traitor. Come on, I've been reading about the Battle. There's a trail we can walk, and then we can have an early dinner. I'm starved and way overdue for a dessert fix."

They exited the church then turned left down Gloucester Road towards the Avon River. Before crossing the bridge they found the first of the Battle Trail signs - a rose with two crossed swords - and plunged down onto the flat field enclosed by a tributary of the Avon on one side and the abbey grounds on the other. Laura looked up towards the impressive spires of the Abbey Church set high above the flood plain. To her left, across Gloucester Road, was another branch of the Avon, commonly called the Mill Avon since this water had been diverted for use by the monastery. They walked along the edge of the battlefield in the area called 'Bloody Meadow'.

Used as a playing field now, it once entertained a sport of a different kind. It was here that hundreds of the Duke of Somerset's men were believed to have perished, trapped between the river and the forces of the House of York. In the confusion that followed, King Edward scattered the remaining Lancastrian forces. Prince Edouard of Lancaster was slain while trying to reach the sanctuary of the Abbey, while others managed to reach the high altar only to be seized and executed for treason.

It had begun to rain heavily, so they abandoned their walk and hurried back to the Abbey, twisting and turning amid the tombstones as they made their way towards a covered porch, ignoring the pathway provided. Laura sat on a stone bench, drying herself off with some tissues from her purse. "Sit down," she suggested, making room for Gail.

"Didn't your mother tell you that you could get haemorrhoids sitting on cold stone?" Gail said derisively.

"Ah, no, she must have missed that one." Laura said as she lit a cigarette and smiled up at Gail. "Maybe we should have made a run for the hotel instead. It's not very comfortable here sitting on haemorrhoidal-inducing stones, watching the rain fall on the tombs. Depressing, don't you think?"

Gail shrugged. "Too bad we're so far from the big cities here. No mortsafes around I suppose and yet I was quite looking forward to seeing one." She turned to Laura, but it was obvious that she didn't have a clue of what Gail was talking about. "It was a popular device used in the 1800's to keep grave robbers from snatching the corpse. Flat tabletop tombstones like those over there were used too. Seems like a terrible waste of money to me, since after a couple of weeks in the ground, body snatchers lost interest." She chuckled.. "Mind you, I doubt if a place like Tewkesbury had to worry about 'Resurrectionists'. It's too far from any medical schools."

"Body snatchers?" Laura said, incredulous.

"Right. It was big business in places like London and Edinburgh at one time. The medical schools needed lots and lots of cadavers, fresh ones, for dissection, but except for the corpse of the occasional criminal released by authorities after execution, the demand far exceeded the supply. In order to keep their students, medical schools were forced to purchase bodies, no questions asked. Gangs of grave robbers competed with each other, often attending the funeral of the dearly departed, grieving along with the rest. At midnight though, they'd be back with a sack, shovels, a length of rope and ... "

"Have you been researching this?"

"Well, I did read a book on the subject recently." Gail said, smiling. "It was very interesting."

"I bet. Shouldn't you be reading Good Housekeeping or something?"

"What about your reading material lately?" Gail replied in self-defence.

"You're right, sorry I interrupted. I can't think of a better subject to discuss in our present locale. Please, continue."

"Thank you." Gail smiled. "They didn't dig up the whole grave but just the top half or so, moving the dirt onto a sheet. Once they reached the coffin, it was easy to smash it open, reach inside, slip a noose around the neck, and gently pull the body out and up.

"Now, this is interesting. Technically there was no law against stealing dead bodies, but there certainly was one for stealing the clothes, so the grave robbers would strip the corpse, throw everything back into the grave, replace the soil, bag the corpse and off they would go to whomever they knew would pay a good price for a fresh 'thing', as the cadavers were called in the trade."

"Jeez Gail."

Gail chuckled, warming to her subject. "When body snatching, grave robbing, whatever you want to call it, reached its peak in the 1830's I think, people began to take action to protect the graves, so things like the mortsafe and stone slabs became popular. Some graves were booby trapped, or family and friends would guard the site for a couple of weeks until the body was so decomposed that it was worthless."

"Thank heavens we don't have to worry about things like that in this day and age." Laura said, shaking her head.

"I'm not so sure. Medical schools still need bodies for dissection, morticians have to practice on something, and the car industry can only use dummies for so long before they have to try out collision protection devices on the real thing and I'm not talking about a bottle of Coke."

Laura laughed.

"Of course, there are laws against it now, but still, an attempt was made once to steal Elvis, and Charlie Chaplin's body was actually snatched and held for ransom. President Lincoln's corpse just about suffered the same fate. The authorities were so worried that they kept moving his huge lead coffin around inside the Washington Memorial before finally burying him and his wife together in solid concrete."

"Isn't it true," Laura said hesitantly, "that not all the cadavers presented for sale to the medical schools died of natural causes?"

"Murdered, you mean? Oh, yes, especially after various safeguards were put into place. It got harder and harder for grave robbers to even invade the cemeteries, let alone the grave sites. In the meantime, the homeless roamed the streets of London and Edinburgh. By degrees the grave robbers began to harvest this wealth of human flotsam and jetsam, no questions asked. Remember at Madam Tussaud's, Burke and Hare? They were two Irish immigrants in the business of snatching bodies for a local medical school in Edinburgh, and they didn't bother going to the local cemetery either. I think they eventually despatched something like fifteen victims before the police finally caught up with them."

"Congratulations," Laura said with a chuckle, "you're stories have been officially deemed as disgusting as mine."

"Thank you, thank you." Gail replied with a shallow bow.

They took turns holding up both umbrellas while first Gail, then Laura, extracted what was needed from the boot of the car. Returning to the hotel via the back door, they negotiated the narrow stairway to the top floor where their room was located. The rain continued.

While Gail busied herself in the bathroom, Laura laid out all the books she had purchased regarding King Richard III. Rosemary Horrox - *Richard III, A Study in Service; The Princes in the Tower* by Alison Weir; Anthony Cheetham - *The Life and Times of Richard III;* Jeremy Potter - *Good King Richard?;* and finally, Charles Ross - *Richard*

III. Laura surveyed the collection with dismay. So much to learn, so little time. She was standing beside the bed, hands on hips, when Gail came out of the bathroom.

"Oh boy," she said peering across at the books. "How about I wander out, find a liquor store, and bring back a bottle of something?"

"No need," Laura said, still staring at the books as if willing one to present itself as the definitive version, the talisman edition which would reveal all. "I've got a bottle of wine in my bag." Absent-mindedly she wandered over to her suitcase, found the bottle and gave it to Gail.

While Laura searched for the corkscrew, Gail approached the bed and picked up the Potter book. The portrait on the cover was similar to the postcard pinned up by Rachael, but the face was harder, the eyes colder and more calculating, the lips no more than a thin line. Gail didn't like this Richard, so she put the book down quickly before moving away, quietly disconcerted.

"Damn, where did I put that Swiss Army knife?" Laura was still searching through her suitcase. "Gail, choose one of those books for me please. I can't decide which one to start with."

"Potter's book." Gail said casually, her voice flat.

"You mean 'Good King Richard', question mark? Okay. Eureka. There you are." Laura held the instrument firmly while she extracted the cork screw attachment. Expertly she opened the bottle while Gail watched.

"Done it before, have you?

"Once or twice." Laura said, totally unconcerned by Gail's implication. "Where are the glasses?"

"Oh, sorry." Gail raced into the bathroom and returned with two small tumblers which Laura proceeded to fill to the brim.

"What are you planning to do if I decide to read for a bit?"

"Read too." Gail turned to her bag and pulled out David Williamson's *Kings & Queens of Britain.*

"I'm impressed. You didn't believe me about the Royal Malady, so check out what Williamson has to say about James I. What a nutter he was."

They presented themselves for dinner at 7:45, but rather than eat in the restaurant, they decided instead on the more casual atmosphere offered by the lounge bar. They took a table in the corner under a large bay window. Once their order was taken, they both leaned back and relaxed. Laura closed her eyes and drifted.

Then she was interrupted by Gail. "Are you all right?"

"Yes," Laura said with a sigh. She turned and looked out the window at the driving rain. "A little tired perhaps, that's all."

Gail nodded towards Laura's hand. "Does it still hurt?"

"No."

"I'm sorry. If I'd known that something like that could happen, I wouldn't have … "

"Forget it Gail. It doesn't matter. Let's talk about something else."

"Okay. Maybe, if you're not too tired, you could tell me more of the Story? I mean, assuming we do meet some Ricardians, I would like to know as much as possible." It was obvious that Laura was not in the mood. "We'll be in Market Bosworth the day after tomorrow."

"Yes, I know. All right," Laura said, sighing deeply, "buy me a very large dry white and you've got a deal."

Well practised by now, Gail was back with the drinks in record time. "Okay, go."

Slowly Laura pulled her notes from her bag. "Poor Richard, you've got to feel sorry for the guy. His reign had hardly begun and already there was trouble. When he learned of the 'Sanctuary Plot', he wrote to his Lord Chancellor Russell in London and ordered him to secure Westminister Abbey and have the conspirators questioned by the Council and prosecuted if necessary. Unfortunately, by the time Russell took action, all the conspirators had gone underground. The Abbey precincts became like an armed camp at the centre of which sat Elizabeth Wydville and her daughters.

"Margaret Beaufort, alias Henry Tudor's mother, on the other hand, moved with impunity since she was the wife of Thomas Stanley, a man Richard trusted - well, sort of. At her side were men like Bray and Urswick scurrying about like hungry rats from one group of conspirators to another, suggesting, encouraging, plotting. Into this mix we add Morton and Buckingham."

"As I said before, Buckingham met up with Richard in Gloucester, they had an argument and Buckingham left hurriedly. Richard continued his progress, visiting Tewkesbury, Worcester, Warwick, Coventry, Leicester, Nottingham, Pontefract and then finally York which he entered on the 29th of August.

"Many authors have suggested that the Progress was nothing more than a series of well-staged PR exercises; propaganda cloaked in pageants and ceremony. It probably was." Laura added with a shrug. "Towns like Gloucester and Worcester offered Richard money which he declined saying that *'he would rather have their love than their treasure'*. In the meantime however, he had unleased his massive spy network, sensing trouble.

"He spent three and a half weeks in York. We know for sure that Richard's secretary John Kendall organized numerous shows and pageants designed to display his master in the most favourable light possible. Anne and Richard participated in a Corpus Christi procession to the Minster, followed by a service of Thanksgiving.

"On the 8th of September, young Edward of Middleham was invested as Prince of Wales, but not by the Bishop of York, Thomas Rotherham, who you may remember, was roughed up by Richard way back in June when Hastings was executed. Rotherham would remain unwilling to endorse Richard's ascension to the throne, so he didn't attend the elaborate feast which was held in his palace, even though he had been released from custody just prior to Richard's coronation."

"A little embarrassing for Richard, wasn't it?"

Laura shrugged. "Perhaps, but I'm sure Rotherham made some plausible excuse which would be calculated to appease both the King and the commons. He certainly allowed his people to make up their own minds on the issue, although Richard probably helped in that."

"What do you mean?"

"Richard made all sorts of grants and gifts to local churches and religious bodies. He reduced the City of York's annual fee-farm, and elevated the City Mayor to King's Chief Sergeant-at-Arms. All and all he was quite a hit in York, which isn't surprising I suppose.

"By the 20th of September it was time to head south. Anne and young Edward were sent back to Middleham, which was a good idea since Richard was now fully aware of the conspiracies underway in the south, led principally by a certain Margaret Beaufort. There were also rumours that the Princes were dead. Deciding to give the rebels just enough rope, Richard waited at Pontefract.

"On or about the 18th of October, open rebellion finally broke in a series of isolated incidents, especially in Kent. By then Richard knew that Buckingham was in the thick of it. He moved fast, first to Nottingham, then Oxford and finally Salisbury.

"Buckingham's role in the uprising was short and sweet. Unable to raise the support he had hoped for - his family was hated by the locals - he tried to flee but was caught and brought to Richard at Salisbury, where he was promptly executed."

Laura chuckled. "Richard offered a a substantial reward for Buckingham's capture so it was not surprising that, when a servant found Buckingham hiding in a cottage, he was promptly handed over."

"So, at the end Buckingham was betrayed too?"

"Yep. Fun, eh? The rebellion collapsed in a heap. Actually, the rebels didn't really stand a chance since it would appear that Richard's spies had infiltrated to the very core and were well aware of every plan. After that, it was a mopping up exercise.

"His spy network caught several fish including William Colyngbourne who had penned a scurrilous little doggerel, remember? *The Cat, the Rat and Lovell our Dog, Rule all England under an Hog.* William made the mistake of pinning his little effort on the door of St. Paul's for all the world to see. Fair to say Richard took more than a dim view of the rhyme and the rhymester. William was convicted of high treason and condemned to be hanged, drawn, and quartered. Richard even provided a brand new gallows on Tower Hill for the occasion.

"Obviously the rhyme didn't help, but William's real crime was that he was a secret agent, representing men who corresponded directly with Tudor - shades of Urswick and Bray. What I find interesting is that Colynbourne had had an excellent career in the service of the crown and was apparently a member of the household of Richard's mother, since Richard wrote to her asking that his Chamberlain be her officer in Wiltshire *'as Colyngborne had'* - obviously before he met an untimely death.

"Mistress Shore had another run-in with Richard too, according to a proclamation dated the 23rd of October. She was accused of harbouring the Marquess of Dorset in her boudoir - holds in adultery - it said, and was sent packing to Ludgate - again. Poor Jane. That's when Richard's solicitor Thomas Lynom visited her to interrogate her on the King's behalf and fell in love instead." Laura chuckled. "When Thomas begged permission to marry her, Richard was thunderstruck. He referred to Lynom's infatuation as a *'full great marvel'*, so obviously he wasn't as captivated by Jane's physical charms as so many others were which suggests more than a strong puritanical streak in his makeup. He asked Bishop Russell to try to talk some sense into Lynom, but eventually Richard relented and ordered her to be released from prison into the care of her father. Lynom married her and she dropped from history."

"I'm curious about one thing." Gail mused. "You haven't

mentioned Richard's wife Anne, yet she was married to him for how many years?"

"About twelve or thirteen, I think."

"As his wife, she must have been about as close to him as anyone. Didn't she realize the extent of his ambition, in the early days I mean, while things were on the boil in London? Was she as ambitious as her husband, or what?"

"From what I've been able to find out so far, Anne was more or less obliged to marry Richard. Forced might be a better word. He wanted her estates and her valuable connections to the northern 'in' crowd. Politically speaking, her position was delicate, so he offered her an out, and she took it. They probably cared for each other, but I wouldn't call it a love match, especially since Richard insisted that she sign a contract which left him in control of all her estates should the marriage be annulled, which if you remember, was a distinct possibility since there was no papal dispensation prior to the marriage.

"Personally, I think she was a bit of a doormat. Ruled by a tyrannical father who treated her as nothing more than a political pawn, she probably learned at a young age to bend with the breeze. As far as her own ambitions were concerned, I think she did exactly as she was told. Her relationship with Richard could best be described as tenuous since she had produced only one frail child, followed by a string of miscarriages.

"When the boy died, he doomed his parent's marriage, and ultimately his father's throne. Caught between the anguish at the loss of his only heir and the need to provide another, any love Richard may have had for Anne turned not to hate, as you might suppose, but to a kind of indifference. Anne failed to recover from the loss of her son and died, it is believed, of tuberculosis. She may also have died of a broken heart."

Laura paused. "I'm sorry, I'm tired, so could we please continue with this another time?"

"Sure." Gail said, suddenly concerned.

As Gail looked over the dessert menu, Laura lit a cigarette and idly watched the rain, induced by gusts of wind into an all-out assault on the window from which she gazed. The streets were deserted, the light reduced to a dull greyness rendered duller still against the stone buildings. Laura's mood matched perfectly.

Hours later Laura woke with a start. She lay rigid in the silent darkness, trying desperately to quell the fear which sought to engulf her while the dream pressed down upon her, horrific and all too real.

She had seen the manner of George, Duke of Clarence's death by murder and, worst of all, she knew without a doubt who the murderer was.

"Could someone hate that much?" She thought, although instinctively she knew that the answer was 'yes'.

"Are you okay?" Gail whispered.

"I'm sorry." Laura said, her voice tight and breathless. "Did I wake you?"

"You cried out."

"I had a bad dream, that's all. Sorry to wake you."

Slowly, almost painfully, Laura rose from the bed and gathered together several of the books which had been left on top of her suitcase.

"Do you mind if I go into the bathroom and read for a bit?"

"I don't mind, but it's three in the morning!" Gail said as she set her watch back on the night table then snuggled deeper into the bed.

"Won't be long."

Beneath the garish bathroom light, Laura referenced then cross-referenced each of the books until she was able to confirm a truth which she feared to find.

"You bastard. You cold-blooded murdering bastard." Her hands trembled as she gathered the books together before turning to extinguished the light. She stood, silent and alone in the darkness, crushed by the knowledge and saddened to the point of tears. Unseen, the first pale hint of dawn assailed the window shades, heralding a new day.

Day 4
Tewkesbury - Ludlow

Duke of York:

She-Wolf of France, but worse than wolves of France
Whose tongue more poisons than the adder's tooth! . . .
O tiger's heart wrapp'd in a womans hide!

Shakespeare -
The Third Part of King Henry the Sixth
[Act I, Scene 4]

Laura sat perched on the window sill, watching the sunrise, while all the while carefully and methodically working through a multitude of conflicting emotions.

So, Richard had stayed on in London after George was convicted of treason despite the fact that he hated it there and would have gladly returned north at the earliest opportunity. Casually she twirled her cigarette around and around between long, slender fingers. Opportunity, yes, that was the key word. Opportunity and a hatred so intense that it defied understanding.

"Well, Richard, my dear, it seems to me that I can no longer afford you the benefit of any doubt. So, just how did you murder the Princes?"

"Have you been awake all this time?"

Laura turned to find Gail sitting up, pillows piled behind her, watching Laura intently

"I couldn't get back to sleep."

"Do you want to talk about it - the dream I mean?"

"No."

To prevent further probing on Gail's part, Laura quickly made her way to the bathroom, shutting the door behind her. A few minutes later she reappeared, dressed in a pair of faded jeans, cotton blouse and heeled leather boots.

"I want to get going as soon as possible, if you don't mind." She stood leaning against the doorframe, her arms folded across her chest, her impatience blatantly obvious. "It's just after seven. I'll be downstairs in the breakfast room. Don't be long."

Without waiting for a reply, she grabbed her jacket, purse and the road atlas, leaving Gail behind to get herself ready as quickly as possible.

Over a typical English cooked breakfast, Gail scanned the map, following Laura's finger as she traced their route north to Ludlow. "Do you want to visit the Abbey again before we go?"

"No. Why should I?"

"Sorry, just thought you might want to, that's all. Tell me, why was George buried here and not beside his father and brother?"

"Because his wife Isabel was buried here, so naturally he would join her. Come on, let's go. It's a relatively short drive today compared to yesterday, but still."

As Laura rose, Gail step out in time to block her way. "Did Richard arrange the murder of his brother?"

"Arrange it?" Laura smiled thinly. "No, he didn't arrange it. Will Shakespeare really did have it wrong, especially when he has Richard describing George as simple, plain Clarence. He was far from it."

"*I do love thee so, that I will shortly send thy soul to heaven, if heaven will take the present at our hand.* Finish the passage Laura, just as Shakespeare wrote it."

"Gail, I'm not prepared to stand in the middle of the restaurant discussing murder, so get out of my way." Laura hissed in a half whisper tinged with malice.

Once back in their room, Laura turned on Gail. "What the hell's wrong with you or do you think fratricide is a subject to be discussed in an open forum."

"Is that what you call it - fratricide?" Gail said sarcastically. "Fratricide is the murder of one's own brother, so just what are you saying Laura? Was Richard responsible for George's death? A simple yes or no will do."

Laura glared at her sister-in-law. "George Clarence was a royal duke. Tell me Gail, do you think Richard would be stupid enough to hire thugs to murder his brother? Rather a nasty precedence, don't you think?"

Gail blanched. "So who ... Are you saying that Richard killed his own brother?"

"Do you believe he was capable of such a thing?"

"Yes." Gail gasped.

"Then perhaps it's true."

Laura slipped the car into fifth gear as they passed the open road sign just north and west of Tewkesbury. She remained tight lipped, acknowledging Gail's navigational instructions with a nod, although occasionally she would glance at her for no apparent reason.

Just north of Leominster, Laura casually asked: "Do you know Sharon Waxman?"

"Yes." Gail said tersely.

"And Roger knows her?"

"I went to school with her. After her marriage broke up she went back to college, got some sort of degree in accounting and was looking for a job. Roger said he would help her find something. No big deal." She shrugged.

"You're not a very good liar Gail, and so it would seem, either is Roger since he steadfastly maintains that he's never heard of her. You two should really get your act together, especially when dealing with me, don't you think?"

"Is that why you're angry at me, because of Sharon? There's nothing going on between her and Roger."

"Who said there was? Besides," she shrugged, "even if Roger was having an affair, would I know - would you?

Gail looked away.

"Well, never mind. To be quite honest, I don't really care right now. But, do me a favour. Quit dabbling in things which you know nothing about, like at Littledean or the manner of George Clarence's death. You're relying on intuition, which is not only an inexact science, but potentially dangerous. Stay within the mainstream. You're of more use to me there."

Gail was instantly alarmed. "Laura, what have you got planned?"

"I've told you, wait and see."

Perhaps Britain's loveliest town, Ludlow was also the seat of power for the House of York. It is likely that Richard was conceived here, and it was also here that he was to have perhaps his happiest memories and most terrifying experience as a boy.

"We've got reservations at the Cliffe Hotel, guaranteed late arrival, so let's go see a castle." Laura suggested as she practically leapt from the car, only to rummage in the back seat for her video camera.

"I want to do some shopping too." Gail announced with a fair degree of determination.

"And so do I, but afterwards, if you don't mind." Slowly Laura raised her camera and began filming. "Don't go all bent and twisted on me Gail. Just relax and enjoy yourself, okay?"

"Sure." Gail said as she turned away.

They entered through an archway set into the stone wall, then along a pathway to the outer gatehouse. At one time it had been much taller, stronger and more impressive as befitting the most vulnerable part of the castle. The walls on either side were buttressed to add additional strength.

Once inside, Laura and Gail found themselves in a large, open grassed area called the outer bailey. In times of trouble the townspeople would camp there with their animals and personal belongings until it was safe to return home. Here too were staged mock battles and tournaments. No doubt young Richard would have watched with pride as his elder brothers, Edward and Edmund, would vie for their father's praise.

With Laura slightly in the lead, they continued across the bailey towards the entrance to the inner ward, which lay on the other side of a dry moat. During Tudor times the original wooden drawbridge was replaced by a stone bridge with a high parapet. The steeply pitched moat relied for its defence on brambles, thorn bushes and sharp stakes driven into the ground at an angle.

Just within, on the left side stood the remains of a once massive keep or donjon, the main stronghold and defensive core of any medieval castle. Beyond was a collection of lesser buildings, the remains of the kitchen complex were meals were prepared, bread baked, meat butchered. Much of the cooking was done over brick hearths while elsewhere large cauldrons boiled and bubbled over an open flame. Spits of various sizes roasted items as small as game birds and as a large as the carcass of a full grown bullock. On the other side of the bailey stood the domestic buildings. The Great Hall in the middle, the block known as Prince Arthur's apartments to the left and on the right, the Great Chamber block, Pendover Tower and standing alone, the circular chapel.

Together Laura and Gail climbed the steps leading to the ruins of a once magnificent set of wooden doors. At the top Laura turned and face outwards, looking down into the inner bailey and back towards the entranceway. Although Gail was eager to go inside, she stayed with Laura, trying to see what it was that attracted such interest.

"I think I mentioned before that young Richard, not yet seven years of age, enjoyed some time here with his parents, brothers and sisters. How he must have enjoyed himself during that brief summer of 1459.

"Then disaster struck. On the 13th of October, a royal army appeared near Ludlow, lead by Queen Margaret. It is likely that she was bent on avenging the death of her lover Somerset and she wasn't going to be satisfied with anything less then the Duke of York's head. Warned in time, Richard's father and brothers, Edward and Edmund, slipped out of Ludlow castle along with the earls of Warwick and Salisbury, leaving the Duchess, young Richard and his brother George behind. Queen Margaret was no doubt furious when she learned that York had fled into Ireland.

"We're standing, perhaps on the very spot where young Richard stood, clutching his mother's skirt as she stood bravely at the top of this stair, waiting for the arrival of Margaret and her entourage.

"A formidable woman at the best of times, Margaret swooped through that gateway like an avenging demon from hell. She was only thirty years old, knew power and how to wield it. I can almost see her, dressed totally in black and riding a coal black stallion, steaming sweat, all nervous energy as it moved closer and closer to the base of these stairs. And Richard, clutching his mother's skirts even tighter as he stared fascinated and in terror at this woman whom he knew wanted to kill his father.

"Margaret did not dismount but brought her horse to a halt as she studied first the mother, cool and resolute, before she turned her attention to the two young boys. At eleven, George would still be considered too small a fry, innocent yet of the sins of the father. Margaret's eyes moved slowly from George, to rest on the little, dark-haired boy so like her own son Edouard. Through his tears Richard may have seen her smile at him tenderly before the lines of her face melted, twisting in hatred and contempt as her attention was drawn once more to the mother.

"In high-born French, a language Richard would refuse to learn, Margaret pronounced sentence on the House of York. Attainted of treason, all their lands were forfeited to the Crown.

Cecily Neville was no longer Duchess of York but the wife of a traitor. She was to leave immediately with her two brats in the clothes in which they stood, under guard to the Duke of Buckingham, where it was hoped, they will learn that the House of Lancaster rules England. Margaret may also have expressed the hope that Cecily Neville was able to bid her husband and sons a warm adieu, since she would not rest until she had achieved their deaths."

"Stop. I'm getting goose bumps all up and down." Gail interrupted, rubbing first one arm and then the other. "And so it began here? Richard's hatred of Queen Margaret I mean?"

"Definitely. He was at a very impressionable age. Years later, the boy who had become a man would remember that day, standing here, so frightened and vulnerable. We may not condone it, but we can understand better, I think, how easy it would be for Richard to participate perhaps in the death of her son and a short while later, the murder of her husband."

Laura turned then, and together they wandered through the ruins of the Great Hall, relying on their imagination to reconstruct what life might have been like there, so many years before.

Later, they shopped the length of Ludlow, finishing up at the 500-year-old *Feathers Inn*. When Laura returned from the bar, drinks in hand, Gail was talking with two young men dressed in business suits. She hesitated for a moment, but Gail had seen her and waved her over.

"This is my sister-in-law, Laura. Laura, Jean and Peter. They're with the EEC. Isn't that interesting?"

Peter chuckled, somewhat embarrassed. "Boring stuff really. Certainly not nearly as interesting as say, Richard Gloucester."

"I've been telling them all about our tour." Gail cut in.

"Excellent." Laura said, smiling evenly. "You must know

your history quite well Peter - Richard Gloucester?"

He smiled shyly. "It's my mother who's the Ricardian in the family, not me. I settled on Dick the Thrice in school when we had to do a piece on an historical character."

"Dick the Thrice." Gail started to laugh.

"Yes well, I'm afraid old Dickie got me into a spot of bother with my mother, since I ended up taking a somewhat different stance from hers. She quite likes the fellow you see, but frankly, I wrote him up as a murdering SOB - excuse me - so, my mother refused to talk to me for weeks afterwards."

He checked his watch, then spoke to Jean in rapid French. "It's been delightful ladies, but we must go. We have a colleague we have yet to find and a work session to attend. It's been lovely to meet you both. I hope your trip is a success and your flight home, safe and comfortable."

He rose, taking Jean with him. Jean bowed politely and wished them adieu before following Peter out of the bar.

"So," Gail mused, "Dick the Thrice was a murdering SOB. That's nice to know."

"Old news to you." Laura said with a wry smile. "Come on, I'll buy you a newspaper full of fish and chips."

St. Albans, that same evening

"So, Rachael, do we have an understanding?" Stephen stood back from the open suitcase spread across the four-poster bed and looked directly at his wife.

Rachael sat on the edge of the bed, her head averted, her hands reduced to two fists of pure fury.

"All right, let's go through it again, shall we? This weekend you will tell everyone, and I mean everyone, that you will be resigning from the Society, effective immediately. I don't give a damn what excuse you use as long as you make it very clear that you will no longer be involved in any way with the Society, or any of its activities. I want you at home, Rachael. I want to start a family just like we planned and I refuse to put up with any more of this nonsense or your obsession with this man."

"You're jealous." Rachael shouted, her voice harsh with tears already shed.

"Damn right, I'm jealous! No man, and I don't care who the hell he is, is going to put up with sharing his wife with the ghost of a dead king for Christ's sake. I want you back on track, do you hear me? The university is still interested in that Stuart manuscript you promised them. Half our friends refuse to visit anymore because all you want to talk about is the life and times of that bastard. Now, either you resign immediately or I'll do it for you."

Rachael began to sob again. "How can you be so cruel to me?"

"Cruel?" Stephen snapped back. "If you don't do as I say, then I'll show you what cruel is. Do I make myself clear?"

Rachael nodded her head slowly as she rose. She hesitated near the door, then turned. She watch him abstractly for a moment or two as he finished packing. "I refuse to have your children Stephen."

The blow from the back of his hand sent her reeling. Her head struck the doorframe, momentarily dazing her. Fresh tears welled up as she realized in horror that the man she loved and been married to for four years could abuse her in such a way.

Before she could sufficiently regain her equalibrium, he grabbed her by the throat, pinning her against the door. His pale blue eyes regarded her with open hostility. "But you'd have his child wouldn't you Rachael? The child of a psychotic killer. Is that what you'd prefer over a child by a mere Systems Analyst? Have you decided in your warped little mind that I'm now unworthy to father your children, but he is?"

He pulled her away from the door and threw her into the hallway. Paralyzed with fear, she sank to the floor. She cringed as he stood over her, suitcase in hand.

"I've decided to leave now. I'll spend the night somewhere downcountry, so you have extra time to think things through, but do so carefully Rachael. Unless you do exactly as I've asked of you, then don't bother coming back here because you won't be welcome. This is my family home, remember?"

Day 5
Warwick - Ambion Hill - Dadlington

King Richard:

> *March on, join bravely, let us to 't pell-mell;*
> *If not to heaven, than hand in hand to hell.*

Shakespeare -
The Tragedy of King Richard the Third
[Act V, Scene 3]

"Well, it looks like we've made it." Laura said, adding a sigh of relief as she geared down in preparation for yet another roundabout.

Gail groaned as she allowed the road atlas to slip off her lap.

"I love driving in the UK - what a challenge!"

"Laura, stick it in your ear." Gail shot back good-naturedly, their little tiff forgotten. "I thought we were never going to find the M42. I had visions of our skeletal remains going around and around through all eternity, lost forever in a roundabout. I need a drink."

"It's nowhere near four o'clock, you souse. You're developing some decidedly bad habits on this trip my dear and I ... think ..." One look at Gail's face and Laura decided she had better shut up. Stopped at a traffic light, she turned, then smiled broadly. "You did real good babe."

"Hey, I did, didn't I?" Gail said, pleased with herself.

"Strange, though, I thought Coventry was larger."

"Coventry! I thought we were going to Warwick."

Gail panicked as she dived to retrieve the map. Laura started to laugh, prompting Gail to deliver a glancing blow just as Laura pulled into the designated parking area near the castle.

As Laura prepared to exit the car, she noticed a dark shape which loomed up on Gail's side. Her first impression was of a suit but when it turned to reveal brass buttons, she erased the word 'suit' and replace it with 'uniform' as in 'police'. Gail remained blissfully unaware of potential danger as she searched the back seat for her purse and camera. Suddenly a moustached face appeared at the window. "Gail."

"What?"

It was obvious that Laura was looking beyond her so, when Gail turned to see what it was, she just about jumped into the back seat. The face remained impassive however, while an index finger ordered the window lowered. Laura calmly turned the ignition key while Gail frantically sought the button which opened the window.

"Good afternoon ladies. I couldn't help but notice your antics in the car just before pulling in." Addressing Gail directly, he asked, "Do you make a regular habit of striking your driver whilst he or she is in control of a motor vehicle?"

"No sir." Gail squeaked.

"I trust not. Such behaviour could lead to some nasty surprises." He paused for a moment as he check the interior of the car. "On holidays, are we?"

"Yes sir," Laura said, keeping her voice calm and in control. "Sorry about what happened officer. My sister-in-law does not make a habit of belting me about. She's just excitable, that's all. It's the first time she's been away from home you see, and well, the cloak of international traveller is still a loose fit, if you take my meaning."

Gail shot Laura a look of pure malice, but held her tongue.

"I see." He said carefully. "You intend to visit the castle I presume? Are you staying in Warwick?"

"Unfortunately, no. We have reservations in a place near Market Bosworth tonight. Gail here is a great fan of King Richard III, you see." Laura smiled wickedly.

"Oh, is she now?"

That did it, Gail had been officially declared a certified nut case.

The officer stood up then and wandered around to Laura's side of the car. He reappeared, framed this time in the driver's window and asked for Laura's licence. He took his time as he compared the picture to real life and read the relevant details. As he handed it back, he wished them a good day. With a final warning glance in Gail's direction, he proceeded on his way.

"You're evil." Gail growled, "and I'm going to get you for this."

"Okay," Laura shrugged, "but could you wait until after I've had a cup of coffee and something to eat."

"Sure, take you time."

They stared at each other for a moment, then simultaneously burst into laughter.

Described at the 'finest medieval castle in England', Warwick is strategically located in the centre of the country on the River Avon. It is in such a remarkable state of preservation that it should come as no surprise to learn that it was a private residence until 1978 when it was sold to the Tussauds Group. For centuries Warwick Castle was home to the powerful Earls of Warwick, including Richard Neville the famous 'Kingmaker' who changed sides during the Wars of the Roses and met his death on the battlefield of Barnet.

After George Clarence's untimely death in 1478, Richard, then Duke of Gloucester, came into possession of the castle. Later it became a Parliamentarian stronghold during the English Civil War and was thus spared the destruction which was visited upon so many castles throughout England.

Laura and Gail purchased their tickets and a guidebook near the stables then walked down a slight incline and along a pathway towards the gatehouse complex. To their left was a delightful Victorian rose garden, while to their right loomed the massive fortification, with Guy's Tower surmounting the ramparts - 128 feet and five storeys high. Further along the wall was the barbican and gatehouse, both massively built and cunningly crafted to repel the fiercest attack.

The first line of defence was the barbican and its drawbridge, which reached out over the dry ditch. Next came a massive wooden door and beyond that, the first of two iron portcullis. Should enemy troops get pass the first portcullis, they would find themselves in a narrow roofed passageway with arrow slits to either side and worse, murder holes in the ceiling from which stones and missiles could be dropped. Any who survived this initial barrage were greeted by the gatehouse with its own door, portcullis and another series of murder holes.

They passed through the gatehouse safely, although their imaginations were working overtime. The walk through this impressive entranceway was angled upwards slightly, the cobblestones deadly under foot. Beyond stretched a beautiful expanse of lawn, while at the far end a earthen mound marked all that remains of the site of the original wooden structure built in 1068.

Laura resorted to the guidebook then to get her bearings, so it was Gail who first saw the sign pointing the way to the Armoury, Dungeon and Torture Chamber. Laura had to practically run to catch up with her.

"Just looking, or are you planning to buy?" Laura whispered.

"Don't tempt me."

Predictably the dungeon lay deep beneath the earth in the lowest chamber of Caesar's Tower. Laura felt her throat constrict as they descended the steep, narrow stone steps. The air grew substantially cooler, damper and, although Gail didn't seem to notice, there was a stale nauseating smell, as of decay, which Laura found disconcerting. Despite the electric lighting, the atmosphere remained oppressive.

Gail spread-eagled herself against a section of wall pretending to be shackled. "Water, water." She gasped.

Laura eyed her without enthusiasm. "Sorry, no ladies allowed. From the looks of it, this was an exclusive men's club, so pack your rags and bags, collect your lice and get out."

"No female prisoners?" Gail seemed disappointed.

"Oh, great, so that's what women's lib has taught you? You're disappointed because you can't be down here being treated like one of the guys? Listened to what it says here. *The dungeon was more than a place of confinement; it was intended to be a pit of despair. Whatever degradations the body underwent, the mental suffering was even greater.'* Still want to sign up?"

"Hum, maybe not. What's this?" Gail said as she poked her head inside a closet-size recess in the wall.

"Careful, I think that's the 'oubliette'."

Laura joined Gail and together they looked down into the blackness. Gail shuddered. Through the middle of the room ran a ditch, the only form of sanitation, while above, suspended by a chain was an iron cage known as the *Scavenger's Daughter*. Within its cold embrace the condemned would die slowly of starvation, a vivid example to others. Often the body would remain there for months, while the flesh rotted away or was eaten by birds and rats.

"I wonder what the 'rack rate' was for this hotel?" Laura mused, smiling at Gail.

"Ha, ha."

"Actually, do you know what this place really is? It's a medieval 'Fat Farm'. A month or two down here and even your closest friends wouldn't recognise you."

"Let's go." Gail said as she made her way back to the stairs. Laura followed gladly. Although they had been in the dungeon for perhaps fifteen minutes, they both breathed the fresh air in deeply, luxuriating in the warmth of the sun. Laura consulted the guidebook again.

"Ah, Guy of Warwick." Laura said with a romantic sigh. "Here's a hero for you Gail."

"Who?"

"Sir Guy. He started out as a squire in love with the boss's daughter. To make himself presentable as a potential suitor, he sought wealth and fame by entering all the jousting competitions around the country. He must have been very good, because eventually he came back to Warwick and claimed the fair Belize, I think her name was. All this happened in the 900's, when the legend was born of a monstrous beast which terrorized Dunsmow Heath. Anyhow, before Guy could claim his bride, the king at the time - Athelstan - order Guy to kill the beastie."

"What was it?" Gail said, looking grim.

"Well, that's why I thought you'd like Guy, because the beastie was a cow. Mind you, a very large cow, but a cow nevertheless.

"You're making this up."

"It's true, it says so right here - see." Laura pointed to the spot in the guidebook. "Now, that's all it says about Sir Guy, and we don't have the time now for the rest of his story, but remind me later. A tale of true love."

Gail just shook her head as Laura continued to read the guidebook.

"This should be interesting." She said as she flipped through several pages. "Remember Warwick, the 'Kingmaker'?"

"He died early on in the piece, didn't he?" Gail moved to Laura's side to look at the guidebook. "Wasn't he the one who couldn't decide whether to paint his roses red or white?"

"Yeah, something like that." Laura replied derisively. "He was called the 'Kingmaker' because he helped to put Edward IV on the throne and then, when Edward refused to do as he was told, Warwick manipulated George into turning against his brother the king and making a bid for the crown himself. When that failed Warwick really turned traitor, joined Queen Margaret, married his younger daughter Anne - Richard's Anne - to Margaret beastly son Edouard , and for awhile at least, the scheme worked. Remember Edward, Richard and a few others were caught napping and narrowly escaped to the continent?

For a time Warwick ruled supreme with old King Henry back on the throne and all the roses painted Lancastrian red.

Well, our Eddie wasn't about to be pushed off his throne, so back he came in the spring of 1471 with Richard and a good size army. Warwick was here at this castle with George, who was none too pleased with the way he had been sidestepped by Warwick in favour of Edouard, so when Edward and Richard called on their brother to join them, he did, taking a sizeable force with him. Edward hurried to London, reclaimed the throne, kissed his wife and new born son, then focused his attention on bringing Warwick down in a heap.

"Warwick Castle is now owned by the Tussauds Group and they've put together a series of scenes with wax figures over there in the Undercroft. It depicts Warwick preparing to go to battle against King Edward."

"Just a minute. The battle Warwick was preparing for, he died in it, didn't he?"

"Right. Butchered, it is said, trying to escape the field. His brother Montagu too. That's what should make this very interesting. I just hope we're not expected to be sympathetic towards Warwick though, because quite frankly I don't like him very much. Too many people died unnecessarily because of his distorted vision of himself. Besides," she shrugged, "what kind of man would join forces with the very side that murdered his own father?"

"Maybe he didn't like his father." Gail offered.

"There's a thought."

The display was thoroughly impressive. Laura and Gail were able to walk at their own pace through room after room, each containing life-size wax figures engaged in a variety of activities from the blacksmith forging horseshoes to a wheelwright repairing a cart.

The atmosphere of each tableaux was enhanced by an audio system so Laura and Gail really felt part of the preparations as men shouted, grunted and groaned under the weight of the work required, while children laughed, horses whined and lumber creaked. Warwick's powerful warhorse stood ready in its stall, decked out in a caparison, tail twitching, all nervous, pent up energy. Armour was being polished, carts loaded, bows checked and readied for deployment.

They progressed slowly, taking in every detail of the extraordinary display. In a recreation of a medieval apartment, a woman is depicted sewing a battle standard while another mends a pavilion. A young girl, almost lost in the folds, giggled as she played, the sound echoing through the chamber. Laura and Gail wandered around at length examining the chamber's many details before proceeding through into the final room where they came face to face with the 'Kingmaker'.

A handsome, powerfully built man, Warwick was displayed with sword raised as he extols his men to fight. Laura listened to his little speech dispassionately. Knowing that in a very short while all the preparation and fine ideals would come to grief and eventual death at Barnet, Laura moved away before the audio system began again. They exited into a shop.

"Shades of Disneyworld." Gail exclaimed.

"What?"

"It's like coming out of the 'Pirates of the Caribbean' ride at Disneyworld. Have you ever tried to get through the shop at the exit with a kid in tow? Impossible. Worse then the candy counter at a supermarket check-out." Gail paused. "I feel sorry for Warwick."

"Okay." Laura shrugged as she rummaged through a basket piled high with plastic swords and miniature helmets. "I'm looking for something suitable to wear at Bosworth Field, but it looks like they only have kid sizes. Tell me, why do you feel sorry for Warwick?"

"I don't know. He went to all that trouble and ended up being butchered, you said. It doesn't seem fair." Gail sighed.

Laura straightened and turned to face Gail, unable at first to determine whether she was pulling the proverbial leg or not. "Fair, I'll give you fair. According to this," Laura brandished the guidebook, "Warwick was caught, stripped naked and then killed. Now that's not fair. Based on that little titbit of information, it's not beyond the realm of possibility that our young Richard might have arrived in time to witness Warwick's death and may even have been forced to participate. Richard had to stand and watch while his sometime mentor and friend was humiliated and then executed, probably by decapitation.

"Warwick lived by the sword and sure enough, he died by it. Under the circumstances, that was about as fair as he could expect. He was probably grateful. It could have been worse. Traitors usually got the HDQ treatment. The man was a menace Gail, he had to die."

"What's HDQ?"

"Hang, draw and quarter."

"Oh." Gail muttered. "Still, it doesn't seem fair."

Laura sighed and continued shopping, leaving Gail to work it through. Independently they wandered around, quickly selecting small gifts to augment their substantial hoard of souvenirs and trinkets destined for export. As Laura was about to exit the shop, she overheard a woman behind the counter give directions to a young couple.

"'Tis back where you came in luv, and up the stairs. Quite an interesting exhibit on the life and times of King Richard." Laura wheeled around, looking for Gail. In the end she practically had to pull her from the shop bodily.

"Hey, where are we going?"

"Wait and see." Laura replied, increasing her pace.

To the right of the Gatehouse was a flight of stone stairs which lead upwards into the gloom.

"What's up there?"

Laura stepped back to reveal a small sign attached to the wall

- Richard III Museum   "Oh, oh, we're in trouble now. Did you know this was here?"

"No." Laura checked her camera. "Coming up?"

"Sure," Gail said with a shrug.

The first room was furnished in a style typical of the 15th century - fireplace, wooden table and chair, a bench, a straw mat on the floor. Typical, yes, but not for someone of Richard's degree of birth. The next area could be best described as 'general information', and included pictures of all the principal characters including Richard, Edward IV, Tudor as well as copies of various correspondence, enlarged for easy reading. Beyond, a small hallway contained a medieval loo and more written material, mainly from chronicles. The next room listed in chronological order important events during Richard's reign, plus pictures of tomb effigies, a description of Bosworth field, and background information regarding Richard's choice of the boar as a symbol and the number of occasions the badge appeared in its various forms.

From there they descended down a vice to the next room in which the two Princes in the Tower were featured, plus a family tree and finally, various depictions of Richard, some of them humorous, some not, as the wicked uncle of Shakespearean fame.

Laura lingered, so Gail continued on, standing atop an arched bridge which spanned the gateway, watching the flow of visitors beneath. After perhaps fifteen minutes, she turned back to look for Laura. She was leaning up against the wall, legs casually crossed at the ankles, writing in her notebook.

"Find something interesting?" Gail said as she moved closer.

"Do you know," Laura replied, not looking up, "this whole display has been organized by the Richard III Society. There's a plaque on the wall over there."

"So, it's biased?"

"No, I won't say that - just careful." Laura straightened and smiled as she slipped her notebook into her bag. "Anyhow, I'm finished. Where to now?"

"Let's wall-walk a bit. There's a section that Richard built, according to this." Gail waved the guidebook. "He named one of the towers after brother George. Nice touch don't you think?"

"Okay." Laura replied, easing herself free of the wall.

The stairs up to the ramparts were steep, but once surmounted, Laura and Gail were able to walk with ease along the section of the wall where two stunted towers formed part of the Tower House which Richard, then Duke of Gloucester, began building in 1478. The complex which he had in mind was substantial.

"It says here," Laura paused to read from her guidebook, "that these two towers - the Bear and the Clarence - were meant to be part of a four-tower Royal Keep constructed in part to protect against a mutinous attack from **within** the castle. Richard's hold on the English crown was so precarious, according to this, that he lived in fear and distrust for the final two years of his life. I think that's called paranoia."

"Let's see now," Gail said, working her fingers, "so far we have Richard - a paranoiac, psychotic, murdering, SOB. Right?"

"Does this mean that you're not going to join the Richard III Society now?" Laura said in counterfeit shock. "Not to worry, half an hour with a Ricardian and you'll think he's 'Mr. Nice Guy' again."

"I will not! Frankly, I think he was a bastard of the highest order."

"No you don't."

"And why not, Miss Smartypants?"

"Because, my dear Gail, you're a hopeless optimist who always manages to see the good in everyone. Evil doesn't exist for you, not really. Your perpetual sense of charity has forgiven Warwick as it will forgive Richard. That's why everyone loves you. Come on, let's have lunch. I'm starved."

The Crypt Restaurant, situated as the name suggests, beneath the Great Hall, was delightful. Cafeteria style, they were able to select what they wanted from the items displayed or from a posted menu, complete with prices.

Suddenly Gail laughed. "What's Spotted Dick?" She nodded towards the desserts list.

"Stodge pudding." Laura replied. "If you're going to have it, you'd better stick with a very small main because that stuff's deadly. When it goes off, it's used to anchor boats with."

"Spotted, what does that mean?"

"It's filled with currents usually or at least that's what my grandmother used. She didn't make it very often though because my grandfather insisted upon calling it 'fly cemetery pudding' just to annoy her. Mind you, he could have been right." She shrugged. "No screens in those days and well, a squished fly does look a bit like a cooked current, especially …"

"I think I'll have cheesecake instead."

"Good choice."

They found a table in a small alcove. Outside the window at the end of their table was a fine view of the parkland which surrounds the castle and the River Avon, perhaps fifty feet below. The room was large enough to easily seat 200 people or more, although it was difficult to tell since it was divided into separate areas by massive stone columns which supported the upper floors, the roof domed for extra strength. The walls were plastered and painted with bright designs typical of the medieval age.

While they ate, Gail asked about Sir Guy.

"Ah yes," Laura said with a romantic sigh, "Sir Guy, the 'Bovine Basher' married his beloved Belize and eventually became Guy of Warwick. Obviously, having dispatched the Dun Cow, he considered himself **udderly** invincible - ouch Gail, that hurt - so, he signed up for the Crusades. Now, if you've studied anything about the first Crusade, you know that it was a thoroughly not nice adventure, so by the time Sir Guy made it home, he was fed up to the teeth - if he had any left - with death, torture, murder, rape, pillage, poor food, bad weather, bad roads, bad breath, bad manners, and the Crusade itself, which was a bad idea. Anyhow, he didn't rush into the arms of his beloved, but hid out in a cave near here, supposedly to spend the rest of his life in prayer and meditation. Strange. He did see his wife once, though, when he begged alms at the castle door, but by then he knew he was dying, so he let it be. At the end, however he wrote to her and she rushed to his side and held him close as he died. Boohoo."

"Why do I get the feeling that the story isn't finished?"

"Well, you have to ask yourself - prayer and meditation? I don't think so. Most likely he had developed leprosy, or he had become a raving lunatic, or a homosexual, in which case, he couldn't face his wife."

"Boy, you sure can take the romance out of things in a hurry." Gail shook her head.

"Personally, I opt for leprosy."

"Tell me about the road to Bosworth." Gail said as she settled back in the passenger seat, the road atlas across her lap.

"Well, we go north on the Foss Way to Watling Street, east then north … "

"No silly, the road Richard took - Tudor and the rest."

"I haven't got my notes."

"But nevertheless you know the story so, out with it."

"All right." Laura said as she settled the car into fifth gear. "Tudor landed near Milford Haven, Wales, on August 7th, 1485. He received very little in the way of aid at the start, despite promises from men like Rhys ap Thomas, a Welshmen and friend to a Doctor Lewis who just happened to be Margaret Beaufort's personal physician. Now, there's a coincidence for you. Anyhow, Tudor's army consisted mainly of French troops, about 600 English exiles with nothing to lose, soldiers of fortune of indeterminate parentage, and Scots mercenaries. He made his way north then east, finally gaining support in Shropshire. He wrote to his mother and to the Stanley brothers, begging for their support.

"Richard, in the meantime, was jubilant. The long awaited Tudor had landed and he was ready for him. Now, prior to Tudor's arrival, Thomas Stanley had requested leave to visit his estates. Richard, obviously distrustful of Stanley, insisted that he leave his son George behind as a hostage. When Richard ordered troops to be brought to Nottingham, Stanley replied that he was too ill with the sweating sickness to attend upon his King. Under pressure - or torture perhaps - the son revealed that his uncle William and others were planning to aid Tudor, but that his father - Tudor's own stepfather remember - was ever faithful to Richard. I doubt if Richard was convinced because he kept the kid close to him to the very end."

"So, let me get this straight." Gail said. "Richard told Stanley to muster his troops, but Stanley didn't relish the idea, so Richard told him that he had better catch-up, or he would make hamburger of his son Georgie. Right?"

Laura smiled sardonically as she shot Gail a withering glance. "You **must** have a death wish."

Gail chuckled. "Sorry, couldn't resist."

"Well, are you ready for this?" Laura asked as she turned off the A447, past the signpost marking the route to the Bosworth Field Battle Site.

"No problem. I'm going to sit on the fence and smile a lot." Gail said, adding a broad grin which only succeeded in making her look demented.

"You know, I've been thinking about Rachael. We may have to be careful with her."

"What do you mean?"

"Why was she on that bus with a bunch of old ladies?"

"She'd have no control over that."

"Ah, but then again, she might. And, what was she doing visiting Minster Lovell Hall, a place she's seen before?"

"So, what are you getting at?" Gail said as she offered Laura a mint.

"No thanks. Let's suppose that Rachael was the tour director for that enterprise. Let's suppose that she is, in fact, a bigwig Ricardian who recruits in her spare time."

"The way you say it, you make her sound like one of the aliens in the *Invasion of the Body Snatchers*." Gail chuckled.

"It's just a gut feeling that's all. I guess I don't want to disappoint her if she does try her spiel and I have to tell her that I'm not buying."

"Ah well, play it by ear. What's that?" Gail asked staring out her side window. "Pull over - quick."

Alarmed, Laura put on the emergency flashers and brought the car to a halt at the edge of the road. The car had barely stopped when Gail eased herself out, nearly falling into the ditch which ran along the edge of the road. Although there was no traffic, Laura took considerable care in getting out and around the car to join Gail.

Resting against the front of the car, arms folded across her chest, Gail calmly chewed on the remnant of her second mint while she gazed across an open field. "I think we're here." She announced without emotion.

Laura turned and followed Gail's line of vision up a moderately steep hill to its top. On the stiff afternoon breeze flew a massive banner, twenty-two feet long.

"It's his battle standard." Laura said with more than a hint of excitement. "Where that was, so too was his army. See, it bears the cross of St. George, the white rose of York with the sunburst, and of course his personal emblem, the white boar. It's huge! Someone must have more money than brains. Come on, let's go."

A road climbed the hill then forked around a massive oak before merging at the crest. As they drove up, Gail continued to watch the banner. "If there's anything which would attract Richard back from the nether world to refight the battle, that would be it." She nodded. "Tomorrow's the anniversary, right?"

"Monday." Laura said, gripping the wheel tighter. Her thumbs prickled, whether from the pressure or something else. She began to feel uneasy.

Parking was to the right beyond a large flat area which was being roped off by a team of men while another group wrestled to unfold a massive marquee lying on the ground in a tangle of ropes and wire. Preparations were well underway for tomorrow's tournament.

The impressive Visitors Centre stood to one side. This was more than a typical Visitors Centre. Everything within related in some way to the age, but more particularly to King Richard, from the post cards to the inevitable paper weights, coffee mugs, books and bookmarks and wall plaques. They both looked but decided to delay purchasing anything until later. At the far end of the shop was the museum. Laura swooped through, unaware that there was an admission charge which Gail quickly paid while mumbling apologies to the startled lady behind the counter.

Gail found herself in almost total darkness, caught within a room meant to depict a corner of a medieval street perhaps. She grew accustomed to the dim light but not to the all pervasive smell of urine which made her gag. Laura was just on the other side, waiting for her. Here the light was brighter but subtle to emphasize the displays.

"Great atmosphere, eh?" Laura said laughingly.

"Thanks, but I'd prefer to use my own imagination when it comes to what it smelt like around here in 1485. Wow, you're right about the money. This place must have cost a fortune."

As Laura and Gail moved away from the malodorous zone they were confronted with a vast array of information relating to the Battle of Bosworth Field. A brief description of the two antagonists set Gail reading while Laura inspected a map on the opposite wall which indicated where the various battles were fought during the Wars of the Roses, the dates and most interesting of all, the appalling loss of life on both sides. The display was cunningly devised behind non-reflecting glass. In the front at the bottom, lay a helmet resting in long grass, while arrows studded the site. A grim reminder of just what the battlefields might have looked like when arrows were launched from longbows at the rate of ten to fifteen per minute.

Just around the corner a waxen figure of a widow, dressed in black, was depicted kneeling in prayer. Her whole appearance was typical of the age, from the 'pregnant look' fashion of her gown to the elaborate headdress designed so that no hair showed. To achieve this, women shaved the hair at the back of their necks, exaggerating the neckline.

The 'Brasses Room' included a recreation of the tomb effigy of Sir William Harcourt, a Yorkist Knight who died in 1482. The original, Laura read on the accompanying plaque is to be found at Aston Church in Birmingham.

There was a splendid display of weapons which would have been in use at the time, plus mannequins dressed in the costumes appropriate to both sides on the day. The lethal looking pikes, halberds, swords and daggers made Gail and Laura wince as they were reminded that war in the 15th-century was a gory, horrific exercise where even a slight wound could mean death - eventually.

In the second section there was a detailed topographical map of the battle site complete with miniature soldiers on foot or horseback. The scene was quite extensive so it took Laura and Gail some time to find the centre of the action at the very front of the glassed display. Tiny figures represented Richard and his few companions practically within the Tudor camp. Richard actually got close enough to Henry to kill his standard bearer William Brandon and unseat the giant Sir John Cheyney. In the near distance and on the move were the forces of the Stanleys.

Gail looked at Laura, perplexed. "Why is Richard, Tudor and the rest shown way down here in the corner practically? What was going on out here, where we're standing?"

"Nothing." Laura said sadly.

"This is it?" Gail was incredulous. "Richard left his main army behind him on the hill?"

"Richard felt that if he could kill Tudor, then he would win the day. One death and it would be all over. He didn't reckon on whose."

"I'm beginning to think that our Richard was a paranoid, psychotic, murdering, SOB, dummy." Gail whispered, since there were other visitors close by.

Laura smiled thinly. "I'm sure he thought so afterwards."

Towards the far end of the room was a glass case containing a miniature of a knight on horseback, splendidly attired for a jousting tournament. Beside him stood a squire while the knight's lady stood ready to hand her lord a favour to wear. "Guess who it is?" Gail whispered.

Laura shrugged, not recognizing the devices.

"Hastings." Gail cleared her throat.

At the far end of the room was a magnificent stature of Richard astride his horse White Surrey, depicted as they both might have appeared just prior to battle. The rendering was exquisite in its detail of both horse and rider. Laura quickly turned away, quietly disconcerted.

"Hey, guess what's in the next room?" Gail whispered excitedly. "They're showing the final scenes from Olivier's film." Gail gripped Laura's arm and pulled her through. "It's being rewound the girl said and should start any second."

"I don't think I ..." Laura was interrupted as the audio system burst into life and the film began just as Sir Lawrence Olivier - as King Richard - exits his tent prior to the battle. Gail had already settled in to watch the production, joined by several others, so Laura was forced to do the same as Gail pulled her down beside her. At the end there was complete silence from the audience as they filed out, grim faced.

As Laura stood she noticed a final tableaux which had been missed in their hurry to see the film. Depicted life-size, Henry Tudor was shown seated at a table with papers spread out in front of him. Behind and slightly to one side, stood Oxford. The scene is called 'The Act of Conciliation'.

"Do you know," Laura said in hushed tones, "after Henry was proclaimed king, he backdated his reign to before Bosworth so that all those who participated on Richard's side could be declared traitors?"

"That's not fair!"

"Fair, as we have determined, has nothing to do with it. The winner takes all and can make, break or alter the rules."

Beyond the screening room was a smaller gift shop. There Laura purchased a book entitled, *The Battle of Bosworth* plus a sheet map depicting the layout of the battle site and the various pathways for visitors to follow. From there they exited into a courtyard which contained toilet facilities and a coffee shop.

"Let's have a quick coffee while …"

"… you look over your new book. I know, I know." Gail nodded. "Loo first."

Gail hurried away, leaving Laura to crack the book as she walked slowly towards the restaurant area. By the time Gail joined her, Laura had purchased two coffees and had settled at a table in the far corner, next to the windows. Gail seemed disappointed.

"Didn't you get some sweets or something? How I am going to walk the killing grounds without a bit of sustenance?"

"According to this," Laura said, indicating her new book, "Richard went into battle without celebrating Mass first. Very unusual."

"I don't care about Mass, what about mess. I'm going to see what desserts they have. Want something?"

But Laura was too busy reading to hear Gail's question. When she returned, Laura was even deeper into the book and didn't acknowledge Gail's presence for some time. Contenting herself with her brownie, Gail waited patiently. Laura's one big fault, if it could be called a fault, was her insatiable thirst for knowledge. Hers was the type of mind that rarely forgot anything, provided that she was given the opportunity to deposit the information under control conditions. Distracted or hurried, the logical laying down of data in sequential order was disturbed, resulting in its total loss, or more likely, its drift to a region of Laura's subconscious where the data was stored for retrieval by instinct or when its owner was pressed. This Laura found both disconcerting, and annoying.

"I'm sorry Gail."

"That's okay. So, what have you found out?"

"Well, Richard should have won this battle. He had the superior force, years of experience in warfare, while Tudor had none. Richard had cannon, the benefit of the high ground and he was King. Henry's army was made up of French and Scottish mercenaries and Welsh archers who, it seems, were not well provisioned. Henry's force was substantially smaller too. But, there was treason in the air and ultimately Richard was betrayed."

"*Jockey of Norfolk be not so bold, Richard thy master has been bought and sold.* That's what Shakespeare said, and it doesn't look like he was too far off the mark." Gail said as she rose from her seat.

"No." Laura said sadly.

The beginning of the battlefield trail was on the far side of the parking area. As they walked, Laura told Gail more of what she had learned. "Not only did Richard miss Mass, but it would seem that he ended up fighting on an empty stomach, poor lad. There was a mix-up or something with the wine and the Host for the Eucharist, so no Mass and no sticky buns either. Someone should have gone to the donut shop.

"Anyhow, Tudor was on the move early so Richard hurried his army into action. Apparently he was more than his usual grim self, ashen faced and given to outbursts of rage. He had had a fitful night's sleep, perhaps as Shakespeare suggested, visited by the spectres of those he had slain. During the night there had been defections from the royal army, possibly as a result of Norfolk's anonymous note, and if that wasn't enough, he had serious doubts about the loyalty of Northumberland and, of course, the Stanleys who were camped away over near Dadlington. Now I know what Rachael meant by sleeping with the enemy."

They walked to the crest of Ambion Hill, as it was called, to stand near the huge Royal standard. Looking out towards the north they could see the village of Market Bosworth with its square church tower. To the right, hidden in the trees, was Sutton Cheney while to the left and below flew the red dragon standard of Henry Tudor, barely moving in the sheltered valley, while the Royal standard snapped and groaned on the hilltop, driven by a stiff wind.

Richard's battle strategy depended, in part, on a show of force as he positioned his troops along the crest of the hill were Laura and Gail now stood. The hill could barely support the large numbers involved. It is generally believed that the royal host was divided into three 'battles', with Norfolk leading the vanguard, the main body under the King, and a rearguard under Northumberland.

"Tudor's forces, with the bulk of the army under the experienced leadership of the Earl of Oxford, began to skirt the southern edge of the hill towards Shenton over there." Laura pointed. "The Stanleys followed at a discreet distance. Typically, they decided to take a 'wait and see' approach, not committing themselves to either side at this stage. It must have been extremely frustrating for both the King and Tudor. The combined armies of Thomas Stanley and his brother William amounted to about 5,000 men in arms. Remember, Tudor was Lord Stanley's stepson, and his son George was a hostage held within arm's reach of Richard, so he had to be very careful. Tudor appealed several times for help, while Richard delivered ugly threats, hoping to force their hand. There seems to have been some members of William Stanley's force who did go over to Tudor, while the remainder of the army drew back, effectively withdrawing from the field. All this was observed by Richard from his vantage point atop this hill. Richard sent one final order to Stanley, insisting that he deploy his troops or George would die. Apparently Stanley replied that he had other sons. Swearing vengeance, Richard ordered the immediate execution of Georgie."

"No!"

"Oh, yes. Fortunately, cooler heads prevailed and Richard was persuaded to delay the execution until he could top all the Stanleys together."

"And Tudor too."

"Not Tudor." Laura reacted savagely. "Richard had to kill him on the field. This was trial by battle, a duel to the death if you like. Both sides firmly believed that God would be on hand to determine the fate of England's throne. Richard didn't think much of Tudor, calling him a 'Welsh milksop', a pretender, a rebel, as well as a few other derogatory words not fit for the ears of ladies. Probably most of them were true. Henry Tudor could never hope to match Richard's power in the field. For all his size, Richard was a true 'Warrior King', and dressed in full armour astride White Surrey, he must have been an impressive and frightening sight.

"Unfortunately for Richard, John de la Vere, 13th Earl of Oxford, was also on the field, and he was no milksop. He represented the oldest surviving noble house in England and Richard needed to fear him. Oxford had good reasons for hating the House of York and Richard in particular. Way back in 1473 his father and brother Aubrey were executed by King Edward IV on charges of treason, and it was Richard who wrestled the estates from de Vere's mother, remember, frightening the old lady half to death in the process?

"Anyhow, even the book here admits that the details of the battle are sketchy. One thing, though, seems clear. Most of the fighting took place down there on the borders of a marsh on the southwest slope of this hill. Richard must have watched, perhaps right where we are standing as the battle raged, taking note of the lacklustre performance of his troops. Lord Stanley had proven false, his ally Northumberland remained in the rear, sullen and uncooperative. Some time during the fighting, Oxford found his way through to Richard's chief supporter, Norfolk, and killed him. Richard had to take the initiative, and soon, or the day would be lost. Scanning the field below him, he picked out Tudor in the company of a small group of supporters, separate from the main body of his army. Richard selected a group of men he knew he could trust, donned his gilt helmet with its bejewelled coronet, and with banners unfurled, led a cavalry charge at full speed down the hill towards Tudor." Laura sighed. "It would be the last time ever in English history that a ruling monarch would actually participate in battle. Those few men who witnessed Richard's bloodcurdling charge down this hill saw the end of an era - the swan-song of medieval English chivalry."

Laura started to laugh suddenly. "Poor old Henry must have wet his pants as Richard and Co slashed and skewered their way ever closer. A protective ring was thrown around Tudor, but, it seems clear that Richard was able to get within possibly of few feet of his quarry before the unthinkable happened.

"The forces of Sir William Stanley arrived just in the nick of time with a host of red-coated soldiers swarming in in increasing numbers. Richard fought valiantly. Even the most obstinate anti-Ricardian testified to his bravery at the end. Some sources suggest that White Surrey was either mired in the mud or shot from beneath Richard, since a horse of this calibre would be dangerous to approach if you wish to pull the rider from the saddle. It's also suggested that, at one point, Richard was offered a fresh mount and an avenue of escape from the field. Whatever, he refused, preferring to stay and fight, to live or die a king. The English held back, fearful of dealing a death blow to an anointed king, so it was left to the Welsh, who not only killed Richard, but desecrate the body by mutilation. Even the Croyland Chronicle grudgingly admitted that the treatment of Richard's remains were 'not exactly in accordance with the laws of humanity'. The corpse was stripped naked, slung over a horse and ... "

Laura stopped abruptly and turned to Gail. She stood as if frozen, staring out towards the distant hills, her head held high as the wind pulled her hair back from her face. Silent tears coursed down her cheek.

"How dare you!" She said, wiping the tears away as her anger grew. "We've talked so much about him, got to know him a little and then you stand here like some damn machine and tell me that he was betrayed? That he came down this hill risking everything to secure the crown fairly in the sight of God and the whole kingdom, and then he's pulled from his horse by a band of Welsh cut-throats, commoners, who butcher him?"

"Gail," Laura whispered, "he died the way he wanted to die."

"You don't know that! Go away and leave me alone."

"All right." Laura said as she backed away, leaving Gail to work it through. She followed the pathway which dropped approximately half the height of the hill before it turned left, flattened briefly, before finishing its descent into the valley. Near Tudor's standard Laura lit a cigarette and waited, watching the sheep graze contentedly on the hillside.

From this vantage point she could clearly see the Royal standard, but Gail had disappeared. She stood alone, although twice she felt as if she were being watched. On both occasions she turned abruptly, expecting to see someone, but all remained silent and still. Even the air hung heavy, oppressive almost. The red dragon banner stirred listlessly, moved by a wind Laura could not feel. Not a bird, not an insect. Even the sheep seemed to be painted against the brilliant green of the pasture. She felt a presence, a sense of something, vague and indistinct yet ...

"As I supposed," she whispered, half in fear, half in excitement as her eyes narrowed. She turned then and hurriedly began to retrace her steps, only to be greeted by the spectacle of Gail and Rachael coming towards her.

"Hi," Rachael shouted enthusiastically. "Gail said you'd be

down here somewhere. What a meany you are, getting her all upset."

"She does a good job of upsetting herself, she doesn't need help from me." Laura was angry and defensive.

Rachael eyed her at close range, weighing, measuring. "You must have realized that Gail would see the unfairness of Richard's death? You only make it worse, you know, when you talk about how his body were desecrated."

"Unfairness! This had nothing to do with fairness! This isn't a playing field with referees, end zones, penalty points and time-outs. This is a field of war. Rachael, I try to deal in fact, and the fact of the matter is, Richard died here somewhere, betrayed both of his crown and his life. None of this happened by chance or just bad luck. Richard sowed the seeds of his own destruction. A trait, it seems, that runs in the family."

Gail hung back behind Rachael as if seeking protection there. Laura cast her a quick glance and found her anger rising.

"Well," Rachael said, trying to keep the situation light and friendly, "I'm going to take Gail across and show her the memorial stone. Come along, if you want to."

"No thanks. I think I'll go back and get another coffee and read some more."

Laura had already began to move up the hill, detaching herself from this petite tableaux, so Rachael and Gail continued on their way, still close together, engaged in whispered conversation.

Near to the top of the rise, Laura looked back but both Gail and Rachael had disappeared. She sighed, turned to her book and examined the maps. After a few minutes she stopped reading and allowed the book to drop to her side as she gazed out over the battle site. "Richard, why did you do it? Why?" She shouted to the wind.

Suddenly she again had the vague sense of a presence, as if whatever it was, had followed her up from the valley and stood now very close, watching her, listening perhaps. Although she could see nothing unusual, subconsciously she could hear the slow, metallic click of metal against metal, like the heartbeat of a giant clock. The air grew strangely chill around her as she retreated, hurriedly following the pathway back the way she had come.

The day was drawing in, and although the sky had cleared, the wind has risen in strength, mercilessly clawing at every bush and tree, setting up a dull moaning sound punctuated by the snap of Richard's standard as it flew in mock triumph from its massive metal pole.

Laura was on her third cup of coffee when Gail and Rachael entered the restaurant. So engrossed was she in her book that she didn't realise they had arrived until Gail swooped into the chair opposite, setting down a cup of hot chocolate. Laura knew immediately that things weren't right. Gail hated hot chocolate. Tentatively at first, Rachael joined them, but she sat on the edge of the chair facing outwards as if ready to flee at a moment's notice.

In the relatively dim light, Gail was dismayed to see that Laura had removed her dark sunglasses in favour of her reading glasses. She removed even these as she turned towards Gail, smiling, her eyes scanning every detail of her face. Gail did not like to look at Laura's eyes directly. Coloured approximately the same shade as her hair, Laura normally wore tinted glasses to hide the fact that her eyes were a malkin yellow. A colour which many people found just as disconcerting as Gail did now.

"Did you have fun?" Laura said, her eyes more than typically predatory.

"Yes I did, as a matter of fact. Rachael showed me where Richard died. There's a lovely stone there to mark the spot. According to Rachael, more people visit that site then ever visit Henry VII in Westminster Abbey."

Rachael cleared her throat. "I've invited Gail to attend the memorial service for Richard at Sutton Cheney tomorrow at noon, if you want to come too. It's just a short service with a luncheon afterwards, although that's booked out, I'm afraid."

Uncertainly hung in the air. Rachael looked away as Laura turned in her direction. "So, there'll be all sorts of Ricardian about then?"

Rachael turned to meet Laura's gaze directly. "Of course. No matter what Richard Plantagenet was in life, he deserved a better death, and a better remembrance then a corpse hacked to pieces. So, if you want to come, consider yourself invited. Sorry about the luncheon, but you probably wouldn't be interested anyway. It's just a bunch of R-Three types getting together to talk and share information."

The implication was not lost on Laura. "I'm sorry," she said with a deep sigh, "I guess we got off on this round left-footed."

"That's all right." Rachael said as she rose from her chair. "Some friends are getting together tomorrow night at the New Black Horse Inn in Market Bosworth. You can join us if you like. Have a bit of dinner. Historically it's usually a pretty wild evening so you just might enjoy it, although it usually degenerates into a brawl." She laughed lightly. "We'll see you tomorrow then, well before noon though, if you want a seat in the church. I've got to run. Bye for now."

Laura and Gail watched her go, then slowly turned to face each other again.

"So tell me," Laura asked, tilting her head to the side and smiling, "when did she ask you to join the Society?"

"I asked her actually." Gail said with a shrug. "It sounds like a lot of fun. Every year, on his birthday, the members dress up in period costumes and enjoy a medieval feast. Papers are produced on a wide variety of topics and everyone has a good time. Rachael says you don't have to be on Richard's side either to join. All they're trying to do is have the truth told Laura. What's wrong with that?"

"Ah, the truth. A precious commodity then, as now. Well," Laura said as she stood and stretched, "it's getting late, so we'd better go and find our hotel. I need to use the loo and it looks like they're closing for the day. I'll meet you over at the big gift shop. Okay?"

Gail nodded, concentrating on her chocolate.

By the time Gail joined her, Laura had added substantially to her library.

Dadlington was well signposted, so it didn't take them long to find it atop a small hill, tucked in between the battlefield and Stoke Golding. It was smaller even then village size, but contained a large Green set next to an old church which caught Laura's attention. Their hotel, fittingly called the Ambion Court, stood at one corner of the Green. Although it looked relatively modern, it was over 200 years old, but carefully and thoughtfully restored. Their room on the second floor looked out over the Green in one direction, the courtyard and their car, in the other. Beautifully appointed, large and comfortable, they settled in immediately. After freshening up, they went back downstairs to the bar lounge. Their host quickly appeared, took their order, then left behind a menu for the evening meal.

Laura sighed deeply as she settled into a large, soft leather wing chair and closed her eyes, while Gail wandered about the room, studying the various objects which decorated it. She gratefully accepted her wine, while Laura's glass was quietly delivered by their host to the sidetable beside her. He arrived back a few minutes later to start the gas heater and adjust the room's lighting.

"The church," Laura said, "it looks old enough to have been around in 1485."

"Indeed it was." He replied enthusiastically. "In fact, many of those who died in the battle were buried in the churchyard there."

"But not Richard Plantagenet, eh John?" Boomed the voice of a guest as he and his wife entered the room. "Now, that would be good for business." He chuckled. "Imagine having old Dickie buried just across the way. Hello."

Laura's first impression was of size. It had always amazed Laura why extremely large men marry tiny women, and here before her was a case in point. Not only was he tall, but powerfully built, or at least he had been until the years began to take their toll, softening the robustness. His wife, on the other hand, was a fraction of his size.

"I'm Ian, and this is my wife, Anne."

"Gail, and I'm Laura. Please to meet you both. We were beginning to think we were the only guests."

Their host, John, was behind the bar by then preparing drinks for the new arrivals. "Others are coming, but quite late, I believe." He said as he poured out two large scotch whiskeys and added just a dash of water, no ice.

"Ah, well done John." Ian beamed as he took possession of his drink before turning his attention once more to Laura and Gail. "You're both from North American, I believe. There's a surprising number of Ricardians in the US and Canada."

"We're not members." Laura returned his smile.

"Oh, assumed you were. Place is crawling with them this time of year. I'm not, but Anne here has been a member of the Society for what, twenty years, I guess." She nodded, smiling shyly. "Haven't got time for it myself, but she trots me out now and again to attend functions. More women then men, of course. Frankly, I think it's a load of rubbish. Let the poor man alone to expiate his own sins. He doesn't need the help of a bunch of old fuddy-duddys."

"Thank you very much!" Anne said, casting her husband a withering glance. "Pay no attention to him. He's jealous of Richard and he won't admit it."

"Jealous! How can I be jealous of a man who barely topped five feet and weighed less than nine stone, soaking wet."

"Size has nothing to do with it." Anne huffed.

"Oh, you're right there, Anne. For all his size he was still capable of ordering more than a few public executions and private murders." He turned to Laura and Gail, smiled and winked while Anne fumed.

"I trust you're going to behave yourself tomorrow Ian, or …"

"Of course my dear, I always do. I can only imagine what horrors might await an individual who dares to utter treasonous remarks against Richard Plantagenet at one of these meetings." He laughed heartily. "Gail, Laura, if you mix it up with these Ricardians, don't mention Hastings, the Princes, or Richard's bastard children, otherwise you'll find yourselves in a right stew."

John arrived just then to escort his guests to their tables. The evening meal was excellent. Anne seemed particularly interested in hearing all about Gail and Laura's trip. She was gratified to learn that, yes, they would be going to Middleham and York. She offered a few suggestions on additional places to see before settling down to enjoy her dinner. They picked up their conversation again over dessert and coffee in the lounge when Anne mentioned the church service at Sutton Cheney.

"Well," Gail said hesitantly, "I would like to go, but Laura and I haven't had a chance to talk about it yet. We've met another member of the Society. Her name is Rachael and she suggested that we go."

"Rachael? Pretty girl with short brown hair, very energetic?" Anne asked.

"Yes."

"Ah, Rachael Ward-Thomas. She lives in St. Albans I believe. A very active member. She's American, if I'm not mistaken, but has lived in England now for years. Married an Englishman. Her father is a professor I think, something like that. She's written several papers on King Richard and is quite well respected within the Society.

"You know, of course that there will be a medieval tournament in the afternoon, at the battlesite? It's put on by a group, quite professional, who tour around the country."

"Do they ever do a re-enactment of the Battle of Bosworth?" Laura asked over the top of her coffee cup.

"Oh, sometimes, but not very often." Anne said sadly.

Ian chuckled. "Mind you, if Richard had won the day, it would be a different story."

"It isn't just that Ian. You see Laura, Henry Tudor wasn't a popular king. It is said that he was more feared than loved. He was exceedingly greedy, sly and secretive.

"In the north particularly, Richard's death was keenly felt. Four years after Bosworth, Henry Percy - Northumberland - was dragged from an inn near Thirsk and hanged while trying to collect taxes for the new regime. The men of Yorkshire, you see, rendered their own judgement on Percy's betrayal of King Richard. The city of York wrote in its records the news of his death saying *King Richard, late mercifully reigning over us was piteously slain and murdered to the great heaviness of this city*. If King Richard had lived, he would have been a great king. To re-enact the tragic story of the betrayal of a fine man? No, it's too sad a portion of our history."

Laura addressed Anne directly. "Tell me, do you really believe he was a fine man, Anne?"

"Of course." She said, surprised at the question.

Laura nodded as she turned away, prepared to focused once more on her coffee.

Laura came out of the bathroom to find Gail lying in bed, propped up by two large pillows, her hands folded neatly across her chest. "What are you doing, practising your funeral effigy?"

"I was just thinking, I hope you behave yourself tomorrow too."

"Oh, I see, it's gag order time is it? I'm not allowed to ask questions, offer an opinion?" Laura threw herself on her bed then turned on her side to face Gail.

"Sure you are, but there's no need to step on toes or hurt feelings in the process. In case you're not aware of it, you're coming down pretty hard. What's the matter? Ever since we arrived here you've been a real pain. You hardly ate your dinner, you were very rude to Rachael and to me too, for that matter. Something's bothering you, so out with it."

Laura sighed. "Maybe it's this place. Walking around the battlefield. Good God Gail, over half the men who died didn't even want to be there and certainly not under the command of leaders they hardly knew, let alone trusted. The other half used the occasion to settle petty feuds. It was a mess. A horrible, cruel joke. What Richard did was an act of unparallelled desperation. He killed himself Gail, just as surely as if he had pointed a gun to his head."

"Damn it, you don't know that!" Gail was angry and confused. "Yes I do."

Gail caught her breath.

Day 6
Bosworth Field - Sutton Cheney

Margaret: *From forth the kennel of thy womb hath crept*
                   A hell-hound that doth hunt us all to death:

Shakespeare -
The Tragedy of King Richard the Third
[Act IV, Scene 4]

When Gail came out of the bathroom the electric jug was beginning to boil, so at first she didn't notice Laura, perched by the window overlooking the Green, quietly smoking a cigarette. Because of the high sill and the window's deep recess, she was forced to practically climb into the space to ensure the smoke trailed outwards. Gail appreciated the effort, although Laura's resemblance to a bird of prey was somewhat disconcerting.

"Stay where you are, I'll make the coffee." Gail announced.

"Thanks and good morning. Sleep well?" Laura said as she repositioned herself.

"Okay I guess. Dreamed about something or other, but I can't remember now. How about you?"

"Out like a light." Laura lied effortlessly, but the truth was that she, too, had had a dream, but she had been awake for most of it, swathed in moonlight, sitting where she now sat, with the Green below. She had seen the carts bearing the bloodied, naked bodies of the soldiers who had perished on the battlefield; had witnessed their hurried internment in shallow graves while villagers watched, anxious and afraid as news of the Tudor victory was passed in a series of whispers.

The power which Laura was able to bring to bear to elicit the image was well practised, although seldom used in recent times. Satisfied, she mentally unravelled what could best be described as her secret agenda, in the middle of which stood the ultimate prize - King Richard. She had felt his presence and another's, and although she had also felt a strong sense of evil, she was not afraid, at least not yet.

Laura watched with mild interest as Gail ploughed through a massive breakfast which included two fried eggs, mushrooms in sour cream, bacon, sausage, fried tomatoes and toast slathered with marmalade. "Excuse me, are we going on safari?"

"Is that all you're having?" Gail replied in self-defence.

Laura had declined a cooked breakfast in favour of dry toast, orange juice and coffee. "It's enough." She replied with a shrug just as Ian and Anne arrived.

It was obvious that Anne was excited by the day's events. Ian far less so. "What a load of rot." He exclaimed as he looked over the list of subjects to be discussed at the various seminars.

"Ian, behave yourself." Anne growled good-naturedly as she offered an apologetic smile.

They settled down to enjoy a quiet breakfast, so it was some time before Laura mentioned the churchyard. "Last night Ian, you said something about the bodies buried here."

"Buried in the churchyard yes, and here, there and everywhere from the sounds of it. Hold on, John has a reprint of an article published back in the twenties, I think." He was back moments later. "Right, it's entitled *A Church for Bosworth Field,* reprint The Hinckley Guardian December, 1922.

'The sounds of the great battle had surged up from the plain below, and the strife had ebbed and flowed to St. James Church, Dadlington, walls. When the clang of arms had subsided, and the groans of the dying had ceased, within this enclosure were brought their shattered remains. With no gentle sowing were they consigned to mother earth; no dibbling out of tender plants; but into

shallow and unshaped trenches they were pitched as weeds to rot; and to this day their bleached bones peep through the soil'."

"How many?" Gail asked, openly appalled.

"Oh, it's hard to say." Ian shrugged. "About eighty odd, I think, died in the battle, but most of the bodies were returned home for burial, which left the common soldiers, mercenaries and the like to be shoved into common graves without markers. Once Richard was dead, the killing stopped, well, more or less. Battles like this were often used to settle petty feuds, so it's reasonable to assume that a few met their end by what we would call 'friendly fire'. Bloody awful stuff really. Well, my dear, shall we?"

When Laura looked up, Gail was staring straight at her from across the table.

"See you two at the church." Anne whispered before she hurriedly followed Ian from the room.

"Laura, I think that maybe … "

"Too late, Gail. Relax will you, everything's under control. Besides," she shrugged, "I very much doubt if anything unusual will happen, but if it does, you'll be first to know. That I promise you." She chuckled wickedly.

By the time Laura and Gail were organized and on the road, it was nearly ten o'clock. At the battlefield site, preparations for the day's events were well advanced. The pavilion had been successfully raised, the jousting ground roped off, while at the far end of the parking lot could be seen a large horse van with several large horses tethered along its length. A small caravan at the edge of the ground half-way along contained all the electronics equipment, with massive speakers on the roof and heavy cables draped to one side.

They wandered around, did some more shopping, then decided to visit the museum again. They shot through the 'stinky part' as Gail called it, then settled down to take their time and see everything again, properly.

Gail lingered over the movie again, so Laura proceeded on to the gift shop alone During the course of her conversation with the woman there, Laura learned that it would be better if she left the car where it was and walk the short distance to the church at Sutton Cheney. She assured Laura that, by the end of the service, they would find parking a problem since the day's events were very popular.

"Now, what you do," said the woman, "is go out and around the Visitors Centre and through the gate. Follow the fence line straight along until you're there. It's a twenty minute walk and level most of the way."

Laura thanked her then wandered outside to enjoy the morning sunshine. The day was perfect. Richard's battle standard was flying well, but not as lively as yesterday. The parking lot was filling rapidly. Laura told Gail what the woman had suggested, so they returned to the car to get their walking shoes and stow away the few items they had purchased. The service would began at noon. It was now nearly eleven, so they decided to begin their journey, setting a leisurely pace. In the second paddock, they encountered cows.

"I'm not going in there." Gail announced firmly.

"They're away up the other end. They probably won't even notice us. Come on, hurry."

Gail hesitated, measured the distance between her and the cows then slipped through the gate. She fairly bolted, moving faster than Laura ever thought possible. The cows neither moved, nor looked up.

"See." Laura said with a chuckle as she opened the gate and ushered Gail through.

Typically, tall hedgerows separate each paddock, and although there is a fence, it is often buried in deep brush. Gail swept through the gateway at speed and nearly collided with a sizeable, cud chewing Holstein hidden behind the hedge. She froze. The cow's interest in Gail was casual, although she did extend her neck to sniff at Gail's shoulder bag.

"Oh, oh," Laura whispered, trying desperately to keep a

straight face, "isn't that the bag you bought in Ludlow? It's probably made from her second born."

"It's Moroccan leather." Gail whispered tightly. "Do something, damn it!"

"Like what?"

"I don't know. Just get her to move away."

"Excuse me Mrs. Cow, could you please shove off so we can walk through your backyard. Nice day isn't it, although everyone's saying we need rain now because its been almost a week and you know, in this part of the world, going a week without rain is practically unnatural, unhealthy really, and well, just a few more days of this and you cows will think there was a drought on, but that's silly because you don't know anything about droughts, not like in Australia where ..."

"What the hell are you doing?" Gail hissed.

"Trying to bore her with my conversation. Works a treat at parties if you want to get rid of someone you don't want to talk to particularly." Just to prove Laura's point, 'Gail's cow' huffed a great sigh, turned and ambled away. Laura smiled in triumphant as she watched the beast depart, tail swishing nonchalantly back and forth across its bony backside. "Tell me Gail, just how are you going to manage an apparition or two if you can't even get past a living, breathing bovine?"

"Ghosts are harmless, cows aren't."

"Oh, I see." Laura laughed, derisively. "Keep that thought Gail, it could come in handy."

The rest of their journey was uneventful, so they arrived at the church in good time. Several buses were parked at the edge of the road and from them issued a steady stream of passengers of all age, size, and degree of enthusiasm. Collectively they could have been just another group of like-minded individuals on a day trip, but, in fact, they were all Ricardians, so Laura studied them with particular interest.

"Rachael said that if we want to get a good seat, we best be here early, so let's go in." Gail suggested as she pulled Laura from her reverie.

The church of Saint James the Great, Sutton Cheney, is considered to be 'Richard's Church' since it was there, tradition says, that he heard his last Mass the evening before the battle. As they entered, they were each handed an Order of Service. Just ahead of the bus loads, Laura and Gail had their choice of seats. The church was crowded with chairs to augment the pews, so it was impossible to wander around.

They seated themselves quickly, close up against a stone pillar near the front. Neither of them were surprised to see the large bouquet of white roses which graced the area beneath the pulpit. Laura leafed through the Order of Service in which she found printed Richard's personal prayer from his Book of Hours. She read it carefully, along with the prayer for those who had fallen at Bosworth Field. She had a feeling that this was not to be a happy service.

The church filled rapidly. A young girl, in the company of an elderly woman, took a seat directly in front of them. She was dressed in a muted brown print dress which reached down to her ankles. Her hair was tied in a ponytail. Everything about her reminded Laura of the hippies of the 1960's. As she turned and smiled at Gail, Laura realized that she wasn't as young as first supposed, but her excitement was obvious. She engaged Gail in a vigorous conversation, mostly about how this was her first time here, and wasn't it wonderful, and how she was looking forward to meeting all the other Ricardians. Her manner bordered on the fanatical. Laura marked her down as a nut case. This was confirmed moments later when Gail asked her why she had joined the Richard III Society.

"Well, I was dreaming of him night after night you see, so I guess he wanted me to join. So I did."

"Do you still dream of him?" Gail asked warily.

"Oh yes." She gushed, then smiled, her face radiant.

Laura slithered in her seat and prepared to concentrated again on the Order of Service, although she kept wondering what 'nut case' would think if she met her hero in a darken alleyway. She smiled to herself at the thought, then instantly sobered as she realized that, in a sense, she was planning to initiate just such an encounter, although, unlike this not-so-young lady, she would be prepared, well practised and on guard.

Moments later, the service began.

"Over five hundred years ago, a battle was fought near this church. A battle which would herald both an end, and a beginning for this country, and its people. How often, it seems, that from the ashes of war arises …"

Laura turned in her seat. The little church could barely contain the congregation which pressed in upon it, trailing those who arrived late out, beyond the open door, to stand, listening intently. Her eyes were drawn to the foremost reaches of the church, to an elderly woman dressed in a simple pink flowered flock. Cherub features made more ethereal by the memorial wreath which she clutched tenderly to her breast. Her eyes were closed but, as Laura stared, they opened and the old woman smiled the most joyous smile Laura had ever seen.

"… for those who gave their life in the service …"

Suddenly a woman screamed, then another. "Close the door, close the door." The church barely registered the echo before the storm hit, drumming the lead roof with massive hailstones, drowning out the cries of those caught outside. Laura had only the briefest glimpse of two women, their faces slashed by ice, screaming in terror as elongated wounds erupted blood. Quickly they were brought inside then laid on the stone floor, while the hailstones, as if seeking fresh victims, pounded on the door before landing, only to ricochet upwards into the astonished faces of those who watched, enthralled.

Instinctively the crowd drew back from the open doorway, pressing against each other in a vain attempt to escape the threat.

Laura grabbed Gail's arm. "Quick," she screamed over

top of the tumult, "get on the other side of the pillar." Gail slowly eased around, clutching the stone with both hands, trying to keep her balance. The pillar shuddered as the assault intensified. Then, as quickly as it started, the storm stopped. Everyone froze in anticipation as the last of the stones rolled from the roof, along gutters, coming to a halt at the apex of their momentum only to fall back, stalled.

"Mother of God," someone gasped. In two and threes, people began to file from the church only to stand, bewildered, in a sea of ice. Each about the size of a golf ball, the hailstones covered everything in a glittering, unbroken wave beneath a clear blue, cloudless sky.

"Jack, call an ambulance." Laura turned, recognising Rachael's voice immediately. "Are you two all right?" Without waiting for a reply, Rachael moved on, checking others, while soothing those still too frightened to move "I know, it's terrible … yes, Jack Monroe will call on his mobile … it's okay Mary … I'm sure it's over, so …"

"Rachael, quick, it's Nell."

Laura followed Rachael's line of sight. The elderly woman lay on her side, the wreath almost lost from sight beneath her. Rachael bolted for the back of the church, weaving between pews and overturned chairs, pushing people aside in her haste. Laura followed close behind.

"Nell?" Rachael whispered as she knelt down. 'It's Rachael. Can you hear me?" The old woman's lips trembled. "Here, I'll help you sit up. There, is that better?" Gently she rested her against the stone wall. "Nell?"

Slowly Nell opened her eyes, then smiled. "I saw him Rachael." She whispered, while joy danced in periwinkle blue eyes studded with tears.

"Saw him? Who did you see Nell?"

"Richard. He … he was here Rachael. I saw him. Rachael, they … he … " She groaned.

"Hold on Nell, there's an ambulance coming - hold on."

Gently Rachael tried to pull the wreath away, but the old woman clung to it with tiny, blue-veined hands, gnarled with arthritis. "Nay lass, 'tis mine yet awhile." She drew the wreath closer, then gasped as another spasm of pain rocked her. She looked up, past Rachel to where Laura stood. "Come closer child." Laura knelt down beside Rachael. "Ye must finish what ye have started. Strength ye will need, aye, and more than strength, for he will fight for that which is promised him." She pushed the wreath towards Laura. "Take it and see it placed now, with the words that he would hear. My time is done. It is for you … " Slowly both hands parted from the wreath as she slumped to one side.

"Nell?" Rachael reached out. "Oh my God," she cried, "she's gone." Her hand began to tremble as she moved her fingertips across Nell's face. "She … she was the one who first got me interested in Richard. I don't know how many hours we spent together researching, talking. Nell please, don't leave me. Please." Rachael sobbed.

Laura reverently lifted the wreath. She stared at it a moment, marvelling at the layers of laurel intertwined with white rose buds and pale blue heather. "She wanted it placed, Rachael."

Rachael nodded. Slowly she stood, then turned abruptly, wiping her tears away with the tips of her fingers. "Nell Turner has just died." Shouts of disbelief mingled with shocked surprise reverberated throughout the church. "She ah … the last thing she wanted was for the service to continue. I think we should do just that, if you don't mind. This is Laura." Rachael moved to one side. "Nell asked that she take her place so, if you would please take up your Order of Service and turn to Richard's prayer."

Slowly Rachael began. "Most Merciful Lord Jesus Christ … deign to release me from the affliction, temptation, grief, infirmity, poverty and peril in which I am held, and give me aid. Extend Thine arm to me; pour Thy grace over me, and free me from all the distresses and griefs by which I find myself troubled."

Hesitantly at first, Laura moved forward and placed the wreath on the wall next to a plaque which commemorated the battle while remembering all those who lost their lives on both sides of the conflict. Her heart grew tight within her as the words of the prayer echoed in her mind.

"… keep me and to defend me from all evil and from my evil enemy, and from all danger, present, past, and to come … from damnation to everlasting life. I ask Thee, O Most gentle Jesus Christ to save me from all perils of body and soul, and after the course of this life, to bring me to Thee, the living and true God, who livest and reignest, O God, through Jesus Christ, the living and true Lord, Amen."

"Amen." Laura whispered.

When she looked up, Rachael was staring at her fixedly. "It's done."

Rachael stepped back as the ambulance slowly began to move away. Laura and Gail stood together nearby. Rachael smile weakly as she joined them. "She was ninety-one years old. Hard to believe, isn't it?" She wiped away more tears. "You know, if she had to go, this would be exactly the way she would want it. Here, in his church."

"Rachael, I … Gail and I had better get back and see if the car's okay." Laura paused as she looked around her. Was it an eternity ago that she had seen these same people, happily greeting each other before the service began? Before the storm … before, when Nell Turner breathed and all the world seemed at rest, content for a few brief moments to remember. "These people need you now."

Rachael nodded. "Come to dinner tonight, at the Black Horse in Market Bosworth - please." She took Laura's hand and squeezed it tight. "I think we need to talk."

"We'll be there." Laura said in a hushed whisper.

The hailstones were all but melted by the time Laura and Gail began to make their way back, this time along the road. It was a perilous journey. Hedged in on one side by a deep ditch, cars flew by at speed as the spectators on Ambion Hill dispersed. News of the cancellation of the jousting tournament spread rapidly. Two of the horses had bolted, while a third lay in the middle of the field, sedated, while the attending vet worked feverishly to save its eyesight, and its life.

The refreshment tent, which had enjoyed a profitable day until the storm hit, had been turned into a makeshift hospital. Inside were perhaps a dozen people, all of whom had been hit by especially large pellets. As Gail and Laura walked by, their shoes crunched on the last vestiges of ice. Laura stooped and picked up a piece. As she held it in the palm of her hand, it quickly melted, leaving behind a miniature pool of blood. She turned full circle. "Strange. The storm hit the field but missed the tent. It ignored the Visitors Centre and yet it fell with full fury on the church. Like a tornado, hit and miss, as if it were tracking along some prearranged path."

"What does it mean?" Gail's voice betrayed her fear.

"It's just a freak storm. There've been cases like this before." She chuckled. "Aren't you glad you're not a superstitious serf?"

"Look at the sky, Laura. It's cloudless. How could a storm of that intensity happen?"

"I don't know. Come on, I'm almost afraid to see what the car might look like."

The car sat neglected and forlorn looking in an almost empty car park. A few random hailstones clustered deep in, beside the windshield wipers, but the car had not received any damage that they could see. Relieved, Laura slid in behind the wheel and started the engine without difficulty.

As she eased the car back down Ambion Hill, Gail said, "When we get to the road, turn left."

"I thought we were … "

"Then left again at the intersection." Gail was on the verge of tears.

"All right, but where are we going?"

"To the Deathstone."

Laura gripped the wheel tighter. "She was an old lady Gail. You heard what was said? She had a heart condition, a bad one, and when the storm hit, she … "

"I don't want to talk about it right now."

Two minutes later Laura pulled the car off the road then stopped beneath a massive oak tree. Across the road was a small, open area in grass, the 'Deathstone' monument clearly visible despite the wooden fence which protected it from casual intrusion.

Laura followed Gail through a side gate, being careful to secure the latch again. As she moved from the shadow of the trees into the sunlight, she looked up into a sky totally devoid of clouds. She could hear birds singing somewhere close by, feel the warmth of the grass beneath her, fragrant and freshly cut.

Gail waited, hands clasped in front of her, head bowed. The plaque on the granite monument was simple enough.

Richard, the last Plantagenet King of
England was slain here 22nd August, 1485

Gail barely moved as she phrased her question. "Why did she ask you to place the wreath? She didn't know you. You're not a member."

"I don't know. Perhaps she thought I was someone else."

Gail shook her head. "I heard what she said before she … she … "

"Died? That's the word you're looking for, isn't it?" Gail gasped. "You've never seen death before, have you? Never seen something die right before your eyes. Tell me Gail, was Nell's death unfair too? Was his?" Laura nodded towards the Deathstone. "Three score and ten. That's our lot. He had thirty-two and she, ninety-one. I guess that balances out about right."

"You're so cold, so unfeeling." The tears Gail had held back finally erupted. "Ever since your parents were killed, you've been different."

"Perhaps because they weren't killed Gail, they were murdered - remember? Murdered by a pair of deficients for two hundred dollars, a portable TV and half a bottle of gin. I guess that wasn't fair either." Laura glanced at the monument, read the inscription again, then walked away.

At the edge of the park, almost lost amongst the trees, Laura encountered a set of steps cut in the hillside. She hesitated, then turned.

Gail was only a few feet away. "I'm sorry," she said, her voice wavering, "it's just that you worry me. I'm frightened for you and I don't know how, or what ... " She choked as more tears came.

"Hey, we're suppose to be having fun. Come on, enough of this. Look what I've found." She indicated the steps. "Want to see what's at the top?"

Gail wiped her eyes, then blew her nose, the sound reminiscent of a bull horn. They both laughed.

"Last one to the top is a rotten egg." Laura shouted childlike, as she began the climb.

Neither of them were prepared, however, for what they found at the top. So astonished were they, in fact, that the elderly couple sitting, enjoying the afternoon sun on board their canal boat, chuckled.

"We've had quite a few people caught out today after climbin' them steps." The old man called out. His pale blue eyes twinkled in delight. "Not what you might be expecting now, is it?"

Laura and Gail moved closer to admire the beautifully sculptured and painted wooden craft. She was called 'The Rosa'. Thirty feet long, slender and flat bottomed as befitting a canal boat, her colour scheme was predominately black over-painted with flowers, birds and plant life in a profusion of colours. She was simply magnificent.

Suddenly the man frowned. "Have ye cum from the field then?" Laura and Gail nodded. "Aye, nasty business that."

"Did the storm … I mean, did you … " Gail stammered.

"Not a bit of it. We was down below fixin' lunch, so we missed it. Mae 'ere says she 'eard it though, far off like."

"How deep is the water?" Gail asked, hoping to change the subject.

"Four feet I guess, is it Herbert?" Mae said, shading her eyes to see Laura and Gail better.

"Aye, it would be that or else sum'it less. This 'ere's the Ashby Canal. If'n you drive along road down there, you goes over it as it bends 'round and tucks up against Ambion Wood. Mae says its 'aunted and won't abide a night there or anywheres near. We puts ourselves 'ere like and watch folks come up them steps and get themselves surprised. But come dusk, I'll be movin' her down a space, well away from the Deathstone. There's none I knows what spends a night 'ere."

"Who, or what do you think haunts the Wood?" Laura asked, although she knew for certain what the answer would be.

"Why, King Richard dear, looking for his crown." Mae said in a hushed voice. "On certain nights, it is said, ye can hear the battle; men crying out, horses screaming in pain and fear, the cannon booming. Even the word *treason* shouted wild like on the night wind."

Day 6
Market Bosworth - The Dinner

King Richard: *A horse! A horse! My kindom for a horse!*
Catesby: *Withdraw, my lord; I'll help you to a horse.*
King Richard: *Slave! I have set my life upon a cast,*
  And I will stand the hazard of the die.

Shakespeare -
The Tragedy of King Richard the Third
[Act V, Scene 4]

Laura and Gail found Rachael near the bar in the first room off the parking lot. "Hi." She waved through the crowd clustered around her. "Glad you two could make it. I was just organizing the dessert trolley. Come on, I'll introduce you both, although, I guess almost everyone knows who you are Laura." She smiled thinly as she tucked them, one under each arm, and began to led them through to the private functions room. "I thought about cancelling tonight but I know Nell wouldn't want that."

The room receded into the background, overwhelmed by a massive wooden table, beautifully prepared and covered by a deep, blood red tablecloth which threw a small bouquet of white roses into sharp contrast. Several bottles of wine stood clustered together near the centre, some already open, breathing. A fireplace was in evidence against the exterior wall, its hearth partly obscured by a dried flower arrangement.

Interspersed throughout the small room were Rachael's fellow Ricardians, some engaged in heated debate, while others stood by watching and listening. Their arrival caused a stir and the cessation of conversation.

"Everyone," Rachael said, "I want you to meet Gail and Laura, although some of you may remember Laura from the service."

General mummerings as Rachael began the task of introducing each person individually.

"Laura, Gail, John and Claire Delt. John is a self-professed, lapsed Ricardian - a heathen in our midst. If it weren't for Claire, we would have given him the boot ages ago. I warn you, he's extremely charming, so watch yourselves."

"Rachael," he shouted, hand on heart as if mortally wounded, "you do me wrong. I am but a seeker after truth, nothing more." He smiled broadly then winkled at Laura. She had the briefest impression of impish, hazel green eyes before she turned away in time to be introduced to another pair of sister-in-laws from York.

Mary and Beth, however, were similar enough to be full sisters. Both had a puritanical air about them which manifested itself in their mutual disapproval of John's antics. They apologised for him which Laura found amusing, wondering why. Neat, prim and trim, they seemed at variance with the rest of the group and kept to themselves, or rather, tried to.

Next came a loosely knit circle of three women, each representing a different age group. The youngest, Jenny, was perhaps twenty-five and was, no doubt, a close friend of Rachael. In the middle, representing the thirty's group was Pet, a housewife and mother of three from Coventry. Then Stephanie, forty-five perhaps and judging from her clothes and mannerisms, well bred and well cared for.

Moments later Ian and Anne arrived and it was Laura and Gail's turn to offer explanations where introductions were unnecessary.

Rachael had her back to the door, so their next arrival took full advantage and pinched her, causing her to jump in alarm.

"Peter! Do that again and I swear to God I'll do you a major injury."

"Don't swear my darling Rachael. It's so unbecoming. You know I adore you, worship you and so I understand, find you without Stephen - yet again." He eyed her lecherously before turning his attention to Gail and Laura. "Ah, we have young ones have we? Converts perhaps. Doing missionary work again Rachael?"

"Laura, Gail, Peter Downing." Rachael was obviously flustered. Peter was much too attractive and he appeared, on the surface at least, to have cracked Rachael's veneer of self-control. Laura took note, smiling up into Peter's suntanned, too perfect features. He returned her gaze with pale blue eyes, totally devoid of warm despite his apparent affability. Laura quickly turned away, quietly disconcerted.

Jenny approached Rachael just then and pulled her to one side. "Don't seat Pet close to the wine. She's already on her fourth glass," she whispered, although Laura and Gail were able to hear quiet clearly, but pretended not to. Casually glancing in Pet's direction, they both noted that she seemed to be listing to starboard slightly, waving her arms about as she harangued Mary and Beth on an unknown topic. Both women hung back, holding their ground so far, but obviously unhappy with the situation. Rachael, with Jenny following close behind, proceeded to extricate Pet to the obvious relief of the beleaguered matrons.

"There are thirteen people here." Gail whispered in Laura's ear. "Thirteen."

"An interesting number for I hope, an interesting evening. Not to worry, a seance requires only twelve Gail, so unless Pet passes out or something, we're safe."

"I don't like this." Gail said grasping Laura's arm as she tried to turn away. "It's all disjointed, out of phase. There's something wrong here." Gail's voice was tight with fear.

"Your imagining things. It's just a group of people getting together for dinner and conversation. It's obvious that Nell should have been here to make the numbers even."

Gail frowned.

"Come on Gail, " Laura urged, "isn't this what you wanted? An opportunity to prove your theory? Who knows, maybe we can manage to tease old Dickie back from hell to join us after all." She chuckled sardonically.

Gail stared at her sister-in-law in horror. "Don't do it, please." She pleaded.

The smile on Laura's face died. "Sit down Gail." She demanded.

Gail backed away several paces and was caught just in time by Rachael, who showed her to her seat. Rachael looked briefly at Laura, before turning away.

The stage was set. Laura was shown to a seat at the end of the table facing directly down its length. On her right sat Rachael, then Ian and Anne while Gail sat between Stephanie and John near the other end. On the side wall to John's right hung the now familiar portrait of King Richard, set in a gilt frame.

Rachael cleared her throat. "Before we begin, I think it would be nice if we could join hands in silent prayer, in remembrance of a dear friend and fellow Ricardian, Nell Turner." General approval ringed the table as hands were offered and heads bowed.

After perhaps a minute, Rachael broke the silence. "Thank you. I know Nell would want us to carry on." She paused, biting her lower lip, fighting back tears. "The choice of menu tonight is pretty basic, I'm afraid. Salad to start and then a choice between fish, chicken and roast beef, so let the waiter know what you would like when he brings the salads. There's a good selection of wines as you can see, from John's ghastly malmsey to some excellent clarets. Enjoy." She sat down then amid general rumblings of appreciation and anticipation.

John turned to Gail. "How do you know when you're at an anti-Ricardian feast?" Gail smiled weakly then shook her head. "They serve Welsh rarebit and Cock-a-leekie soup."

"And Spotted Dick for dessert?" She added, her courage and natural good humour rebounding. Both Ian and John laughed uproariously.

"Rachael," Peter said, pouting, "I'm disappointed. No goose, no lamprey, not even a muggety pie."

"And thank heaven's too." Ian said. "The food in Richard's day was much too rich. Full of spices, all jumbled up. My liver goes crook for day's after one of those feasts."

"Well, at least we're not having roast sucking pig." Gail said laughingly. Silence descended as everyone looked in her direction. "I mean, it was quite a common ... well, you know, at medieval feasts you read ..."

Laura hastened to Gail's rescue. "Roast pig, or boar if you like, would be inappropriate considering that, in a sense, one might well have been sacrificed here just over five hundred years ago."

Claire broke the silence. "Sacrificed!" She shouted, patently horrified.

John chuckled wickedly as he reached for a bottle of wine.

"Yes." Laura said calmly as she carefully prepared the bed of contention from which, she hoped, would rise the emotional pitch necessary to achieve her goal. "Richard would have been a fool to believe that even if he managed to kill Tudor, he could escape the field alive and I don't think any of you consider him a fool."

Stephanie put her wine glass down then turned in her chair to consider Laura more evenly. "I understand Laura that you are not a Ricardian. If you were, you would know that once Tudor was dead, the throne of England would have be at rest under the management and good government of King Richard."

"Do you believe that?" Laura asked pointedly.

"Yes I do." Stephanie replied with haughty disdain. "King Richard would have gone on to be one of the finest kings in English history."

"Well," Ian interjected, "I agree with Laura. Bloody foolish trick racing down that hill with so few men at his back and wearing his crown for all the world to see. He might as well have painted 'King' on his armour along with a bull's-eye, or an 'X' with the words 'kill me here'. So, if he wasn't a fool, then why would he do such a thing unless he saw himself as a sacrifice at the end. Only thing that makes sense - that or suicide."

Laura smiled at Ian. "All we have to do is look at the logic of the situation. Henry Tudor was no soldier, but Oxford was. Assuming that Richard, after killing Tudor, was able to extricate himself from the tangle, he'd have to face Oxford in one direction, and presumably, the Stanleys in another. They had already proven themselves traitors and so could expect nothing from the good government of King Richard except perhaps a splendid execution. In the mood that Richard was in, he would have wiped out the whole clan on the spot, and they knew it. Do you honestly believe that Richard could have stood up to such an onslaught?"

"That's nonsense." Jenny interjected. "Who would have dared to touch Richard, an anointed king?"

"Oxford for starters." Laura smiled. "Oxford hated Richard so much he would have killed him just for fun. But, there was profit too. Oxford could pick up where Tudor left off, marry the fair Elizabeth of York perhaps and established the House of de Vere. We're talking power here. Tudor would have died trying to defend himself against a man who knew a thing or two about warfare. With Oxford it would have been a fairer fight.

"Kings are created in three ways. By common consent, by right of birth and by combat. Richard would have been challenged by Oxford, and ladies and gentlemen, I don't think for a moment that Richard would have won, or to put it in a rougher form, he wouldn't have been allowed to win."

"And," Rachael said sadly, "you believe that Richard knew this even before he began to move down Ambion Hill?"

"Yes Rachel, I think he did. As far as God's judgement is concerned, Richard knew God's answer on the day his only son and heir died. In his heart, he knew God had abandoned him.

Perhaps at the end he hoped for redemption, but as he stood poised at the top of that hill, surrounded by traitors, he must have realized without a doubt, that the end was near. It is to his credit that he died exceedingly well."

At that moment two waiters arrived, carrying trays bearing heaping plates of toss salad and a selection of dressings. Orders for the main course were quickly taken before they departed.

"I'm curious Laura," said Peter as he leaned forward, "why do you suggest that his death was a sacrifice and not a suicide?"

"At first I thought it was suicide, but now I'm convinced that he saw what was to come as something more then just his death."

"Perhaps I can answer that," interrupted Rachael, "if Laura doesn't mind? Richard's background, indeed his whole being was centred around a code of chivalry. He had read the classics, the Arthurian legends and most likely, had some knowledge of Celtic folklore. In the old religion the king was sacrificed to ensure the land's renewal. Regrowth, fertility, it was all bound up in the ritualistic shedding of the blood of the One. At one time, when a king showed signs of old age or illness, he was ritualistically slain to ensure that the spirit of the God/King would remain strong, reincarnated in the king's successor. He had three choices of death. By fire, after which the ashes would be thrown into a river or stream. By asphyxiation and dismemberment, with the pieces placed in sacred places or burned and the ashes scattered. Or finally, killed in such a way that his blood soaked the earth."

"Just a minute!" John barked, "you're assuming that Richard believed himself worthy of the role of God/King. Give me a break! An anointed king he might have been, but at the end, he was betrayed by his own. Why? Because there was something wrong with the man - something dark and evil."

"John!" Claire turned to her husband, more shocked then angry.

Ignoring her, John continued. "Richard Plantagenet died a bloody death, and who knows, maybe you're right Rachael. Maybe the Welshmen who pulled him down did carry out a form of ritualistic murder, cutting his throat for instance, allowing the blood to soak into the earth, thus ensuring the success of Henry Tudor's reign."

"Really John." Stephanie huffed as she turned away in disgust. "Rachael, must we put up with this? Claire is the member here, not her husband."

"We have four nonmembers here tonight, Steph. It's not a meeting. Everyone's welcome to participate." Rachael smiled indulgently, trying to defuse Stephanie's obvious indignation.

"Thank you Rachael." John said, returning her smile. "So, if the Welsh knew what they were about, how shall we explain the two Princes who were supposedly asphyxiated? Was that done to ensure Richard's sacred succession through the uncrowned boy-king? If he believed it at the end, it's reasonable to assume that he believed it at the beginning. The only difference is that those kids were murdered without, I fancy, any ritualistic intent. It was infanticide, the murder of the innocent, pure and simple and he paid for it big time. His manner of death was, I think, nothing more than an attempt to atone for his own sins, and in the process the bastard took most of his closest friends and supporters with him, all the way to hell."

"John, that's enough." Claire demanded.

"I'm sorry Claire," John said sadly, "but I've always felt this way, even when you would go on and on about how wonderful he was. Well, he wasn't! He murdered his way to the throne Claire. The boys, Hastings, even his own brother, George. He murdered the old king too, helped in the execution of Warwick and Edouard, and may even have murdered his wife. I've wanted to tell you for years. Well, now you know."

Everyone stared in open astonishment.

"Well, well." Laura whispered as she turned to Rachael.

"I can't understand what's gotten into John this evening. It's so unlike him." Rachael was in shock.

Laura turned to her left. "Peter, what do you think?"

"About what John said?" Peter shrugged. "There are a lot of inconsistencies in Richard's character. He certainly wasn't as fine a fellow as these ladies seem to think he was." Peter indicated Claire, Pet, Jenny and Anne, all of whom sat opposite him. "If I'm not mistaken however, there's no other recorded king whose remains eventually ended up in one of England's premier rivers."

"What?" Gail exclaimed. "Sorry, excuse me?"

"Laura," Peter tut-tutted, "you haven't told Gail the whole sad story? Then I shall. After his death, Richard's body was taken to the Greyfrairs in Leicester, near the river. After his corpse was exposed to public view for two days, he was quietly buried without stone or epitaph. Henry VII eventually managed a modest tomb but when Greyfairs was dissolved by Henry VIII, the bones were thrown into the River Soar. The coffin became a horse-trough outside the Whitehorse Inn until it eventually perished.

Peter straightened in his chair then turned to Rachael. "Going back to what you said earlier Rachel. In the old religion, kings were sacrificed not just because they were old or ill, but also because they failed to uphold the briefs and principles of their subjects. If we wish to believe that he was ritualistically murdered, the bones inadvertently thrown into the river, then we have the full Celtic God/King rites observed, which means that Richard III cannot die, not in the traditional sense of the word that is." The room descended into complete silence. "Well, is there any other king, short of Elvis perhaps, who has such a following?"

John began to laugh as he raised his glass. "Ladies and gentlemen, the king is dead - long live the king." The smile died on his lips however, when he glanced at Laura. Her eyes, catlike, regarded him triumphantly.

Peter continued, ignoring John. "As far as being a cold-blooded murderer, I'm not convinced or rather, I'm prepared to give him the proverbial benefit of the doubt." He shrugged as he too raised his glass in silent salute.

"We met a fellow in Ludlow who called Richard a murdering SOB." Gail added.

"That sounds about right." John growled as he looked down the length of the table.

"Ian?" Laura looked past Rachael to Ian, who sat brooding. Something had obviously been said to him by his wife and he was none too pleased about it.

"All of us," he started, glancing at each one of them in turn, "all of us has the potential to commit murder. We might contemplate it, we may even mentally slaughter on a grand scale, but we're civilized now you see. Richard had an enormous amount of power and influence and he knew how to use both to optimum effect. Combined with a sizeable force of retainers totally loyal to him and the knowledge that he was an anointed king and earlier, the brother of a king, he was capable of anything, including murder."

"Well," Stephanie huffed, "if Richard was so capable of murder, why did he let that horrid little man Stanley, Tudor's own stepfather, live and eventually betray him? I would have gladly attended his execution, the traitor!"

"Steph!" Anne was scandalized.

"I agree with Stephanie and Laura too." Jenny said angrily. "Richard should have had all the Stanleys disposed of before the battle even started, then he could have substituted men he really trusted and well …"

"Bloody hell Jenny." John shouted. "You don't lead an army with a stick and you don't go around murdering its commanders either."

"Shut up John!" Jenny jumped up from her chair and glared at him. "If Thomas and William Stanley had been executed before the battle, then Richard would still be alive."

The room fell silent. Jenny stood stock still as she realized what she had just said. "Excuse me." She rushed from the room on the point of tears. Anne rose, made her apologies and hurriedly followed Jenny.

Laura smiled at Rachael. "You're right, it's been an entertaining evening already and we're not even on the main course yet."

Rachael turned and looked straight into Laura's eyes. "At first I thought it might be the wine. Everyone seems so different all of a sudden, but now I'm not so sure. Gail said something to me about you being . . . I don't know exactly. I feel like I'm looking into a mirror. It seems real, but it's not. What do you want Laura?"

"What do **I** want? It was you remember, who invited Gail and I here, so you must have had a reason. What I want is the same as what you want, Rachael. The exchange of ideas, nothing more, and the truth too, of course. Richard Plantagenet was just a man who belongs in an age we can't begin to understand. A ruthless, violent era, full of superstition and sudden death. Considering his childhood, it's amazing that we all assume he was quite sane."

Laura eyes hardened. "I found it offensive when the Tudors blackened his reputation, turning him into evil personified. But I also find it equally offensive when it goes too far the other way and he somehow becomes a saint, endowed with qualities far beyond the reach of the man. It seems obvious that Jenny is distressed by Richard's death, but I bet if he walked through that door right now, he would scare the hell out of all of us and perhaps Jenny most of all because she's so vulnerable. Don't worry Rachael, please. Everything's going to be just fine."

"All right." Rachael said as she tore her eyes free of Laura's.

When Laura looked down to the far end of the table, she found John studying her intently. Gail and Stephanie were engaged in conversation, but when Gail glanced at Laura, she quickly dropped her eyes and looked away.

Anne, with Jenny just behind, returned to their places at the table. Rachael rose, walked around and leaned over between the two. Jenny was fine, embarrassed certainly, but she insisted that the evening continue just as planned. To make her point, she smiled at Laura then gave Rachael's hand a reassuring pat before sending her back to her seat. Laura did notice however, that she drank deeply from the ornate wine goblet she had brought with her, and that her hand trembled.

Rachael called for everyone's attention. "Yesterday I had a lengthy conversation with Gail during which she proposed an interesting theory regarding the manner of King Henry VI's death."

As Rachael began to relate the misericord idea, Laura eased back in her chair, closed her eyes and mentally drew the company together, pulling their combined subconsciousness close around her, focusing the force as she willed the one. Semi-tranced, she whispered in her mind. "My lord?"

"*Madam.*"

"... that Richard was forced into performing the execution, but . . ."

Laura froze. Time skipped a beat, then another as she reached forward in her mind, took hold and in so doing fractured the known concepts of life and death; inadvertently reaching a point of no return. Attracted by her life force, he stood at the perimeter of her consciousness. He was not alone.

"... that the murder was carry out ritualistically using only this sacred instrument and that the victim embraced death willingly at Richard's hand."

Laura felt herself sinking inside as he whispered in her mind.

"You would have this Truth. Aye, and more methinks. I shall satisfy thee in this - for a price. Close do you come madam in the knowing. Closer still shall I bring thee, to look even upon the mouth of doom. But mark me well, for as God is my witness, I did not want to do this thing. Damn my brother Edward's soul to hell where he has sent mine.

At prayer I found him clutching, as was his wont, the hem of heavenly grace. His addled wits mistaken me for Edouard, his son. Tenderly he embraced me, calling me by that name. He asked news of his queen, whom he called my mother and told me now she did love me. Then he espied my companion and in that instant, knew who I was and why I had come. In kingly grace stood he then, throneless aye, but majesty doth know itself even 'tho imprisoned, with hope fled and the executioner nigh.

Mercilessly he cursed me and my House saying that, like the scorpio, we would sting each the other to the death in treachery and betrayal. Brother against brother, unto the last of our line.

My knees quaked as he prophized my doom. Proclaiming with outstretched arm he cried 'Richard Gloucester, you will weep pitious tears upon thy death for the downfall of thy House, as I have mine. If ye have son, then let him die begging for the protection of his father, as did mine. May ye not see him breath his last, kiss his lips and enfold him tenderly in thine arms, for all this is denied thee, as I have been denied. Your end will be cruel, thy corpse will bled, as mine, to wash away the last of all our being. Death will come to claim thy soul unshiven and God's divine salvation will be beyond thy grasp. They body will know no sepulchre and thy soul will wander upon thy place of execution, a dark and piteous wraith.'

Ah wretched, embittered king, I cry for thee now in my understanding. But alas, I was as yet untutored in treachery, deceit and despair.

I drew forth that terrible instrument of death. Aye, beauty and deadly malice entwined, plaited together. A blessed thing cursed in the service of mankind. The jewels flashed in the light and within I saw my father and my brother Edmund and I grew angry at this Henry, who called himself king. Revenge spoke to me from the blade, steadying my trembling hand. 'Speak not to me of curses old man, for thou hadst been a curse upon this land. Thy death wilt ensure a new beginning.'

He drew back from me as I moved nearer him, then dropped he his eyes from mine to gazed but an instant upon the blade. He smiled, then turned and knelt in silent prayer before the altar. As I grew closer still, my companion caught my arm and whispered . . . whispered . . .

'It must be done with care, so as to appear a death natural'.

I gazed down upon the deadly instrument. Felt the weight of the hilt as I turned the tip of the blade. So beautiful to look at . . . so beautiful. I struck him once, twice and on the third blow his skull cracked. My companion looked to see that he was dead, and he was.

Thus fell the first evil."

"Madam? Madam?" Rachael started as if from a dream and turned to the waiter who stood beside her.

"I'm sorry, what did you say?"

"Shall I served the main course now madam?"

Rachael blinked, then blinked again. Her head ached and she felt dizzy. "Yes . . . yes, of course, thank you."

Laura was not in her seat but stood instead resting against the fireplace, smiling benignly as she watched Rachael's every move. Slowly she headed back towards the table. As she sat down, Rachael shrank away slightly. Ignoring her, Laura poured herself a glass of claret, took a sip and thanked the waiter as her plate was placed in front of her. Many of the company stared dumbfounded at Rachael, while Anne slipped her hand protectively into Ian's. Gail's eyes remain fixed on Laura. Something was wrong, terribly, terribly wrong yet Laura sat quietly, refusing to acknowledge Gail's obvious distress. Mary arranged and rearranged her dinnerware, while Beth watched her, unable to accept the monstrous implication. Surely Richard was much to young to be involved in such a crime, or so she had always believed.

Gail swallowed hard. "The old king, Henry. He ... he was bludgeoned to death, not stabbed?"

John cleared his throat. "The concept of a ritualistic murder is unique, I must admit, but in 1910, Henry VI's body was exhumed and examined. It was reported then that the cause of death was, most probably, the result of a severe blow to the head, or perhaps several blows, since the skull was described as 'much broken'. Sorry."

"But ... but what about the blood?" Gail was both confused and frightened as she looked to Laura.

"A contrivance Gail by the enemies of the House of York." Laura said as she set her knife and fork aside. "The medieval mind was full of superstition and one such was the belief that the body of the deceased would bleed in the presence of its murderer. King Edward publically claimed that Henry had died of melancholy, and I guess, if you looked at the corpse with its head capped and resting on a pillow, the death might indeed have appeared to have been from 'natural causes'. Richard had done a good job. Too good for those who wished to see the creation of a martyr, so pig's blood in a bladder was placed between the inner and outer coffin, or in the coffin itself. Pierced at the appropriate moment, the blood would seep out. Alternatively, the body itself may have been penetrated from below, straight through the coffin, allowing the bodily fluids, which would have collected, to slowly drain away. A simple bunghole would ensure the flow of blood on cue. Instant martyrdom for Henry and instant vilification for the House of York and Richard, Duke of Gloucester, in particular."

"The Great Chronicle of London, yes, it said something to the effect that *'the common fame then went that the Duke of Gloucester was not all guiltless of Henry's death.'* Peter said in surprise, remembering something he had thought forgotten.

Laura continued. "Richard probably gave himself away, no doubt in public, when the corpse began to bleed as he drew near it. It's hard to say whether he was more angry then frightened, since he knew better than anyone that it was a ruse, although, he might have been sufficiently superstitious himself to recoil in horror and guilt. Years later, of course, he moved Henry's body from Chertsey Abbey to Windsor where it was reverently laid to rest in a vault near Edward.

"Unable to stem the tide of pilgrims, Richard ordered that some of Henry's personal possessions be put on display, including a velvet cap. Pilgrims were allowed to touch the cap in the belief that it was an effective cure for headaches. The connection between the cap and Henry's manner of death was probably lost on the general populace, but Richard knew."

"But," Beth said, her voice hushed and full of emotion, "Richard did try to make amends?" She looked at Laura, her eyes pleading.

"Richard's son died in April, 1484. Henry's reburial took place in August of the same year. Perhaps as you say, he tried to put things right or perhaps the exercise was nothing more than a form of damage control."

Ian leaned forward to catch Laura's eye. "Why do you feel that Richard was forced, I think that was the word Rachael used, into murdering the old king?"

Laura shrugged. "Richard was praised constantly for his loyalty to his brother, Edward. Richard's motto, Loyaultie me lie - Loyalty binds me. What do you think it really means?"

She canvassed the room but no one was prepared to offer any form of explanation.

Laura sighed. "After George Clarence's nonsense with Warwick, Edward could never bring himself to trust him again. He had to be sure of Richard's loyalty at least, and what better way then to order him to do the unthinkable. Sadly, Richard was caught either way. Edward was a brutal man beneath that suave exterior. If Richard refused, Edward would exclude him from council and overlook him when the lands formally held by Warwick and his co-conspirators were redistributed. If Richard did the deed, he was then bound to his brother. A form of blackmail, if you will. Loyalty did bind him, to the knowledge that, in a twinkling of an eye, Edward could turn on him and let it be known that the old king did not die of natural causes but was murdered. That's why Richard stayed away from court as much as possible and why it was easy for him later on to contemplate the destruction of his brother's progeny."

Several of the company gasped. Pet dropped her fork and knife. The knife fell from the table, landing on the carpeted floor with a dull thud.

Laura continued as she watched Pet closely. "Sheer common sense suggests that Richard would be the only one Edward could trust well enough to do the job. You don't get underlings to murder kings, even deposed ones."

"Do you think then," John said, "that Richard actually hated his brother?"

"Yes, I think he did. He turned Richard into an assassin after all. Ransomed his soul. Not a nice thing to do to your baby brother, is it?" She smiled thinly. "In his youth, Richard adored Edward but, as the years past, Richard became more and more disillusioned."

"Edward's sexual exploits certainly put Richard off." Peter suggested.

"Richard was a prig." John shouted overtop of his wine glass. "Everyone had extramarital affairs in those days. He was hardly in the position to be self-righteous with two bastard children."

"Oh, I don't know." Laura said as she relaxed slightly, then smiled. "I don't see Richard as a prig exactly, although I doubt that he was much fun in bed."

"How dare you!" Stephanie growled, openly indignant.

Both Ian and John chuckled, relishing Stephanie's strident overreaction.

"Laura thinks that Richard liked to sleep with doormats." Gail said, her manner curt and offhand.

Stephanie's look of annoyance deepened to Ian and John's delight. Pet had recovered herself and her cutlery, and was listening now intently.

"I just think that he preferred women who posed no personal threat, that's all." Laura said with a shrug. "He liked to stay in control, you see. He hated domineering bitches, like Liz Wydville and Margaret of Anjou. His beloved Anne, on the other hand, was acquiescence personified."

"In other words, a doormat." John said laughingly. Ian joined in, oblivious to his wife's displeasure.

"To understand Richard," Laura continued, glancing briefly at Rachael, "we have to establish what it was that he held in the highest regard."

"Law and justice for the common man." Claire suggested. "He set up the Court of Requests, a Council of the North and law courts were everyone had access to an impartial trial."

"An excellent clue." Laura nodded. "But what really drove Richard was an insatiable thirst for power. Twice exiled and penniless, he was determined never again to find himself as the victim. It's not difficult then to understand his motivation in setting up courts of law to assist other victims. Mind you, he was in a win-win situation as King. The courts provided justice, but unlike in the old days, when people were flogged or degraded in public, the new system provided a system of fines as punishment. The money, of course, went to the Crown.

"In every bit of research I've done on Richard Plantagenet, I've kept in mind that one word - power. To achieve it, he needed land first, which generated wealth, which attracted supporters, which in turn, led to prestige and ultimately the determination to seize a throne when the opportunity presented itself. To be King then became the ultimate power trip, although it has been suggested elsewhere that committing murder, control over life and death if you will, is supreme above all."

The room descended into dead silence.

When Laura drew inward and tried to make contact, he refused her, deflecting her intent, content for now to listen. She could, however, detect a vague clicking sound. What wasn't vague, was a strong sense of annoyance.

"But, where's this leading us?" Jenny asked, confused.

"To Richard's murder of his beloved brother George, that's where." John announced.

Gail asked for a sample of the malmsey but nearly gagged on the sweet, heavy wine. "Imagine being drowned in it?" John whispered darkly.

"Do you really think that's what happened? Gail said, making a face. "Seems a terrible waste to me, even if it is an awful wine John."

"But, what about poor George?" Peter said, his tone petulant. "Is there no sympathy for the man?"

"Bah," Ian sneered, "he was a walking disaster looking for a place to happen. Edward was as patient as he could possibly be, but treason is treason, and in the end he had no choice. Clarence was nothing but an abusive drunk."

"His wife Isabel was barely cold in her grave," huffed Beth, "before Clarence conspired to marry the Duke of Burgundy's daughter, Mary. Quite disgusting."

Laura smiled into her plate.

"I can't believe that Richard was in any way responsible for Clarence's death." Mary said forcibly. "He did everything he could to save his brother."

"Why?" Laura asked pointedly.

"Well … well because he was his brother, that's why."

"And," Laura added, "the holder of vast estates which Richard thought might look better in his portfolio."

"Still," Anne added, "there's absolutely no proof that Richard had anything to do with George's death."

"All right, let's try a scenario." Laura said, leaning back in her chair. "As you all know, George Clarence was convicted of treason in a court of law. He was imprisoned in the Tower under heavy guard, and no doubt, lived in morbid fear. To ease that fear and to make his confinement more tolerable, he was probably given more then enough to drink. He drank alone however, distrustful of anyone who came close with one exception - Richard. He was the one man Clarence could trust. He was, as Mary said, his brother after all. It was Richard who had acted as a go-between the two brothers which resulted in Clarence's defection from Warwick, so again, it's reasonable to assume that he placed some trust in Richard. Perhaps Richard visited him on several occasions and they drank together.

"Clarence had a secret and during a particularly heavy drinking session, let's suppose he told that secret to Richard. Jealousy, spite, and malice, how Clarence hated his brother the king, so he told Richard what Bishop Stillington had inadvertently disclosed. Edward's marriage was invalid, his children bastards. As soon as the secret had passed his lips, he had signed his own death warrant.

"It would have taken Richard only a matter of seconds to realize the implications of such knowledge. If Edward's heirs could be declared illegitimate, then only the King and Clarence now stood between him and the throne. It's my belief that Richard was able to get Clarence so drunk that he passed out cold. In such a state, it was easy to drown him in just inches of water, or wine if you prefer."

The room erupted into chaos, while Laura mentally slipped away to where he waited.

"Thou art cunning madam. Dost thou not marvel in the knowing? Attend, and I shall tell thee of the why, for now hast come the time of Truth. The second evil, aye and Henry's curse made manifest, 'tho I cared not, for truly I rejoiced in the destruction of this one.

Brother Clarence! Canst thou hear me? Thou evil, twisted aberration of the House of York, I prayed thy soul to hell even as I murdered thee. Drink slowly of the draught I hast prepared thee, beloved brother, and remember how I was tormented by thee, even when a child, too young as yet to understand thy cruelty. Remember Clarence, the bitch whelp given me by Burgundy, and how ye did drown it in the mill pond, heedless of my anguish and my tears?

Drink deep Clarence, as I recall the taunts I endured when ye did call me elfin child and changling. Laughing at my littleness and my darkness, while the memory of our father dimmed.

Drink deeper Clarence, for all the world knew of thy cruelty to women, defenseless against thy rage and drunkenness. Anne did tell me of it, did ye think that she would not? How she lived in mortal terror of thee while ye tried to keep her from me, her estates thine. She risked a perilous course when she flew from thee, yet even in the search for her, thy cursed spite offered me no aid.

Drink deeper still Clarence, and remember the woman thou condemned, in innocence, to a death upon the gallows. Slayer of women, most cursed of God's creatures.

Hast thou tears Clarence? Shed them now for our noble house, ransomed by thy greed and corruption. Traitor thou art, thrice heralded traitor and none shall mourn thy passing.

Farewell brother, I thank thee for the telling of thy secret and for thy final insult. But in this, thou hast err'd. I shall not shrink from use of this new found knowledge to my advantage.

I send thee this final farewell that ye may wake unto the gates of hell and know who sent thee hither and how much I hated thee."

Trembling with fear, Laura rose slowly, turning her back to the others. "And the place?"

"Does thou not know, nor guess? 'Twas Coldharbour where he breathed his last on a sourfait of wine, or so it was believed."

"And is there pity now?"

"None."

The two waiters returned to clear the table while a third rolled in a large dessert trolley which he parked practically at Gail's elbow.

She chose the trifle then turned to Laura. "May I speak with you please - in private?"

Not waiting for a reply she stood up and made her way out of the room towards the patio area at the back of the hotel. Laura hesitated momentarily, then followed.

Gail had her back to Laura but she turned abruptly, her face contorted in anger and fear. "Stop it!" She shouted.

"What are you going on about?" Laura said, her voice low and soothing.

"You know what I mean. These are Ricardians - nice people. They don't want to hear any of your damn theories, especially about Richard killing his own brother. It's ... it's too grotesque."

"Grotesque! Then I shall tell you something else for nothing. It's very likely that Richard's mother encouraged him rather than risk the spectre of even a private execution and more negative PR for the House of York. Who knows, maybe she learned from Eddie that her youngest son was a professional assassin. A regular double-0-seven with a licence to kill by royal warrant. There's nothing like keeping something like that in the family, is there? Whether you like it or not Gail, Richard murdered his brother. I know it, and so do you."

"Don't say that! Look, I think we'd better go, now, before you ... you ... "

"Before I what?" Laura asked, her anger rising.

Gail was breathing hard, trying to catch pace with the pounding of her heart. Tears sprang into her eyes.

"Come into the washroom." Laura said as she took hold of Gail's elbow.

Laura leaned against the edge of the sink facing Gail, watching her carefully as she ran cold water across her wrists. Her eyes shone back brilliantly from the mirror, a reflection Laura was at pains to avoid.

"Feel better now?" Laura asked, her voice tinged with concern.

Gail nodded as she slipped past Laura, being careful not to touch her as she edged towards the door. "Laura?" She whispered, her back turned. "Promise me you won't try, you know, what we talked about?"

Laura laughed harshly. "How do you know that I haven't?"

Gail hand froze on the handle of the door. "Please Laura, don't play games." She pleaded.

"I don't play games, as well you know." Slowly she moved closer to Gail. "The evening is young yet, the group entertaining. So, why don't you just sit quietly, eat the trifle you managed to ordered before dragging me out here, and let what might happen, happen."

Gail knew instinctively that she was powerless. Desperately she wanted to turn, to confront Laura, but she was suddenly very afraid. For a fraction of a second more she hesitated before continuing her progress back to the table.

Laura monitored Gail closely as she made her way to her seat but she was interrupted when Rachael took her arm.

"Gail said that you don't like desserts so I ordered you an Irish Coffee instead. I'm having one too." Laura thanked her with a generous smile.

Rachael's eyes were as brilliant as Gail's. "We were just talking about whether or not Richard was a Political Realist."

"Or," said Ian, "Niccolo Machiavelli's 'The Prince'. Cunning, amoral and an opportunist. Machiavelli was a contemporary so he was obviously able to write about what he knew."

"Richard was not immoral." Beth insisted.

"Not immoral, my dear lady, amoral." Ian intoned. "Immoral is applied to that which infringes moral rules. A transgression of accepted moral values, usually in matters sexual. Amoral is only used of that to which considerations of morality are irrelevant, or of persons who lack any moral code whatsoever, sexual or otherwise."

"Are you suggesting that Machiavelli used Richard as a model?" Laura asked. Ian smiled thinly.

"Oh please," John begged, "anything but the Dracula connection."

Laura rounded on John. "What do you mean?"

John chuckled wickedly. "Missed that, did we?" Warming to the topic instantly, he leaned forward. "Vlad the Impaler - Prince Dracula to some. It was Bram Stoker who made him a Count. He existed in real life, every inch the monster that history records, and what history recorded was, in part, during Richard's lifetime. He's the model for Machiavelli's 'The Prince'. Richard was nothing more than a brash beginner.

"Now, let's see if I can remember the statistics on Vlad. Something in the order of forty to one hundred thousand victims were blinded, strangled, hanged, burned, boiled, skinned, roasted, hacked, nailed, buried alive, stabbed, tortured, and preferably impaled by this bloodthirsty, murdering bastard. He didn't have to drink the blood of his enemies, his country was saturated in it. Quite a remarkable career considering the relatively small population of the time." He chuckled sardonically. "Even Robespierre couldn't manage more than twenty to twenty-five thousand and that was with the help of Madame Guillotine.

"The connection to Richard Plantagenet Laura? John Tiptoft - Earl of Worcester - called the 'Butcher of England'. He learned his craft while at Dracula court then returned to England to take his place at Edward IV's side and … "

"John," Claire shouted. "that's enough!"

John leaned back, shrugged, then reached for his wine.

"Ian?" Laura said, trying to hide her concern.

Ian cleared his throat. "Machiavelli's 'Prince' was Vlad Dracula, no doubt about it, but well, we can only speculate on just how much Richard may have learned from Tiptoft, especially with regard to statecraft."

"Let's talk about something else." Claire said flatly.

"No, please," Laura pleaded, "I want to learn more about Dracula."

John rubbed his hands in glee as he turned to his wife. "Then so you shall, with Claire's permission of course."

She presented him with a withering glance, but said nothing.

John continued. "Dracula lacked both the looks and the essential charisma to rule successfully, so he inspired his countrymen with raw terror, and a fair measure of social engineering. Do you know, even to this day he is regarded as something of a folk hero in eastern Europe?"

"Why?" Laura was perplexed.

"Good question." John replied derisively. "Maybe it has something to do with the fact that many of his victims were what we would call 'undesirables'- beggars, thieves, vagabonds. He wiped them out. He was a earnest advocate of hard work and dedication to family. He valued thrift, honesty, morality too, if you can believe it. He gave generously to religious institutions which was probably why both the Roman and Eastern Orthodox Churches turned a blind eye to his atrocities. Plus, the geographical location of his country provided a natural frontline against incursions from the infidel Turks." John sighed. "You know, he was not unlike Richard in so many respects." He paused, then smiled wickedly. "Oh, did I mention that he wasn't adverse to impaling women and children too?"

"That's it," Claire demanded, "enough."

Laura frowned. "Are you suggesting that Tiptoft instilled in Richard some of Dracula's ideas? Tiptoft was executed when?"

"1470, before a capacity crowd on Tower Hill. He was the fellow who insisted that he be decapitated in three blows, in honour of the Trinity. Richard was around eighteen years old by then, and yes I believe and so does Ian, that young Dickon learned a lot from the Butcher of England. Perhaps more than was wise - or necessary.

"Tiptoft was an extraordinary man. Handsome, well-read, a Latin scholar of some note. He had perhaps the largest library in all of England and was described as pious and flamboyant, when he wasn't being called ruthless and sadistic that is."

"Strange." Laura mused.

Ian chuckled. "Well, let's just say that Tiptoft had a slight personality disorder."

John smiled, genuinely amused. "Yes, I'll say. He was certainly an excellent example of the crossover between a man of learning and a brutal monster. Not uncommon then or now, for that matter. What an impression he would have made on a rising young star like Richard Plantagenet. Next time you're near Ely Cathedral, pop in and say hello. He has quite a remarkable tomb - and two wives."

"I agree with Claire, let's talk about something else. This whole Dracula nonsense is pure speculation." Stephanie said, her manner brisk and condescending.

"But interesting nevertheless." Laura added, tapping her fingernail against the side of her glass. She looked away then towards the other side of the table. "What do you think Richard really looked like?" She asked, tilting her head and looking straight at Pet.

"Like Hitler sans moustache." John growled, then yelped as Claire kicked him under the table.

"You're asking me?" Pet said, suddenly flustered. "Well, he was slender, strong obviously despite his size, he had beautiful, long tapered fingers ... "

"So he could pick your pocket." John cut in, laughing, before moving quickly to one side to avoid a second blow.

"And blue eyes, just like in the portrait." Pet added quickly.

"His eyes weren't blue. They were more a hazel colour, I'm sure." Stephanie added.

"Oh God, here we go." John grumbled.

Ignoring him, Stephanie continued. "I'm sure his eyes were darker, like his father's. Certainly not blue, although I know of lots of people who believe they were pale blue, or even grey."

"He bit his lower lip, according to Shakespeare, whenever he was angry or upset." Ian remarked. "I want to read to you what Vergil said in describing him. Ian reached inside his jacket and extracted a piece of paper. "Vergil wrote: *he was wont to be ever with his right hand pulling out of the sheath to the midst and putting in again, the dagger which he always wears.* That little quirk alone would have been sufficient to intimidate anyone. Knowing what I know about our friend Richard Plantagenet, it would have scared the living daylights out of me."

Laura smiled at Ian. "Come on Ian, he was half your size."

"Yes," Ian allowed, shifting his weight in his chair, "and fifty times more predatory."

"Well, one thing we know for sure then, thanks to Ian." Laura chuckled. "Richard was probably right-handed and presumably, was prone to nervous affectations."

"Or murderous posturings." John cut in.

"Or murderous posturings." Laura allowed, with a slight bow of the head. "Now, why do you think Richard felt it was necessary to execute Hastings?"

No one was prepared to answer. It was Jenny who finally spoke up, her voice tentative. "I talked to a elderly man at my library a few weeks back. When we got talking about Hastings's execution, he admitted that Richard shouldn't have done that."

"Well," Laura said laughing, "I guess that's the understatement of the week."

"Intimidation, unadulterated intimidation." John mumbled. "Today, when someone tries to swim against the corporate tide, he finds his office has been moved under the stairwell. Guaranteed to keep the others in line. In Richard's day, you chopped off a head or two. Worked a treat. Richard was in the process of ursurping the throne. It was a power play, but Hastings was dragging his feet and apparently consorting with the enemy, so he was singled out for special consideration, to put it politely. Once Hastings was out of the way, Richard had no more trouble with Council."

"I've heard it suggested that perhaps Richard was just clearing the way so he could have it off with Lady Hastings?" Peter look scandalized as he twilled his dessert fork.

"We know Peter," Stephenie said, her voice bored and condescending, "and Edward's mistress Jane Shore too. I think most of us have heard this story before. Well, just remember, Jane ended up in prison and not in Richard's bed."

"That's where she eventually ended up after Richard propositioned her and she told him to get lost because she didn't date short guys."

Laura in particular thought this was very amusing.

"Don't listen to him." Jenny remarked, turning to Laura. "Last year he tried to get us all to believe that Richard and Buckingham were lovers. You really are quite disgusting, Peter."

Laura laughed as Jenny stuck her tongue out at him.

Peter ignored her as he leaned forward, rubbing his hands together gleefully. "Talking about love and lust, how about Bess, the young, though perhaps not so innocent niece? She and Richard's wife Anne wore identical dresses at the Christmas party. Why?" He glanced at Laura, who just smiled and shrugged. "I will tell you. His wife was seated on one side, Bess on the other. Should he be caught with his hand up the wrong skirt, he could blame it on the confusion of identical dresses."

"Rachael," Jenny shouted, "will you please smack Peter. He's too far away from me."

Peter just laughed and continued, his eyes dancing with impish delight. "And, where do you suppose Henry Tudor had to go to find his intended after Bosworth? To Richard's stronghold of strongholds at Sheriff Hutton, that's where. Richard had her on ice so that, after he had despatched Tudor, he could marry her. His success in battle would be so profound, or so he thought, that he would be in a position to defy everyone, including the church. He didn't wait for a papal dispensation to marry his cousin, why bother for a niece?

"Besides," Peter added nonchalantly, "Bess was all over him like a rash. Richard should have married her off to some lord somewhere to keep her from Tudor, but he didn't because he wanted her for himself. Chances are she gave herself to him too, which would have suited Richard down to the ground, so just in case he lost at Bosworth, he could send Tudor the ultimate raspberry."

Gail started to laugh so hard she nearly choked. John patted her politely on the back.

Peter chuckled. "I wonder what Tudor did when he realized that not only was Bess not a virgin, but who it was that got in first?"

"Shut up Peter." Jenny growled. "You're too disgusting for words."

"I think he's funny." Gail coughed.

"There, you see," Peter said with a flourish, "at least one of you lovely ladies appreciates me."

"It would be interesting though, to speculate on what would have happened if Elizabeth of York had been pregnant with Richard's child." Jenny mused.

"I think Tudor was away ahead of you on that one Jenny." Rachael suggested. "He didn't marry Bess until January, 1486, which suggests that he was aware of rumours circulating regarding her and Richard. He was too shrewd a man to be caught in any short-duration pregnancy. Once he was sure, then he married her. His first son, Arthur, was born almost exactly nine months later. If Bess had been pregnant by Richard, I can't begin to guess what would have happened, beyond all hell breaking loose."

Stephanie sniffed, her indignation obvious. "I categorically refuse to believe that Richard ever touched her. He was much too highly principled. Peter's talking a load of rubbish, as usual. No one should pay the least attention."

"I agree." Mary said. "The Church of Rome would never have condoned such a incestuous marriage."

"The Church of Rome would have condoned anything if the price was right." John huffed. "The Church turned a blind eye to corruption even within its own ranks. What do you know about Rodrigo Lanzol Borgia, Mary?"

Mary, it seemed, knew absolutely nothing, beyond the fact that she thought he was Italian.

"Oh, he was Italian all right." John chuckled. "He was about twenty years old when Richard was born. At twenty-five he was made a Cardinal by his uncle, Pope Calixtus III. Borgia became famous, or perhaps infamous, for his sexual excesses. At one of his orgies, servants kept track of each man's orgasms, so that later he could award prizes.

"He had a particular fondness for bedding married women, usually immediately after he had presided at their wedding. In later years he and his son, Cesare, took turns sleeping with the stunningly beautiful Lucrezia, his own daughter and Cesare's sister. Now, that's what I call incestuous! Rodrigo Borgia went by another name - Pope Alexander VI."

Mary stared, open-mouthed.

"That's enough John." Claire snapped.

"John has made a valid point though." Ian said as he leaned forward. "Corruption within the Church was legendary, not only in Rome, but elsewhere. Most priests had mistresses and children by them. I read an interesting statistic recently. Something like twenty-three percent of the men indicted for sex crimes against English women were clerics, although they representative less than two percent of the population. Women were offered absolution right in the confessional in exchange for sex on the spot. The Church's 'do as I say, not as I do' approach was wearing pretty thin by the time Richard came of age. What do you think Laura, was Richard a deeply religious man?"

Laura shrugged. "I doubt it. Typical of the age he lived in, he would have hedged his bets by attending Mass, contributing to charities, doing what was expected of him, but personally I think it was all show, nothing more. Anne, I think, was religious but here again, her patron saint - Katherine - was invoked by women to prevent miscarriages. Richard would have gone along with Anne on this, until it became apparent that Katherine wasn't doing her job."

"But," Beth interrupted, "Richard founded chantries at Windsor, Southampton, and at Wem, in Shropshire. He advanced the parish church at Middleham by funding and incorporating a college there and did much to improve the nearby abbey of Coverham. His acts of charity and declarations of faith are well-attested."

Laura smiled. "I'm not suggesting that he didn't do some wonderful, Christian things, but I'm suspicious of the motives behind his supposed acts of piety. As far as building is concern, man's desire to erect any sort of structure which will survive as a monument for future generations, is an almost primeval urge, and has absolutely nothing to do with Christian faith as we know it. The chantries Richard built satisfied, in the first instance, this urge. They also provided a venue where perpetual Masses were offered for the souls of those members of his family who had died and for himself, his Duchess and his son in future time."

"You make him sound like a hypocrite." Beth said defensively.

Laura shrugged. "John and Ian have already established, I think, that hypocrisy was the flavour of the century. Let's try it another way then. Just because someone parades down the streets of New York City on St. Patrick's Day, are we to assume that he or she is Irish? Because someone gives generously to the Church, does that automatically confer piety?"

"It's been my experience," Ian added, clearing his throat, "that often those individuals who donate the most are the biggest sinners of the lot."

"And the biggest hypocrites." Laura added. "However, the Church was still a powerful institution and Richard was wise to keep on the positive side of it Conversely, dukes and kings were both forces to be reckoned with on the earthly plane where ecclesiastical preferments were granted. It all comes back to wealth and power, doesn't it?"

"So," John said leaning back in his chair, "where were we on the killing chain?"

"I think Buckingham is next, but he hardly counts since he was publically executed as a traitor." Ian shrugged.

"Has anyone figured out Buckingham yet?" Laura asked, canvassing the room. "Now, there's a character that gives me the creeps."

"Why?" Rachael asked.

"I can't figure out for the life of me why Richard ever trusted the man. He must have known that Buckingham was a closet Lancastrian."

"The malice of him that had best cause to be true . . . the most untrue creature living." Intoned John. "Isn't that what Richard said of him when he found out that he had gone over to Tudor?"

"I think it was Buckingham who killed the Princes." Stephanie said flatly.

"No, it doesn't work Steph." Rachael said. "If Richard knew, or even guessed, that Buckingham had killed the boys, he would have wrung a confession from him and made it public. Conversely, if Richard had killed the boys and Buckingham knew of it, why didn't he proclaim it for all the world to hear? As was, Buckingham didn't say anything at all prior to his execution which suggests that he had no idea about what happened to them either."

"Before his execution," Anne said, "didn't Buckingham plead on several occasions to be allowed to speak with Richard, but Richard refused?"

"Yes," Rachael replied, "I think whatever happened between Richard and Buckingham happened in Gloucester, when they last saw each other and had that terrible row. Unfortunately, no one knows what it was all about, although, as Laura suggested, it could have been a power struggle. After his coronation, Richard had time to see the bigger picture and realised then that Buckingham as an 'over-mighty subject' and decided to clip his wings. Buckingham threw a fit and stormed out. Obviously Richard didn't take his blustering very seriously because he continued to correspond with him, in a conciliatory manner, hoping to make amends. But the damage had been done and Buckingham switched to plan 'B' sooner than he intended. Whatever Richard or Buckingham knew of the Princes' fate is purely academic. Richard refused to talk to Buckingham because he had nothing to say to him, while Buckingham, at the end, had plenty to say to Richard, and I suspect, it may have been knowledge that Richard could have used to his advantage. Mostly about the activities of a certain Margaret Beaufort.

"Certainly Buckingham would not be fool enough to think that he could cut a deal with Richard. In fact, Buckingham's downfall left Richard with a veritable treasure-trove of patronage appointments to dole out to his supporters. It's my belief that Richard used Buckingham's oratory talents and prestige to gain the throne, but once King, Richard ceased to trust him, and in fact, had him carefully watched."

"I agree," Laura said, "I don't think the use of the phrase 'untrue creature' means anything more than, say, 'lying toady' or 'false sycophant'. But Richard should have done more than just keep tabs on him. He should have put him on a short leash."

"In a sense that's what Richard did." Rachael replied in defence of her case. "His spy network kept him well informed. I think he was hoping to net not only Buckingham, but Margaret Beaufort, alias Mrs. Stanley, amongst others."

"Like Margaret's little weasels, Bray and Urswick?" Laura asked.

"Exactly."

Laura smiled. "You know, when Gail and I were in St. George's Chapel, Windsor, I began to wonder about men like Bray, Urswick, and Oliver King too. Where could they have found the money, and it must have been considerable, to assist the building fund and erect such fine monuments for themselves? Very suspicious. Bray bequeathed his total fortune, almost as if he and the others where trying to atone for some great sin. What do you think, could these men have conspired together to murder the Princes?"

"Men like that couldn't have gained access to the Princes." Ian cut in.

"With Buckingham's help they could, just after Richard left London and before Brackenbury took up his new appointment as Constable." Laura suggested.

"You're assuming again that Buckingham knew what happened to the boys, and I don't think he did." Rachael pointed out.

"I don't know," Laura said, shaking her head, "there's something so perverse in Buckingham's character that, even if, as you suggested, Richard tried to force a confession from him, Buckingham would have resisted, hating Richard enough not to give him the satisfaction."

"But why? Why would Buckingham hate Richard so?" Stephanie asked, perplexed.

"I told you," Peter interrupted, "they were lovers."

"Shut up Peter!" Both Stephanie and Jenny shouted simultaneously to everyone's amusement, including Peter's.

"It goes full circle then, back to why Richard ever trusted Buckingham in the first place." Rachael explained. "Buckingham's mother was a Beaufort. His aunt by marriage was Margaret Beaufort - Henry Tudor's mother. If you look at the genealogical tables, the Beauforts married just about anything that moved. They were all Lancasterians and that would be reason enough for Buckingham to hate the House of York. I think it all comes down to Richard's use of Buckingham when he seized the throne, but I still maintain that Richard had plans to do away with this 'over mighty duke' in due course."

"Nice thought Rachael." John laughed.

"Perhaps," Ian mused, "Richard's attitude was similar to a US President - Johnson, I think - who, it is said, disliked Hoover but put up with him on the theory that it was 'better to have him inside the test pissing out, than outside pissing in'."

"Well," John added, chuckling, "Richard sure got pissed off with Buckingham. He went so far as to have him executed on a Sunday. Most unpopular with the church."

"Yes, but Buckingham's rebellion, on the surface at least, made everything so much easier." Rachael continued. "Richard was able to either execute or attaint a goodly number of individuals. Estates confiscated to the crown were redistributed to those loyal to the House of York."

By chance Laura happened to be looking at Rachael at that moment, so she was able to observe her sudden, mild distress.

John picked up on it even sooner. "Come on Rachael, out with it. Let's hear again about how clever Richard was in doling out the estates of traitors to his loyal supporters."

"Enough John," Claire said with a sigh, "no one wants to talk about that again."

"No? Well I do." John thundered.

Laura turn from Rachael to concentrate on John, who seemed to go angrier by the second. "Well, hasn't anyone got anything to say?"

"Come on John, let's talk about something else." Peter insisted.

"Typical Ricardian reaction." John huffed. "You can call Richard anything you like. Murderer, seducer, whatever, but, for heaven's sake, don't call him stupid. Well, he was stupid. He filled all those vacancies with Northerners. Planted them up and down the country and caused nothing but strife. Even to this day there is a natural antipathy between the north and the south of this country, so you can imagine what it was like back then. Northerners were regarded as something just short of barbarians and here they were taking over the neighbourhood. England was not that far out of the feudal thicket for us to ignore, as obviously Richard did, the fine tuned and balanced affinity which existed in each region. Based on a history of loyalty, bound by marriages and agreements between like-minded individuals from peasant to lord, Richard tried to cut through all that and impose his will on people who saw things within the perspective of their region, not nationally. England didn't exist in the minds of most, but Kent did, Devon did. Richard's policy succeeded in bringing about the slow erosion of his authority, not from the top but from the bottom. It doesn't look like this lot are going to say anything. What about you, Laura?"

Laura consider the problem briefly. "If I'm not mistaken, there were about a hundred individuals attained for treason in Richard's parliament in January, 1484. It was an unfortunate situation, but I'm sure that Richard reasoned that those regions you spoke of deserved their fate for harbouring traitors. If it were you John, what would you have done?"

John laughed. "Probably the same thing."

"There you go then." Laura shrugged. "But, you're certainly correct when you suggest that it was the middle and lower classes who failed to support Richard's rule. The majority of the magnates accepted their new king; certainly the church did. Unfortunately, the fate of the two Princes cast a long shadow which would eventually overwhelmed him."

Everyone fell silent.

"The two boys, now that's a subject I definitely do not want to get into." Peter said firmly. "Let's talk about Richard's Anne. Did he murder her or no? She's last on the list, isn't she?"

"Of course he didn't murder her." Stephanie huffed, thoroughly disgusted. "The poor woman was already dying, so why bother? Besides, he loved her."

"But," Peter replied, "she wasn't dying fast enough. After the loss of his son, Richard would have been in a dead panic to ensure the survival of the House of York. And, there was little Elizabeth of York, ever at her uncle's side. Do you know, according to the reports of ambassadors visiting at the time, she had large breasts and was considered 'comely'."

"Peter, give it a rest." Jenny sighed. "Richard could have had his marriage to Anne annulled at any time. He didn't need to resort to poison to rid himself of her."

"Nonsense!" Ian huffed. "The north would never have condoned the setting aside of Queen Anne, especially if it meant that Richard could then marry his own niece. All of Richard's Northerners told him so too, in no uncertain terms. After the death of Edward of Middleham, Anne … Generally believed … lost no time …"

Laura drifted. "Elizabeth of York … my beloved Bess …"

"Aye, my beloved Bess, cursed child of thy mother's ambition, released upon a sleeping world all seeming innocence. Proud thou art, and in thy pride did call me Uncle, not as others might - my lord or Majesty. Haughty vain trull, I would cleave thee to my breast and hold thee tight 'til thou would match me breath for breath. Do I hate thee Bess, or is it thy mother I reach for through thee? Let her bear witness then to the cruelty I mean to visit upon thee even as I raise thee to my high estate, chained to my bed 'til thou hast given me a son to keep my tottering house upright. Close too will I keep her that fears me most, and I will fed upon that fear, unto her death."

"What do you think Laura?" Ian asked.

Laura was at first unaware that everyone was looking in her direction. Resting with her forehead against the tips of the fingers of her right hand, elbow on the table, she appeared distressed, her eyes closed. When she opened them, they were full of tears. "I'm sorry, I ah …" She frowned. "What did you say?"

"Do you think Richard murdered his wife?"

Taking a deep breath, her voice trembling at the start, she began to answer Ian's question. "I ah … I think he hastened Anne's death, but not by poison, which would have been a very risky undertaking." She paused to sip at her wine, partly to calm herself.

"Perhaps he staged a few, carefully chosen moments of pure cruelty like reminding her of her barrenness which now jeopardised his throne, lavished all his attention on a pretty, vivacious and healthy young girl, abandon the marriage bed under the guise of doctor's orders, perhaps for another's, or at least rumours of another's and presto, one brokenhearted, dead queen."

She paused, suddenly fearful, as she looked down the length of the table. "After his son's death, Richard was not the same man and he never would be again. The political realism mentioned earlier was about all that sustained him now." Laura paused again, breathing hard, trying to stay calm, to ride the fear which was beginning to engulf her. After a moment she continued.

"I agree with Peter. I think Richard had every intention of marrying his niece once he had disposed of Tudor. As the rightful heiress of the House of York, he either had to marry her and make her his queen, or destroy her." Laura clutched at her chest as a knifelike pain shot through her.

"God in heaven." Mary whispered, crossing herself.

Laura turned inward as her anger and fear rose. "Damn you, you go too far ... too far."

"This knowledge lies old within thee. Trouble me not with thy petty cries when ye do know, in thy heart, this Truth above all. Thou art perlous Madam, yet thou needs be held in reason lest thy heart o'rule thy head. Have I come to be so injured, yea, and damned by such as thee?"

The room fell silent, watching as Laura fought to regain her equilibrium.

Gail jumped from her chair and ran to Laura's side. "Are you all right?"

Rachael relinquished her seat, to allow Gail to sit beside Laura. Gail took her hand. It was icy cold.

"I'm fine Gail, really." Laura said, trying to catch her breath.

"Please Laura," Gail whispered urgently, "don't do this. Oh God, please don't."

Laura clutched Gail's hand tightly as she tried desperately to regain control, although she knew he stood close, aware of her distress yet seemingly unconcerned.

Ian leaned forward. "Laura, any theories on the Princes?"

Laura laughed, trying to ease the pain and fear which gripped her heart. "Ian, it was you who ... who warned me away from any discussion of Hastings, the Princes and ... and, what was it, oh yes, Richard's bastard children." She panted, unable to catch her breath. "Now you want me to put my head ... in the noose?"

"Do you think Richard had the two boys murdered?" Peter asked pointedly, his concern for Laura lost in his need to know.

Gail interrupted. "I think we've all had enough for one evening, so I ..."

"No!" Laura insisted. She pulled her hand free of Gail's and sent her back to her seat. "It was for this one reason alone that I've come." Breathing deeply, she watched as Gail took her seat, then she turned to John, who sat casually and self-assured. "John," she demanded, her voice sharp, "ask the question again."

John smiled, somewhat embarrassed. "All right, did Richard murder, or order the murders of Edward V and his brother Richard, Duke of York?"

"No, I don't think he did." Laura replied flatly. "However, " she added, looking first at Peter and then each in turn, "you must all realize that no matter what happened to them, they were his responsibility. As his wards, he was morally bound to protect them and this he failed to do. On the contrary, he had them so deeply incarcerated within the Tower that some historians supposed them lost. No, I don't believe that he murdered them, but he did the next best thing."

"Step warily lest ye dash thyself against the rocks. In this thou shalt have no answer. All who have loved me have sworn to keep this secret unto death and even then beyond the grave to eternity's end. If ye seek this truth, then get ye to the high moors of Middleham which was my home and death place of my sweet Prince Edward. There, entreat the wind that blew the day my hope died and it will answer thee. If not, then thy last hope rests in a

place forsaken of the living world, where time is measured in drops of blood as through an hour glass. Search alone on pain of eternal damnation, for that which thou seekest cuts to my very heart, and so, to prove thy love, thou must promise now to keep the truth to thine own self. Swear ....."

"I swear."

". . . at King Richard's Well tomorrow morning at 10:30 am. It will be a short service." Rachael finished her speech then turned to Laura and smiled. "Are you okay?" Laura nodded. "Good. It's been a long day so perhaps we can talk tomorrow, after the service."

"An excellent idea." Laura replied, her eyes shining brilliantly, while her smile remained distant and artificial. Slowly she turned and pulled Gail to her with a gesture.

Laura stood on the patio deck, breathing in the warm, scented night air. All the goodbyes had been said, the last few lingering questions answered, topics briefly discussed then dismissed with conclusions tentatively reached, until the evening ended with promises made for a new day. She was beyond exhausted when Gail slipped her arm inside hers. "Are you all right?" She whispered.

"Yes, I'm fine." She turned as Ian and Anne appeared, arm in arm. "Ian, would you take Gail back to the hotel with you please." "Yes, of course." Ian said without hesitation.

"Where are you going?" Gail asked, instantly alarmed.

"To a place I dare not take you." Laura replied flatly. "I'll be back in an hour."

Laura parked the car by the side of the road. As she got out, the Deathstone took shape, its surface dull, shadowed. Carefully she climbed the wooden fence which separated the park area from the roadside. Despite the darkness and the hushed silence, Laura was unafraid, although tall trees formed a canopy above, blocking out even the stars. She walked past the stone, turned slightly to the left then dropped down, allowing the woods to find her as she sat huddled on the edge of its whispered secrets.

Gathering her strength and concentrating tightly, she called forth another time, but all remained silent. She tried again and again to no avail. After a time, she rose, disappointed but secretly relieved.

She turned and began to retrace her steps, then stopped abruptly. For a moment her consciousness was unwilling, indeed unable, to fathom the power of the entity which stood so near to her.

"So, ye have come even as a slave unbidden to slake thy thirst in duty to me, or 'tis it for another master which ye call Truth? That One I have satisfied, which makes thee mine."

Laura felt a rush of wind, a sudden blinding movement before she was rendered unconscious. As she fell, the trees swayed and moaned, startling the rooks into flight as a deeper darkness beyond earthly reason, descended.

She awoke in absolute silence save for the beating of her heart. She felt cold despite the warmth of the night. Her whole body ached and she could taste blood in her mouth. Trembling with fear, she managed to ease herself into a sitting position despite the pain, and although she wanted desperately to cry, to scream, she forced herself to remain calm as she regained her senses.

The night lay close around her, hushed but no longer silent. Deep within her, a voice cried, 'run, get away, go', but still she sat, breathing deeply, trying to quell a primeval fear which sought to overwhelm her. Suddenly she froze as she felt the air around her grow cold, then colder still. Something brushed her cheek. Panic took her.

Kicking free of her shoes, she scrambled to her feet and raced for the car, fumbling at the end to extract the car key from her jacket pocket. The moon had risen. Its nocturnal rays lit the Deathstone, transforming it with a pale white light which cast a shadow like a crouched beast. She shuddered when she glanced at it as she scrambled over the fence, nearly losing her footing on the other side.

Once inside the car, she locked the doors then cursed aloud as her trembling fingers lost control of the key and it fell to the floor beneath her just as the car's internal lighting system timed out. Retrieving it, she blindly sought the ignition, her whole body trembling uncontrollably, her breathing reduced to ragged gasps. Finally she found home, turned the key and the car's engine burst into life. Relieved, she put the car into gear but her foot slipped off the clutch and the car stalled. Breathing deeply, she tried to settle herself down before trying again. Ignoring the seat belt, she willed the vehicle back to life, then carefully eased it onto the roadway, concentrating as she increased her speed, successfully transferring the car into second gear.

As she drove her terror lessened so that by the time she pulled into the hotel parking area, she was almost calm. It was five minutes to one in the morning.

Gail raced out of the hotel door just in time to help Laura out of the car. "My God, look at you!" She gasped.

Laura's pantsuit was covered in dirt and grass stains, her hair was badly snarled and contained bits of debris. The back of both hands were scratched and bleeding and there was a nasty welt on the side of her neck.

"Sorry," Laura said weakly, 'I fell."

"Come on, let's get you inside."

Gail took Laura's right arm and guided her in and up the stairs. Settling her on the bed, Gail hurried back down to shut and lock the door as she had promised, then raced back up to Laura. She was sitting exactly as she had been left, her eyes remote, her body motionless.

Grimly Gail began to help Laura undress, ignoring her halfhearted protests as she pulled her free of her suit jacket. Suddenly Gail gasped then stood back, staring in horror at the marks on Laura's body.

"What happened Laura?" Gail demanded, her fear replaced by anger.

"I told you, I fell." Laura replied defensively, avoiding Gail's eyes.

"You look like you've been savaged by a wild animal or ... I'm calling the police."

"You'll do no such thing!" Laura growled at her as she rose. "I'm going to have a shower then go to bed. I fell Gail, and that's the end of it. Understand?" She focused the force of her whole being on Gail.

"Okay, if that's what you want." Gail backed away as Laura moved past her and into the bathroom.

The sound of the water drowned out Laura's sobs as she touched some of the larger bruises, while washing away the blood from several finely made cuts.

"Murderous, cold blooded bastard, you're not going to get away with this." She said, her voice nothing more than an angry whisper, tinged with hate and fear.

Day 7
Dadlington - Preston

King Richard:

> *Look, what is done cannot be now amended:*
> *Men shall deal unadvisedly sometimes,*
> *Which after-hours given leisure to repent.*

Shakespeare -
The Tragedy of King Richard the Third
[Act IV, Scene 4]

ail sat on the edge of her bed and watched Laura. It was a little past eight o'clock and still she slept, and as far as Gail could see, it was a dreamless sleep. Leaving her then, Gail quietly dressed and went downstairs. As soon as the door closed Laura rolled on to her back and opened her eyes. She had been awake for some time. Unable, as yet, to come to terms with what had happened she was unwilling to risk any discussion, and the more she thought about last night, the more fearful and unsettled she became until finally she flung back the bed covers, rose painfully and went into the bathroom.

Successive cold compresses calmed her as she breathed deeply, relishing the cool morning air which filtered through the small window. When she viewed herself in the mirror however, she was shocked to see how pale and drawn she appeared. Moving closer, she inspected the welt on her neck, while just below her collarbone was a line of small bruises as if her body had been gripped hard once, then once again. She shuddered and backed away out of the room

When Gail returned, Laura was back in bed, awake, propped up on several pillows.

"How are you feeling?" Gail asked, her concerned obvious.

"I'm fine. What time is it?"

"Just past nine. I had breakfast with Ian and Anne. I told them you were still asleep so they suggested that I come with them to the service at the well. It's not until 10:30 so you've lots of time, I mean, if you want to come and …"

Laura sudden, almost hysterical laughter caught Gail totally by surprise. "I'm sorry Gail," she said, pulling herself together as she sat up to adjust her pillows, "it just struck me as funny somehow. You go. Give my regards to Rachael and the others. Get Rachael's telephone number and address in St. Albans and tell her, I hope to see her again before we go home."

"Okay," Gail said, backing away, "I'll organize a breakfast tray and bring it up to you."

"Thanks. Hey, don't look so glum, I'm fine. Just a little tired, that's all. I'll sit here quietly and read my books. Okay?" Gail nodded and turned to leave. "Oh, and by the way, don't mention last night to anyone please. Falling into ditches is definitely not a cool act."

"Is that the story you're sticking with, because if it is, then why didn't you plan to fall into a ditch in Dadlington? There's lots here you know, but you went to Ambion Wood, didn't you?"

Laura sighed, "just some dry toast and coffee would be fine." Her voice was as hard as crystal as she glared at Gail intently, challenging her.

Gail stormed out of the room slamming the door behind her. A few minutes later she returned with Laura's tray, set it down on the small side table then left without saying a word.

Laura lay for several minutes thinking but the smell of fresh-perked coffee cut through her reverie and she turned to the tray. Lying by the side of the plate was a single white rose. Tenderly she picked it up and twirled it around and around just as the morning sun burst into the room, bathing both the bloom and Laura in an almost gauzelike wreath of light. A single drop of dew trickled down her thumb. "Apology not accepted, you bastard."

Once she was sure that everyone was gone, Laura leaped from her bed, hurriedly dressed and was on her way back to the wood to retrieve her shoes. She gripped the wheel with steady determination, more angry now then frightened. She parked the car in the same spot, scaled the fence and walked resolutely across the open space, ignoring the Deathstone. The sound of so many birds singing in the trees above eased any fears she might have had as she gathered her dew-drenched shoes into her arms, turned and retraced her steps.

By the time Gail returned Laura was ready to go. Back to her cheerful self, she apologized to Gail, hugged her and soothed her so that by the time Gail was ready, she was wondering what all the fuss had been about. Just as they finished packing the car, Ian and Anne arrived with their luggage eager to return to Oxford.

"Laura!" Ian shouted, all smiles and bonhomie. "We were hoping to see you before we left. Thank you for such a wonderful, enlightening evening - thoroughly enjoyable. You certainly gave them all plenty of food for thought." He chuckled. "Anne couldn't sleep for the longest time thinking about what you had said about Elizabeth of York."

"Sorry if I caused you any distress." Laura smiled at Anne.

"Oh, it's all right dear. It's just that I've never thought of him as being in any way cruel; not to women anyway." She smiled, a little embarrassed and more than a little sad.

The smile on Laura's lips faded as she looked into Anne face. "None of us are what we seem Anne. The course of Richard's life was written perhaps even before he was born. We can't begin to understand most of it nor should we try for we stand as outsiders looking back to a time interwoven with events inexplicable to us. Continue to grieve for his loss, love him still if you can and dream of what might have been. I think he would like that."

Anne's eyes filled with tears as she turned on Ian's arm and was helped into the car.

Laura sat behind the wheel as Gail studied the road map. "Would you mind if we pressed on through to Middleham as soon as possible?" She asked as she ran her finger tips lightly back and forth across the steering wheel.

"Sure, I don't care." Gail said casually. "I'm really looking forward to seeing the Yorkshire moors."

"Good, good." Laura nodded as she started the car.

"Excuse me," their host John flew out the door just in time to stop the car, "there's a call waiting - a Miss Ward-Thomas, I believe. You can take it on the phone in the lounge if you like."

"Hi Rachael, sorry we didn't have our little chat this morning but, I ah … "

"Yeah, Gail told me. It's what she didn't tell me that concerns me most." Rachael paused, as if searching for just the right words. "Nell's family will be here any minute so I can't talk long, but look, can I see you next week? When are you heading south?"

"We have to be back in London by the 29th."

"I want to see you before you go. My life's a little unsettled right now but maybe you guys can stay the night in St. Albans. Give us a chance to talk. What do you think?"

"All right," Laura said, biting at her lower lip, "how about I call you. Gail's got your number?"

"Yes. If I'm not in, leave a message on the machine." For a moment Rachael thought the line had gone dead. "Laura?"

"Yes, I'm still here."

"Nell said she saw Richard."

"I know." Laura replied, sadly. She could hear a disturbance in the background.

"They're here. I've got to go. Promise me you'll call."

"I promise. Maybe sooner than you think."

"You'd better," Rachael chuckled, "Gail gave me your e-mail address. Have a good trip. I'll see you in a week or so."

Slowly Laura lowered the phone. Gail stood a few feet away. "She's invited us to stay with her in St. Albans."

It was almost noon by the time they left Dadlington. Laura set a punishing pace northwest on the A50 before turning north on the M6. They stopped briefly at a roadside cafe, filled the car and had a late lunch in a modern, sanitized cafeteria.

Laura seemed agitated and inattentive at times, smiling assurances at Gail before withdrawing into her own troubled thoughts. Gail watched the English countryside fly by while she waited and worried, glancing briefly at Laura now and again as she drove. Perhaps it was her imagination but Laura seemed diminished somehow, as if a portion of herself had collapsed inwards. Gail was determined not to allow it to continue.

It was early evening by the time Laura pulled off the M6 at Preston, unable to drive further.

Although 'The Tickled Trout' was modern and lacked much of the atmosphere they had grown to know and love, it suited. Their room on the second floor overlooked a stream lazy with long tendrils of grass, waving back and forth, pulled relentlessly by the river's steady flow. Beyond was a large open field where a herd of dairy cows grazed contentedly while in the distance could be heard the dull hum of traffic on the M6. Laura watched from the window as the evening drew in and the first star appeared. Despite the serene backdrop, her thoughts were fearful and morose.

"Come on," Gail encouraged, "let's have some dinner. I'm hungry." Laura smiled as she turned but Gail had already moved away by then to retrieve her purse. "I know, bring your notes along. You haven't told me about his life between Buckingham's rebellion and Bosworth. I'm curious about what Peter said about the two dresses and Richard's relationship with his niece."

Laura stared at Gail's back, unable to decide what to say or do. "All right, give me a moment to hunt them out and then we're off."

The hotel's restaurant area was large and thankfully, sparsely populated. The menu was extensive and varied. Gail was the one who was really hungry, so she dove into the vast selection of starters and mains before planning an attack on the desserts list. Laura quickly chose the smoked salmon and a Caesar salad while Gail opted for the same smoked salmon followed by filet mignon, roast potatoes and vegetables. The desserts could wait - for now.

"Well." Laura sighed, as she eased back in her chair.

"Well?" Gail replied in imitation. "Do you want to talk about ancient or recent history?"

"What do you mean?" Laura asked casually as she crossed her legs and looked around the room.

"Are you going to tell me what happened?" Gail asked, her voice low and even.

"Well, that might prove a little difficult, since I don't remember much."

"Then tell me what you do remember."

"I think that would be unwise. Believe me Gail when I say that it would be better if you stayed just as you are, on the outside, where it's safe. I'm having enough trouble sorting it out myself. As soon as I have, then I'll tell you everything. Okay?"

"What's there to sort out! Laura, you were criminally assaulted. There are laws against that sort of thing, you know."

"I wasn't violated if that's what's worrying you."

"Oh God, how calmly she says it. Well, thank heavens for that. So, all we have to do now is decide what sort of monster would knock you unconscious, as I guess you were, then spends his time bruising the hell out of you and cutting into you with what looked like a very sharp, pointed knife." Gail paused then and looked straight at Laura. "What did you mean 'where it's safe'? We're a day's journey from Bosworth, why shouldn't I be safe?" Gail caught you breath. "You know who did it, don't you?"

Laura closed her eyes, fighting for control. "Please, let me handle this. I don't want you involved, not if it can be help. It could be dangerous and you aren't equipment in any case, so please, let it be."

"All right." Gail stammered, her eyes filling with tears. Mentally she backed off, appalled by a truth she refused to believe.

Moments later their salmon arrived. They ate in silence for a while, enjoying the delicate sliver-thin morsels. Occasionally Gail would cast Laura a sorrowful look before turning away quickly, until Laura could stand it no longer.

"I brought my notes so how about we explore the last year and a half of King Richard's life? It's a blast. Liz Wydville finally leaves sanctuary, Richard's son dies, Anne is diagnosed with a terminal disease and Tudor becomes a household name. It's really quite the most interesting part. Full of incestuous passion, betrayal and sudden death, and a few wild parties." Laura laughed lightly, the sound hollow, brittle.

"At the dinner, when the talk was going around and around the table, I didn't understand some of it so, yes please, let's do it. I want to know the truth."

..... *Truth. That One I have satisfied which makes thee mine.*

Gail was too busy finishing her salmon to notice Laura's face suddenly turn pale as the memory descended, crashing like a wave over her. With a quick apology she slipped from the table and hurried to the washroom in the lobby before Gail had a chance to realize that anything was amiss.

"Ye must finish what ye have started. Strength ye will need, aye, and more than strength, for he will fight for that which is promised him."

Laura leaned heavily against the sink counter and stared at her reflection in the mirror. "What did you mean, Nell?" She whispered. "What did you mean?"

"Calm thyself child." Nell's voice soothed. "The truth must be spoken, 'tho lies and deceit be his weapons. Beware of him, for he knows of thee, yet he fears thee mightily. The Lord is at thy side. Trust in him. Be strong. Be strong."

"Nell please, who is he?" Laura pleaded, but there was no reply beyond the echoing words 'be strong, be strong'.

"I'm sorry Gail, I should have gone before we came downstairs." Laura laughed lightly. Just then their main course arrived. "Excellent." She proclaimed as she took her seat.

Between mouthfuls Laura entertained Gail with details of their route tomorrow, up through the infamous Pendle Hills, lunch at Skipton and a quick look at the castle there before the journey across the high, wild moors of Yorkshire, to Middleham. Gail was both happy and relieved to see the 'old Laura' back as she flourished her fork about, talking in rapid good humour, her eyes ablaze with enthusiasm for tomorrow's adventure.

When Gail asked to hear more of the Story, Laura paused only briefly before extracting her notes and making room on the table.

"Let's see, let's see." She mumbled, as she flipped through the pages, picking up the story just after Buckingham's rebellion.

"Buckingham was executed in the market place at Salisbury. Several of the lesser conspirators ended up at Tyburn. Richard had his brother-in-law, St Leger, remember, executed in Exeter and even turned on our Lady Margaret Beaufort and if she wasn't married to Stanley, Richard would probably have done her more of an injury. She lost the title of Countess of Richmond, all her personal property was removed to her husband and, in effect, she was placed under Stanley's jurisdiction where, on Richard's insistence, she was told to shut up and behave herself.

"Stanley was made Lord High Constable and continued on at Richard's side right up to the day he died." She cleared her throat suggestively. "Having done all that, Richard returned to London in November 1483 in triumph, no doubt believing that his victory over Buckingham and Co had vindicated him.

"In the meantime people began to notice that the two Princes were not eating up their breakfasts, or lunches - not even dinner. Even allowing for the fact that both of them were dead set against eating their broccoli, this was getting ridiculous. It soon became apparent to even the densest Tower troll that the boys were not where they were suppose to be.

"Richard had a super Christmas season at Westminster Palace, spending money like a drunken sailor, while Henry Tudor knelt in the Cathedral at Rennes and made a solemn vow to marry Elizabeth of York once he was king. Now, there's a guy who kept the horse before the cart.

"In January Richard pushed through the Act of Settlement in parliament. Known as the 'Titulus Regius', it basically reconfirmed his legal title to the crown. The document was based on Edward IV's invalid marriage to Elizabeth Wydville but this decision really belonged to an ecclesiastical court and not to a bunch of layman sitting in parliament. However, Richard obviously made it very clear that he wanted the Act passed, and it was."

"So," Gail interrupted, "Richard put the heavy word on."

"Terror tactics more like. But, he did pass some good legislation including the abolition of the hated benevolences or forced financial gifts to the Crown. So, you give a little, take a little, but all and all he did try very hard to come out on top as a champion of justice. Unfortunately, almost everyone also believed that he had murdered his nephews, so I think it is fair to say that the guy had a credibility problem."

Gail chuckled.

"Now, into this mix we add Elizabeth Wydville who probably had season tickets for the theatre and here she was, stuck in sanctuary with her daughters driving her nuts. Believe it or not, Liz and Dickie came to an understanding in February and Liz walked out of her nine-month confinement, right into Richard's arms. Mind you, he had to submit to a public oath beforehand but what's a little legalize against the knowledge that he no longer had this thorn in his side but standing right there, close enough to grab by the throat. Wonderful!" If Gail took Laura's derisive tone as a form of humour, she couldn't have been more wrong.

"What did his oath say, do you know?"

"Oh yes, I've got a copy right here. It's not long, so shall I read it?" Gail nodded so Laura searched her files briefly before coming up with the document that Richard read aloud at Westminster before the lords of the realm, churchmen, the Lord Mayor and other chief citizens of London.

I, Richard, by the Grace of God King of England, in the presence of my lords spiritual and temporal, promise and swear on the word of a king that if the daughters of Dame Elizabeth Grey, late calling herself Queen of England, will come to me out of Sanctuary at Westminster, and be guided, ruled and demeaned after me, that I shall see that they be in surety of their lives, and also not suffer any manner of hurt by any manner person, nor any of them imprison within the Tower of London or any other prison, but that I shall put them in honest places of good name and fame, and them honestly and courteously shall see to be entreated and to have all things requisite and necessary as my kinswomen, and every one of them given in marriage to gentlemen born. And such gentlemen as shall hap to marry with them I shall charge, from time to time, lovingly to love and entreat them as their wives and my kinswomen, as they will avoid and eschew my displeasure.

"Did you notice the bit about the Tower of London? The Ricardians maintain that Elizabeth Wydville would never have released her daughters into the care of the very man who she believed had murdered her two sons, but it's obvious from the oath, that she not only believed it, but tried to protect her daughters through it. Based on the oath, Richard would not have dared to move against the girls, or at least not right away.

"Anyhow, Richard not only agreed to the oath but offered Elizabeth Wydville the handsome sum of 700 marks which she gladly accepted. Then Richard took it one step further and promised to pardon her son Dorset, if he would leave Tudor and return to England. Can you believe it, she actually wrote to him, urging him to come home, that all was forgiven? Dorset went for it too, but was stopped by Henry's spies and warned off the idea before he took ship. If Richard was a Political Realist, then Elizabeth must have been a supreme Pragmatist, especially when you realize that Richard had ordered the execution of her son, Richard Grey and her brother, Lord Rivers." Laura shook her head in disbelief.

"Anyhow, in early April, Richard and Anne went to Nottingham, taking the two elder nieces - Elizabeth and Cecily - with them. While there, news reached them that Edward of Middleham had died, exactly one year to the day after the death of Edward IV. Both Richard and Anne were beyond prostrate with grief. It's even hinted that Richard was so overcome that he was deranged for a time."

"How did the boy die?" Gail asked, almost in a whisper.

"Officially the cause is unknown although whatever it was, it took him swiftly and violently, which suggests something like appendicitis. Certainly something so quick that his parents had no prior knowledge. It is said the child died scream ... ah ... screaming for his father at the end." Laura shifted in her seat. "Is that enough?" She asked Gail as her voice clouded.

Laura put her notes away and they finished the evening talking about anything but the Story. The conversation was light and humorous, as they reminisced about past adventures together.

Occasionally Gail would pause and grow serious however, worried about what was to happened - the storm about to break around them, for she could sense Laura's anxiety yet she was powerless to either help or prevent what was to come. All she could do was trust in Laura and pray that she would be there to help in any way she could, when the time came.

Meanwhile, she matched Laura's upbeat mood, selecting for

dessert a piece of chocolate fudge cake which was so rich she was unable to finish it, although she did try. Laura made the usual comments and Gail the expected replies until the evening faded and the day drew to a close.

Back in their room, Laura stood by the open window and listened to the night sounds while Gail readied herself for bed. The moon hung like a beacon, nearly full now and heavy, its perpetual nocturnal splendour illuminating the fields beyond, turning the river into an incandescent silver stream of light.

"Middleham tomorrow. What then?" Laura whispered as she stared at her reflection in the glass.

Day 8

Newchurch-in-Pendle - Skipton Castle - Middleham

King Richard:

> *Conscience is but a word that cowards use,*
> *Devised at first to keep the strong in awe:*

Shakespeare -
The Tragedy of King Richard the Third
[Act V, Scene 3]

Laura was awake at first light. As the sun rose, the clouds parted then dissipated, leaving behind the promise of another sunny day, although the wind had picked up during the night, bending and twisting the branches of the trees along the river's edge. The herd of cows reappeared in the paddock opposite. Delivered of their burden of milk, they slowly meandered back into the fields to begin the cycle again. Laura stood and watched their progress, then with a sigh, turned from the window.

Gail continued to sleep soundly, huddled in her usual manner, deep beneath the covers, her head barely visible. Laura stared at her for a moment then slipped into the bathroom. By the time she came out, Gail was awake, lying on her back staring up at the ceiling.

"Hi, sleep well?" Laura asked, bouncing on Gail's bed.

"Okay, I guess. I woke just at dawn. You were standing by the window smoking your damn cigarettes. You'd get a good night's sleep you know, if you gave up smoking."

"Undoubtedly, but then again, no one would find me still abed with such a day as this to rush into. Get up."

Laura bounced hard five or six times before leaving Gail to begin a search through her suitcase for the hair dryer. With a sigh, Gail rose and padded off to the bathroom muttering something about monkeys.

A generous buffet breakfast greeted them as they entered the restaurant. Offering everything from stewed prunes to smoked kippers, Gail quickly took the lead, piling her plate high with more than a representative sampling. As she prepared to turn away, she added several individually wrapped pieces of Camembert cheese to the side of her plate. Once back at their table however, she quickly slipped them into her purse.

Laura watched this performance with mild interest. "Should I take the salt and peppers?"

"No smarty, but there's some miniature bread rolls if you can manage to grab a few. We can have a snack at this witch place you told me about." She smiled wickedly.

"Oh, so you want to go there, do you?"

"Sure. You're probably low on supplies."

Laura chuckled good-naturedly. "Well, you're going to need your own brand of magic to navigate this one." Laura pulled the road atlas up from under her chair. "There's our destination - Newchurch - right in the middle of the Forest of Pendle. As you can see, it's surrounded by all those nasty little white, no-number roads disguised as driveways, so I think it's fair to say that you're about to encounter yet another navigational nightmare. Up to it?"

"Piece of cake." Gail intoned with confidence.

Laura smiled. "What an appropriate turn of phrase."

After studying the map further, they decided to tackle Newchurch from the west, risking a crossing of the high land rather then through the valley. They headed vaguely north towards

Clitheroe as the land slowly rose on their right, building ever higher to eventually form the crest called Pendle Hill. Laura turned right at the sign to Pendleton and began to climb immediately. The further they drove, the rougher the terrain became as the soil gave out and the land grew progressively poorer, and rockier.

Laura brought the car to a halt inches from a metal cattle grid laid flush with the roadway. Beyond, resting directly in their path were three sheep, lazily ruminating. It was impossible to go around them since there was a series of large boulders on one side and a not-nice drop on the other.

"Gail, you're going to have to shoo them out of the way."

"Me?"

"Okay, never mind, I'll ask one of the Gails in the back seat." Laura turned and glared at Gail overtop of her sunglasses.

"What do I do?"

"Bark like a sheep dog."

"And if they don't move?"

"Bark like a Doberman sheep dog."

Gail slid out of the car and approached the sheep. They looked her up and down, and after a few cursory barks from her, continued to look her up and down. Laura was thoroughly enjoying this but aware of the time factor, she finally broke down and got out to help.

"Your barking idea isn't working so I suggest you bite them." Gail growled as she moved away to let Laura have a turn.

"There you see," Laura said as she began to prod one of the sheep with the toe of her boot, "it just proves that you aren't a bitch afterall. Come on old girl, up you get." Shocked by such inappropriate behaviour, the ewe rose and sauntered away, taking the others with her.

Except for making a wrong turn somewhere near Sabden and stopping several times to enjoy the view, their progress was reasonable and so they finally arrived at Newchurch-on-Pendle, home of the Pendle Witches of the 16th and 17th centuries.

Laura had to park the car carefully on the narrow, steep road in front of the witches' shop she had heard so much about. It was easy to recognise. Decked out in traditional Halloween fashion, the door was guarded by two life-size, over-stuffed figures dressed in black and in need of beauty treatments. Above the door, written in old English were the words which roughly translated said 'there are no pockets in shrouds'. "Nice thought." Laura remarked.

Gail was first in the door only to be greeted by a young, attractive girl who did not look like a trafficker in eye of gnat or bat's blood. She did, however, tell them about the witches, ten of whom were tried at Lancaster Castle in 1612, then promptly hanged.

They wandered around the shop, selecting several small items to augment their arsenal of souvenirs. Just as they were about to leave, Laura asked, "do you have a talisman of some sort to ward off evil spirits?"

"Well, we have this." The girl said, holding up a nondescript stone, pierced through the middle and dangling from a leather thong. "People buy them at tax time to prevent being audited."

Laura fingered the piece briefly before handing it back "I don't think it'll be strong enough."

"Oh?" The young girl replied, arching her eyebrows.

If being lost is defined as not knowing where you are, then they were indeed lost, but travelling more or less in the right direction until they broke through to the A59 just on the outskirts of Skipton, the southern gateway to the Yorkshire Dales.

Because of the open market stalls all along the edge of the road, Laura found it difficult to find a parking spot on the main street as it rose gently towards the castle at the far end. Just as she was about to give up, a car backed out in front so she was able to block the traffic behind, then nip into the space. Gail and Laura smiled at each other then leapt out of the car to shop. The castle loomed just ahead, lost from sight behind two massive stone towers which guarded the entrance. The stalls proved a disappointment however since neither of them were interested in buying vegetables, cut flowers or cheap socks, so they headed towards the castle.

As they walked, Laura filled Gail in on a few details. "Originally the castle belonged to the Clifford family but after the battle of Towton, King Edward IV seized it for the crown. Sir William Stanley held it until it was acquired by Richard, then Duke of Gloucester, in 1475 as part of his plan to secure a power base in the north." Laura chuckled. "It's doubtful if Richard's decision to appropriate the castle was appreciated by Stanley.

"The Cliffords, by the way, were hunted almost to extinction since it was 'Butcher Clifford' who murdered Richard's seventeen year old brother Edmund in cold blood. The poor kid had surrendered. Anyhow, Clifford died shortly afterwards under mysterious circumstances. His body was never found."

"Hum, shades of Lovell." Gail remarked casually.

Laura stopped dead in her tracks. "Yes," she muttered, "shades of Lovell."

They purchased their tickets just inside the entrance way at the colourful Shell Room before proceeding through the archway beneath the Watch Tower. Once inside, they found themselves in a large open area with the private apartments to the right. Ahead and slightly to the left was a flight of stone stairs called the Lady Anne steps which led to the original entrance arch of Norman design. Within was a magnificent courtyard called the Conduit Court, so named because it was the termination point for the spring water which was piped into the castle. In the middle of this enclosed area was a huge yew tree, planted by Lade Anne Clifford over 300 years ago. The courtyard was a delight. Laura and Gail lingered for some time, enjoying the intimacy of scale before turning their attention to the various rooms leading off this central court.

Despite the fact that they wandered around for nearly two hours, they did not see everything, although they did manage to work they way through to the dungeon, deep beneath the original

Norman gatehouse.

They had lunch sitting in the sun by the river, eating fish and chips right from the newspaper it had been wrapped in. Laughingly Gail pronounced this one of their finest meals. Laura couldn't help but agree. It was a little past two when Laura eased the car out of its parking spot and headed north towards the high moors of Yorkshire.

They virtually had the road to themselves which was just as well, since it was extremely narrow, full of bends and offered some excellent drops to the river valley below.

Occasionally Gail would lean over and groan as she viewed the stony depths. "I hope we don't meet anything larger than a bicycle coming the other way."

"Relax," Laura chuckled, "after a while, you get use to it, especially if you don't look."

At Kettlewell, the road turned sharply away from the river and began to rise alarmingly. Occasionally Laura was forced to gear down quickly to negotiate hairbend turns at angles so steep that their relatively powerful car was barely able to surmount the course. Gail held tight, making gurgling sounds now and again, until they were high enough to find relatively flat land, wide open and wind blown.

At the first opportunity, Laura eased the car to the side of the road and got out. The wind blew wild and free here. Turning her face into it, she relished the fresh clean air and the magnificent desolation, the expanse of rock and heather and heath.

Gail was far less enthusiastic. "Don't go far," she shouted as Laura began to wander away from the car, "there are cows everywhere in case you haven't noticed."

"I've noticed." Laura said as she plucked a sprig of heather. "Beautiful, isn't it?"

"It's bleak, that's what it is - windswept, cold, treeless, desolate, barren, rocky - take your pick. I can't even see a Seven-Eleven, let alone a McDonalds."

Laura stood, hands on hips. "You're a complete heathen, aren't you?" She took several more deep draughts of air before slowly making her way back. "Richard loved it up here, away from court and all the hassles associated with being a royal duke. They didn't have much in the way of privacy in those days, so it must have been wonderful for him to get away - for awhile at least." Her voice trailed off in sadness.

"Let's go before I get chilblains." Gail urged.

All the signposts indicated Leyburn so they were surprised when Middleham Castle suddenly burst out from amongst the trees, grey stone against a pale blue sky.

Their hotel - the Black Swan - stood on the main street just off the market square so Laura was able to park the car within just a few feet of the front door. The castle was behind, lost from view by the buildings which now encroached upon the original outer bailey. Their room was at the back of the hotel, overlooking a delightful, flower-filled patio area called the 'Bear Garden'. Just beyond loomed a corner of the castle's outer wall, barely a stone's throw away.

The room was small but beautifully appointed. In the closet were extra pillows, blankets, an ironing board and iron plus laundry bags, tags and forms. It would cost them the earth, but reasoning that time was an important and valuable factor, they decided to take advantage of the offer and mentally for now, began to separate the cleans from the not-so-cleans.

Finally Laura gave it up. "Come on, I'll buy you a drink and then, if you like, we can walk around a bit before dinner."

Unbeknown to Laura and Gail just yet, Middleham is famous not only as the home of King Richard III in history, but in modern times, for its racehorses which explains why, when they wandered into the bar area, they were confronted by a group of casually dressed men, none of whom were over 5'6" tall. Gail boldly allowed herself to be 'chatted up' while Laura ordered two wines. The truth was soon revealed.

"We exercise the animals first off in the mornin', so if'n ye 'ave a mind to gets up early like, then you'll be seein' us atop the 'orses." A senior member of the group shouted as Gail moved away, smiling politely before joining Laura.

"Jockeys and exercise grooms." She pronounced sagely.

"Aye, that's right, listen to old Ned 'ere. He knows all about it. Exercises that great lump of a bay all day he does, then exercises his drinkin' arm all night. Right, Ned?" General warm-hearted laughter all around.

Before they left for their walk their host, George, reserved a table for them for dinner that evening. Gail's eyes sparkled at the prospect of choosing between Yorkshire lamb with all the trimmings or fresh Scottish salmon, poached in a light dill and butter sauce.

On impulse Laura asked him if it would be possible for them to stay an extra night.

While he was checking the reservations book Laura turned to Gail. "Sorry, it just occurred to me that there's so much to see and do right in this area, one more day might be a good idea. I like this place, so except for contacting the hotel in York and delaying our arrival by a day, there's no problem. We have the time."

"Yeah, well sure, if you want to." Gail shrugged nonchalantly, hiding in a gesture the distinct feeling that somehow she was being manipulated by Laura for reasons she could not, as yet, understand.

George returned moments later to confirm that yes, the room was available. Laura smiled. She would need that extra day or rather, night. Casually she reached into her pocket and massaged the two keys given her. One for their room and one for the back entrance, just two steps from their door.

Middleham is small, little more than village size, but oversupplied with gift shops, B&B's and hotels, all eager to take advantage of the tourists drawn by the castle and its history. Together they wandered through a few shops but it was obvious that Laura wasn't in the mood. Half an hour later, Gail found her standing in the market square.

"I bought you something." Gail said as she handed Laura a small paper bag.

"What is it?"

"Open it and find out."

Laura tipped the bag into her open palm and out tumbled a paperweight made of white stone, carved into the likeness of a boar.

"I ah . . . thought you might like to carry it around with you when you get bored." She laughed, or rather she tried to. "The lady in the shop said that it was an exact replica of the ones worn by his retainers. Is that the right word?"

Laura nodded. "Thank you." Quickly she turned away.

"Come on," Gail said as she slipped her arm inside Laura's, "let's go see his country home."

Closed at this hour, they were still able to view Middleham Castle up close, across the dry moat although their initial impression was one of disappointment since the castle was now virtually a ruin. Unlike Skipton however, most of what there was to see belonged to the time of Richard Plantagenet, with very few exceptions.

They followed the line of the wall around two sides of the perimeter and it was then that Laura noticed that the castle was atypically situated on the lesser ground, while behind, the land rose to the site of the original motte and-bailey set on the high ground to the southwest. "That's strange."

"What?" Gail asked.

"I wonder why the old site was abandoned, when it was more common to build on top, incorporating the old construction into the new."

Gail shrugged. "Maybe it was too exposed up there."

"Yes, you're probably right. Well," Laura sighed, "sorry it's not in very good shape. Do you know, in its heyday Middleham was referred to as the 'Windsor of the North'? It was Richard's favourite residence, but I don't think he had the opportunity to visit it much after he became king. His son Edward, was born here and died here, so I guess the memories were both bitter and sweet."

Gail looked at her watch. "It's almost seven. The table's booked for eight, so if you want to get cleaned up and organize our laundry then maybe we should head back."

"Good idea." Slowly Laura turned away.

Promptly at eight they arrived at the doorway leading into the hotel's private diningroom. Dinner was a massive success. The food, the delightfully small, almost intimate dining room and attentive service of their host, provided the perfect ambience for a perfect meal. Laura seemed totally relaxed although Gail did notice that occasionally she would pause during the course of their conversation as if she were either listening to something, or for something.

Gail ate herself almost into oblivion so she agreed to another walk before bed. The summer evening was cooler than they had, as yet, experienced. The village was almost totally silent as they strolled around the square then sat for a while on the steps of the stone market cross where, Gail felt sure, malefactors were flogged almost daily for petty crimes like overindulgence. The sweet, almost pungent odour of night flowers hung in the air, dissolving away any trace of automobiles and modern pollution. The wind had dropped to a zephyr.

Slowly they retraced their steps back up the hill, following the roadway before turning left into the lane which fronted the castle. The ruins appeared stark against the night sky, distant and remote as if brooding over its state, remembering happier times when it enjoyed special privileges granted to it by one of its own, who had become a king.

Laura stood and stared at the massive structure until Gail finally took her arm, complaining of the cold.

Day 9

Bolton Castle - Askrigg - Tan Hill - William's Hill

Duchess of York:
> *O! My accursed womb, the bed of death*
> *A cockatrice hast thou hatch'd to the world,*
> *Whose unavoided eye is murderous.*

Shakespeare -
The Tragedy of King Richard the Third
[Act IV, Scene 1]

Laura woke with a start. The room lay deep in shadow, silent. She had slept fitfully and now her head ached, making her feel nauseous. Quietly she slipped into the bathroom and splashed her face with cold water. Clutching the edge of the basin, she shut her eyes and breathed deeply, in part to quell a sense of foreboding which wrapped then rewrapped itself around her.

Desperately she tried to remember the dream, to piece the fragments together. John, angry and defiant, his face contorted in rage. Peter, lewd and mischievous, unaware of the black vale through which he walked. Rachael, smiling and self-assured, while forces beyond the limits of her understanding whirled ever closer to her. Anne, fearful of an evil which she knew existed, but could not accept. Stephanie, cool and aloof, her life a tragic play performed by weary actors. Ian, who guessed a truth his logic could not acknowledge. And Jenny, desperately seeking an equilibrium she would find impossible to sustain.

It was a clamorous dream, disjointed and chaotic but through it Laura could sense the others, scattered now, but in some way inexplicably connected. Tears welled up as she turned from the mirror and forced herself to dress hurriedly before slipping from the room, glancing back only briefly to make sure Gail had not been disturbed.

As she emerged into the sunlight at the back of the hotel she could hear the sound of horses as they clip-clopped down the broad main street, whinnying and snorting, while their riders called out to each other and to their mounts. There was a narrow, arched laneway which joined the Bear Garden to the street so Laura took it, arriving just in time to see a dozen magnificent thoroughbreds move by at a walk. They were perhaps the tallest horses Laura had ever seen or at least they appeared to be against the backdrop of the deserted street. She wandered over to the car to get the road atlas just as one of the horses drew close on the other side.

"Daft bloody bugger!" Yelled its rider. "Sorry Miss, Clovis here, he likes to look in the windows. Quite fancies himself, he does. Get out of it, you bloody great burk!" Reluctantly the horse pulled itself free of its image and rejoined the others.

Laura smiled as she leaned against the car and watched them as they continued on, past the market square, then down the hill, heading roughly eastwards towards York.

Suddenly the image shifted as the buildings dissolved, leaving only open fields and a muddy, wheel-rutted road, pockmarked with pools of water which mirrored a dull, overcast sky. Men dressed in deepest black rode two abreast, their forms indistinct, blending into horses draped in funeral crepe. Then the image wavered, turned in upon itself and was gone.

"God help me." She whispered in a trembling voice. She spun around only to encountered a deserted street with everything as it should be but she could not erase the feeling of being watched by a maleficent presence. A mouse under the eye of a voracious cat.

The cool morning air proved the perfect tonic for her as she walked along the main street, moving by degrees towards the castle. The unease within her increased however, the closer she came until finally she broke off from her intent and hurried back to the room.

Gail turned as Laura entered. She had just plugged in the jug and was busy arranging the coffee cups. "Hi! Thought you probably went for a walk or something. God you look awful! Didn't you sleep well?"

"I slept just fine thank you very much." Laura replied defensively. "Hurry up and get dressed. I'll meet you in the breakfast room. At least there I can get a real cup of coffee."

Gail nodded towards the road atlas. "I thought we were going to see the castle today?"

"We are, but I thought we'd start with Bolton Castle since it is largely intact and then we can see some of the lovely villages scattered along the river valley. After that, we'll take to the hills and see a little of the Pennine Way. Sound good?"

"Sure," Gail shrugged, "but, I guess I thought you'd be eager to see Middleham Castle first."

"It can wait." Laura said flatly. "Besides, Bolton has a slight Mary Queen of Scots connection, which should please you. She was held prisoner there for a brief time before Liz really put her on ice further south." Rolling the road atlas in her hand, Laura rose from the breakfast table. "Ready?"

Except for the northwest tower, Bolton Castle is in an excellent state of preservation so Laura and Gail were able to wander around, climb stairs, navigate spiral staircases and guidebook in hand, poke into corners, crannies and recesses without hindrance. Occasionally they came across wax figures in costumes, busy going about their duties, thrashing grain in the mill or working iron at the forge.

They were both quite taken by the private apartments, including the Solar and a little room leading off of it, which may have been a nursery and Lord and Lady Scrope's Bed Chambers. Some of the rooms were used by Mary Queen of Scots during her brief imprisonment and still reveal much of the original plaster work.

Laura turned to find Gail sniffing the plaster walls. "What are you doing?"

Gail made a face. "See the way its peeled into two layers? According to the guidebook, the inner one is probably medieval. Do you know what it was made from?"

"I've no idea."

"A mixture of cow manure, horse hair, lime, sand and milk. Yuck!"

"Now you know why they whitewashed the walls." Laura said as she turned to inspect three more wax figures representing servants of Queen Mary, frozen in time as they went about their duties preparing clothes and linen for their mistress.

Gail scrutinized a magnificently carved four-poster, canopied bed from every angle. Frowning, she called out to Laura. "Didn't you say that Mary was five feet, eleven inches tall?"

"Yes."

"Then this bed can't be hers. It's much too short."

"I don't know, after her execution it would have been just about right."

Gail cast her a withering glance before disappearing into Lord Scrope's private garderobe. She sat on the edge of the loo for awhile reading the guidebook while admiring the view until Laura stuck her head around the corner just long enough to remind her that she could get haemorrhoids doing that.

"It says in this," Gail said as she exited the privy waving the guidebook, "that the medieval plumbing was so good here that it was still in use during the Victorian age. There was a chute or discharge pipe connected to each loo and this led to a pit, a sort of sceptic system below ground level. Where to now?"

Together they climbed the narrow staircase to the roof and battlements, ninety-seven feet above the ground. The view across the Dales was superb. After a time they returned and gradually worked their way back to ground level.

"We haven't seen the dungeon yet." Gail whispered to Laura as they exited into the courtyard. "It's through here." Gail led the way to the north curtain wall, then down its base, to a small chamber excavated from solid rock. "An arm bone was found down here once, still bearing its heavy iron manacles. Wooooo. Prisoners were chained to that rock over there in the corner."

"Gail," Laura whispered, "I think you should write a book - *Dungeons I Have Known and Loved.*"

"Great idea!" Gail smiled. "Do you think Richard visited the castle often?"

"Maybe." Laura replied as they gradually made their way back to the gatehouse. "Sir John Scrope, Fifth Lord Scrope of Bolton, was Richard's Captain and Governor of the fleet. He fought at Bosworth, survived and was pardoned by Tudor."

"He survived?" Gail said, amazed. "You mean he wasn't with Richard at the end?"

"No," Laura said turning away, "strange isn't it, especially since he and Richard were so closely related - cousins I think."

Laura continued to drive west, avoiding the main road in favour of lesser ones despite the fact that she was halted by farm machinery on two occasions and by a flock of sheep once, just outside Askrigg. A handsome village, Askrigg was the venue for the filming of the television series *All Creatures Great & Small*, based on James Harriot's books. Naturally, Laura and Gail wandered around, shopped a bit before having lunch at a delightful outdoor cafe in the centre of town. Several huge lorries loaded with bales of hay managed to spoil the tranquillity only briefly. Harvest had begun and soon, winter would arrive.

The afternoon was spent high in the Dales, atop Tan Hill, where they met and chatted with a group of trampers walking the Pennine Way. Laura was quite enthusiastic, Gail far less so, since she considered walking necessary only as a means of getting from Shop A to Shop B, not from mountain top to mountain top.

Laura wandered off, leaving Gail to investigate the Tan Hill Inn, reputed to be the highest pub in England. The views were out of this world, the area devoid of trees which, for some reason, seemed to please Laura. Gail considered her quite mad as she watched her go, humming softly amid the stark landscape.

Laura stopped now and again to listen to the wind which paused only long enough to rumple her hair and clutch at her clothes before hurrying on. She came to rest on a moss covered boulder surrounded by coarse grasses, cropped by sheep. With her legs drawn up to her chest, enfolded in her arms, she hummed softly as she watched a few, scattered patches of cloud move rapidly across the open sky, hurried by the wind. Above her a hawk cried out a vociferous warning as it rode the thermals higher and higher, its passage marked in silhouette against the sky. She was ready for anything now, or at least she thought she was.

Suddenly she felt cold. The wind direction changed then changed again, creating a maelstrom around her, obscuring her vision. She was no longer alone.

"Do not touch her!"

"But, my lord, you promised . . ."

". . . nothing!"

She froze in fear.

"Thou wilt come to me alone this night upon William's Hill, when all the world is silent. I shall aid thee in thy quest, as ye shalt aid me in mine. We shall be as one and Truth shall be our slave."

Instantly the wind died then resumed its normal course. Laura remained where she was for what seemed an eternity while the knowledge that somehow he had found her cut into her, leaving her breathless with fear. "Oh my God, what have I done? What have I done? She whispered to the wind, her voice ragged with fear.

"Stop it! Calm down and think, damn it!" In one quick movement she leapt from the rock. Angry and defensive now, she turned around and around, seeking him despite the tears which welled up, obscuring her vision, blunting her senses.

In the distance stood the Inn, a solid bulwark, a symbol of a real world in which she suddenly felt alienated. She squared her shoulders, took a deep breath then went in search of Gail.

She was sitting atop a bar stool surrounded by a least ten trampers ranging in age from eighteen perhaps to twenty-five, maximum. Everyone was drinking soft drinks except Gail who admitted, with casual defiance, that she was on her second glass of wine.

"Hi, we were just talking about what a moor is." Gail shouted, then giggled as one of the older boys whispered something in her ear, nearly causing her to fall from her perch. "So Laura, here's your chance. What's a moor?"

"Someone from North Africa?" Laura shot back with a wry smile.

"Oh, so clever! Not Moor capital M, moor small M, like where we are now, atop Arken . . . Arkengarty . . . what is it again?"

"Arkengarthdale Moor," offered her friend.

"Right! Come on, how would you define a moor?" Gail persisted.

Laura thought for a moment. "Well, it's high land, usually open, unfenced, the soil is of poor quality, badly drained, so only vegetation like heather, coarse grass, bracken and moss can grow. What's my prize?"

"I get the prize." Gail shouted triumphantly "I bet them that you would know because you're ever so smart - too damn smart." She snapped.

Laura took hold of Gail's arm. "Gail, I think . . ."

"Do you know,' Gail interrupted, pulling her arm free with some force, "all this land around here use to be wonderful for hunting deer, bear, if you can believe it and wild boar. Yeah, especially wild boar! One damn pig too many if you ask me." She laughed hysterically, her eyes bright with tears.

"Gail, are you all right?" Laura asked.

"Of course I'm all right, damn it!"

"Come on, I think we should go."

At a table near the fireplace an old man looked up from his glass of beer, clucked disapprovingly then smiled a toothless grin. Laura ignored him as she took Gail's arm but, just before leaving, she paused long enough to look back. The chair was empty, although the glass remained exactly where she had seen it, only now is was filled with a dark red liquid - like blood.

"Don't touch me." Gail warned as she got into the car, tilted her seat back, closed her eyes and instantly fell asleep.

Both shocked and worried, Laura stood beside the car unable to decide what to do. Finally she got in, started the engine and began to head back to Middleham.

Just north of Leyburn, Gail turned her head towards Laura then opened her eyes. Alarmed, Laura pulled the car to the side of the road.

"He will kill you." Gail's voice was low and even as she stared at Laura, her eyes vacant. Then slowly she closed them and turned away, falling back into a sleep again.

Laura sat for some time behind the wheel, her hands alternately gripping then releasing the hard plastic until her fingers ached while Gail lay like a limp doll beside her. When Laura touched her hand it was cold and damp, almost lifeless although minutes later, when she stopped in front of their hotel, Gail woke with a start.

"Gosh, did I sleep all the way back! Sorry." She oozed.

Laura kept an eye on Gail for the rest of the evening but she seemed herself again although she did admit that she was tired and could do with an early night. All things considered, Laura couldn't help but agree. However, to ensure that she enjoyed a restful night's sleep, Laura reduced a sleeping pill to a fine powder and introduced it into a cup of decaffeinated coffee, heavy with milk and sugar. Ten minutes after drinking it, Gail was fast asleep.

Laura quickly extinguished all the lights then changed into a full length skirt and black silk blouse. Knowing the night would be cool, she wrapped herself in a large woollen shawl woven in shades of grey and dark purple. Before opening the door she turned. "I'm sorry Gail, for lots of things." She whispered sadly then she was gone into the night.

The streets were deserted, the village silent. She hurried across the brightly lit Bear Garden to the lane beyond, turned right then left, following the laneway which skirted the eastern edge of the castle. Beyond was a wide open field. In the distance, silhouetted against the night sky, stood the ragged outline of the motte upon which the original castle was built perhaps during the time of William the Conqueror - William's Hill.

Desperately she fumbled with the latches on two gates. Her whole body trembled with fear while tears welled up making it impossible for her to see. She stopped several times, too afraid to continue, yet too afraid to turn back. Whatever it was, she needed to protect Gail. Over and over in her mind she tried to rationalize, to come to some sort of logical reason, to make sense of . . . of what?

The night enfolded her in a sea of shadows puckered at the edges by a silvery paleness as the moon rose into a sky bright with stars.

Gathering her skirt in her left hand, she crossed an earthen bridge which connected the field to the base of the hill. On either side, ditches had been dug perhaps to form a moat. A scar in the side of the hill revealed a path, well worn but narrow, which brought her up the face of the hill to the top. Her heart raced and her breathing was rapid and shallow as she surmounted the final portion and stood on the rim of William's Hill before she turned to look back towards Middleham Castle and its village nestled below.

The central portion of the hill consisted of a large open area perhaps five feet below the rim where she now stood. The grass sides sloped gently downwards into this amphitheatre-like interior, while the rim rose higher on either side of her. The outer drop to the base of the hill was considerable.

She trembled, but held herself in check as she slowly turned, seeking him but all remained silent, the night hushed and still. Breathing deeply to quell a rising sense of panic, her eyes swept the muted landscape around her as the wind rose suddenly, stirring the small trees and shrubs nearby.

"Conserve thy sight madam, for it will avail thee not. Know only that I stand near to thee. Close enough to see thy beauty and feel thy fear. 'Tis unwarranted. I mean thee no harm. Thy warmth hast brought me life, thy thoughts have awaken mine. I shall draw from thee and grow the stronger for it. All that thou art is mine, now and for evermore."

Laura turned abruptly then backed away, tracing the narrow ridge of the hill with the toe of her boot. Although she could not see him, she knew without a doubt that he stood perhaps ten feet from her. She was appalled by the raw sense of power which seemed to emanated from him.

"You shall not claim me neither in body nor in soul, for that which is not freely given can never be yours."

He laughed, low and malicious. *"Eyes like a tiger, hast thou claws to match? I have endured enough of thee madam. Presume no more upon my patience. I have set for thee a task and you will perform it. Come to me."*

She had neither the strength nor the resilience to disobey. Inexplicably she found herself being drawn forward, to the very brink of the hill. Below, in the middle distance stood the ruined castle.

"Steel thy mind madam for this thing which I would have of thee to do. From the vale of time draw forth the image of my son's death."

"I can't." Laura sobbed. "Please, I . . ."

"Nay madam, thou wilt do as I command in this, as in all else. Come, I will aid thee. Look."

Slowly the vision blurred, contorted then rapidly expanded and before her stood the castle as it had once been, ablaze with light from a hundred torches. A massive stone structure rising from the earth three storeys and more. The image caught and held, bathed in the unnatural light of a moon belonging to another time. Camp fires burned low along the periphery while men moved in silent motion before coming to rest as the night wore on. To the east Laura could clearly see stables, store houses, numerous other buildings behind a stone wall. Beyond lay a massive fortified ditch.

Suddenly the night was shattered as a child screamed then screamed again. Shadows danced on walls as torches moved first one way then another while the screaming continued. After a moment which seemed an eternity, the screaming stopped only to be replaced with a pitiful, sobbing cry as the child cried - 'father, father, please help me' - then absolute silence.

Past and present drew apart slowly, straining at the image before it dissolved, leaving Laura alone in a world of silence.

The death of Edward of Middleham cut like shattered glass. In a state of shock, exhausted, she sank to her knees, huddled deep within the shawl, unmoving until the first dull grey streaks of dawn touched her. In the distance a cock crowed.

She stood slowly, gaining her footing but swaying slightly. Gradually she made her way carefully down from the hill and across the open field. As she passed the ruins she clutched the shawl closer to her with fingers numbed with cold.

The room was dark and silent. She paused to look at Gail before going into the bathroom, closing the door behind her before turning on the light. It hurt her eyes. She ran a corner of a towel under cold water then pressed it tightly to her face. Her hands trembled. The coldness revived her somewhat although she felt deathly tired, her head ached again and the nausea returned.

Suddenly the full weight of what had occurred crashed down upon her and she was terrified. Slowly she allowed the towel to slip away. It fell into the sink unheeded as she lifted her head and stared in horror at the image of herself reflected in the mirror.

"I shall draw from thee and grow the stronger for it. All that thou art is mine, now and for evermore."

Day 10
Middleham

Margaret: *O Buckingham! take heed of yonder dog*
Look, when he fawns, he bites; and when he bites,
His venom tooth will rankle to the death;
Have not to do with him, beware of him;
Sin, death and hell have set their marks on him,
And all their ministers attend on him.

Shakespeare -
The Tragedy of King Richard the Third
[Act I, Scene 3]

Gail was surprised to find Laura still asleep when she came out of the bathroom after her shower. Usually Laura would growl good-naturedly about how all the noise Gail made was enough to wake the proverbial dead. She quickly dressed then prepared coffee, allowing the fumes to waft in Laura's direction but still she slept, on her side, facing the wall.

Suddenly fearful, Gail drew near then touched her. She was deathly cold. Laura moaned then gasped for breath, her fingers clawing at the sheets before she relaxed once more into sleep. Quickly Gail turned on the electric blanket, twisting the dial to medium-high.

"It's a virus." She laughed to herself nervously. "The bane of international travel, when germs and viruses stand poise to capture tourists unawares. Isn't that what Laura always said? Yes, I'm sure it is. She'll be fine. She just needs to rest, that's all." But even as she said the words, her heart grew tight within her, prompted by a fear she could not as yet comprehend. Slowly she backed away. Not knowing what else to do, she fled the room to organize a breakfast tray. When she returned, Laura was awake. "Hi! I ah . . . thought you might be hungry, so I . . . Are you all right?"

"Sure." Laura smiled thinly.

"Do you want me to call a doctor? There must be one here, somewhere."

"Why, whatever for? I feel great. A cup of coffee and I'll be fine." She reached for the cup Gail offered her and drank deeply, allowing the hot liquid to penetrate deep within, warming her.

"Laura, you might feel great, but you look terrible." Gail said matter-of-factly.

"Thank you Doctor Gail." Laura replied as she set the drink down and reached for her watch. "Wow, look at the time!" She leapt from her bed and padded quickly towards the bathroom. She was almost there before Gail caught her arm.

"I woke up last night just past midnight, but you were gone. What the hell's going on Laura?"

Their eyes met briefly before Laura pulled herself free and disappeared into the bathroom, closing the door behind her.

"Laura! Damn it, don't lock me out - please." Gail sobbed in anger and frustration as she pounded on the door. "Laura please, I know you're in danger and I want to help. Please, talk to me. I have to know what's happening. Please, you have to tell me the truth."

Gail backed away as the door slowly opened. Laura glared at her as she moved forward. In one quick motion she grabbed her arm and threw her on her bed. "So, it's truth you seek, is it?" She hissed, inches for Gail's ear, "then you shall have it."

She backed away from Gail then, breathing deeply as she fought to control herself. Gail cringed in fear. Suddenly Laura laughed, the sound hollow and brittle. "And truth shall set us free." She fell on the bed opposite Gail. "Well," she said smiling, "that's a truism if I've ever heard one."

She sobered then as she realized just how frightened Gail was. "I'm sorry." She said, her voice level as she tried to reassure Gail. "It's all my fault. I planned it all along you see, but never in my wildest dreams did I really believe I would succeed until … until I realized that he was there, so close Gail you wouldn't have believed it! The dinner, the night, the right combination of individuals. It all came together. The temptation was just too great - I had to try." Laura paused, breathing deeply. "Well, it seems that somehow I have managed to … to … God, how can I describe it, when I'm not sure myself." She leapt from the bed to wander around the room. "How can I stand here, in broad daylight, and tell you that I've managed to bring him from the spirit world into ours?"

Gail's eyes widened in disbelief. "Richard?"

Laura nodded then turned away. "Crazy, isn't it? Well, it may be crazy, but it's the truth and I'm scared to death. I can't see him, but he sure as hell can see me, right down to the colour of my eyes. He's wicked Gail, charming and cruel and I'm powerless to defend myself against him."

She moved away then to stand by the window, looking out at the beautiful courtyard, bathed in the morning light. "Life's not a game Gail. There are pits of hell on this earth so deep as to defy understanding. The dark side exists, whether we want to believe it or not and evil, like goodness, love, faith - thrives."

"What does he want?" Gail gasped.

Slowly Laura turned. "What he has always wanted – power."

"I knew it! God in heaven, how could you do such a thing? Damn it - damn you! What happened to you back in Bosworth - the cuts, the bruises. He did that, didn't he?" Laura turned away. "Answer me, damn it!"

"I think you should know something else."

"What?" Gail snapped, her voice tight with anger and fear.

"He seems to be focused on me and only when I'm alone. As far as I can tell he's unaware of you but I can't be sure. I get the vague feeling of another entity too. Something really nasty." She paused as tears welled up. "Forgive me Gail."

Gail rushed to comfort her and they held each other close.

"Laura, what are we going to do?"

Laura shrugged. "We're going to visit a castle and a church. Have some lunch, shop a bit maybe and try to carry on just the same as always. Beyond that, I haven't a clue." She bit at her lower lip. "You see," she whispered, her voice trembling, "I don't think it's my show anymore."

As they walked along the lane towards the castle arm and arm, Laura suddenly started to laugh. "So, here we are two thirty-something tourist ladies on our way to see one of the local attractions once owned by a man who lived over 500 years ago, and who I also spent some time with last night."

Gail stopped short, throwing Laura off balance. "Last night? You were with him last night?"

"He asked me to - well, more like ordered. I thought about sending a note of apology. You know - 'Dear Mr. Plantagenet: I regret that, due to a prior commitment ...' - something like that, but then I figured he probably wouldn't appreciate that very much and might just decide to come and collect me anyhow. Hey, don't look at me like that."

"How you can joke about it?" Gail was incredulous.

"Gail, it's my sense of humour that is about all that is sustaining me right now. That, and a very healthy hatred for this bastard. If I get the chance, I promise you, I'll send him straight back to hell where he belongs."

She sighed then turned and looked at the castle. "In the meantime, let's walk all over his front lawn, poke through his closets and strangle the first enthusiast who goes on and on about what a great guy he was."

Smiling, she hooked her arm through Gail's and together they proceeded up the incline towards the entrance way to Middleham Castle.

As they walked through the gatehouse, Laura took careful note of where the original wooden gates would have been and beyond, the portcullis. Within the courtyard which encircled the massive keep, was a small wooden building where they purchased their tickets. On the wall behind the counter was a large, framed print of the now familiar portrait. Laura caught the briefest glimpse before she turned away, uneasy.

Beneath a perspex dome was a replica of the 'Middleham Jewel', a 15th century pendant with a sapphire and an engraving of the Trinity on the front and the Nativity on the back. It was found near a footpath at the edge of the castle grounds in 1985, almost 500 years to the day after Richard III's death. Laura frowned as she stared down at it.

"It's beautiful, isn't it?" asked the woman who ran the shop. She stood, hands clasped in front of her, smiling not at Laura but down at the exquisite gold, lozenge-shaped piece. "The original is in the Yorkshire Museum if you want to go and see it."

"Is it worth a lot of money?" Gail asked.

"Oh my dear, some consider it priceless. It was almost lost to England when it was sold not long after it was found, but with the support of all sorts of people and organizations all around the world, it was purchased in time.

"For how much?"

"Gail," Laura cut in, "just read the info."

Quickly Gail scanned the card pinned to the side of the case. She looked up, surprise evident in every facet of her face. "Two and half million pounds!"

The woman's face lit up with pride. "It is impossible to know who the owner was of course, but it would have been a lady of substance. From the general style of it, experts believe that it dates from the third quarter of the fifteenth century, so it is possible that it might have belonged to Queen Anne. The sapphire was valued in medieval times not only for its beauty but it was believed that it protected the wearer from disease and helped promote peace and harmony. It would have been worn as a necklace, with the Trinity facing outwards and the Nativity in, nearest to the body of the wearer. The inscription reads 'Behold the Lamb of God who takest away the sins of the world' plus the phrase miserere nobis."

"Have mercy on us." Gail translated in a whisper.

"Yes," the woman allowed, "and the single word Tetragrammaton - the Hebrew word for God."

Laura swallowed hard. "How could something so precious be lost?"

She was standing just outside the hut with her hands on her hips when Gail joined her. "What a mess! I'm sure glad we saw Bolton because we're sure going to have to use our imagination on this lot."

"Ah, but I've bought a guidebook. Here's what it looked like in its prime, circa 1480."

Together they studied the aerial sketch. Between the various drawings, photographs, and the well written text, they did extremely well reconstructing in their minds what it might have looked like. Laura had already had a preview; one she would like to forget.

After a full circuit, and an easy climb up the spiral staircase to the top of the southeast tower, they settled down atop a small stone wall near the Princes Tower where, tradition says, Richard's son - Edward of Middleham - was born and subsequently died.

For a second or two Gail thought it was her grandmother. Certainly the elderly lady who took a seat not far from her was of the same vintage.

She smiled at Gail, then began to fan herself with her guidebook. "Getting too old for clambering around ruins." She said with a breathless chuckle. "Come on over here Dotti and have a wee rest." She called to another woman, much the same age, but it would appear, in a lot worse physical condition. Gail smiled pleasantly. Laura smelled Ricardians.

Gail turned towards Laura, who was watching Dotti intently as she negotiate the final few yards. "What do you think life was like here?"

"When he was at home, or away?" Laura asked with a malicious smile.

"Come on, in general."

"Like living in a sculptured cave with tapestries." Laura allowed as she sought a more comfortable perch.

"Oh, it was a wonderful life," the old lady cut in, waxing potentially poetic Laura thought, as she talked to no one in particular. "Beautiful, sweeping dresses; servants catering to your every whim; magnificent banquets. By King Richard's day, life had moved into a renaissance of culture and good living."

Which meant, Laura assumed, that they killed each other with da Vinci paintings since Leonardo and Richard were both born in the same year. She smiled politely. "I'm sure life was wonderful, if you were of the purple that is, otherwise I think things tended to be more in the shades of grey category."

"I agree," said Dotti, as she sat down with an audible sigh next to Gail. "Margaret here has been daft most of her life, poor thing. Quiet fancies herself the lady of the manor." Dotti huffed.

Margaret eyed her companion with contempt. "That's your problem Dotti, you haven't got one ounce of imagination. Too many years married to that worthless Fred and now that he's gone, you're quite incapable of finding an interest for yourself."

"Well, for your information, I've been reading the guidebook and before we left York, I purchased a book all about life in the Middle Ages, so there. For breakfast Richard and his wife, Anne and guests would have had lovely white bread, a bit of cheese and sliced meat, wine perhaps, while downstairs it was a hunk of horse bread and, if you were lucky, a slurp of ale. The downstairs crowd were then expected to work until the main meal at noon and even then it was leftovers from the lord's table, if you were lucky, and quick.

"The fireplaces smoked, the latrines stunk, the water was unfit to drink. Almost everyone was drunk half the time. A servant who made a mistake was beaten privately or taken before the lord of the manor in severe cases and God help him then. Marriages were arranged even within the lower classes and often by the lord who wished to secure some advantage. In winter, the windows were sealed to keep out the draft, so the rooms were dark and dreary, especially this far north. Oh, it was wonderful for the lords and ladies I dare say, but for the rest, it was drudgery.

"Well then, you would have fitted right in." Margaret huffed. "When King Richard was lord here, life was very pleasant. The windows were glassed, the fireplaces did not smoke, because they had elaborate hoods and louvred panels to let the smoke escape. Most of the squires and pages came from the new, wealthy merchant class so they were certainly not treated like glorified slaves. Richard was a kind and considerate man. A great lord who attracted loyal retainers from amongst his own, not like some, with their foreign mercenaries."

"You mean like King Henry VII?" Gail ask, innocently.

"Oh no, now you've done it my dear," Dotti whispered.

"King! Tudor was no king. Not a drop of English blood in him to speak of and a bastard, milksop coward to boot." Margaret's face grew florid as her blood pressure rose. "Tudor, with his Welsh cut-throats; his French whore-soldiers." She huffed in disgust.

"Honestly Margaret, why you get so upset about such things. It's quite beyond me, really it is." Dotti shook her head in disbelief.

"King Richard," Laura said, standing in profile as she viewed the ruins of the keep, "now, he was totally English, wasn't he? Does it make a difference do you think?"

"Absolutely," Margaret replied, "the Tudors introduced more

French blood, Spanish, and the Stuarts! What a disaster they were. Then later, Germans on the throne. Couldn't even speak English for heaven's sake."

It was a short walk down the hill from the castle to the Church of St. Mary and St. Alkelda. Laura and Gail skirted the cemetery, pausing only briefly to inspect a few of the more interesting tombstones. They entered the church through the 13th-Century porch which housed a stout pair of oaken doors. Old by any standard, the building was in an excellent state of repair, although yet again stripped of all its original magnificence. To their right, just inside the door, was the 'Richard III Window' dedicated to his memory in 1934 by the Richard III Society.

Laura barely glanced at it before moving across to the back of the nave to inspect a 14th-Century font, capped by a ten foot high 15th-Century Perpendicular canopy. To the right, set into the wall was another replica of the Middleham Jewel displayed with a mirror behind and a timed light, activated by a button. Slowly they both wandered up the north aisle where medieval grave covers were used as lintels above the three windows.

Gail fell behind slightly as Laura moved towards the Sanctuary to stand between the two sets of four choir stalls, beautifully carved. In setting up the College, King Richard named each stall after various saints; the names carved above each seat - St. George, St. Ninian, St. Anthony, St. Barbara, St. Cuthbert, St. Catherine, St. Margaret and the Virgin Mary.

Near to the chancel rail Gail noticed a Saxon knotwork stone set into the floor. Believed to be a portion of the tomb cover of Saint Alkelda, the patron saint of the church, Saxon remains were found during restoration work in 1878. As Laura began to make her way towards Gail, she stopped suddenly, turned full circle and frowned as she looked down the length of the nave.

"What's wrong?" Gail asked, perplexed and somewhat alarmed.

"Does anyone know for sure if Edward of Middleham is, in fact, buried in Sheriff Hutton?"

"I haven't a clue. Why, what are you thinking?"

"I'm thinking that the boy is here and he's not alone."

"Where?"

"I'm not sure yet but close, very close." Laura straightened as she caught a sense of something. "Gail," she said, her voice low and even, "promise me something."

"What?"

"If I tell you to get out of here in a hurry, promise me you will, no questions. Just get out - fast. Okay?"

Gail nodded, biting at her lower lip as she backed away from Laura. She was almost at the far end of the church when suddenly the great oaken doors flew open, pushed by a mighty gust of wind which bore earth, leaves and twigs in with it.

"Gail, get out - quick!" Laura screamed.

As if in anticipation, the doors slammed shut, sending a series of echoes through the church. Just beyond the entrance could be heard unearthly, maniacal laughter.

Paralysed with fear, Gail pressed close to the wall as she felt his presence - pure rage, cold and dreadful. She tried to scream but no sound came as her knees buckled under her and she slid down the wall.

Laura raced forward and stood squarely atop the spot where she had felt the child's presence. Turning around and around, she could see nothing although she knew he was close. "Gail, are you okay?" She shouted down the length of the nave then she caught her breath as he drew near to her and she realized the extent of his rage.

"Stand away!"

Laura breath came in jolting gasps but she stood her ground. "He's buried here, isn't he? Your son Edward is here, beneath this stone?"

"Stand away, I say!"

"No!" Laura shouted, angry and defiant though her voice trembled. "I must have the Truth!" She shut her eyes, too frightened to even imagine what he might do. She pulled the ragged fragments of her consciousness together in preparation for the onslaught, feeling his anger increase as he gazed upon her, contemplating her insolence.

"How dare you gainsay me. Thou art common. Yea, less than common. I call thee witch and harlot by thy dress. Thou knowest me but little madam if ye do think thyself safe in this place. Do as I command, or by Saint Paul, I shall strike thee dead."

Laura backed away towards the altar as if to claim sanctuary there, then realized in horror that she would have no refuge there or anywhere, not from this one. She had overplayed her hand and she, and Gail perhaps too, stood in mortal danger. "Forgive me," she gasped, dropping to her knees.

"Nay, 'tis not enough. Forgiveness, like Truth, is held in high esteem and dearly purchased. 'Tis fear that has set thee upon thy knees madam, not contrition. Now thou must beg both."

"Then humbly I beg forgiveness of thee for my effrontery." Laura hesitated, trying desperately to remain calm. "I am but a seeker after truth and mean no harm. Your son …"

"Is dead."

"I grieve for you in your loss."

"Do you madam?" He paused for a moment, as if considering. *"My beloved son, scarce half grown then tossed from this world to pay the ransom for his father's sins. In blood he died, so it is said. Thou knowest how he cried, seeking succour in his father's arms. So frail he was in death. Lips pale blue in imitation of his living eyes that once did shine in joyful, childlike innocence.*

"None shall have him. None shall gaze upon his face. Secretly he will lie, as were the others, where none shall know the place. So it was ordered, so it was done in the darkest time of night. A priest was brought to say the Latin but I trusted him not. Sly, ambitious, deceitful fool, I slew him here upon this place that he might be guardian to my son's tomb. My

sins were added to by not one whit more, for God had turned his face from me, taking my son, my hope, my life."

Laura felt his closeness, the raw cold chill of him as he whispered to her, his voice heavy with anger and malice. *"This Truth thou hast learned comes highly prized and for it, thou shalt pay the price. And for the other, thy companion shall reap a bitter harvest of pain for thy insolence."*

In sheer terror, Laura knees gave way and she sank to the floor.

The doors, shaken in their hinges, swung open with a dull, metallic groan before coming to rest against the stone wall.

Suddenly Gail screamed. Laura scrambled to her feet then leaned heavily against a stone pillar while she fought to regain her equilibrium. "Gail!" No reply.

Slowly, painfully, Laura clawed her way to the back of the church, moving from pillar to pillar to prevent herself from falling. Gail lay close to the wall, drawn into a foetal position. Laura sank to her knees beside her. "Oh please God. Gail, are you all right? Gail, please, it's okay now. He's gone - they've gone. I've …"

"It's wrong!" Gail stammered, her voice almost hysterical as she drew herself apart then reached out to clutch Laura's hand. "This is a church, his church. It can't happen … not here."

"I felt him Laura. He brushed by me so close I ... You've got to stop this! Make him go away."

They were seated in the Bear Garden at a wooden picnic table beneath a broad sun umbrella advertising a local beer. It all seemed so very normal.

"Make him go away? Go away where? Gail, you know as well as I do what we're dealing with here. For heaven's sake, please understand that. Look, it's only two o'clock. Plenty of time to get you a room in Masham or somewhere, well away from here."

"Me? What about you? I'm not going anywhere, not without you."

"Gail, I could be in very big trouble." She smiled tightly as she traced the pattern of the wood with a fingernail. "This is all my fault, so it's up to me to put things right. I don't want you anywhere near, just in case."

"Tell me what happened." Gail asked, trying to keep her voice even.

Laura told her, but left out the priest which, she reasoned, was an extra piece of information which would only serve to prove that Richard had, indeed, become homicidal following his son's death. As far as his threat regarding Gail, Laura was not prepared to even hint at any possible danger. Gail had enough to contend with without that.

"He specifically said that Edward was buried secretly 'as were the others', which can only mean the two Princes. He killed those kids Gail, goddamn it!" She smashed the table with the fist of her right hand. "Stay here, I'll be right back."

She hurried up to their room, returning moments later with a pad of paper and a pen. "Right, I'm going to write down everything I know and hopefully, I can decide upon some sort of plan of attack."

"Attack!"

"What is the saying? The best form of defence is a good offence." Laura headed up the page 'Strategic Offence - RIII'. She smiled. "Okay, what do I know for sure?

"One - he can see me clearly, certainly up to fifteen feet, maybe more. Two - he is capable of acquiring a physical presence but visually he is shrouded, indistinct. It may be too difficult to manage an apparition. Who knows, maybe it takes too much juice. Which brings us to three. Like a vampire ..." Laura started to laugh then in anger threw the pen against the stone wall. "Why don't I just have myself committed and save everyone the trouble."

"You're not crazy, Laura. I saw what happened. I felt the sudden cold, a sense of his presence. Come on, like a vampire ..."

Laura moved across and retrieved the pen. Her hand trembled

as she picked it up. "After being with him, when he's near, I feel … drained. It's like he's extracting my soul, taking what I am away. Intangible things like integrity, faith, moral values, personal pride. But, he isn't taking the knowledge, just the essence, the power in all of us which makes those things real, that make us human - kind and gentle, forgiving and understanding. He's converting it into something else, I'm sure, because God help me, I don't think he believes any of it anymore. Like Ian said, he's amoral. Incapable of any concept of morality and that is what I fear most. If allowed to continue, he will increase in strength and I will degenerate. It's happening already. You know what I mean? Do I usually throw you around like I did this morning? There's a displacement going on here and it has to stop. He didn't touch you, did he?"

"No." Gail replied flatly, although secretly she was unsure, aware only of a brief lapse of time when …

"Good, good." Laura sighed deeply as she fought to control a rising tide of panic. "Four - he seems centred on me which means that he is either totally unaware of your existence, which seems unlikely now or, I'm sorry Gail, he's keeping you back, watching you, evaluating you for future use. I know, I know, but we have to think that way. It's no good is it if I can deflect him away from me only to find him focused on you instead?

"I don't want to scare you but we have to face the fact that he has another with him. An entity to do his dirty work. Whatever it is, it's probably subservient which means it's incapable of independent action … I hope." Laura paused, breathing deeply, trying desperately to quell a rising sense of dread.

"Five - I'm convinced that there are two Richards, probably three. Middleham of all places offers us the best possible ground. This was his home for years when he was young. He was happy here. He met Anne and developed a strong love for her, of that I have no doubt. Later, he brought her here as his bride. His son was born here. Here is to be found the Ricardian Richard. The good lord, the man who endowed churches, brought law and good government to an unruly land and best of all, attracted the finest, who for love of him declared themselves loyal until death.

"But after his brother died, self-preservation, personal ambition, a lust for power, the lure of the crown, it all conspired to corrupted, and ultimately, corrupt absolutely. Then a new Richard was created and probably after the death of his son, yet another - cold, cruel and destructive - a paranoiac, psychotic murderer. This is the one we must deal with." Laura laughed thinly, then hugged Gail. "Other then that, everything's just fine."

Tears slowly trickled down Gail's cheek. "He'll kill you, I know he will."

Laura rocked Gail back and forth gently, her head resting on Laura's shoulder. "I don't think so because you see, he believes, I think, that if he kills me, he will cease to exist so he won't dare threaten the source of his new freedom. At least, that is, not until he knows for sure what my worth is." Laura voice hardened. "He needs me, I sure as hell don't need him which, if I'm not mistaken, puts me at a decided advantage."

"What are you going to do?"

"I still think I should get you away from here."

"No."

"Gail, this is my fight and besides, if something should happened to you, I would never forgive myself. You've got kids, remember? I'm expendable, you're not."

"Hey, it's women and children first, not women with children."

Laura smiled. "Okay." She rose, stretched then turned to admire the beautiful garden, the potted plants and the flowering shrubs. "There's one thing more which I think you should be aware of - Richard was the seventh son." She paused, biting at her lower lip. "It's all superstition perhaps but it was believed at one time that the sacred number seven endowed such an individual with extraordinary powers including 'second sight'. Wittingly or not, they attract a familiar - usually a dog." She smiled almost shyly.

"So my dear, we had better come up with something very good - and soon.

"An idea has occurred to me but it depends a great deal on how well he can hear and more importantly, understand me. I should take a crash course in Shakespeare and Chaucer." She sighed, trying not to let her anxiety show. "I've got to go to him again."

"No." Gail gasped.

"Gail, if I don't he will only come after me. I've incurred a debt for which he expects payment. I can't take the chance that you may be caught in the middle. I'm going to try to reason with him, talk to him if I can. As long as I can stay far enough away from him, then I stand a pretty good chance. I need a costume too."

"What kind of costume?"

"Something decidedly up-market 15th century. A dress suitable for a lady. Rich, not gaudy, for as Shakespeare said, 'clothes do 'oft proclaim the man', or woman in this case. I'm going to blow the socks off this bastard with something discrete, yet sexy."

"Explain to me just how you expect to keep him away from you in something 'discrete, yet sexy'?"

"That's just the point. He may feel more comfortable dealing with a woman dressed as a lady. If I show up in modern clothes, there'll be no rapport. I have to establish a common ground. If he thinks I'm a lady, he will be less likely to … It's just a good idea, that's all so come on, let's go find George."

It was ridiculously easy to find costumes amid the theatrical and re-enactment groups in the area. In fact, Laura had a choice of several, many in vibrant colours. In the end however, she chose a black dress not unlike the one she had seen at the museum in Bosworth.

The costume was excess to requirements according to Mrs. Shields who handled the wardrobe department. "I talked to the

Director, and she said that the Company would prefer it if you purchased it outright since, well, it's too small a size for most of the players, you see. Would sixty pounds be all right, with the headpiece too of course? It's not real velvet you understand and the fur is rabbit." Laura agreed readily. "Good, now try the cap on while I look for the jewellery designed for the dress. Not real jewels of course, but ... Now, where did I put it?"

Laura busied herself with the headpiece which fit a little too snug. Try as she might, her hair kept spilling out all around, spoiling the affect. A few minutes later Mrs. Shields returned having found what she was looking for.

"This should be worn tied around the waist like so." Before Laura had a chance to see properly, Mrs. Shields had the ornament in place. "Of course on the stage the cross would appear gold, the beads pearls I suppose."

The rosary hung from Laura's waist almost to the hem of the gown. Her heart leapt then grew tight within her.

By the time they arrived back at the hotel it was nearly dark. Laura reverently laid the gown across the bed. It was really quite lovely with its trim of fur along the neck line and the cuffs. It had fit her perfectly; accenting her bust line and slender waist.

"Are you sure this is a good idea?" Gail said, eyeing the costume from across the room, "black is the colour for widows. If he thinks you're unattached, what then?"

"It's not my marital status I'm trying to confirm Gail, it's my class. Now, how do I use this?" Laura asked, fingering the rosary.

Laura flipped to a fresh page, ignoring for the moment the glass of wine George had discreetly placed at her elbow. "The curse - King Henry's curse."

"What are you talking about?" Gail whispered.

"Before he was murdered King Henry cursed Richard to his face and the House of York. Oh, please God, what was it?

Something about Richard's son dying, as his son had died, crying for his father. Yes, that's right. Neither Richard nor Henry were present when their sons died. What else, what else?" Laura closed her eyes tightly, trying to remember while outside the last of the day dwindled away. "That's it! Henry prophesied a violent death for Richard and that his soul would remain earthbound where he died - Bosworth. But he's not at Bosworth now, he's here, so it's like the curse has run its course and ... and maybe all this was meant to be. Gail, I think that's it! Richard's soul has been in a sort of limbo for the last five hundred years. No wonder he's been acting like such a jerk. The poor guy has got to be very confused."

Gail sat bolt upright, her body rigid as she listened, her eyes wide in undisguised horror.

"Gail look, I've been thinking about what you said in the church. Nothing's changed. It's still a sacred repository of faith, I'm sure of it. We're dealing with a man who once lived and died tragically. His soul is still earthbound, caught between heaven and hell and we're caught with him in some inexplicable cosmic game."

Their meals arrived just then although Gail made no move to start. "Come on Gail, eat up. Even the gladiators ate a hardy meal before going into the arena. Just to please you, tonight I think I'll have dessert."

Gail gasped while tears welled up. She stared at Laura, then began to sob. Suddenly she pushed her chair back and ran from the room. Laura sighed and signalled for George, asking him to please keep Gail's plate warm. She sat quietly and watched as the last vestige of dusk faded into night, her own dinner barely touched.

Gail returned fifteen minutes later, slipped into her seat and began to make apologies but Laura cut her short. "Gail, I'm the one who should be doing all the apologising. I've had days in which to try to come to grips with all of this, you haven't. It's hit you all at once and I'm sorry. I wanted to keep you totally out of it but I'm glad I didn't because of what happened in the church."

A fresh steak was put in front of Gail by their host who smiled indulgently, assuming perhaps that the two had had a tiff. "What can I do to help?" Gail asked, her face a wreak.

"That's the spirit! Where's your copy of the Order of Service from Sutton Cheney?"

"In our room I think."

"Good, because I want you to read Richard's personal prayer aloud, over and over again while I'm gone. Don't stop, don't even hesitate. Okay?"

Gail nodded, took a deep breath and began to eat her steak. She avoided Laura's eyes, concentrating instead on her plate and its immediate surroundings while Laura watched her and mentally laid her plans.

Laura did join Gail in dessert - an apple pudding with daubs of rich Yorkshire cream. She had several cups of coffee too, to counter any affects of the wine. She needed to be ice cold sober and have every wit she owned in full working order. As fearful as she was, she was also excited by the challenge. She smiled just as Gail looked up.

"What's so funny?"

"Just me and my perverse sense of humour." Laura chuckled.

"What?"

"Well, I was just thinking. If he kills me how are you going to explain it to everyone back home? Promise me Gail, if anything happens, sue the Richard III Society." She started to laugh but quickly sobered as Gail's eyes once more clouded with tears.

"Damn!" Laura growled. "Gail, I'm going to have to cut my hair," she shouted from the bathroom. "I need your help."

"You're what?"

"Here, give me a hand. I think about an inch all along the hairline should do it. Cut it first, then I'll shave the rest." Gail looked at Laura in disbelief. "The headpiece won't fit. There's too much hair in the way."

Half an hour later Laura presented herself for inspection. "Well, how do I look?"

"Thin, pale and ..." The tears came. "Laura, I . . ."

"Gail please, I know what you're about to say and I don't want to hear it. I need your strength now. What is past is done with - over. There's no going back especially to what might have been. Have you got the prayer? Good." She kissed Gail quickly on the cheek then squeezed her hand. "Wish me luck."

The night embraced her in its fragrant warmth while above, stars danced with a moon already high. She turned right from the Bear Garden and down the lane towards the castle. From there she retraced her steps to the top of William's Hill. No one saw her - no one living that is.

Gail didn't go into the bar as she had promised. Instead, she changed into dark clothes, congratulating herself for including an oversized jersey-knit top with hood, black as jet. Gail too had been toying with a few ideas. Foremost in her mind was the knowledge that Laura needed her, that the spirit she had encountered was not only aware of her, but wary, afraid to come any closer than it had - thankfully.

Ignoring the 'Beware of Bull' sign hung on the first gate, Gail hurried across the open field heading for the eastern slope of William's Hill. Although easier to climb, she soon found herself engulfed in a small forest of stunted trees while an uneven terrain of gullies and mounds slowed her progress and thistles clawed at her in the dark.

Laura's entire body was alert for even a hint of wind in the still silence which surrounded her. As hard as she tried, no prayers would come, no divine inspiration and no peace from the terrible fear which sought to engulf her. Aware of her vulnerability, her mind began to search for him and the other but she could detect nothing, although …

He stood alone, just beyond the border of her consciousness, watching her.

"Thy manner is as counterfeit as thy dress madam tho', in truth, 'tis a pretty picture. Get up! 'Tis blasphemy for one such as thee to seek God's grace."

Slowly Laura rose while she carefully gathered the rosary into her hand before gently kissing the crucifix. "Good my lord, would a witch dare such a gesture? Would God in his infinite wisdom allow such misuse of this holy relic of Mother Church? Sir, I am not a witch nor have I done anything displeasing in the sight of God."

"Indeed, then thou art fortunate madam. Thou must think thyself a saint to be so blessed yet thy haughty nature matches not thy pretended sanctity. I shall ask of thee but once, to satisfy my knowing. What art thou?"

"I shall endeavour to . . . to please thee in my reply, my lord, but first, one question - where is the other?" Desperately she tried to keep her voice steady, her mind clear.

"My companion is sent to wait upon events. Thy mind is shrewd madam. Too shrewd methinks to live long within a breathing world. I say again, what art thou?"

"One who seeks to intervene on your behalf. Five hundred years and more you have been held a prisoner of King Henry's curse. It is finished. You are free now to seek redemption in the sight of God. Many love you, and would have it so."

"And do you love me and would you have it so?"

"Aye, my lord, tho' loving prayers for your salvation have long ere this been lost when you turned your face from God."

"He turned his face from me! Enough! Speak not to me of God's salvation for it is undeserved, as well you know. I shall tell thee of thy purpose, so mark me well. Thou art to me as a vessel from which I shall draw the strength I seek and with it knowledge which, like a beacon, shall light my way and illuminate the darkened corners of this my conscious state. For this thou were ordained, and I shall teach thee obedience."

"In that you are mistaken!" Laura retorted in a voice dappled with fear.

"*I think not.*"

Laura recoiled in horror but kept herself firmly in check. "If I am to be thy instrument of knowledge, know this. The other, thy companion, is not what him seems."

"*Francis is my friend, both in life and death madam. You do him wrong.*"

Laura's heart skipped a beat. "Francis Lovell, I knew it!" She mentally exclaimed. "My lord, in life he was never thy friend nor did he met his end at thy side as you would suppose. His passing is unrecorded as was Clifford, the one called 'Butcher', who murdered thy brother Edmund upon Wakefield Bridge. Evil has many names but one purpose. And now he awaits thee. Sent from Hell to bring you as a trophy to lay before his true Master. Your cruelty is his doing for he breathes evil in your ear and malice in your heart. But he is afraid, for in your awakening you did speak to me and opened your heart to the confession of your sins. In fear he will seek my destruction and your own."

"*You lie. Never friend was truer.*"

"Nor more feared. Know then that it was he who drove the priests from the field at Redemore, denying thee and all thy host, absolution. From thence thy hope was lost. Buckingham tried to warn thee of the evil but ye cast him out to die a traitor's death. Thy own sweet Bess …"

Her love for me turned to fear then loathing. She must not be lost to me."

"Closely then was she confined at Sheriff Hutton to prevent her escape?"

"*Yes.*"

"Child that she was she knew the extent of the evil that sought to rule thee and through thee, all of England. Please, my lord, there is not much time. If ye do not believe me then ask of him. No longer does he need to play the actor. The demon within will reveal its true self to thee, then ye shalt know the truth. Richard, please I . . ."

"*Richard! Thou wouldst dare to so presume!*" His voice was razor sharp, the tone heavy with malice. Laura screamed as he drew closer to her, drawing a net of blackness cold as death about her. "*Be silent!*" he whispered urgently, "*thy companion stands in peril. Yet, unless I do mistaken it, this device shall bring him swiftly to my side.*"

Desperate to help, Gail began to move from her hiding place but was stopped cold by a sound like a hissing snake. As she turned she was confronted by the image of a man dressed in partial armour. He smiled at her hungrily, his black eyes flashing as he drew closer. Gail knew without a doubt that she was face to face with a demon.

Laura tried to scream again as the coldness bit into her flesh, bearing down on her as he prepared to draw from her the last of all her being. She felt herself sinking, falling into unconsciousness, dying. With the last of her strength she cried, "Slayer of women, most cursed of God's creatures."

Instantly he drew back, releasing her. "*Well played madam. Now, come to me thou treacherous fiend.*"

Inches away from Gail the demon turned suddenly, aware that his plans had been interrupted.

"Murder the witch my lord."

Vaguely Laura saw a flash of armour, the sound of metal against metal as the companion moved closer. She forced her mind to focus, but he drew back from her, suddenly wary, though she sensed a dreadful evil. "Nell, please, I need you," she pleaded. "He needs you."

"I have the other near to hand, my lord. Both must die."

"*By what judgement?*"

"They know too much."

"*Hast that become a crime in our realm, Francis? Would you council me now to murder truth? Get back from her for I know what thou art.*"

Fiend, hell spawn slave of Satan. No more will I listen to thee. Get thee gone."

The demon barked like a dog then angrily replied. "The bitch speaks true Plantagenet, for thy soul hangs by a thread above my Master's gaping jaws and I will deliver thee. Too long has he waited for that which does belong to him. He goes impatient. For the Other, there is no hope for thee, for He must hear thy full confession and that thou wilt not do for thee alone must bear the guilt for those young souls so casually tossed to me. Thy brother's sons. Destroyer of children thou art, thy soul damned."

"No — "

The demon moved closer and tried to touch Laura but found his way blocked. He laughed wickedly as he drew back. "I will have her and the companion both, in good time. Splendid prizes aye, but this one I shall pin like a butterfly to grace the abyss which has long awaited thee."

"I ask Thee, O Most gentle Christ Jesus, to keep me and to defend me from all evil and from my evil enemy, and from all danger, present, past, and to come . . . "

"Pretty words sown upon rock for thy God hears them not. He has turned his love from thee and this mortal here cannot change what must be. Long hast thy soul been forfeit as well thou knowest. Murder her now and thy true Lord and Master will smile the more in the taking of this gift at thy hand, as he has the others."

"NO!" Laura cried, marshalling a strength which was more than her own. Gail gasped as an aura of fine white light appeared to emanate from Laura. "You lie, foul beast that thou art, for God's love and forgiveness is eternal. He has not forgotten, nor is he unaware of the struggle, for many there are who do love this man still and will see him safely delivered. Get thee gone evil toad of perdition, for this one thou shalt not have."

Laura fixed the demon with raging eyes then watched in horror as it twisted and bent in upon itself, turning from a manlike image into its true shape, a dog but more serpent then dog, with fanglike teeth sharp as razors, hair and scales combined. It hissed and snarled as it backed away from her. Then it was gone in an explosion of wind which tore at the earth.

Gail drew back in terror as the trees above her bent and moaned, lashing her with their branches. Then all fell silent.

"Gail!" Laura screamed.

"She is well and has but swooned. But what of thee lady? Have I done thee harm?"

But Laura did not hear nor could she answer. Weaken to the point of death, she lost hold of her conscious self and dropped like a stricken bird to the ground while her gown billowed out around her, cushioning her fall.

Gail lay motionless, half submerged beneath a ancient dog rose, its gnarled and blackened branches ladened with small white blooms which seemed to dance, dreamlike all around her. The moon, pale as death, rode the cloudless night sky, shamming the stars into insignificance. For a moment she thought she was dead. Then she began to tremble as the image of the demon rose in her mind. Terror seized her yet again and she scream. "Laura!" Silence.

Painfully she eased herself free of the bush which sought to contain her before slowly making her way across the open amphitheatre, carefully skirting the spot where the demon had stood. "Laura!" She cried, but all remained silent. Then she saw her, silhouetted against the night sky on the apex of the hill, bent forward on her knees, motionless.

"Laura?" Gail whispered tenderly. "It's okay, I'm here." When Gail touched her however, her hand came away slick with blood. "Oh my God, what has he done to you?"

Gently Gail eased Laura backwards, cradling her head in her lap. She used the hem of her top to stanch the flow of blood from Laura's nose as she slowly rocked her back and forth.

Gradually Laura could feel her strength returning and after a few minutes, when the bleeding had subsided, they made their way back.   Several times Laura collapsed but each time Gail was able to rouse her, forcing her at the end by sheer willpower to complete the course.

She lay as still as death while Gail used a wet cloth to gently wipe away the blood from her face, neck and chest. Holding her hand then, Gail could feel the warmth returning although Laura remained in a state of shock, unable to speak. Gradually she shut her eyes, while Gail sat and watched her safely into a dreamless sleep.

Day 11
Middleham - Jervaulx Abbey - York

Duke of York:

> *Open Thy gate of mercy, gracious God!*
> *My soul flies through these wounds to seek out Thee.*

(Dies)
Queen Margaret:

> *Off with his head, and set it on York gates:*
> *So York may overlook the town of York.*

Shakespeare -
The Third Part of King Henry VI
[Act I, Scene 4]

You shouldn't have gone up there Gail. Damn it, I told you to … "

"Don't you tell me what I should have done. If I hadn't been there you could have bled to death. Look at you! I've never seen you so thin. You're pale as a ghost. You can't even hold a glass without your hand shaking." Gail's voice broke as the tears came. "He's sucking the life right out of you. Can't you see that? Look, I think we should head straight back to London right now. Maybe catch an earlier flight home."

"No!" Laura shot back. "I don't know how much you heard or saw, but believe me, this isn't finished. Damn it Gail, I never wanted you involved in the first place. You go back to London. Get the hell out of here but I'm staying to see this through. Now, get me Rachael's phone number."

Gail watched from the window as Laura tried the number several times. "Come on Rachael, get off the phone," she growled before finally giving up in disgust. "I'll try again from York. Hopefully she can meet me in Fotheringhay."

"I'm coming with you." Gail announced with conviction.

"No you're not. You're getting on transportation south - bus, plane, train - whatever."

"I'm not leaving you Laura, at least not until ... if Rachael can help then . . ." She caught her breath. "Richard was born in Fotheringhay wasn't he?" Gail asked in sudden alarm. Laura nodded. "Your birthday and his birthplace. Laura, I don't think this is a good idea."

Laura smiled thinly. "It's said that those born on the stroke of midnight are doomed to die then too and neither heaven nor hell will claim the soul in that brief hush of time while the clock strikes the hour. It will be my thirty-third birthday; one he never achieved."

"Bull shit!" Gail exploded. "That's one of your grandmother's old country superstitions. Not for a moment will I believe that your soul might be in peril so stop this nonsense right now! If he goes to hell or to heaven, it will be at his choosing, not yours. The time, not even the place matters. He should have gone to hell five hundred years ago. You know it, I know it and I bet you a month of lunches, he knows it too."

She grabbed Laura by the arm. "Now, you listen to me. If I ever thought for a moment that you would yield your soul up in his stead and damn it I know you and that's just what you're thinking, I'd rather have left you to bleed to death. He deserves to go to hell, do you hear me? To use your words, he is cruel and amoral. Let the Devil have him unless he makes an effort to reach to God."

Laura nodded then turned away, her face a tragic mask. "God in heaven, Laura! After what he's put you though? Send the bastard to hell and that . . . that monster with him."

Laura jumped up from her bed, nearly colliding with Gail as she stormed into the bathroom, slamming the door behind her. As she looked into the mirror, her eyes clouded with tears. Yes she understood, but it didn't make what might be any easier.

Together they walked to the breakfast room, neither saying a word. Laura played with her food much to Gail's distress. "I'm driving to York." She announced flatly.

Laura merely nodded her head while pushing her poached egg from place to place on her plate. "I want to stop at Jervaulx Abbey, if you don't mind. I read somewhere that White Surrey was born and bred there," she paused, biting at her lower lip, "and I think it would be a good place to talk."

"All right." Gail whispered as she slipped her hand atop Laura's.

They paid their bill, packed and were on their way by eleven. The car offered Gail some excellent challenges, all of which she was eventually able to surmount. Laura seemed unconcerned, ignoring the occasional gear grinds, high RPM's, and second would be better than fourth opportunities. Gail was upset and it had nothing to do with the car's performance.

"I'm all right now Gail, really."

"Yeah, you're just as normal as blueberry pie. Do you want to talk about it now?"

"No, let's wait until we're inside the Abbey where it's, ah …"

"Safe?" Gail suggested. Laura just nodded her head then turned away. "Is anywhere 'safe' any more Laura?"

If she heard her she didn't acknowledge and Gail decided to let it go - for now.

Jervaulx Abbey dates back to 1156. It was a Cistercian Abbey, an order of monks whose rule prescribed strict silence, hard work, study and of course prayer. They ate frugally, shunning such foods as meat, eggs and cheese. At its zenith of wealth and prestige, the

Abbey owned half of the valley of the Ure. It is reasonable to assume that they bred horses.

Severely mutilated during the Dissolution, much of the stone was carried away for the construction of local buildings although enough of the structures which once made up this massive religious complex still exist, standing in a pleasant park-like setting just five miles from Middleham. Gail parked in the area provided and together they crossed the road, through a gate and across the fields, criss-crossed now with footpaths, dotted with giant oaks.

"It's amazing!" Laura said, shaking her head.

"What?"

"Well, this whole area of the country in the 12th Century was wild, uncharted land and yet, well, look at the size of this place. Life must have been very difficult; their faith absolute. The monks here lived a fraction of our life span yet they gave all they had and would ever have - their lives - to God. I feel ashamed that we have absolutely no comparison in our time."

A metal honesty box was screwed into a weathered table just inside the enclosure gate which marked the precincts of the Abbey itself. Beside it, beneath a wooden canopy was an assortment of information sheets, pamphlets, guidebooks and postcards depicting a portion of the ruins - all available for sale. Laura casually ran her finger tips across the surface of a stone slab nearby.

"What's that?" Gail asked.

"It was used for embalming. See the cutaway portion of the lip where the body fluids would be allowed to drain away. Couldn't have been used very much though. Only Abbots were embalmed."

"You're a real repository of little known facts, aren't you? Here, I bought you a guidebook - get busy."

Laura flipped through the pages quickly. "Listen to this." Laura said, guidebook raised. "The nave, just the nave, was 162 feet long and 63 feet wide including the aisles and was divided into ten bays - that's huge."

They began their tour by walking through the ruins of what

was once the Lay Brothers Frater or dining hall with dormer above. "Lay brothers weren't monks though were they?" Gail asked.

"No, they did most of the manual labour and took care of the external affairs of the Abbey. They enjoyed the same social status as monks but they didn't take monastic vows - including the rule of silence. Most were illiterate I guess, so they were probably excluded from any important decision-making within the community. They couldn't have been married since women weren't allowed or, if they did have a wife and family, they'd need the abbot's permission to leave."

"Not much of a life."

"With war, pestilence, disease, lawlessness and savagery just beyond the wall, a place like this must have been a welcome haven. An oasis of peace and security. For many, it would have appealed. Evil wasn't welcomed here." She whispered, her voice tight with emotion.

Nothing remains now of the Abbey church itself, except for the foundations and a few stone tomb-covers set flush in the earth, too weathered now to read. The length of the structure was astounding. While Gail wandered around, Laura walked briskly towards the high altar. She stopped just short of the sanctuary steps, reduced through time to nothing more than a vague pattern in the earth, leading to a raised field of grass. A gentle breeze played with her hair, tickling her neck, while the sun, high now in a pale blue, cloudless sky, cast a tight shadow about her feet. Gradually she sunk to her knees in prayer.

Gail watched, a bouquet of wild roses clutched to her breast. "Miserere nobis." She whispered.

Gail waited in the Chapter House which stood just beyond the south transept of the church. Here the monks met daily for chapter and notices of the dead, followed by confession of monastic offences and the acceptance of discipline. Stone seats ringed the perimeter which measured forty-eight feet long by thirty-six feet wide, divided into three aisles by two rows of three columns, five of which still remain. The Abbot sat in the middle of the east side and so too did Gail, keeping silent company with four abbots whose tomb-covers lay side by side at her feet. Set six steps below the level of the Cloister just beyond, Gail found this portion of the Abbey extremely attractive perhaps because it is still substantially intact, the walls perfect to the height of the springing of the vaulting.

Gail's thoughts were interrupted as Laura poked her head through one of the arched windows at the far end. "There you are."

"Come here, I think you'll like this place."

Laura disappeared momentarily then reappeared at the top of the stairs. They were typically narrow, so she took care as she descended. Gail made room for her. They sat quietly for a few minutes, savouring the tranquillity around them, the sense of peace that was assumed, measured, constant. "How did you know it was Francis Lovell?" Gail asked in a half whisper.

"I didn't, although I suppose that's not quite true. I felt something at Minister Lovell. Something vague, but there nevertheless. It wasn't just a feeling either, it was a peculiar smell like nothing I've ever encountered before. I smelt it again when we left the church at Middleham. I don't think Richard has any physical power so it must have been the demon that smashed open the doors. He left his calling card." She smiled thinly. "Gail, what did you mean when you said that Richard would have to reach to God, yet it seems the Devil in near to hand?"

Gail shrugged. "Perhaps the truth lies in the way of mankind. Always it seems, that which is easily achieved is held in low esteem. Who knows, maybe God feels the same way. Doesn't it say in the Bible somewhere that the way to heaven is a torturous path where the faithful are tested, yet the road to hell is broad, a pleasant run ever downwards into Satan's maw?"

"I've never heard you talk like this before."

"I guess we've never needed to think about religion much. We live in our cosy homes, we have our health, the bank accounts are sufficiently swollen, the cars paid for." She shrugged. "We don't need God. We live in an artificial world in which we believe we have power over our existence, our future. Science has replaced God or so it seems to a large portion of mankind. Sublime indifference, that's us. So typical of our age, we ignore God while the Devil dances.

"Richard, on the other hand, knew better. In his time, belief in God, the Devil, heaven and hell, was as much a part of life as eating and drinking. For him to turn away, to allow evil in when he bore the devices of sovereignty, vowing to uphold the kingdom of God on earth, well frankly, I don't fancy his chances right now. God does not offer salvation on a platter, for he is the Master, not the servant."

"But, there is hope?".

"Hope? Ah yes, Pandora's box, opened in disobedience to release upon mankind all the ills of the world leaving only Hope within. A gift from the true God cloaked in Greek mythology." Gail smiled tightly. "You better have something more than hope in your arsenal."

"The prayers of so many for Richard's soul. What of them?"

"A mummer in a howling storm."

Laura turned away, tears forming across her vision. "Still, we must try."

"Yes," Gail murmured, "we'll try. Come on, we better get going."

"Just one thing." Laura said as she looked up at Gail. "Why can't I see him?"

"Oh Laura." Gail sighed as she sat down again. "It may be that he doesn't want you to."

"What do you mean?"

"No one knows for sure of course, but it is generally believed that when someone dies, the spirit, ghost, whatever you want to call it, bears the marks of their death up to the moment of quietus, just as Christ bore the stigmata. Laura," Gail paused as she looked at her, "he could be one hell of a mess. You know that, don't you?"

Laura nodded then turned away.

Silently they returned to the car. Gail slipped deftly behind the wheel while Laura eased the passenger seat as far back as it would go. "We'll never be the same people again, will we? Not after this." Laura whispered as she settled into her seat. "Oh Gail, I'm so tired and ... and I'm so very, very sorry." Tears coursed down her cheek.

Gail patted her hand. "Sleep." She demanded. And Laura did, fitfully and dream-possessed all the way to the very walls of York. Gail concentrated on her driving, while fear mounted within her.

Gail turned right off Blossom Street and brought the car to a halt beside a parking lot. "Where are we?" Laura said as she sat bolt upright.

"In York I guess, but I haven't a clue where the hotel is. You'll have to do the rest. I'm lost."

They changed places. Laura readjusted the mirrors and Gail the passenger seat then together they studied the road atlas map of York. "Our hotel is here, right next to the Minster so, if we can make our way around to Botham Bar here, we should be right. All this part," Laura indicated the centre of the walled portion of the city, "is probably closed to cars. If I can find the railway station then I can get my bearings. We'll cross the river at Lendel Bridge, here."

Laura turned the car around, stopped at the edge of Blossom Street and waited for a break in the traffic. Turning to the right to monitor the flow in that direction, she gasped, lost the clutch and stalled the car. "Micklegate!"

"What?"

"It's Micklegate Bar."

"Good, so you know where we are. Where's the hotel from here?"

"It was atop Micklegate that Margaret of Anjou displayed the heads of Richard's father, brother, uncle." Laura quickly restarted the car, backed it up to the entrance to the parking area and drove in. "I want to have a closer look."

The walls and gates, called Bars, are substantially the same as they were in medieval times. Built mainly of magnesium limestone quarried from Tadcaster, the walls stand fifteen to twenty-five feet in height and are built atop the original earthworks. The walls appear almost stark white in the sun. There are four main gates: Micklegate, the premier bar which guards the approaches from the south; Bootham, the northwest; Monk Bar, the northeast and Walmgate, the east.

As the second city of England, Micklegate bore the brunt of the medieval practice of displaying the spiked heads of traitors. Perhaps the most famous was Richard, Duke of York, his bloodied head, it is said, decorated with a paper crown.

Traffic moved slowly beneath the central arch so it was necessary for Laura to view the famous gateway from the side. Gail remained silent as she followed Laura through to the other side and up a flight of stone steps to a museum housed within the towered gate. They were greeted by a jovial fellow seated at a counter, surrounded by a wide assortment of souvenirs, maps, postcards, books. Laura smiled thinly then turned away to survey the interior. Immediately her eyes fell upon a life-size wax image of a head impaled upon a spike. Imitation blood and gore plastered the model while its lifeless eyes stared out beneath half-closed lids. Laura had guessed even before she read the sign below - *Richard, Duke of York*.

"This is in questionable taste sir," she growled, turning to the proprietor.

"Ah well, it's the tourists you see. They like that sort of thing but I can see that it has upset your sensibilities, and I do apologise." He turned his head slightly to one side, studying Laura. "Most Ricardians do find it offensive." He smiled knowingly.

"I'll keep that in mind should I ever meet one!" Laura snapped back, smiling wickedly. "The likeness is wrong in any case. Your poor waxen fellow here is more representative of the Earl of Devon after Towton, then York, murdered by treason on Wakefield Green. It would do well to change the name." Laura stormed from the room. Gail was in shock.

"Takes all kinds," he muttered, shaking his head. "If your friend is so bloody keen on the House of York, take her to see the Richard III museum at Monk Bar if you haven't been there already. She can get into that lot, boots and all." He laughed spuriously.

Gail purchased a booklet entitled 'Haunted York' as well as a few postcards and a detailed map of the city before hurrying from the shop.

"How could you be so damn rude!" Gail demanded, facing Laura straight on.

"I wasn't rude, he was and his wax monstrosity! Come on, let's go and find the hotel."

Without waiting for Gail's reply Laura turned and retraced her steps back to the car. Gail navigated, using the small 'pop out' map she had purchased at Micklegate. Laura drove in silence, her face stern, her grip on the wheel of the car tight and unyielding. Within minutes they were easing their way into a vacant slot outside the Dean Court Hotel just across the square from the impressive west facing entrance to York Minster.

Knowing that the car would be taken from them and stored heaven knows were, Gail busied herself sorting through her luggage while Laura leaned against the side of the car studying this most beautiful of medieval cathedrals. Gail slammed the boot shut. "Right."

"I'm starved!" Laura announced. "How about we check in

then go and find somewhere to eat on our way to Monk Bar."

"I don't think you should go to Monk Bar." Gail replied, suddenly uneasy. "I agree about lunch, a walk around but then I want you to have a rest before the Cathedral. I'll go if you want. I'll tell you all about it but you're not going and that's final."

Laura eyed Gail for a moment then relented. "You're right, it probably wouldn't be a good idea."

"No, it would not." Gail mumbled.

Their room was pleasant enough, with high ceilings and decorative wallpaper in vague pastels. The window offered a magnificent view of the Minster to the left. The hotel itself was another warren of additions, annexes and dislocated extensions. They got lost trying to find the elevator so they took the stairs instead.

Laura was so weary that she had to force herself to show even the vaguest interest in what was around her. Gail took the lead, map unfolded around the Cathedral to College Street where she found a small bistro with tables sent beneath young maple trees.

An advertisement for cappuccino caught Laura's attention. She smiled almost shyly. "Do you know what I feel like? A peanut butter and strawberry jam sandwich." She laughed lightly as she tried to lit a cigarette with trembling hands. Gail watched her briefly before quickly looking away.

"See what I can do."

Laura watched indifferently as a vast assortment of tourists passed by in every direction. Her mind, normally alert, refused to process the myriad bits of information presented to it. She sighed, closed her eyes and if it wasn't for Gail, she may well have drifted off into a deep and potentially dangerous, sleep.

"I bet your blood sugar level is off the scale. Here drink this, then the coffee." Gail pushed a plastic container of pure, fresh squeezed orange juice at Laura.

"Gosh Gail, you're just like a sister to me."

"I am your sister, nut case. Now, drink it!"

"You're also a bully and I love you. I haven't thanked you for last night."

"Last night seems an eternity ago. Sitting here in broad day light, it's as if it were all a horrible dream - a nightmare." Laura nodded.

She got her sandwich, inch-thick French bread slathered with whole berry jam and a fair measure of peanut butter too. As she ate, the filling oozed out, much to her delight. For a moment Gail saw the child that was once Laura then realized sadly that no matter what happened, neither of them would ever be the same again. Laura's face was pale, wasted and lined with care and when she did smile now, it was quick and although it still lit her face brilliantly, it lacked its usual warmth and generosity of spirit. What had she said about displacement?

"Feel better now?"

"I can't finish this." Laura dropped the remainder of the sandwich onto the plate then pushed the plate away. She lifted the cappuccino cup up in both hands ignoring the handle, her fingers spread wide, delicate and pale against the whiteness of the china. Gail realized with a shock that Laura's skin was almost translucent, as if she were fading. She must be made to rest.

"'Haunted York.'" Laura said as she pulled the booklet from the side pocket of Gail's bag.

"Never mind that. You promised to rest and its nearly three."

"No, I will read this and you will get for me another of these." Laura ordered, looking briefly at Gail before returning to the booklet. Gail went back into the restaurant and ordered another cappuccino. She was badly shaken by Laura's rapid mood changes, so uncharacteristic of her. She could only pray that Rachael would be able to meet them in Fotheringhay. When she returned, coffee in hand, Laura had finished reading.

"Find anything of interest?"

Laura shrugged. "York is full of ghosts from spectral dogs

to Roman troops to victims of duels at dawn and phantom cavaliers. Just over there for instance, the cottage at number five? During the plague - it didn't say which visitation - the cottage was sealed shut to contain the infection, locking in a whole family. Everyone in the house died except a little girl who survived the disease only to die of starvation before the quarantine was lifted. Her ghost haunts the top floor and is said to cry piteously."

"Rachael Ward-Thomas."

"Rachael, it's Gail."

"Hi, where are you?"

"In York."

"Super place, lots of history. Have you been to the cathedral yet?"

"Ah … no, not yet. We only arrived a short while ago. We ah … came over from Middleham this morning, and ah … well … "

"Gail, are you all right? Is Laura with you?"

"Yes, she's here. Maybe you should talk to her. Rachael, we need your help. We've gotten ourselves into a real … Well, maybe you should talk to Laura." Gail handed Laura the phone, then backed away.

"Rachael?"

"Hi, what's going on?"

"It's kind of hard to explain, especially over the phone. Can you join us in Fotheringhay tomorrow? It's very important that you do, I think."

"Fotheringhay? Sure, I guess so. Stephen is … well, he's still out of town and I'm sort of between things right now. Have you made reservations?"

"Not yet."

"Trouble is, Fotheringhay is really small. Look, give me your number there. I've got a friend who runs a B&B right next to the ruins of the castle. I'll give her a call, and fingers crossed, she can fit us in for what, one night?"

"One night? Yes, I think that's all we'll need." Laura gave her the hotel's phone number, all the while watching Gail as she paced the room like a caged animal.

"Great, okay. I'll call you right back. Bye for now."

"Thanks Rachael."

Ten minutes later the phone rang. Laura picked it up.

"Talk about good luck. She just got a cancellation so the Coal Room is ours."

"Coal Room?"

Rachael laughed. "It's an old farm house. They renovated a whole wing, turning the coal room and the old apple store upstairs into accommodation. Did a great job. It's a proper working farm too, of course, right next to the site of the castle where Richard was born. Nothing left of it I'm afraid which is a shame since, as you know, Mary Queen of Scots was executed there. Anyhow, you can't miss it. It's right on the corner, just past the pub and the church if you're coming from the north. When do you think you'll get there?"

"I'm not quite sure."

"It looks a long way but believe me, if you get on the M1, you can drop like a stone right through the middle of the country. Are you planning to see Towton on the way?"

"Hadn't thought about it."

"Wrong time of year because the fields will be planted but worth a stop I think, especially since it's so close to York. It's not everyday you can walk the site of a battle in which 28,000 men died. A bit gruesome perhaps. Burial mounds all over the place."

"I don't know Rachael, I think we've had enough of the horrific lately."

"Oh." Rachael said softly. "Jeez Laura, you're sending chills up and down my spine."

Laura laughed lightly. "Rachael, by the time we've finished with you, you'll be lucky if your hair doesn't turn white."

"Interesting!" Rachael exclaimed, more fascinated then alarmed. "Tell me though, has all this got something to do with Richard?"

"Yes Rachael, it has a lot to do with Richard." Laura replied in a whisper.

The phone seemed to go dead for a moment. "See you both tomorrow."

"See you then. Drive carefully and Rachael? - thanks."

Laura lowered the phone and turned to Gail. "She's coming."

"I just hope we aren't making a mistake, inviting her in on this mess."

"Yes." Laura replied sadly as she moved towards the window to admire the view. "But I think we need her, although …" Laura paused as her eyes fell on the massive cathedral. "I've got to go."

"Hey, I thought you were going to rest?"

"That was your idea, not mine. Are you going to the museum?"

"Yes, I'll go there while you are in the church."

"Good. I'll be interested in hearing all about it." Laura said as she gathered up her purse.

"Yes, I bet you will." Gail shot back.

Laura glanced at her briefly then dismissed the comment.

They split up in front of the west entrance to The Minster. Gail retraced her steps back towards the bistro then continued down Deangate to Monk Bar.

Laura stood in front of the imposing west-facing doors, suddenly very afraid. Breathing deeply, she fought to control herself, to calm her fears and a rising sense of panic as she slowly, reverently entered the Cathedral. It was dark and cool inside.

She hurried along the length of the nave the sound of her footsteps barely registering in the deep silence which surrounded her. At the junction of the north and south transepts, in the very heart of the cathedral, stood the statues of fifteen kings - from

William I to Henry VI - carved in stone. She stopped and stared fixedly at the last before turning away.

Briefly she paused at the high altar as if considering before continuing on to the most eastern end of the cathedral to stand before the massive east window. The largest medieval stained glass in a single window to be found anywhere in the world.

She dropped a coin into a small wooden box, then took a candle, lit it from another, and placed it in the black wrought iron holder. A symbol of mankind's hope, she watched it burn brightly. Then she knelt on the floor of the Lady Chapel, ignoring the cushions provided. In a whisper she spoke the 8th Century prayer of Alcuin of York.

Eternal light, shine in our hearts,
Eternal goodness, deliver us from evil,
Eternal power, be our support,
Eternal wisdom scatter the darkness of ignorance,
Eternal pity, have mercy on us,
That with all our heart and mind and soul and strength we may seek thy face,
And be brought by thine infinite mercy to thy holy presence.
- Amen -

"Amen"

She could not see him but he was near to her. In the quiet sanctity of the church, she sought to measure him, to get a sense of him but each time he drew back, turning her mind, deflecting her from her purpose. He was wary.

"Can you see the window Sire?" She asked nervously.

"Aye madam, in my remembrances."

"The writings of God portrayed scene after scene, the suffering of man. So it must be 'til the end of recorded time."

"Why?"

"To atone perhaps for our disobedience in the garden of our beginning. Our first sin and then the next. In the first row see, the second - Cain kills Abel."

"That hast been spoken of. I will not indulge thee. Choose another. Not of man's suffering, but of love and fealty. A speck of coloured glass that speaks of the immortality of a king, his crown and of the love he bore his country, its laws, its customs."

"'Tis written elsewhere Sire and read by more than could ever hope to see this window."

"Why do you weep?"

"The words of man - 'tis not enough to see thee safely home."

"Home! A word as foreign on my tongue as loyalty and trust. Words sent to bend our minds and break our hearts. There is no home, loyalty is fled and trust in a word that fools employ. I will have none of it. Thou knowest why I have come?"

"Yes my lord through it grieves my heart."

"Still, in this brief measure of time yet left me, thou shalt yield to me the sum of all thy knowledge. Leave all within. Spare naught from me in the telling for much has been rendered me beforetimes. Now madam, what of my son John?"

Laura steeled herself as best she could. "Betrayed Sire by Lovell, both Tyrell and your son were confined within the Tower. Tyrell escaped his fate for a time, but your son and your brother's son both died upon Tower Hill.

"A traitor's death?"

"By the axe my lord, as Tudor, of late called Henry the Seventh ordered. The House of York was to be extinguished." She could feel the anger in him grow.

"And what of Lincoln?"

"Long did he defy the new regime 'til he was deceived into open conflict at the Battle of Stoke. He died, fighting bravely to the end, 'though his troops were greatly outnumbered. Lovell escaped the carnage yet again only to disappear from all known records of the time." Suddenly fearful, Laura caught her breath then shivered involuntarily.

"Calm thyself madam. Lovell sits even now within my mind's eye. I will be avenged. Leave him to me. There are other matters more pressing.

Attend. On the eve of battle a child was brought me. Long did I reject the claim that this boy was my bastard son, 'though when I looked into his face and saw the image of my father there, I knew he was mine own."

"The mother named him Richard."

"Aye, then you know of him."

"Only of the possibility of such a child. I know but little and what there is speaks more of legend then truth. The child was born within the bounds of thy marriage to Anne?"

"'Tis of no consequence to thee." He snapped, his voice chill.

Taken back, Laura answered. "He lived a full life, so it is recorded. He was called Richard of Eastwell, 'though it is said that he lies buried beneath the name Plantagenet. Of children, I know naught." She felt him turn from her. A dark cloud suddenly dulled the radiance of the window. She shivered again. "My lord?"

"Was she happy?"

Laura knew instantly of whom he spoke yet she hesitated, considering her reply carefully. "No Sire, she was not. He kept her closely confined, jealous perhaps of the love that the commons bore her, but never him. Three sons she had and four daughters. The second son, called Henry, would live to ascend the throne in the second generation. After the third, the House of Tudor would cease to exist by direct issue."

"How came her death?"

"She died nine days after the birth of a daughter, thirty-seven years to the day when first she entered into the world."

"'Tis young."

"Aye, my lord." Laura replied, as tears welled up anew. "She died within the Tower where it is believed that her brothers met their end."

"Believed?" He paused, considering. *"Then one question alone remains unanswered. What is writ of me?"*

"Many bemoan the brevity of thy reign. Thy laws and goodly works left half made up."

"And what else?" His voice grew cold. Laura hesitated. *"I will have this truth from thee. Say on."*

"That you murdered your brother's sons."

- SILENCE -

"Please, you must ..."

*"Do **not** speak to me of what I must do! Long have I borne this burden. 'Tis none of thy concern."*

Laura gasped. Tears flooded her eyes and she began to sob uncontrollably. Pushed to the brink, her nerves gave way and she slumped to the floor where she lay for several minutes while the sun danced, bathing her in the reflected beauty of radiant light from the magnificent window. Gradually she regained her senses, but when she sought him, he was gone.

Strangely devoid of tourists at this hour, the massive cathedral stood silent, watching as Laura slowly retraced her steps. Halfway to the door, she halted, exhausted and unable to go further. Above her the statues of the kings paraded in silent mockery, heedless of her plight. Slowly she moved forward and stood before the last.

"Will a saint allow a sinner into heaven, Henry? Your curse is ended. Are you satisfied? Has he suffered enough?" She whispered, her anger rising while fresh tears erupted. The dark grey stone continued to stare fixedly ahead, frozen in time, ignoring her. She was about to turn away when she realized in alarm that she was no longer alone.

From the shadows he emerged, catching her completely off guard as she gazed upon his face, recognizing him instantly. Too stunned to move, she watched helplessly as he drew nearer.

"Thou art brave madam to look upon the face of death. But are you resolute enough for the task I would ask of thee?"

He looked past Laura to the image of Henry VI. Laura moved but a fraction but it was sufficient to attract his attention once more to her. He returned her gazed directly with dark grey eyes, cunning and predatory. Deathly pale, thin and careworn, he studied her intently as he appraised her, judging the level of her strength and usefulness to him.

"You shall go to Fotheringhay on the morrow. There seek out the trappings of my House, the tombs of my parents, brother. I shall find thee. Steel thyself madam for this final effort for I need thy strength and purpose of mind if I am to bring thee safely through. Thou art in mortal danger, as ye know, yet I am not without some craft which may prove the undoing of this treacherous fiend. Adieu madam, 'til we met again." He drew back within the shadows and was gone.

Transfixed for a moment, Laura found herself incapable of movement. Her heart beat wildly, leaving her gasping for breath. Painfully she edged closer to the door, his image pressed firmly in her mind, his resolve blending with her own need and determination.

The late afternoon sun nearly blinded her as she exited the cathedral. The fresh air revived her somewhat, giving her the strength to move a few paces more. Towards the edge of the square, a mime artist slowly slithered along the walkway, his arms outstretched, his fingers tracing an imaginary panel of glass. A crowd of about twenty people stood watching, the children especially showing their delight. Suddenly he peeked through an imaginary door, frightening two little girls who squealed and jumped back, giggling nervously.

Laura stood as if rooted, both fascinated and appalled by this grotesque imagery. The stark white face paint only served to exaggerate the black costume worn over a slender frame. His shoulder length black hair hung loose, dirty and unkempt and as he drew closer to her, she could see dirt beneath his fingernails. She shuddered and drew back apace.

He stopped then, removed his barrette and like a robot, moved amongst the crowd, cap outstretched to catch the coins offered in appreciation.

The crowd quickly dispersed. Laura edged backwards, slowly moving towards the door of the church but he knew where she was and turned his full attention upon her.

"Stay!" He shouted, pointing at her with a long, bony finger. His eyes were as black as night and as cruel as death. "I pray thee Madam, have ye no coin to toss in my direction?" He bowed low then moved closer.

"Get away from me!"

"Surely 'tis not much to ask of thee. A groat perhaps or is it that my skill must go unrewarded yet again?" He drew closer, all the while watching her intently. Smiling thinly, he held out his cap.

"I know what you are." She growled, the anger in her voice masking her fear.

"Do you madam? Then alas this ruse has failed in its enterprise as ye shall fail in thine. Such a pretty thing, so wise, so proud." He sighed. "I would have thee on thy knees before me but then I could not see thy beauty, nor the flash of rage in thy eyes which serves only to heighten my desire for thee. He would have thee too, but alas it cannot be for time grows short and my patience with it.

"Did ye think to dismiss me so easily? Fool, for even now the host gathers, smelling victory, smelling blood and souls to capture all unawares. Thou hast provided us with a feast madam, and we do feed, and feed well." He laughed cruelly. "I trust ye bid him a fond adieu, for Fotheringhay he shall not see."

Laura tried to scream but the demon caught her by the throat. "Such a pretty little butterfly. If ye have faith in him best abandon it while ye can. He has no power; not now. Know then that when I call thee, ye will come." He hissed, revealing fanglike teeth. In disgust he flung her against the cathedral door, knocking her unconscious.

"Are you all right my dear?" The elderly lady said as she patted Laura's hand. "You must have fainted. Shall we call someone? Maybe we should Paul, her hands are ever so cold and there is no colour in her. Oh, so pale."

Gail appeared from nowhere. "It's all right, I'm her sister-in-law." She took Laura's hands and pressed them together between her own. "Laura, it's Gail. I'm here. It's okay now." Turning, she smiled up at the old woman and her companion. "I'm sure she's going to be okay." Gail nodded towards the hotel. "If I could just get her ..."

"Aye," said Paul as he stepped forward. Gail was openly amazed by the ease with which he was able to lift Laura into his arms and carry her.

Once back at the hotel, a doctor was called.

"Your sister-in-law has had a terrible fright but she's going to be all right, with a little rest. Her blood-pressure is rising now, and as you can see, her colour is coming back a bit." The doctor seemed so sure, so calming, hiding within himself the distinct belief that this young woman had, for a moment, stood within the shadow of death and had seen what very few mortals will ever see, and survive. "Speak to her, please. Try to get her to talk."

"Laura, it's Gail. We're at our hotel now. Speak to me." Nothing. "Her hands are so cold doctor."

He moved forward, checked her pulse at the wrist but found it too weak to monitor so he pressed against the jugular, finding a trace. "Damn!" He growled. Swiftly he reached into his bag, deftly filled a syringe, swabbed a flat portion of Laura's forearm and inserted the tip of the needle, allowing the fluid to slowly enter her vein. He took her blood pressure again, easing off the instrument but keeping it loosely wrapped about her left arm. A few minutes later he checked it again and her eyes, which were beginning to appear normal - not so dilated, not so distant.

"Tell him," Laura whispered, her voice angry, "tell that hell-spawn seed of perdition ... he can not ... will not have her ... get out of my city ... leave my people ... this place." Her voice trailed off at the end as she lapsed into a deep sleep.

"What was that all about?" The doctor said, amazed. He checked her carefully once more, satisfied this time as all vital signs settled within an acceptable range. He turned to Gail and offered her a reassuring smile. "I think the crisis or whatever it was, is over. She's sleeping nicely now. Here's my mobile number. Call me immediately if there's any change. Right now, she needs the sleep she's getting and, if you don't mind me saying so, you could do with a rest too. You look exhausted."

Gail tried to return his smile but failed miserably. After he left she sat holding Laura's hand, warm now, living. After awhile, and as quietly as possible, she made a cup of instant coffee and prepared to sit with it at the window next to Laura's bed. Outside, she caught a glimpse of tourists milling about. A horse-drawn carriage across the road patiently waiting for passengers. The South African War Memorial outside Norman House nearly lost amongst the trees while pigeons strutted about, finding real or imaginary bits of food to eat.

Then she saw him. A grotesque, evil representation of a man, dressed all in black, with thin strands of equally black hair falling straight to his shoulder. His eyes were the colour of nightshade and just as deadly as they bored through her, seeking the other. Gail stood transfixed, powerless, as he raked her mind.

Suddenly a wind sprang up, grew stronger, sending cart and tourists in every direction, seeking shelter, as a heavy rain began to fall from what, moments before, had been a clear, almost cloudless sky. He neither moved nor appeared to be aware of the storm which rapidly accelerated, whipping the branches of the trees, sending debris in every direction.

In a panic, Gail shut the window and drew the heavy drapes closed. Inside, the room boomed and creaked as the storm raged. She sat huddled up, her ears covered against the sudden violent onslaught, watching Laura's every movement. Twice she screamed, her body pulled rigid. Gail raced into the bathroom and came back with two towels, which she rolled then draped, first in one direction and then another to form a cross atop Laura, allowing her to fall deeper into a fitful sleep, dreaming of things too frightening to even contemplate. As the storm abated somewhat, Gail became aware of a gentle knocking on the door.

"It's Mrs. Galen. I just wanted to know how she is doing? We have been so worried." Gail opened the door to the elderly lady and her companion. "Oh, such a storm! Paul had to close the windows, the wind was coming through our rooms, tossing things about! How is she?" She sat down on the bed beside Laura then, as a mother to a child, touched her forehead tenderly. "Poor thing, poor, poor thing."

From nowhere she produced a small glass phial, stopped with wax. Carefully she removed the top and tipped out a measure of the pale yellow liquid onto her fingertip. Gently, she reached out and anointed Laura's forehead with the sign of the cross.

"Who are you?" Gail gasped in fear. "What are you doing?"

"We are friends dear, do not be afraid. He has been allowed to touch her you see and now he wants her for himself."

"He?" Gail shouted, almost hysterical.

"The creature that watches and waits. The companion of the other. Released now, he hunts alone." She turned then to Paul and handed him the phial. "You must anoint the door and the window too."

Gail watched, fascinated, as he drew the sign of the cross at intervals along the doorframe before turning to the window. She drew back in fear as the curtains were opened. When he was finished with the phial, he returned it, taking instead another, filled with white crystals, which he poured carefully along the sill before closing the drapes.

The old woman nodded and smiled. "It is good. She is safe now and so too are you, my dear." Gail just stared, incredulous. "You have seen this creature?" Gail nodded, unable to speak. "And not for the first time I warrant. Come now, sit here beside her and take her hand. Much has she suffered. More even than can be imagined. I fear some part of her seeks the one. You must help to bring her back before she is lost to us, forever."

"I … I don't understand. I'm so afraid and … and I don't know what to do." Gail began to sob.

"I know child, I know." She patted Gail's hand tenderly. "We are here to help and perhaps, explain as best we can. Whether by accident or design, both of you have become involved in a rare and unusual sequence of events. It is to your credit that you have survived to this point. Forces beyond your control have manipulated circumstances but mistakes have been made necessitating our intervention. In her eagerness to seek the truth, this child has imperilled both her life and her soul." Gail gasped. "I cannot answer the why of what has happened nor shall I try, but I think you must prepared yourself for the worst.

"The one she seeks to save may be beyond redemption. Too close she has come to this spirit and what she offered freely has been misused. Now she is enthralled, her soul entwined. Thus it will remain unless we are able to intervene and call her back. The attraction must be powerful yet she hesitates, fearful perhaps and unsure.

"So much of what has happened to both of you resides in your subconscious where the mind can process information without interfering with your conscious state, without causing an imbalance. When reality becomes too much, when it is no longer possible to cope, the mind goes into shock and unconsciousness results. It may be, however, that she has either forced herself, or been forced, to go beyond what is reasonable for her to sustain. If that is the case, she may run mad.

"I hope and pray that we will succeed in retrieving her totally, with sufficient consciousness for her to be not only aware, but totally in control again. She has been touched by evil, but also by the hand of God. We must trust that He will see her safely returned. Now, you must talk to her. Call her to you." Silently, the old woman moved away.

Gail slid to her knees beside the bed, inches away from Laura's ear. Gently she began to speak in a whisper, her voice as steady and as calm as possible. Over and over again she called Laura's name, pleading with her to open her eyes.

Almost imperceptible at first, Laura slowly moved upwards through the convoluted realms of all her being, like a diver surfacing, level by level. She could hear Gail's voice, dreamlike, distant, but unfaltering. Hesitating, almost at the point of consciousness, she paused and thought to look back, but turned instead in her mind, and reached out. "Hi."

"Hi yourself." Gail voice quivered. She rose then and sat beside Laura, taking her hand, but when she turned, both the woman and the man she called Paul, were gone.

"What time is it?"

"Almost eight. How do you feel? Can you sit up?"

"Sure. Eight o'clock?" Laura sat up, leaning heavily against the headboard. "How did I get here?"

"We'll talk about all that later. Right now I think we both could do with something to eat. "Let's order room service and watch some TV tonight."

Laura frowned. "Don't you want to go out?"

"No! I mean, it's still raining I think, and I'm too tired." Gail searched through the room, found the hotel information booklet and was too busy reading through the menu to notice Laura get out of bed and move rapidly to the window. "Laura, don't!"

Too late, Laura pulled the curtains apart. "Hey, what are you afraid of? See what you mean about the rain. It's pouring out there. What's this stuff?"

"Don't touch it. Close the drapes - quick!"

Laura looked at Gail, then back to the crystals. She started to laugh. "It's salt." Her eyes traced the faint outline of the crosses and she laughed harder, her voice harsh and dry. 'Tell me, is this an attempt to keep something out, or something in?"

Quick as a flash, Gail pulled the curtains closed, then turned on Laura. She hit her hard across the side of the face with the flat of her hand. "How dare you! You almost died! I had to stand by helpless, not knowing what to do, while a doctor desperately tried to find a pulse while your blood pressure plummeted. Do you know what that feels like? Do you? And in Middleham too - blood everywhere! No more! I forbid you to laugh at the puny attempts of others to keep you from him."

Laura stared, dumbfounded.

"And don't pretend with me either. You understand exactly what I'm saying to you. What you don't know, or refuse to admit in that overweening mind of yours is the fact that you wouldn't stand a chance if you ever tried this trick again. Before you would get anywhere near him, the demon would have you."

"Excuse me, I think I'll go and have a bath." Laura moved around Gail, all the while watching her carefully.

"Good idea." Gail snapped. "In the meantime, I'll order a cheese omelette for you, and you had bloody well better eat it!"

They ate in front of the TV, watching nothing in particular. Afterwards they readied themselves for bed, all the while avoiding each other, not speaking, not even looking in each other's direction. Just past ten o'clock, the doctor arrived and insisted upon checking Laura.

She regarded him with mild amusement as he check her blood pressure, eyes, and pulse rate. Satisfied, he turned over to Gail two mild sedatives which he ordered them to take immediately. Gail quickly did so, but Laura needed considerable urging before she finally gave in, just to be rid of him. As soon as Gail turned to see the doctor to the door, Laura coughed, expelling the tablet into her cupped hand.

When Gail turned around after showing the doctor out, Laura was sitting, legs crossed in a chair across the room, smiling benignly. "Do you always do just as ordered, on command?" Laura asked, amused, though her eyes were cold, threatening, as they regarded Gail evenly.

"Shut up." Gail growled as she headed towards the bathroom.

She closed the door behind her, then leaned on it heavily. Fear clawed at her, constricting her breathing.

By the time she exited the bathroom, Laura was already in bed and, so it would appear, asleep. The sedative pulled at Gail's consciousness, sending her into a quiet, gentle rest moments after she settled into her bed.

Outside, the storm continued unabated, causing widespread flooding as swollen rivers tore away banks, uprooting trees and submerging roads. On a darkened stretch of motorway, less than a mile from the Minster, a heavily loaded bus ploughed into the rear of a car, killing twelve, including a family of four. On the other side of the city, a reformed alcoholic drank himself to death on a lethal combination of gin and vodka after first murdering his young wife and infant son. The local police station received numerous calls, complaining of barking dogs, while in the darkened recesses of Micklegate Bar, a prostitute lay dead in a pool of blood, her throat slit.

The demon stared fixedly at the darkened window. "Do ye lie safe abed my beauty, while chaos reigns?" He growled. "Call him to thy side, if ye can, 'tho ye shall pay a price beyond measure for it." His thin lips parted, revealing canine teeth. In anger, he turned away, then thought to hunt elsewhere in the pre-dawn hours when, he knew, mankind was at its most vulnerable.

Day 12
York - Towton - Fotheringhay

Richard, Duke of Gloucester:
>*No more can you distinguish of a man*
>*Than of his outward show; which God he knows,*
>*Seldom or never jumpeth with the heart.*

Shakespeare -
The Tragedy of King Richard the Second
[Act III, Scene 1]

Gail woke with a start just after dawn. Too fearful to pull the curtains back and see for herself, the city of York slowly roused itself from a night of terror, peeling away the darkness like the skin of an onion, layer by layer, revealing by degrees the extent of the chaos visited upon it.

Gail checked Laura several times, but it was almost nine before she actually touch her. Her hand instinctively drew back, repulsed by the cold, clammy feel of her. She called the doctor immediately, but by the time he arrived, Laura was awake.

"All right young lady, you're fine, although I would prefer your BP to be a little higher. You must promise to take better care of yourself and stop doing whatever is was that you were doing which caused your collapse. You almost succeeded in getting yourself in a right pickle - bad for tourism. Now promise." Laura sighed, cast Gail a quick glance, then nodded. "Good. Enjoy the rest of your trip."

Laura leaned heavily against the doorframe as she paused in her effort to negotiate her way into the bathroom. She fought back the nausea which sought to overwhelm her, seeking the relief which a warm shower would, she hope, afford her. Blissfully unaware of Laura's distress, Gail busied herself repacking her suitcase.

Both of them ate a hearty breakfast so by the time they were ready to leave, Laura had managed to stabilized herself, buoyed in part by massive doses of orange juice and several cups of coffee, heavy with sugar and stirred pale with warm milk. Gail watched, intrigued, since Laura usually took her coffee black, and sugarless. While they were checking out, the car was delivered to the front and within minutes they were ready to go.

Laura assumed that she would drive and Gail made no objection as she slipped into the passenger seat. Laura stood on the curb, leaning against the car while she stared at The Minster. Her heart grieved and grew tight within her as tears welled up, unwanted. She repaired herself as best she could before getting into the car, quickly adjusting herself, while Gail watched her closely.

"I was hoping to see Mrs. Galen. That was the name of the lady who helped me. She ...well, she seemed to know what was happening to us and what to do." Gail paused for a moment, wondering if maybe she should make an effort to find her, to say good bye properly and to thank them both of course. Laura sat behind the wheel, her head bowed. "What's the matter?" Gail asked, suddenly alarmed.

"Nothing," Laura said with a shrug, "but, I think if you check, you'll find that GALEN is an anagram of ANGEL." She glanced at Gail briefly before starting the engine. "Interesting company you keep my dear."

Gail was about to say something, then thought better of it.

Using the Railway Station as a reference point again, Laura edged her way clear of York, heading south towards Tadcaster. Gail consulted the map several times. "Where are we going?" She finally asked, perplexed.

"Towton." Laura replied flatly.

"No." Gail groaned.

Fifteen minutes later, Laura pulled onto a gravel roadway beside a stone monument dedicated to the 28,000 men who died in the bloodiest battle ever fought on English soil. She left the car running, while she got out and searched through her bag in the backseat for her notes. All around them were fields planted in wheat, oats and barley. "Are you sure this is it?" Gail asked, somewhat surprised, since it all looked so ordinary. It wasn't.

Laura drove the car down the lane for about 100 yards, then parked close to a fence line. From where the car sat, the land began to fall away dramatically, only to level out in an open area of pasture nestled beside a stream. Sheep grazed contentedly on an abundance of feed. Together they climbed a section of wooden fence, which formed a small enclosure, then wandered down the hill side by side.

Laura headed straight towards to the River Cock which meandered through the valley. An innocent looking killer of men. She brought her notes, which she now extracted from her bag. At the top of the page Gail noted the words '*Towton - The Day of Reckoning*' while beneath, in Laura's handwriting was the notation *28,000 died!* and, scrawled in the margin in red ink, '*biological hazard*'.

"What do you mean - 'biological hazard'?"

Laura glanced quickly at Gail before turning, to allow her eyes to wander across the valley - another bloody meadow. "Most of those slain," Laura said sadly, "were buried in huge pits dotted around the battlesite. Unfortunately, the weather was cold, snowy, so the pits were probably inadequate. To this day, bones and artefacts are said to work their way to the surface."

"Nice one." Gail shivered, then looked down as if to check the earth beneath her feet.

Laura smiled thinly. "I long time ago it seems, you asked me about Richard's childhood. Well, look around you because, in a sense, most of the horror that was to follow began right here."

"Laura, please, let's go." Gail stammered.

"No." Laura snapped. "Rachael suggested that we see this place, and so we shall. Now, let's see - Towton - Palm Sunday, March 29th, 1461. Richard's father, brother Edmund and uncle were slain at Wakefield the previous December. The gloves were off now as Edward of March, soon to become King Edward IV, swore vengeance on the House of Lancaster and death to its adherents. Going back a bit to set the scene, remember Margaret of Anjou was marching on London with her army of wild Northerners, but it was Edward who slipped into London first and won the hearts of the commons who promptly proclaimed him King at St. Paul's Cross? He refused to be crowned until after he had defeated Margaret and Co and so, he left London and turned north to follow Margaret's retreating army. Just south of the village of Towton, Edward found what he was seeking. The Lancastrians had positioned themselves on an east-west line straddling the two roads which converge at Towton. The Yorkists drew a similar battle line to the south. It must have been a terrible night, bivouacked in the open, exposed to a cold south wind with a threat of snow to come.

"The battle started about eleven in the morning on the flat land near the road. The cross marks the traditional site of the Lancastrian right flank. Further south, as I said was York, strung out in a line. All lovely flat land, well drained and hard, I guess, with the cold weather. Typically, the order of battle began with a barrage of arrows but, because of the favourable wind, the Yorkist arrows carried further than normal, straight into the Lancastrian camp. The return fire fell short, much to the glee of the Yorkist, who gathered the arrows up and sent them back, inflicting severe losses and causing panic in the Lancastrian ranks. Then, it was time to get down to it as the two armies closed on each other and archers were replaced with swordsmen and bill men. The carnage was so great in the front lines that a wall of dead began to build up between the opposing forces. When the Duke of Norfolk arrived with 5000 troops, the Lancastrian army began to buckle and many tried to cut and run."

Laura turned vaguely in the direction of Towton, upstream of the River Cock. "Everything south of here was substantially Yorkist. To the north, especially the city of York - where Queen Margaret awaited the outcome of the battle - was either uncommitted, or Lancastrian. North was the only avenue of escape for the fleeing Lancastrian host, and by late in the day, the battle had become a Yorkist rout. Men ran in a panic across the flat fields only to be confronted by the steep slope we just came down, and then this. The River Cock was in flood then, so it was probably a lot deeper and wider than it is now. Remember too, it was snowing. The Yorkists pushed their enemy hard up against the river where literally thousands drowned in a panic to escape the killing ground.

"There was a wooden bridge here somewhere which offered a reliable crossing point, but the sheer volume of men trying to cross at the same time caused the bridge to collapse. So many died there that the river became blocked with bodies, forming a ghastly dam of human corpses across which the living scrambled, hoping to achieve safety on the other side. But, there was no safety there as hundreds were cut down by archers as they tried to scramble up the far slope."

Slowly thay walked along the edge of the River. Neither spoke as they allowed the enormity of the horror and loss of life to impact them both. What made their walk even more disturbing was the knowledge that the battle site has not changed substantially since that fateful day more than five hundred years before.

Gail stopped walking. "How come so many died? I mean …" Her voice trailed off in a shrug of bewilderment.

"Revenge." Laura frowned. "You see, Richard's father, brother, uncle did not die in battle. They were ambushed by the Lancastrians during the Christmas truce."

"Hey, that's not fair."

Laura mentally rolled her eyes. "Ah, no, I guess it wasn't.

Edward was determined to wipe out all Lancastrians, and I mean, **all**." Laura sighed. "He did something totally uncharacteristic of medieval warfare. He commanded that no prisoners be taken."

"You mean he ordered wholesale slaughter." Gail said, her tone savage.

"According to George Neville, the dead littered the field in a swath six miles long by a third of a mile wide. The chase went on into the night and the following morning, right to the gates of York. It was said that the rivers at Towton and Tadcaster ran red with blood for miles."

"Savages, that's what they were!"

"Oh yes, we've come a long way in the art of war, I must say. Now even civilians can get into the act. Vaporize a whole city with a push of a button. Isn't that what modern warfare has become?"

"You know what I mean, killing each other with swords, pikes. Fighting hand to hand, eye to eye."

"Well, at least they were honest about it."

"Come on," Gail growled, "let's go. I think I've just about had my fill of medieval history."

Laura followed Gail back up the hill, pausing now and again to look back towards the River Cock as it meandered through the lowland, almost hidden amongst the trees and long grass.

Relentlessly Laura pushed southward, picking up the A1M south of Doncaster. As she eased the car into fifth gear, then settled back, she glanced briefly at Gail. "You saw the museum at Monk Bar?"

"Yes, but I didn't stay long. While I was there, I kept thinking it was a good idea that you didn't come. It was a little irreverent."

"Oh?"

"Well, it wasn't as good as the one at Warwick Castle, in any case."

"So, what was it like?"

Gail sighed. "Three floors in all. The first was the shop - souvenirs and stuff. The second had a sort of trial and a book you could sign - guilty or not-guilty. On the top floor, more information, pictures and such." She finished her brief description with a shrug.

"The trial, what was that about?"

"You need to ask? The death of the Princes of course. The verdict was about 50/50. Some of the comments were funny though."

"Such as?"

"Statements like 'frankly Scarlet I couldn't give a damn' or 'who cares' or," Gail paused, "'guilty as sin'."

Laura smiled. "Did you write anything, on either side?"

"No." Gail said flatly. She pulled the road atlas onto her lap and began to study the route again. A not too subtle indicator of a conversation closed. Laura wondered what Gail meant by 'irreverent' but decided not to push the issue. Besides, she already had a fairly good idea.

Their journey south past by rapidly, especially since Laura drove at speed, passing all before them. They exited the A1 at Wansford with such force that Laura shifted from fifth to second in just a few feet. The rest of the way to Fotheringhay required sign posts on roads not much wider than one car width in places.

Past the pub, the church, then at the right-hand bend in the road, they found the guesthouse Rachael had mentioned. She was standing in the courtyard when they arrived. Silently they embraced each other, words momentarily unnecessary. Gail looked a little tired perhaps, but much the same. Laura, on the other hand appeared thin, too thin, and aged, her face lined with a deep sadness which frightened Rachael.

Recovering quickly from the initial shock, she made all the necessary introductions to their hostess Joanne, who appeared not much older than Rachael. Afterwards she helped them to settle into their room. It was very pretty in shades of soft blue.

"Not bad for an old coal room, is it?" Rachael asked laughing. "Sorry, but I'll have to bunk in here too. Joanne's got family visiting so we won't see much of her I'm afraid. No other Ricardians either, as far as I know, so you guys will be a lot more fun, and from what little you've told me, a lot more interesting."

"We're not Ricardians Rachael." Gail announced, hands on hips.

"Oh, but I live in hope of both of you joining." Rachael replied, smiling broadly. Laura started to laugh uncontrollably while Gail looked away, busying herself with nothing important. "Hey, what's so funny?" Rachael asked, bewildered by Laura's reaction.

"I'm sorry Rachael," Laura stammered, "maybe you can make us honorary members. Would you like that Gail?"

"Shut up!" She growled as she headed into the bathroom, slamming the door behind her.

Rachael folded her arms and regarded Laura guardedly. "Okay, so what's happened? Have you two had a fight, is that it, and you want me to referee?"

"No," Laura chuckled, "we wouldn't have asked you to come all the way up here for something like that. No, no Gail and I are just fine. She's under a lot of pressure that's all. We both are, and have been for several days now. I'll get my walking boots out of the car and maybe you can give us a tour. Give us a chance to talk."

The guesthouse stood within the very shadow of the mound upon which Fotheringhay Castle's keep was built. Today, there is nothing left but vague impressions in the ground and one large chunk of tumbled stone and mortar protected behind an iron grill near the edge of the River Nine which, at one time, fed the massive moat and lake which surrounded the castle. In 1625, a survey was undertaken and the castle was described then as being in good order, but by 1635, demolition had began, ordered by James I, it is said, to avenge the execution of his mother there. Just inside the gate there was an artist's impression of what the castle looked like in its heyday.

"I can't begin to guess how many times I've been here." Rachael remarked as she walked. "I went to school in Oundle, you see. Sometimes I'd come out here with friends and picnic, run around, neck under the trees. That's how I met Stephen." She laughed lightly, remembering a happier time. "Maybe that's why I joined the Richard III Society, because of a sense of closeness I mean, like I've known him for a long, long time." Her voice trailed off in sadness at the end. "Anyhow, this flat part was the Outer Court, then close to the base of the mound, the Great Hall, then the Keep on top. Other buildings scattered about; all gone now. Come on, let's climb to the top. Great view of the church and the surrounding countryside from up there."

She led the way, taking a well-worn path upwards, bending under the trees and, in the steeper parts, using the branches to steady herself, before the final push to the top. Laura and Gail followed close behind. The view was truly magnificent. "Richard was born somewhere in this area. Not a bad view from a nursery window, is it?"

"How long was he here?" Gail asked.

"Ah, let's see." Rachael said. "His father called his whole family to Ludlow in the spring of 1459. Richard was coming up seven years of age, so it's likely that he spent the first six here."

"So, he wasn't really a true Northerner after all." Gail suggested.

"Well, no," Rachael admitted, "not in terms of his birthplace perhaps, but at heart he was. He loved the wild, open country around Middleham."

Laura moved away towards the edge of the mound and found a spot from which to view the church.

"Pretty isn't it?" Rachael asked.

Indeed it was perhaps the most beautiful church Laura had ever seen. Built entirely in the 'perpendicular' with stately windows of the same style, delicate flying buttresses arched outwards, while a magnificent tower crowned the church and carried atop it a golden weather vane, shaped in the likeness of a falcon - symbol of the House of York. *Fotheringhay he shall not see.* Laura's eyes filled with tears, blinding her. Slowly she sat down, her back to Gail and Rachael.

"Lots of thistles." Gail announced.

"Yeah I know," Rachael said, kicking at a few. "Two varieties. Legend has it that Mary Queen of Scot's ghost sowed the seeds after her execution as an perpetual reminder of what happened here. Hey Laura, I ..."

Gail quickly grabbed Rachael's elbow and pulled her away. "Leave her." She whispered.

Rachael looked back towards Laura. "Is she crying?" She looked again. "Gail, she's crying. What's going on?"

"Do you believe in ghosts?" Gail asked flatly.

"I ... I guess so. Haven't seen any, but you know what it's like in this country? Every second house over a hundred years old seems to have some sort of story about ghosts, haunted barns and ... " Rachael frowned. "Have you two encountered one?"

"Yes."

"Well, tell me!"

"I'll wait for Laura and we'll tell you together."

"Laura said this has something to do with Richard."

Before Gail could answer, Laura turned around, her eyes studded with tears as she beckoned them to her. "I think it's time." She said, her voice low and sad, her face a mask of tragic grief.

They formed a tight circle of three sitting on the grass near to the edge of the mound, while the windows of the church captured the early evening light, bathing the magnificent building in shades of soft pink and gold.

"Are you all right?" Rachael asked as she took Laura's hand. It felt fragile and cold.

"No I'm not," Laura replied as she cast Rachael a shadow of a smile, "and I doubt that I ever will be again."

Gail cleared her throat and looked away, her eyes too began to fill with tears.

Laura took a deep breath and began. "First of all, what happened was my fault entirely and I must accept total responsibility. I . . . I pushed too hard, and in my desire to seek the truth, I penetrated a realm beyond mortal experience. I didn't push the envelope, I punctured it and through it came - came what? Rachael, do you believe in ghosts, demons, angels?"

"Gail has already asked me about ghosts, but demons? Laura please, you're scaring me."

"Then perhaps the conversation should end here, now." Laura replied, turning away.

"That night we were all together at Bosworth?" Rachael asked, her voice unsteady.

Laura slowly turned. "Yes."

"I shared a room with Jenny. She was up half the night, scared to death, but she won't say why. She's had a nervous breakdown before, but this was different. Anyhow, she's in an institution now, 'under observation' they call it. Stephanie too is a basket case. She had a room of her own. Sometime during the night, she called the front desk to complain about a scratching sound at her window. They checked of course, but they couldn't find anything. It continued off and on until dawn. That's why she wasn't at the ceremony at the well, and neither was John and Claire. Now, this is really strange. They had a bit of a tiff after, and John went for a walk around the village, then down the lane that runs from Market Bosworth to Sutton Cheney. I don't hear about this until a couple of days later, but, well . . . Claire said that John was attacked by a large, like in very large dog. He managed to make it to a car parked in the lane. He nearly sat on the girl's head when he jumped into the back seat, but the guy was pretty with it and flashed the lights on. John said that what they saw at the edge of the car's beams was no dog."

"What they saw Rachael was a demon." Laura looked straight into her eyes.

"God help me." Rachael gasped.

"And us all." Gail added in a whisper.

It look them over an hour to tell the story while Rachael sat quietly, listening intently, all the while subconsciously folding and unfolding her hands, twisting them upon occasion in both horror and fascination. When it was finished, Laura stood up and walked away, leaving Rachael to digest what had been said, and what the current implications might be.

"Rachael," Gail whispered, "Laura didn't tell you what happened at York, probably because either she doesn't remember or doesn't what to remember. Something happened, something so terrible that she nearly died as a result." Slowly she shook her head as fresh tears welled up. "I don't know, don't understand, but Rachael, I think she's seen Richard, although she won't say. And, I think she's in a lot more trouble then she's admitted."

"But …"

"Please Rachael, this is important. Please, let me finish. It would seem that Richard allowed, perhaps … perhaps even invited this demon to touch her." Gail was breathing rapidly as she tried to control a rising sense of panic. "That same night in Bosworth, when she came back from the Deathstone, her whole body was covered with small wounds, like they were made by a knife, but now I realize that those marks were made by the claws of this demon, and Rachael, he wants her now."

Rachael was too stunned to speak. Suddenly, she looked down towards the outer basin, trying to find Laura. "Where is she?" Rachael shouted as she stood up, instantly alarmed as she scoured the open field below.

Just then Laura emerged from behind the large section of the castle wall on display. Rachael breathed a sigh of relief, then turn to Gail. "I'm sorry. It's just that … holy shit, I'm having a hell of a lot of trouble understanding this."

"Yeah well, join the club. Look, there's something else you need to know." Gail drew closer to Rachael. "During the times when she's been with him, there's been, and I'll use the same word she used, a displacement going on. I didn't understand what she meant, so in York, I looked the word up in a dictionary." Gail reached into the side pocket of her purse and pulled out a small piece of paper. "Here's the definition: a transferring of emotional feeling from their original object to one that disguises their real nature."

Rachael frowned. "What do you mean?"

"What I mean is that, well, sometimes I get the vague sense that Laura isn't Laura anymore. I don't know. Maybe it's my imagination, but all you have to do is watch her, even the way she moves, her gestures sometimes. Listen to her, the subtle shift to another mind-set. If you get a chance, look into her eyes, then tell me what you see there."

Rachael backed away from Gail. "This is crazy. Are you saying that somehow Richard's personality or whatever has been transferred to Laura?"

"That's exactly what I'm saying." Gail sighed heavily "If you don't believe me, then watch her react to something unexpected. Think of how someone like Richard would have responded if he had been insulted, for instance. Laura always took criticism well, usually with a clever quip back, but not now. Try it. You might just get a glimmer of what your precious Richard was really like, and believe me, it's not a pretty picture, so beware."

"She's … I mean, she's not dangerous or anything, is she?"

"That depends on how much you really think that Richard was dangerous. Come on Rachael, you're the Ricardian. Do you believe he was? Would you be prepared to share a room with him, sleep just a few feet away?"

Rachael stared, open-mouthed.

"Come on," Gail sighed, as she hooked her arm through Rachael's, "let's go see the church and then have some dinner.

Oh, and by the way, it's Laura's birthday today, but right now, I wouldn't mention it, okay?"

Rachael hesitated. "Are we in deep trouble?"

"On a scale of one to ten, I think we rate a nine point five."

"Bloody hell." Rachael muttered as Gail pulled her back towards the lip of the hill.

Laura stood at the base waiting for them. Together they walked back towards the guesthouse, up the drive and along the edge of the road to the walkway which lead through the cemetery to the church porch. Just before the entranceway, Laura stopped and looked to the left, frowning deeply. Gail took her arm tenderly. "Come on." She whispered.

Inside, the church was perhaps even more beautiful as sunlight poured in through the windows on the western side, transfusing the interior with a soft, warm glow. Gail purchased a guidebook with a splendid colour picture of the church on the cover. When she looked up, Laura was standing near the back of the church, staring fixedly towards the altar, her brow knotted.

"Hello Mrs. Gates." Rachael said as she approached an elderly lady seated at a small table in the nave.

"Rachael! Well, this is a surprise. Visiting again are you? Can't stay away from the place for long, can you? Now tell me, how is your father and that naughty brother of yours?"

Rachael smiled warmly, remembering two men in her life at least, whom she unreservedly adored. "They're both fine, thanks. Vic is back in the US right now, but Dad's at home, working on another thesis the last I heard. And how are you?"

"Oh, much the same I dare say - older. You'll be looking around then with your friends? That's fine, yes. Let me know if you have any questions, won't you?"

"Thank you." Rachael said, smiling politely. "Gail, Laura come on. I want you both to see the York Window."

She lead them across to the far side then up the aisle to the end. "It was a gift from the Richard III Society. See, the Royal

Arms of Richard, his queen, Anne Neville, or rather the paternal Arms of Richard, Earl of Warwick. This one's Edmund de Langley, first Duke of York and below the second Duke, Edward Langley. On the other side, Richard, Earl of Cambridge and his wife Anne Mortimer - he was Edward Langley's brother and beneath, Richard Plantagenet, third Duke of York and Cecily Neville - Richard's parents. The badges you know, Richard's White Boar of course, the Falcon and Fetterlock, the White Rose, and the Rose-en-Soleil - all symbols of the House of York. The White Lion is Mortimer. The Society had much to do with furnishing the chapel too. We're kind of proud of it." Rachael added with a wry smile which quickly vanished when she turned towards Laura.

"Where is the balance of the church?"

"What?" Laura cast her a withering glance. "Gone." Rachael retorted, her voice harsh with a fear she could not comprehend. "The collegiate portion of the church was dismantled by the Duke of Northumberland around 1548, leaving only … only the parish church."

Rachael's heart leapt as Laura regarded her fully with eyes suddenly cold, predatory. "Northumberland - that traitor!" She paused then as if considering, while all the while taking in the details of what was now the high altar. Abstractly she chewed on her lower lip. "Where are the tombs?"

"Here." Rachael said in a voice that was barely audible. "Queen Elizabeth the First visited Fotheringhay in about 1573, I think, and saw the sad state of repair of the original tombs so … ah, she ordered that the remains be exhumed and reburied here, on either side of the altar."

Gail gripped Laura's arm. "Stop it," she whispered. "You're acting like it's Rachael's fault that things aren't what they were. Time goes by Laura. Nothing stays the same."

Laura pulled herself free of Gail and turned towards the pulpit. Without hesitating, she mounted the steps. Gail and Rachael exchanged quick glances before following her.

"Are you sure you're allowed up there?" Gail asked. When she didn't receive a reply, she decided to follow her.

"You are wrong," Laura said in a whisper, her back to Gail as she tenderly traced the carved wooden panel at the back with her fingertips. As she drew her hand away, Gail saw the Coat of Arms of Edward IV as well as a Bull - representing George, Duke of Clarence - and the Boar. "Occasionally time does miss a few things."

"Hey you two, I'm dying for a drink and it's getting late. Come on, the Falcon is right next door. They have a fantastic menu too."

Gail joined Rachael. "Sounds great." Gail tried to sound enthusiastic. "Laura?"

"Yes, of course." Laura replied as she emerged from the pulpit obviously in deep and troubled thought. Rachael and Gail had just enough time to glance quickly at each other again. "Gail, does the brochure give any indication of exactly where the original high altar was?"

Gail quickly checked. "It says here that the original collegiate church chancel was 110 feet long." Gail pointed to the drawing of the ground plan printed on page five. "That would include the Lady Chapel at the eastern end, so the high altar must have been about fifty-five feet from the end of the parish church, or roughly half way."

Laura nodded abstractly. "Sounds about right. Let's see if we can find it."

They exited the church together, turned right from the porch and followed the line of the existing church, searching in the grass for telltale evidence of the structure that had once stood there. They soon found themselves in the middle of a cemetery.

"Well," Laura announced, hands on hips, "someone has the hot spot. Fifty-five feet you said, Gail?"

"That's about right."

Laura went back to the eastern end of the church. "Fifty-five feet; eighteen and a bit yards. Quickly she paced out the distance, coming to rest near a headstone. Gail and Rachael joined her.

"We must make him come here." She announced, her voice barely audible.

"I can't read the name on the tombstone." Gail said, trying to brush away the lichen.

"That's okay. Here, we'll borrow from the neighbours, I'm sure they won't mind." Laura rapidly moved a pot of flowers, wilted and half-decayed from a nearby plot and set it down beside Gail. "Right, let's eat!"

"This is crazy!" Rachael shouted.

Laura chuckled. "Not as crazy as it might get. But, you don't have to continue with this, if you don't want to."

"Wouldn't miss it for the world." Rachael replied, swallowing hard.

"Laura?" Rachael voice was careful, hesitant. Laura turned from viewing the church to stare directly into Rachael's eyes.

"I know what you're going to ask of me and the answer is - yes, I have seen him and I know how he died."

Rachael recoiled, both fascinated and appalled.

"Three wounds, one on the forehead just above his right eye, a smashing blow delivered with great force; certainly sufficient to unseated him. On the left side, just below the temple, a deep laceration, probably from a glancing blow. Rendered unconscious I would think, his throat was cut from just beneath the left ear almost to the throat. A professional job, very nasty, which severed the left carotid artery." Laura looked straight ahead. "He bled to death Rachael."

"Oh my God!" Rachael gasped. "They did cut his throat."

Laura nodded sadly, then looked away towards the church again. "You know," Laura continued in a voice tight with emotion, "the clue to the manner of his death was always there, in the proclamation at York. *Piteously slain and murdered*', it said. Richard didn't die in the field, but was ritualistically murdered at Tudor's command."

Rachael recoiled, visibly shaken.

"They stood and watched, Rachael. Ten, perhaps fifteen minutes, before it was accomplished." Tears sprang into both their eyes as they stared at each other. Laura smiled thinly. "If it's any consolation, he probably didn't feel a thing." Gently she took hold of Rachael's hand and watched as she dropped her head and sobbed.

They were seated around a patio table on the lawn. An umbrella, set into the middle, remained open, but redundant now as the evening gathered in. They had ordered dinner. A bottle of claret sat neglected to one side, its bright red liquid reflecting the light as the sun trailed off to an afterglow, taking with it the light breeze which had stirred briefly atop castle hill. Although the evening was warm, most of the dinner crowd preferred to eat inside the pub, so eventually they had the garden area to themselves.

"Laura," Rachel asked in a whisper, her voice trembling, "what does he sound like?"

"What?"

"You talked to him. What does he sound like? How tall is he? What colour are his eyes?"

"Rachael," Gail cut in, her voice nervous and wary, "I think it would be better if ..."

"No Gail, Rachael wants to know, so why shouldn't I tell her? Now, let's see, where to begin? His voice is low, masculine of course and vaguely malicious. Cold as ice, yet warm as a summer breeze when he wants something. He's the ultimate dissembler, just as Shakespeare said, using words calculated to cajole. Naturally, he speaks in what we would call 'old English' which isn't difficult to understand, particularly since he does speak clearly, distinctly, with if anything, a slight lilt. Satisfied so far?" Laura asked, smiling wickedly.

"He's about my height - five six perhaps - maybe less. Slender I think, with sharp features, notably the line of the jaw." Laura sighed. "His eyes are a very dark grey, ringed in black so you can forget all this nonsense about being blue-eyed. Shall I continue?"

Rachael stared open- mouthed.

"Right. He's physically strong, very strong, and use to getting what he wants. I don't think he'd make an ideal guest for a mix-company evening. He uses women like property, treats those of inferior birth with benign impatience, and will murder without a qualm if the need arises."

Rachael started.

"Please, save me the moral indignation. I warned you before Rachael, we're dealing with a man who belongs within the age in which he lived. A man with unlimited power, wealth and privilege. You have no right, indeed no basis in modern time upon which to measure this man. He was what he was. Why won't you and the rest recognise that? You strip him down, dress him over with nothing but good intentions and what have you got? The Ricardian image of a man flopping on the horns of every dilemma. What a joke! There's no loose cannon here but a man who tried to do well, to please the highest number for the longest time. But, beneath that artificial exterior was a cold-blooded, ruthless individual who played for maximum affect.

"If you want to know what he was really like, then you have to chose a Richard. Was it the young man who fathered two, no three, illegitimate children and knew love while at the same time was capable of bludgeoning an old man to death?

"Or perhaps the young Lord of the North, who learned from the best at hand how to wield power and what it meant to loose it? Don't like that? Too bad, because it gets worse.

"How about a Richard, fighting for his life against the Wydville faction who would have cut his heart out as sure as look at him? Turn the page then to Richard, King of England, when he tried so desperately to be the good king of all our mythology. How long did that last - one month - before treachery struck, not only from the Wydville camp, but from a man he trusted and called friend. Now there's a bastard if ever you're looking for one - Lovell. Ah, but then again, bastard just isn't a strong enough word, is it?

"And then what? Ah yes, the death of Richard's only legitimate son and heir. Then what do we have? Violent, raw power. A cold, calculating monster, wary and distrustful, driven at the end to his own doom, unaware perhaps or unwilling to acknowledge the evil which stood at his side. In the final frame, that's your Richard and that was the one I encountered."

Rachael reeled back, horrified. "Why do you seem to hate him so and yet …?"

"Why?" Laura cut in viciously. "I'll tell you why. He has used me with a cruelty unimaginable in our time. His particular brand of courtliness leaves a lot to be desired, I can assure you. Never once did he express concern for me as an individual. He's a taker Rachael, and he goes for the throat." Laura shivered involuntarily. "Excuse me."

In one quick motion she rose and moved around the table only to stop abruptly at Rachael's side. "Oh, and one thing more. If he does show up tonight, don't call him by his first name, he doesn't like it." She smiled down at Rachael, although there was little warmth in it, then she turned and hurried into the pub.

Rachael half rose to follow, but Gail stopped her. "Let her be."

"Gail, I …"

"She'll be fine. The problem you see is that, on one hand she hates him, while at the same time she's attracted - enthralled would be a better word."

"What can we do?"

"Nothing, at least not yet. We'll have to wait and see what happens tonight. Look Rachael, it's not too late if you want to opt out. I wouldn't blame you if …"

"Not a chance."

Their meals arrived just then, but after a few minutes, Laura still had not returned. "I'm going to look for her." Rachael said as she pushed back her chair and rose.

She checked all the usual places without success. "John," she shouted across the bar, "did you see a friend of mine? She's about my height with blond hair, shoulder length, wearing a silk jacket."

"Hi Rachael. Yeah, I saw her in the corridor, standing in front of that picture. You know, the one of that king you fancy." He chuckled.

Rachael's heart skipped a beat. She raced to the corner leading to the corridor then stopped abruptly, steadied herself, then casually moved forward to stand at Laura's side. "Come on Laura, your dinner's ready and Gail's waiting." She whispered.

Laura nodded and slowly backed away. Just as she reached the door to the patio she paused and turned to Rachael. "I'm sorry," she whispered, her voice choked with emotion, "I wish I could say something really positive about him, but well, he was a very bitter man at the end you see." She smiled thinly. "I think too, he was a very honourable man, who realized too late that his decision to go after Tudor was ill-advised. His last thoughts were for those few brave, loyal men who died trying to defend him, and his crown.

She sighed, on the point of tears as her eyes searched out the night. "Rachael, I think you have to know that if Richard had survived Bosworth, he would have initiated a blood bath. If that had happened, he would have legitimately gone down in history as a tyrant of the highest order, so maybe it all worked out for the best." She smiled thinly. "This way, the prize for executing women goes to the Tudors. Come on, we shouldn't leave Gail alone."

The church was brilliantly illuminated by a bank of floodlights Frequently Laura turned towards it, slipping away from the conversation, listening perhaps before being pulled back, as Rachael and Gail kept her focused as much as possible on the here and now. They avoided any further discussion of Richard directly.

"No," Laura said evenly, "not devils - demons. Devils are lesser beings sent to bedevil us. To be demonized, now that's a different story - trouble - big time. Long time practitioners of human frailty, demons will do whatever is necessary to achieve the eventual ruination of the mortals they have selected. Consummate liars, they breath evil in the ear of those who will hearken to them, guiding the unwary to self-destruction, murder; sins for which there is no hope of forgiveness. They can't kill, they don't need to. It's all too easy to bend a mortal to their purpose, instigating ... "

"Please Laura," Gail pleaded, "I don't want to hear anymore."

Laura smiled tightly. "You should be prepared Gail."

"How do you know he's strong?" Rachael asked Laura directly, her eyes unflinching.

"Did I say that?"

"Laura, you said specifically that he is physically strong. How do you know that?"

"Sheer presumption on my part." She replied with a shrug. "He must have been afterall. Ah, here comes our waitress. Dessert Gail?"

"Laura, I'm not talking about what he was, I'm talking about the now. What he is now. Is there a physical presence?" Rachael gripped Laura's arm just below the elbow. "Answer me!"

"Take care Rachael that the obsession you have for his man does not cloud your reason." Laura cautioned as she pulled her arm free with some force.

"And what about your obsession?" Rachael shot back in a hoarse whisper.

Laura sighed, then turned slightly to smile up at their waitress, pointedly ignoring Rachael. "Irish Coffee please."

"I'll have one too." Rachael said, her voice hard and level as she stared at Laura. "Make it a double."

"Aren't you two having dessert?" Gail whined as she

reappeared from behind the oversized menu, her eyes dancing in anticipatory delight as she order the freshberry flan.

". . . and there's a hierarchy of angels from Seraphim at the top, Cherubim, Thrones, to Virtues, Powers, and Dominions, then finally Principalities, Archangels and Angels." Gail paused to glance at Laura who sat listening, her fingers idly shaping and reshaping her table napkin.

"Powers," she said, tossing the napkin aside. "Didn't St. Paul suggested that they work both sides of the fence?"

"What do you mean?" Gail asked, suddenly nervous. Laura's voice had shifted.

"I mean that Powers were designed to stop evil on earth, or at least control it, and the demons, but many were corrupted to such an extent that St. Paul urged caution, that's all." She shrugged. "Satan was a Cherubim I believe, before The Fall that is. Interesting isn't it, that the Cherubim were believed to be the bestowers of knowledge?" Laura offered Gail a smile, subtly vindictive

"I need another drink!" Rachael said, shaking her head in disbelief.

"Tipsy, sotted, boozed, pie-eyed, sloshed, polluted, stinko, smashed, blotto." Do you know how many words there are in the English language to describe drunk? "High, tight, loaded, stewed, bombed, plastered." Rachael chuckled, enjoying herself.

"Ladies are none of those." Laura announced with conviction.

"Oh, I know," Rachael replied in mock sobriety, "we are inebriated. Horses sweat, men perspire and ladies glow." She laughed openly.

"I like three shits in the wind myself." Gail added.

"That's sheets Gail, not shits." Rachael corrected.

All three of them burst into laughter which echoed stridently in the still night air.

Suddenly Laura stiffened. Slowly she rose. "Ladies, I hope we are sufficiently whatever, because I think we have company."

"Come on Laura, you're just trying to scare us. The only spirit here is the one in the bottom of my Irish Coffee."

"I don't need to scare you. There's something very near that can do a far better job than I can." The tone of Laura's voice sobered the other two instantly.

"What is it?" Gail whispered, her voice tight and breathless.

"By the pricking of my thumbs, something wicked this way comes." Laura intoned the famous lines from Macbeth. Gail began to sob hysterically.

"Gail, shut up! Laura hissed. "Rachael, see to her. Keep her quiet or we're all in trouble. Stay well back both of you and for God's sake, don't move and don't make a sound."

Carefully she inched forward, scanning the darker recesses, using the light which filtered through from the church to guide her. A slight breeze began to stir the shrubs which bordered the patio area, shaking the umbrellas as it grew in intensity. She was about ten feet away from the table when the church bells announced eleven. In a whisper she counted each stroke and on the last, the lights were extinguished, plunging the area into semidarkness. The wind rose, then ceased abruptly. Laura's ears popped. Then, perhaps most horrific of all, a deep, impregnable silence descended, still and cold as a tomb. "Richard please, where are you?" Laura whispered in her mind.

"You will pardon me if I decline your intended venue madam, but I am sure you will understand my reluctance to venture upon consecrated ground." The demon's voice was low, malicious. He appeared out of the shadows, moving slowly towards her. He was dressed in a costume of unsurpassed grotesqueness. "Oh come, come madam, art thou not amazed!" He hissed. "'Tis a fiendishly wonderful costume, you must allow. Now, what shall we call it - Contemporary Renaissance perhaps, or Modern Gothic?" He lunged forward, his face inches away from Laura's. "What do you think madam?"

She shrunk back in horror. His breath stank of death and decay.

"Ah, but I know thy thoughts." He growled as he straightened. "Alas, ye hope in vain. My sometime master, lord," he chuckled, "and king will not attend upon thee this night, nor any other. Pity. And here I was quite looking forward to a petite melee but alas, he has surrendered without a qualm, to save thee." He pouted. "Such a pretty show of affection, quite touching."

"Liar!" Laura growled.

"Madam, you do me wrong! Would I play thee false? Nay, for ye do have his ear, is that not so? Canst thou not call him to thy side as ye have done some short time since?" He laughed wickedly then sobered instantly as he regarding Laura with open contempt. "Even now the male child ye shall bear him quickens in thy womb. For this child yet unborn, he hast made this sacrifice."

"No!" Laura screamed as she tried to cover her ears, to block him out as he whispered to her in a voice harsh with malice.

"Thou art but the vessel of his true intent. Thy union an unholy and unnatural alliance, and for it thy soul is damned."

"Leave her alone!" Rachael shouted, as she raced to Laura's side.

"Rachael!" Laura cried. "Get back from him, don't let … " But it was too late.

Caught within the periphery, the demon turned his full attention on Rachael, his cold black eyes taking in the substance of her as she was held rigid with fear. "Ah, yet another beauty and another slave, me thinks, of the Plantagenet." Rachael tried to turn away, but he forced her by sheer force of will to took into his eyes. "Scream for me child, that I might know thee." But the cry that came died upon her lips as he drew forth the quintessence of her terror, breathing in, feeding upon her to the very core before he tossed her aside.

Laura moved forward, her anger rising to fever pitch as she prepared to confront him.

"Spare me thy indignation lady and thy puny threats, for ye are as dust before my storm   Get thee gone into exile madam! I would not have thy bastard whelp birthed within this realm. And take this creature with thee."

He smiled then, his face suddenly angelic as he rubbed his hands together, gleefully. "Well, 'tis been a good night's work, but alas, I must take my leave."   With an exaggerated flourish he bowed towards Laura. "Madam, 'til we meet again and we shall, one day, I promise thee." He smiled wickedly as he began to back away into the darkness.

"Francis!" The voice was low and masculine; hate and malice thinly veiled by authority.

"My lord?" Instinctively the demon responded, then froze in fear and confusion. His eyes combed the area rapidly before turning on Laura. "You would not dare! You have neither the will nor the capacity.   Try it and I will destroy thee and make his pain the greater."

Laura gasped, then drew back in terror.

The demon smiled, revealing teeth sharp as death itself. His eyes flashed triumphantly as he regarded her with open disdain. "As I thought." He hissed. "Adieu madam." He stepped back into the shadows and disappeared.

Laura rushed to where Rachael lay sprawled across the lawn. She fell to her knees, gasping as she tried to stem the flow of tears. Gail hung back, confused and afraid. "Rachael? Rachael, please it's Laura. He's gone, you're okay now." When she didn't respond, Laura gathered her into her arms and rocked her back and forth. "I'm sorry, I'm so … so very sorry." She cried, stroking her hair. Gradually Laura could feel the life returning, surfacing explosively as Rachael regained consciousness.

"That bastard, I'll bloody well have him!" She shouted, twisting in anger within Laura's grasp.

"Yeah well, he's had more than a snoot full of you. Are you all right?" Laura asked as she released the enraged Rachael.

"Who the hell does he think he is anyway? I'm an American citizen! You don't bloody well muck with the likes of us, or you'll be sorry."

"Rachael, shut up!" Laura laughed thinly. "In case you haven't noticed, we didn't win this round, nor are we likely to win the next."

Rachael grabbed Laura by her jacket collar, forcing her to turn and face her directly. "Laura, is it true?"

"Is what true?" Gail ask innocently. Laura and Rachael exchanged brief glances, before turning towards Gail.

"Did you see him?" Laura asked evenly.

"See who? We were sitting at the table and the next thing I know, Rachael is lying all over the lawn." Gail shrugged. "She drank too much and passed out. What's the big deal?"

Laura turned towards Rachael "I don't want to talk about it, not now, not here." She whispered quickly. "Come on you souse, on your feet. Gail, give me a hand."

As they moved towards the side door into the pub, Gail glanced at her watch. "Laura, it's nearly twelve. You promised to call Roger. He'll be waiting to hear from you. Besides," she said almost laughingly, "I think I'd feel better indoors. It's cold out here."

"John, could you pass me the phone please." Rachael demanded.

"Just a minute Rachael."

"No John, I want it now!"

John came down the bar, his face a thundercloud. He reached beneath the bar, grabbed the phone, and dropped it in front of her. "Anything else my lady?" He said with a mock bow.

"Thanks John." Rachael replied, her tone apologetic

Quickly Gail punched the buttons, summoning the overseas

operator. Within a minute she was through to her brother. She didn't talk long before handing the phone to Laura.

Laura hesitated a moment. "Hello Roger, how are you?" She intoned.

"Well, I hope you're having a great time spending money." He shot back, angrily. "Just today I've received three invoices on the equipment you installed at Peter's. Your illustrious suppliers want payment within seven days, but I haven't got a goddamn cent from Peter's yet. Christ Laura, what the hell kind of charity business are you running here? I checked your receivables. There's nearly five grand outstanding. Shit!"

"Nice to hear your voice too." Laura soothed, smiling tightly, aware that Gail was watching her closely.

"Don't give me that BS either. I'm sick of your mind games. Maybe it's just as well over the phone, away from those cat eyes of yours and the claws, but well, I think it's time we called it a day. You're the one with all the goddamn money, thanks to your parents and their lawyer, so you don't need me." His voice broke slightly. "Laura, I can't keep up with your excesses any more. I want a quiet life, kids, all the stuff you think is a load of crap."

"So, what are you saying?"

"You know what I'm saying. I want a divorce Laura, and the sooner the better."

"Granted." Laura replied flatly.

"Good! Well, that's it then. I've got to go. This call is costing me a fortune. Give my love to Gail." As he was about to hang up, he had an afterthought. "Oh, happy birthday."

But Laura had already dropped the headset into its cradle. On a sideboard a few feet away, a miniature of Big Ben tolled the midnight hour and the life that Laura had once known ceased to exist on the final stroke.

Gail and Rachael sat across the table from Laura. Slowly she lifted her head and smiled thinly at Rachael, while pointedly ignoring

Gail. "Well Rachael, has it been a fun evening for you?"

"Yeah right! Look, I could use a drink and last call is coming up. My treat, so here's your chance. What do you want?" Slowly she edged free of her chair, aware of the tension between Laura and Gail.

"Champagne, that's what I want." Laura announced, drumming the table with her finger tips while she mentally calculated the distance to Gail's throat. "Get a bottle Rachael. Gail and I have something to celebrate."

Rachael moved rapidly away from the table.

"You had it all planned, didn't you?" Laura growled. "It's amazing! Despite all that's been going on, you still managed to get in under the wire. Delivered me up to your beloved, bloodless, suckhole of a brother just in the nick. Now that he has tacit approval, good old Roger should put in quite a performance tonight." She smiled wickedly. "Let's see, it's midnight just gone here. Hey, he's got plenty of time for a quick dinner with his lady love and then a nice slow screw in my bed. Does that sound about right?"

"Laura, you don't understand, I ... "

"Now, there's where you're wrong, I understand perfectly."

"Roger wants kids. He wants a son to carry on the family name but you, you ... "

Laura started to laugh. "Listen you little fool. Roger wants kids sure, but he also wants to have nothing to do with them until they're old enough to make a buck. I'll play nursemaid to no one, least of all him, or his snivelling brats. I'm not angry at Roger, nor the break up of my marriage - it was inevitable What I'm upset about is your duplicity. You have betrayed me Gail, and that I cannot, will not, forgive."

Gail's eyes filled with tears. "You haven't been yourself since your parents were killed. Roger tried to ... "

"How dare you mention my parents in the same breath. I'll tell you what Roger tried to do, a big fat nothing - zero. He barely held my hand, let alone support me emotionally through that awful ordeal. The rest of your family, including you, didn't even bother to attend the funeral. Roger told me later, by way of explanation, that none of you like to attend functions which are sad. Well, that's just too goddamn bad, isn't it?"

Tears rolled silently down Gail's face.

"Oh Gail, please don't cry." Laura reached for Gail's hand and squeezed it lightly. "I'm sorry, I really am, but you can't continue to wish for me to love Roger. I've tried and it hasn't worked. You're the sister I never had, and because I love you, I want you away from me. Until I sort this mess out, I would feel a whole lot better knowing you are safe somewhere far away. Do you understand?"

"What about Rachael?" Gail asked, her voice charged with emotion.

"Rachael must make her own decision." Laura replied softly, deftly hiding from Gail the knowledge that Rachael had unwittingly placed herself in Gail's stead, and squarely in the path of eternal damnation.

Rachael swooped into her seat and smiled before presenting a bottle which she described as a befuddled domestic, with indiscriminate parentage, yet a champagne nevertheless and not too bad a drop - considering.

They stayed in the pub until closing time. Rachael was able to persuade John and a friend to escort them back to their room, although John was more than a little annoyed.

"Jeez Rachael, it's been one hell of a night!" He exploded. "I'm just about up to here with the ass holes - excuse my French - around here this evening. One of the new girls was accosted by some creepy jerk who smelt like he hadn't had a bath in months. I told him and his mates to get the hell out, but they said they were going anyway, the cheeky sods. This is Fotheringhay for crying out loud, not bloody Piccadilly!"

Day 13
Fotheringhay - St. Albans

Queen Margaret:

> *Poor painted queen, vain flourish of my fortune!*
> *Why strew'st thou sugar on that bottled spider,*
> *Whose deadly web ensnareth thee about?*

Shakespeare -
The Tragedy of King Richard the Third
[Act I, Scene 3]

ail! Where is she?" Rachael voice betrayed pure panic.

Gail was awake instantly. "I . . . I don't know! Oh my God!" She leapt from her bed and grabbed the first bits of clothing she could find. "Okay, okay, keep calm. Rachael, you go to the castle and I'll go to the church. She's probably at one, or the other."

"Right!"

Rachael was halfway out the door before Gail stopped her. "Rachael, be careful. She may not be herself."

Rachael nodded, trying desperately to remain calm and in control - for everyone's sake. The early morning sun heralded another beautiful summer day, but Rachael saw none of it as she hurried across the courtyard and along the path towards the site of Richard's birthplace. In her mind she peeled back scenario after scenario as her anxiety mounted.

Laura sat huddled up on the brink of the mound, still in her pyjamas, her shawl pulled tightly around her body, leaving only bare feet exposed. The church, below and across the river, dazzled in the sunlight. Rachael approached her slowly and carefully, stopping just behind her on her right side. After a moment, Laura turned and looked up, offering Rachael a mere shadow of a smile.

"Hi," Rachael whispered, "how do you feel?"

"Shattered." Laura replied. She turned to look back towards the church as Rachael sat down near her, but at a slight angle, so she could see her clearly. "Oh God Rachael, I have a lot of truths to confront." She whispered on the point of tears. "I'm asking for your help."

"You've got it."

"Don't be too quick," she cautioned. "There's danger and something worse then death itself closer than either of us would care to imagine. I didn't want you to get involved, but now you are, and I'm sorry. Sorry!" She spat the word out as if the very taste of it was offensive. "What a stupid word."

"Laura, I …"

"No, don't! Rachael, please, don't ask me or I shall go stark raving mad."

"Okay. Look, I want you both to come back and stay with me in St. Albans. Stephen is still downcountry and will be all next week. When do you leave?"

"That's just it, I don't think I want to return home right now. I think Gail should, but I'm staying. I have an aunt in Edinburgh. I can stay there for a while until …"

"But what about Roger?"

"He asked me for a divorce last night."

"And a happy birthday to you too!" Rachael growled. "Jeez Laura, how could he do such a thing?"

"If you knew Roger then . . ." Suddenly Laura rose and turned, all in one movement.

Gail stood perhaps ten feet away, silhouetted against the morning sun. "It's time to say goodbye," she choked as she moved closer, her eyes brilliant with tears.

"Yes." Laura replied in a whisper.

Rachael rose silently to stand just within Laura's shadow.

Joanne put on a lavish breakfast for them, then stayed to entertain them with all the local gossip, especially about the large number of Ricardians who had visited over the past year, goading Rachael good-naturedly with some of the more amusing occurrences. Rachael tried her best to keep pace with Joanne's banter but, under the circumstances, it was impossible.

Later, they helped Gail load her luggage into the rental car. Rachael disappeared then, leaving Laura and Gail alone in the courtyard to say goodbye.

"What am I going to say to Roger?" Gail asked, tearfully.

"Tell him I'll be in touch as soon as … Just tell him that what happened between us was as much my fault as it was his. But, most of all, tell him to be happy. Okay?"

"Okay." Gail replied, nodding her head. "I … I got so scared Laura. I couldn't take any more."

Laura enfolded her in a tight embrace. "I know and that's why I want you away from it, from me. Just drive carefully and have a safe flight. Try not to worry, I'll be fine." She pulled back from Gail and smiled wickedly. "I'm not without resources you know."

Laura stood for sometime alone in the courtyard, her mind a whirlwind. She turned as Rachael walked from the house to join her. "If you don't mind, I would like to go to the church before we leave."

"Sure" Rachael replied, meeting Laura's gaze directly.

There seek out the trappings of my House, the tombs of my parents, brother. I shall find thee.

"He's not here, Rachael." Laura whispered, her voice unsteady. Bathed in the light transfused through the York Window, Laura had tried again and again, but to no avail. Her hand shook as she brushed a piece of hair from the side of her face.

"Are you okay?" Rachael said, seriously concerned.

"Rachael, what the demon said - *an unholy and unnatural alliance and for it thy soul is damned.*" She shuddered, then gasped for breath as her throat tightened and the tears came.

Rachael drew back, appalled. "Oh my God." She gasped. "Look, it's going to be all right. Come on, you're tired, so let's get you home." She whispered gently as she eased Laura to her feet.

Rachael produced a blanket and oversized pillow from the back of her Range Rover, and proceeded to make a bed of sorts for Laura in the back seat. Laura protested all the while Rachael insisted. When Rachael stopped the car in the middle of the bridge for one final look at the church across the open fields which bordered the river, she turned to checked on Laura. She was fast asleep.

Rachael's home was not far from the centre of town on a large corner lot covered in trees. The house was huge, in preparation, Rachael said, for the family she and Stephen were thinking of starting soon. In the meantime, there were two guest rooms. Laura choose the one overlooking the backyard and Rachael's bed of white roses.

"They're beautiful."

"And in need of attention. Keep me company in the kitchen while I make us something to eat."

Laura watched as Rachael busied herself ransacked the refrigerator before pulling out pots and pans, organizing plates, cutlery. "I don't know how hungry you are, but I think you should eat something."

Laura nodded abstractly then turned and crossed the room to stand beside the set of French doors leading to a flagstone patio. "The garden's lovely." She said as she looked out across the expense of open lawn to the grove of oak trees and rhododendrons beyond. She turned to face Rachael. "You and Stephen must be very happy here."

"Yeah well, I don't think happy is quite the word. Steve wants me to quit the Society, stay at home and have kids. It's his parents really. Steve is an only child you see, and well, his family are pushing to extend the blood line. Boy were they upset when he announced that he was planning to marry a colonial."

"I guess the Society takes up a lot of your time."

"It's more than that." Rachael paused, biting at her lower lip. "My preoccupation with Richard has, well ... Steve calls it an obsession. Anyhow, just before the get-together last weekend, he basically said it was either Richard or him. I had to choose."

"And have you?"

"Just after you guys called, Steve rang." Rachael shrugged. "To make a long story short, I told him to go to hell."

"And?"

"And, he told me to get out of this house, his parents house I might add, by Friday. End of story." She shrugged.

Laura sighed. "I'm sorry Rachael."

"Hey, it's not your fault."

Laura eased herself into one of the chairs set beside a small round table in the corner of the kitchen. "Have you ever seen a musical called *Damn Yankees*. There's a song in it. I can't remember. Something about ..."

Rachael smiled. "Yeah, I know the one. *We're two lost souls on the highroad of life, one without a sail and one with no rudder.* There was a demon, devil or something in that show and it was a musical. Do you think it would help if we put all this to music?"

"Sure," Laura replied with a chuckle, "as long as it has a happy ending."

"Well, you're the script writer, so where do we go from here?"

"Do you fancy a trip into London tomorrow?"

"Where, or dare I ask?"

"To the Tower."

"Oh no you're not! I'm not going to let you anywhere ..."

"Rachael, you want to find out what happened to the boys,

the Princes, don't you? That's where the answer is to be found. He said to look for the truth *'in a place forsaken of the living world, where time is measured in drops of blood as through an hour glass'* - the Tower. Rachael, I have to know if he ordered the deaths of those kids."

"Why tomorrow? Why not leave it a few days, until you're rested."

"Because there's not much time left."

"Time left, to do what?"

"To save Richard, of course."

"But I thought …"

"Oh, he has him all right, but he can't hold him." Laura chuckled wickedly, then jumped up and hugged Rachael enthusiastically.

"I … I don't understand." Rachael cried.

"Don't you?" Laura replied. "All the prayers, all the expressions of love. Don't you see, God has heard Rachael, and so He stands poised perhaps, unwilling to interfere yet … We can save him Rachael!"

Rachael just stared, too stunned to speak.

"We stand within the sight of God. He will listen, but only to the truth. On that basis only will He render His judgement. We must see that it's brought to light even if I have to … I **must** believe He is a God of forgiveness and love, otherwise … Rachael, He won't let it happen. He can't." Suddenly, inexplicably she laughed. "Don't worry, we have a very powerful ally."

"Who?"

"Nell Turner of course."

Day 14
The Final Confrontation

Time's glory is to calm contending kings,
To unmask falsehood, and bring Truth to light.

Shakespeare -
The Rape of Lucrece

Laura stood at the window and watched as the storm clouds gathered. The wind tore at the trees, tormenting the branches, stripping them of their leaves, then forcing them to dance before it like heralds screaming *BEWARE.* She turned away then to inspect the black velvet gown which she had worn on William's Hill. "Gail did a good job removing all traces of blood." She thought sadly as she ran the palm of her hand along the fur trim.

"We're in!" Rachael shouted triumphantly as she swept into the room. "Chris insisted that we go as his guests. Thank God he won't be there. Jeez Laura, if we're caught, I'm going to be in one hell of a fix."

"We won't be." Laura replied flatly.

Rachael was appalled when Laura had suggested that not only must they visit the Tower, but after dark. When Rachael had mentioned the idea of attending the 'Ceremony of the Keys' at 10 pm. Laura had jumped at the idea, insisting with some degree of force that Rachael use her influence to 'procure what was required'.

"Where did you get that?" Rachael asked, indicating the gown.

"In Middleham. I was thinking of taking it with me and changing into it when ..." Laura paused.

"When what? Laura, you have to tell me what you've got planned."

"I can't, not yet. You know, he recognized that the dress was wrong right away but, he also said that he thought I looked quite pretty in it. I think he appreciated the effort." She laughed lightly. "Do I sound completely mad?"

"Yeah, a little, but I always figured you were anyway." Rachael shrugged then smiled.

"Thanks a lot."

"You're welcome. Well," she said, her tone upbeat, "if you're getting dressed up, so will I." A few minutes later she returned with a dark green gown, in real velvet, with sleeves cunningly slashed to reveal gold silk beneath. "What do you think?"

"Very nice. Do you wear it to his birthday party?"

"You make it sound like there's balloons, clowns and magicians when, in actual fact, the evening consists of a medieval banquet, music, and . . ."

"... a cake with 500 and whatever candles." Laura smiled, genuinely amused.

"To us, he's thirty-two." Rachael replied derisively.

"And he looks fifty. Next time, give him a party with clowns. He'd love it." Laura chuckled.

"You are crazy!"

"You know, considering what's been going on lately, you're probably right." She sighed. "Pity though that practicality prevents us from taking the gowns. I think between us we could attract just what we want." Laura replied, her expression sober, her eyes distant, guarded.

"Richard?" Rachael whispered, the name almost catching in her throat.

"We'll see."

They were ushered into the Tower, along with perhaps fifty others, including quite a few children. It was almost 10 pm. The ceremony, which dates back 700 years, would begin promptly on the hour, so they were hurried along Water Lane to take their positions before St. Thomas's Tower. In front of them loomed the Wakefield Tower with the Bloody Tower to the left and the fortified gateway in between. Beyond, lost from sight, stood the great central keep - the White Tower. The storm which had threatened all day was gathering in intensity; the smell of rain pronounced on the strong wind which had not diminished, as is so often the case, at sunset.

As they watched, the Chief Yeoman Warder, with military escort, began the task of locking the outer, Middle and Byward Tower gates. From their vantage point, it was impossible to see what was happening, so they were thankful for the commentary supplied by another Yeoman Warder who had already given them advance warning of what to expect, frightening the children by suggesting that they would soon be locked within for the night, unless they could find their way out.

As the Chief Yeoman Warder returned with his escort, Keys in hand, he was challenged by a sentry. Once satisfied that the Keys were those of the Sovereign, he was saluted by the Tower Guard who fell in behind. At this point Laura and Rachael and everyone else, of course, were asked to proceed through the gateway to the base of the stairs leading upwards to Tower Green. The Keys would then be passed to the Governor for the night, but Laura and Rachael would miss this portion of the Ceremony as they held back from the crowd, then slipped unseen hard up against the Wakefield Tower, before merging with the rubble and scaffolding just beyond where repairs were being made to secure the ancient edifice.

"We'll have to wait here for a bit." Laura whispered close to Rachael's ear. She nodded.

The rest of the Ceremony quickly followed and within a few minutes everyone, including the children, who were arguing about various methods of escape, began to make their way back towards the gates. They were locked, of course, but contained postern doors, small enough to allow individual passage through.

"Come!" Laura drew Rachael rapidly along, pass the site of the Great Hall then up the slope, skirting the ruins of the Wardrobe Tower on the eastern side, to the north side of the White Tower. The wind's strength increased alarmingly, thrashing at the branches of the trees, sending up a low moaning sound punctuated by the dull rumble of thunder as the storm rapidly approached from the west.

Laura paused for a moment as the door leading down into the basement of the Tower loomed out of the darkness, solid oak timber and reinforced iron. Closed, but was it locked? Carefully, gently she put her weight against the iron ring and was rewarded with a dull thud as the latch drew back and the door eased open a crack. Once inside, Laura turned, put her body against the door and pushed it closed with an audible metallic groan which echoed through the chambers below. As if to applaud her enterprise, the rains came, accompanied by lightning and thunder, the one hard up against the other as the centre of the tempest spiralled overhead. It was to be the most horrific storm to hit London in fifty years.

"This is the dungeon." Rachael whispered, her voice harsh with fear. "Do you know what went on down here?"

"Yeah, I know. Come on, it'll be better once we get some light on the subject."

"I don't think so." Rachael muttered as she searched through her bag for her flashlight.

Together they made their way towards the vice at the northeast corner then began their slow spiral course upwards towards the Chapel on the second floor. Their soft-soled shoes made not a sound on the stone as they progressed, keeping their beams of light focused at their feet. Every nerve in Laura's body was on the alert for the slightest sound but all she could clearly hear was the beating of her own heart.

Slowly, carefully they inched their way along the inner wall then through the archway and into the Chapel. Laura breathed an audible sigh of relief, although when she smiled at Rachael, the gesture appeared forced and anxious. "Are you ready?"

"As I'll ever be." Rachael shot back.

Just then a terrific bolt of lightning lit even the darkest recesses. The thunder followed seconds later, a massive cracking sound then a deep, resonate boom which jolted the ancient structure. Seconds later the entire Tower complex was plunged into a darkness which radiated outwards, consuming half of Greater London in a massive power failure.

"That was nasty." Laura gasped. "Okay, now all we have to do is find some more light. Come on, give me a hand. We'll get the candlesticks from the altar and bring them back here, near to the archway. Hurry, there isn't much time."

In a few minutes they had everything ready, thanks in part to Rachael's lighter which she had stowed in her coat pocket. "Ever since Minster Lovell." She said in defence. "You may have given up smoking, but not me. Now what?"

"Now it's just a matter of setting out the bait." Laura replied, her voice hard and cold.

"Bait! What bait?" Rachael asked, suddenly fearful.

"Us, my dear." Laura answered, as she knelt in prayer, pulling Rachael down with her.

"Oh my God! Laura, I don't think I'm sufficient qualified to …"

"Richard said that all truth is highly prized and this truth, precious above all. If you want it, then you'll have to be prepared to fight for it. That's the bottom line. Besides, it's too late now - he's here."

Rachael drew as close to Laura as possible, then followed her gaze through the archway which separated the chapel from the chamber beyond. The blackness was impenetrable. They waited, hardly breathing.

The massive explosive effect of the lightning caught them

both offguard. They clung to each other in terror as bolt after bolt lashed the sky. On the last they saw him, perhaps twenty feet away. He smiled wickedly, before the darkness descended again and the thunder rolled.

Gathering herself together, Laura rose to face him, positioning herself squarely between the demon and Rachael. Despite all her best mental preparation however, raw terror clawed at her as he moved within the candle light and she looked into his eyes, deep black, pitiless and awful.

"Bitch! I should have murdered thee at Bosworth! Then, when I had the chance. That brief moment when he let me have thee for a plaything, before he kicked me aside like a cur." Laura gasped. The demon laughed wickedly. "Fool! He loves not thee. Power is his mistress. There is none other."

Laura threw her head back in defiance, her fists clenched. "What do you want?"

"Ah, the whore speaks very like a true knight's lady. So be it then. Let us to the task at hand, for now is not the time for idle prater. What do I want? I am here to give, not to take." He sighed and moved closer to the threshold. Instinctively Laura backed up as many paces, drawing Rachael with her. "How shall I talk with thee at such a distance?"

"Then come closer." Laura growled, her voice low and even.

"Ye dare to mock me madam?" His voice grew angry, the tone cold as ice. "Ye have interfered! Thy quest for truth has torn in sunder the very fragment of order. The balance must be restored, and this cannot be achieved as long as ye continue to seek this knowledge he has withheld from thee. So madam, I will satisfy thee in this, and in return, ye shall promise to release him from thee, now and forevermore. Do we have an accord?"

Laura laughed, derisively. "You must think me a fool to believe he would ever make a deal with you or any of your ilk."

"He has before," the demon added, mocking her with a malicious smile. "Thou hast no knowledge of this man ye have taken so tenderly to thy breast. Speak madam, what is it to be? You want the truth, he wants you to know it now, and make an end. And I? I am merely the messenger yet again and poorly paid for my pains, I might add."

"And if I refuse?"

"That ye will not do. Thy need for truth surpasses all caution, which is why ye have gotten thyself into this mess of pottage in the first place. Ye hast no choice in this. Mortal thou art. Unless ye relinquish this unholy and unnatural bond, ye will be mad before another year, and all that ye know and love will be lost to thee forever. Mark me well madam, that is both a promise and a threat."

Laura nodded.

"Say!"

"I swear."

He smiled tightly.

———

"Ill they were, both of body and of mind. Knowingly he preyed upon their weakness, locking them away deep within the Tower unseen by all, bereft of the company of those they knew and loved. 'Tis a cruel fate, is it not?" He mused. "Cruel, aye and worse than cruel me thinks, as fear became their constant companion and with it, an intolerable hatred for the uncle who would do this thing. In time fear, and even loathing, were supplanted by despair, then thoughts of death, as they sickened the more. This I know for I visited them, talked with them, then helped them to die." He laughed wickedly. "Such young ones, so easily swayed, so easily brought to my purposes." Laura gasped. "Ah, ye see now the truth of what ye surmised, yet refused to believe."

"He can not be held responsible, he ... he tried ..."

"He is responsible and he tried nothing! He let them die. He encouraged me in my endeavour knowingly, then waited."

"Liar!" Laura shouted back. "Not for a moment will I believe that he would ever have trusted you - ever allowed you near them."

"Thou knowest me madam, for I am the Companion. From his youth to his end at Redemore, aye and beyond, I have been at his side. I am the power the force and the will."

"And the sower of the seeds of his destruction. You were the cause."

"Twas I who did his bidding!"

"No!" Laura growled. "You, you were the instigator, the evil that pervaded his whole existence. It was you who brought about his death, and the deaths of so many others, including the Princes. The responsibility is yours, not his." She laughed cruelly, her voice edged with hate and disgust. "Those boys had been called for, but you got there first, didn't you, and made sure they died. What bitter news was brought to him that day. How you must have revelled in the telling."

The demon's smug expression of satisfaction, of pure unadulterated evil drove Laura's anger to a fever pitch.

"You monster! It wasn't enough to frighten them, was it? No, you had to take from them all that they had left, and more. You destroyed hope, the last reservoir of mankind. My God, they were children!"

Laura voice broke with emotion. "How could he confessed to a sin he knew he did not commit? He knew of your pride, the great weakness, and first amongst the sins abhorrent to God. Such arrogance! He knew you could not resist the telling of that awful truth. To brag about it, you bastard!"

Laura tossed her head back, smiling in triumphant. "Now the truth has been spoken, and he can rest in the telling of it. You shall not have him, now or ever! I and others like me will continue to seek God's mercy on his behalf and you .... you hellhound can go back to your infernal master and tell him you have failed."

The demon smiled, revealing teeth as sharp as daggers in a face no longer quite human. "Ye are mistaken whore bitch that thou art! In thy conceit, born of the love ye think he bears thee, thou hast not marked the compass of my course. There is but one task set me, and that ye have failed to espy. The downfall of his House was but a simple task, and from its ruins no great matter to pluck the last of the Plantagenet line. My task was done long since, save for this murderous and licentious creature that thou wouldst cling to while yet knowing the extent of his cruelty, his ambition. Thou art as a pawn to him, thy obsession has enthralled thee, twisting thy soul. Know then that his fate shall be thine."

His eyes glowed blood red with rage. "Ye take refuge in holy sanctuary, and from it spit thy wrath, yet I would draw thee out, as I have said, and ye will come. But first the other, who stands within thy shadow. Come to me child, that I might work thy terror, thy dreams and deep desires into an instrument which will speak of revenge."

Slowing Rachael moved forward, entranced. Laura grabbed her but Rachael turned, her eyes vacant in the candlelight as she fought to free herself from Laura's grasp. Then, in one violent movement, she smashed Laura across the face with the back of her hand, sending her backwards, deeper into the nave. Rachael turned then and stepped across the threshold to where he awaited her.

"Take this into thy hand child. Yea, 'tis wondrous to look upon, is it not? Behold the misericord of all thy mythology. Instrument of revenge, of lust, of sudden death. Born in the fires of hope by a faith gone mad with power. The incorruptible made loathsome in the sight of God. 'Twas his 'til the last - now it is thine."

The blade slipped into Rachael's hand as her fingers tightened around the jewel-encrusted hilt.

He stood inches from her ear and whispered darkly. "Look closely child into the crystal and see how he did use her, taking the place that should have been thine, pressed deep beneath his lust. No unwilling partner was this, for see how she does rise to meet his thrust, measure for measure, writhing in pleasured pain, drenched with the sickly smell of her own desire. Thrice he took her to ensure the passage of his child to this mortal's womb wherein now it lays, an aberration both of God and man. I shall bring her to thee. No more shall she have of him, for ye shall slay her in the here and now, and he shall be thy prize."

"Rachael! No, don't listen to him. Rachael, he lies .... lies!"

"Silence! Husband thy breath madam, for soon it shall be mine. Now, come to me, so ye may know, at the last, the extent of my power over thee. Thou art mine now and forever more, and I shalt have thee, as I have said. Then I shall know the limit of thy insatiable desire, when ye shall screamed through all eternity at my handling of thee. Come madam, tread the path to thine own destruction. Come to me."

Laura screamed then screamed again as she found herself inexplicably drawn forward. The walls of the chapel seemed to press inwards upon her as if forcing her out, while the entrance way loomed, larger then larger still, opening like the jaws of a giant predatory beast.

The moment she crossed the threshold, he grabbed her by the throat, then forced her, in one quick motion to her knees in front of Rachael.

"Now shalt thou do it. Now shalt thee know the sweet taste of revenge upon this wanton harlot who would steal his love from thee. One quick trust and he is thine, now and forever more. Murder her." He whispered, then watched in pure pleasure as the blade was raised high. In the wavering light offered by the candles, the jewels blazed as they had centuries before, speaking of another time in which innocence was murdered.

The demon's moment of triumph vanished in a heartbeat as Rachael paused at the apex of the thrust, tears dissolving her intent. "No-o-o-o." She screamed. The misericord tumbled from her hands, to be caught unseen in its headlong plunge.

The demon turned, confused. Then he felt the icy thrust as the blade cut into his heart and the image of his hated appeared before him.

"Revenge Francis, yea 'tis truth ye speak, but revenge like treason doth oft' come from that quarter where least we expect to find it. And so I have come to thee. My House will be avenged as now my father and my brother are, done to death by thy treason. Here also find reward for the death of Edward's sons, delivered unknowing to thy malevolent embrace. All those that thou hast wronged shall pour their hatred of thee into this wound made fresh by me. There shalt they feed upon the knowledge of thy evil."

"Dickon, I did love thee once, remember, when we were but boys, before ..."

He screamed then the primeval scream born upon the winds when Cain murdered Abel, and all the world was plunged into chaos. Tortured beyond understanding, his body dissolved, disgorging from itself the misericord. From the twisted stump rose a creature of infinite horror ... massive in proportion reeking of the stench of hell. It regarded its adversary with open contempt.

"Plantagenet! None of thy line hast the power." The voice echoed, deep and resonant, the knowledge of dominion, coupled with an intense hate.

"'Til now."

From the shadows came the ravens, brought by the knowledge of the danger to the land, and to the one who would command of them. The creature drew back in fear, then tried to defend itself as the birds attacked, ripping whole sections of the beast with beak and claw. Unable to withstand the onslaught, it bolted for the vice, only to descend into a greater hell beyond earthly understanding, as its demonic master reclaimed its own.

Rachael woke to the sound of wind and rain, and as if far off, the roll of thunder as the storm followed the course of the Thames south and east to the sea. Laura lay unconscious just a few feet away, the anguish on her face softened in the flickering candlelight. Then the wicks sputtered, the flames twisted then died one by one, plunging her into total darkness made more terrifying by flashes of lightning which penetrated through the chapel window. She drew close up beside Laura and called her name, but there was no reply.

Fear heaped upon fear as Rachael tried desperately to remain calm. Then, from the corner of her eye she either saw or sensed movement. She turned, instinctively pulling Laura closer to her as if to protect her. He stood perhaps six feet away although it was difficult for Rachael to judge the distance until a massive bolt of lightning lit up the chapel as if it were day.

"See to the lady." He ordered, his voice even. Rachael had only a heartbeat of time to look deep within his eyes, to feel a sense of deep grief, of a life lived in terror, suspicion and finally betrayal, before the light was gone and the image with it.

"Laura! Laura! It's Gail, where are you? Laura!"

Gail reached the top of the vice next to the chapel, out of breath, a lantern swinging wildly from her left hand. "Oh, thank God I've found you!" She began to cry as she fell to her knees beside Laura. "Are you all right? Oh God, look at you!" Gently she ran her hand along the side of Laura's face. "The whole garrison is out searching for you two. Jeez, you're both in big trouble! I tried to make them understand but ... they just about ... they've got guns!"

"Gail? How ... how did you get here?" Laura gasped.

"I knew you'd try a trick like this. I've been waiting outside the Tower entrance all day, but you didn't come. When I heard about the Ceremony of the Keys, I had a bite to eat and was back in time to see the two of you go in. When you didn't come out I ..."

Gail was interrupted as the electric lights came on, flooding the Tower in bright, artificial light.

"If you three ladies would be kind enough to follow me."

Although the rifles were not trained on them directly, they might just as well have been. The inference was obvious. Together the three of them made their way out of the White Tower, this time under armed escort.

Day 15
Conclusion

Stanley: *Now civil wounds are stopp'd, peace lives again:*
            That she may long live here, God say amen!

Shakespeare -
The Tragedy of King Richard the Third
[Act V, Scene 4]

The Governor of the Tower of London studied each of them in turn, his arms folded across his chest, his manner sufficiently civilized to mask his indignation. "I assume that you realize the enormity of the situation in which you now find yourselves. Ms. Ward-Thomas, Ms. Kempe, Her Majesty's Tower of London is not a playground in which errant young ladies are free to wander in at will after hours. If, as Ms. Frazer has suggested, you had a specific task to perform here, could it not have been accomplished during regular hours?"

Both Laura and Rachael lowered their heads.

"I see. I will not go into the details of Tower security. It is sufficient, I think, for both of you to know that if it were not for Ms. Frazer here, you two might well be in an even worse predicament then the one in which you currently find yourselves." He cleared his throat suggestively. "Now, as I understand it, you two came here not to take, but to give. Am I correct in this?"

Laura stared incredulous.

"Then perhaps this may refresh your memory. It was found on the altar in the Chapel of St. John. Perhaps one of you would be so kind as to tell me just how it got there." Slowly he began to unwrap a small parcel, unveiling in the last fold, the misericord. "Preliminary study of this item has revealed that it is a misericord. Very rare, and I might add, extremely valuable - priceless in fact. Is it yours?" He asked Laura pointedly.

"No sir." She whispered. "It belongs to England."

"I see." He nodded, staring down, entranced by the bejewelled blade. "Ms. Frazer, I believe you have a flight home this afternoon. One of my security staff would be only to pleased to escort you to the airport and make sure you catch your plane.

"As for you two, neither Scotland Yard nor INTERPOL have expressed an interest in either of you, so I can only assume that you are both what you seem. Eccentric young ladies who ought to be at home nursing babies. Ms. Ward-Thomas, a member of staff has vouched for you in glowing terms. Beyond the fact that you are a member of the Fellowship of the White Boar, I foresee no harm in sending you on your way.

"As for you Ms. Kempe, it is my belief that it was you who masterminded this whole expedition. You and your friend are lucky to have survived." He regarded her with open disapproval before drawing himself to attention in a strictly military manner.

"On behalf of her Majesty the Queen, the Tower of London garrison, and the people of this realm, I thank you for this gift which will be a splendid addition to our museum. Beyond that ladies, I think it is best if we consider this little episode closed. Good day."

Gail, Rachael and Laura practically bolted for the door, nearly knocking over the Chief Yeoman Warder standing there. He watched them go in open surprise.

"But sir?"

"Relax Tom, they are quite harmless I can assure you." He sighed as he lifted up the misericord and looked deep within its jewelled surface, while slowly turning the blade around and around between long, slender fingers. "'Tis beautiful, is it not?" He whispered, enthralled.

Epilogue

King Richard was prostrate with shock and grief at the news of the death of the Princes by suicide. The implications were clear, and involved major damage control on his part. Fortunately, very few knew the truth - Lovell, Brackenbury, Tyrell and Green perhaps - all of whom were involved in the secret burial of the bodies. It is the author's contention that the chest containing their remains was placed at the end of a side shaft off a main tunnel which ran parallel with the surface, but some fifteen feet beneath. This tunnel opened at one end into the subterranean crypt beneath the sub-crypt of the Chapel of St. John the Evangelist. The other end lead directly to where the boys died, most likely the original Lanthorn Tower (or Lantern Tower) which was destroyed by fire in 1774. This tunnel may still exist. The burial was not only secret, but silent as well.

Suicide was regarding with such horror in those days, that Richard was forced to extract oaths from everyone involved so as to protect the integrity of his House. If he was aware of the rumours circulating, he choose to ignore them rather than reveal the truth. Ultimately it became a cross he was forced to bear alone. It would eventually destroy him.

Francis Lovell may or may not have taken the secret to his grave. Scholars still live in hope of finding papers written by him which may reveal the truth. It may be a vain hope however. As fantastic as the demon concept may seem, the fact that Lovell not only survived Bosworth Field but the Battle of Stoke, suggests either singular good luck on Lovell's part, or something more. Even his ultimate fate is shrouded in mystery.

It was Brackenbury who probably found the boys. Indebted to Richard for assuming the burden of responsibility, Brackenbury steadfastly stood by his side and died with him at Bosworth.

Sir James Tyrell was able to deflect Tudor successfully for several years, until he was eventually executed on the 6th of May, 1502. He kept the secret, and his promise to Richard, intact.

It is likely that Elizabeth Wydville was told the truth, perhaps by Richard. Naturally, she kept silent although years later, when King Henry VII began his campaign of vilification of Richard's name, she sprang to his defence. Stripped of all her wealth and titles, she was confined in Bermondsey Abbey where she died five years later.

Elizabeth of York probably knew from her mother only that Richard was innocent of the death of her brothers. Cold and unloving by nature, Henry VII kept her very much in the background, often in a state of extreme poverty. Henry VII was perhaps the most vicious king ever to sit on the English throne. His attitude towards his wife was despicable. Both he, and his mother conspired to break her, using the love she bore her uncle as a whipping post of sorts until she neither had the strength nor the will to defend him further. She adopted the motto *Humble and Penitent* which perhaps says it all. The love she bore her uncle endured however. The one and only thing Henry Tudor could not take from her.

When Edward of Middleham died, Richard ordered that he be interred in secret as were the two Princes. It seemed only fitting. The church at Middleham would seem a more likely place than Sheriff Hutton. It is the author's contention that the tomb effigy at Sheriff Hutton, although originally ordered by Richard to complete the mock burial place of his son, was never used for its intended purpose. After Bosworth, work on the monument ceased, and it was not until some time later that it was purchased, remodelled and employed as a memorial for another.

The murder of the priest in Middleham, although pure fiction, may have some elements of truth, since it is believed by many that the young prince was poisoned, perhaps by a priest or more likely, someone impersonating a priest. If Richard found out, then it would not be out of character for him to slay this individual personally. A rash act perhaps from a man unhinged by grief. 'Temporary insanity' - a plausible plea in any modern court of law.

Ultimately it is up to you - the reader - to decide whether King Richard should in all conscious continue to bear the responsibility for the death of the two boys. It is the author's contention that Richard's major weakness was the trust he placed in others. In the case of the Companion, such trust was misplaced and ultimately it would prove disastrous for this last King of the Plantagenet line, and for the House of York which he tried so desperately to preserve.

Conversely, Richard must be held accountable for the murders of King Henry VI and George, Duke of Clarence although, as the reader has learned, there were mitigating circumstances.

Against the background of the age in which he lived, King Richard III was perhaps no better or worse than his contemporaries and that, more than any other single issue, must be born in mind. At the dinner in Market Bosworth, Laura was heard to say *'Why do we all assume he was quite sane?'* Why indeed.

Excerpts from Laura's Notes

Anne, Princess Royal (1475-1511) - daughter of Edward IV/ Elizabeth Wydville. Married Thomas Howard, Earl of Surrey in 1495. This was the same Thomas who had been instrumental in ensuring that Hastings attended the fateful council meeting at The Tower. He fought on Richard's side at Bosworth, was captured and imprisoned. Eventually pardoned and released to fight the Scots at Flodden. Created Duke of Norfolk and Guardian of the Kingdom in 1520. His father died at Bosworth, slain by Oxford's troops.

Argentine, John - physician to Edward V. Dismissed from service by Richard Gloucester.

Beaufort, Margaret - Countess of Richmond (1443-1509) Married Edmund Tudor at the age of twelve. At thirteen she gave birth to her one and only son - the future King Henry VII. Married four times, her last husband was Thomas Stanley. Extremely intelligent and pious, she was also ruthlessly ambitious for her son. If Richard III had won the day at Bosworth, she would have undoubtedly been at the top of his hit list. Buried in Westminister Abbey beneath a magnificent gilt bronze effigy by Torrigiano, the rendering is notable for the fact that her 'eyes' are open which suggests that, even in death, she was not about to be caught napping! By way of a postscript, her father John, 1st Duke of Somerset, died unexpectedly shortly after an humiliating military defeat in France. Rumours at the time suggested that he may have committed suicide.

Catesby, William (1450-85) - lawyer. Originally a member of Lord Hastings' household, he turned spy in the employ of Richard Gloucester. Captured after Bosworth and executed. The 'Cat' referred to in Colyngbourne's rhyme.

Cicely, Princess Royal (1469-1507) - daughter of Edward IV/Elizabeth Wydville. Initially she married Ralph Scope of Upsall, brother of Richard's ally Thomas, lord Scope. This marriage took place early in 1485 and was sanctioned by King Richard who, by this time, had control of the older sister, Elizabeth. Cicely seems to have been a headstrong girl so perhaps King Richard felt it would be best to marry her off to a lesser noble and thus discourage any influence she may have had over the more pliant Elizabeth. Cicely's marriage was dissolved a year later to allow her to marry John, Viscount Welles, half brother to Margaret Beaufort! He fought at Tudor's side at Bosworth. After his death, she secretly married a humble squire - Thomas Kyme - without first seeking royal approval from Henry Tudor. She was banished from court, her estates confiscated. Margaret was able to intercede on Cicely behalf but it took Tudor a year to forgive her, accept the marriage and return her property.

Cecily Neville, Duchess of York (1415-1495) - Richard III's mother. Married Richard, Duke of York in 1425 when she was nine years of age - he was thirteen. The marriage produced a total of twelve children. Celebrated as the 'Rose of Raby', she was considered quite a beauty. She was the youngest of fourteen children born to Ralph Neville and his second wife Lady Jane Beaufort. Thus, Richard's maternal grandmother was a Beaufort; technically illegitimate and of commoner origins. Outlived all her sons. Died age eighty! Buried at Fotheringhay.

Clifford, John de (1435?-61) - called the 'Butcher'. Murdered Edmund, Earl of Rutland at Wakefield Bridge. Killed at Ferrybridge (Battle of Towton) under mysterious circumstances. His body was never recovered.

Edmund, Earl of Rutland (1443-60) - second surviving son of Richard, Duke of York/Cecily Neville. Murdered by 'Butcher' Clifford on Wakefield Bridge after first surrendering. Buried at Fotheringhay.

Edouard Lancaster (1453-71) - Prince of Wales; only son of Henry VI and Margaret of Anjou although likely sired by Henry Beaufort, 3rd Duke of Somerset. Betrothed to Warwick's daughter Anne. Use French spelling to avoid confusion with other Edwards. Slain at Tewkesbury. Buried beneath the choir - Tewkesbury Abbey.

Edward IV, King (1442-83) - Earl of March, eldest son of Richard, Duke of York/Cecily Neville. Married Elizabeth Wydville (1464). Proclaimed king 1461; reclaimed throne 1470. Buried at St. George's Chapel, Windsor.

Edward V, uncrowned (1470-83) - eldest son of Edward IV/Elizabeth Wydville - one of the two children commonly referred to as the 'Princes in the Tower'. Fate - officially unknown.

Edward, Earl of Warwick (1475-1499) - only son of George Clarence/Isabel Neville. Taken into custody after Bosworth at Sheriff Hutton. Imprisoned in the Tower of London until executed by Henry VII on a fabricated charge of treason. After the death of his son, Richard may have considered the young Edward as a possible heir, but seems to have thought better of it because of his youth, limited intelligence and of course his father had been attainted for treason. Henry VII certainly viewed him as a threat to his throne.

Elizabeth Wydville (Woodville) (1437-92) - Queen consort of King Edward IV. Her tomb at St. George's Chapel, Windsor has the spelling as Widvile. Bore a total of ten children, three sons and seven daughters. Described as a glacial beauty. Died within the confines of Bermondsey Abbey.

Elizabeth of York (1466-1503) - eldest daughter of Edward IV/Elizabeth Wydville. Queen Consort to Henry VII, she was not crowned until two years after her marriage. She was kept in relatively obscurity by Tudor although, after the birth of Arthur, public pressure forced her husband to acknowledge her and the royal blood which legitimatized his claim to the throne. He viewed her coronation and the banquet afterwards from behind a lattice screen, taking no part whatsoever in the ceremony or the celebrations. Her marriage to Henry VII could best be described as a 'political match'. Despite the fact that she bore him seven children, it is doubtful if her relationship with her husband went beyond the bounds of duty. Dominated by first her mother, then her mother-in-law Margaret Beaufort, Elizabeth was kept very much in the background for the remainder of her life. She died of puerperal fever. Buried in Westminister Abbey.

George, Duke of Clarence (1449-78) - third surviving son of Richard, Duke of York/Cecily Neville. Married Isabel Neville, daughter of Warwick ('The Kingmaker'). Turned against his brother Edward IV in bid for the throne. Reunited in 1471. Fought at Barnet and Tewkesbury. Plotted against Edward IV again, charged with treason and condemned to death. Undoubtedly murdered in the Tower of London. Buried in Tewkesbury Abbey.

Grey, Sir Richard - Elizabeth Wydville's son by her first marriage. Executed by order of Richard Gloucester at Pontefact.

Grey, Thomas (Marquess of Dorset) (1451-1501) Elizabeth Wydville's son by her first marriage. Conspired with his mother to remove the royal treasure in advance of Richard Gloucester's arrival in London. Fled to France to join Tudor.

Hastings, Lady Katherine - wife of William, Lord Hastings. King Richard was more than generous to her. On the 23rd of July, 1483 he granted her a full pardon for her husband's treason, lifted the attainder on her title and estates and promised *'to protect and defend the widow and to suffer none to do her wrong'*. Her cousin was Reginald Bray, the notorious Lancastrian aid to Margaret Beaufort and conspirator par excellence.

Hastings, William (Lord) (1440-1483) - Richard III's Lord Chamberlain and Governor of Calais, fellow exile and supposed friend and confidant. Hastings shabby treatment of his wife may well have angered Richard who seems to have had two ruling passions - fidelity in marriage and family pride. Hastings renewed liaison with Mistress Shore after King Edward's death would hardly have endeared him to Richard. Hastings may have been either personally unaware or uninformed of Richard's disapproval of him and his lifestyle. By the time Hastings realized just how far out of favour he had become, his head was rolling across Tower Green. Ironically, the land on which the Battle of Bosworth was fought formed a portion of Hastings' estate. Executed by order of Richard

Gloucester on charges of treason and witchcraft. Buried in St. George's Chapel, Windsor.

Henry VI, King (1422-1471) Henry's mental condition was nonviolent unlike his grandfather Charles who, after being startled by the clash of a dropped lance is said to have killed four people before he was restrained. Henry VI's condition might best be described as a depressive stupor; he would lose control of his limbs and was unable to speak. His worst bout of illness lasted eighteen months. Very likely murdered by Richard Gloucester. Buried in St. George's Chapel, Windsor. The poet Pope wrote the following regarding King Henry VI and the close proximity of his tomb to that of King Edward IV.

> *Here, o'er the martyr-king, the marble weeps,*
> *And fast beside him once-feared Edward sleeps;*
> *The grave unites, where e'en the great find rest,*
> *And mingled lie the oppressor and the oppressed*

A private ceremony takes place each year on the anniversary of his death - 21st of May, in the Wakefield Tower. The brief service is conducted by the Provosts of Eton and King's College, Cambridge, both institutions founded by King Henry. The college emblems (lilies and white roses) are laid atop the plaque marking the spot where it is believed he died.

John de la Pole, Earl of Lincoln (1464-87) - Richard's named heir and nephew by his sister Elizabeth. Slain by Oxford's superior cavalry at the Battle of Stoke.

Katherine - Princess Royal (1479-1527) - daughter of Edward IV/Elizabeth Wydville married Sir William Courtenay, Earl of Devon, a firm ally of the House of Tudor which isn't surprising since Richard had presided at the trial and subsequent execution of Henry Courtenay in 1469.

Margaret of Anjou (1430-82) - Queen consort of Henry VI - mother of Edouard Lancaster, Prince of Wales. Conspired with Warwick to reclaim her husband's throne. Captured at Tewkesbury in 1471, imprisoned in the Tower before eking out an existence under house arrest, first in Windsor, then in Wallingford. Eventually ransomed to King Louis of France in 1476. Forced to relinquish all pretensions in England and her inheritance in Anjou, she died in abject poverty, her renowned beauty wasted by disease. Buried beside her parents in Angers Cathedral.

Margaret, Countess of Salisbury (1471-1541) - only daughter of George Clarence/Isabel Neville. Executed, by order of King Henry VIII on yet another trumped up charge of treason.

Morton, Bishop/Archbishop - lived to be a very old man. He succeeded Bourgchier as Archbishop of Canterbury and was soon afterwards appointed Lord Chancellor. He was trusted implicitly by Henry VII who relied heavily on his experience both in finance and diplomacy. Thomas More spent a brief time in his household while still a boy. Morton's almost fanatical hatred of King Richard lead to a series of plots and sub-plots which ultimately weaken Richard's hold on the throne, eventually leading to the destruction of both the monarchy and the House of York. Buried in Canterbury Cathedral.

Neville, Anne (1456-85) - Queen consort of King Richard III. Younger daughter of Warwick ('The Kingmaker'). Betrothed to Edouard, Prince of Wales, son of Henry VI in 1470. Married Richard Gloucester on the 12 of July, 1472. Produced only one frail child - Edward of Middleham. Died at Westminister Palace during a solar eclipse. The Richard III Society provided a beautiful wall plaque to mark her resting place near the high altar in Westminster Abbey.

Northumberland, 4ᵗʰ Earl of - Henry Percy - imprisoned after the Battle of Towton for father's Lancastrian support; pardoned and restored to earldom. Conspiciously absent at both the battles of Barnet and Tewkesbury. Richard Gloucester's pre-eminent position in the north caused considerable friction which is perhaps why Northumberland held his troops back at Bosworth. This is one man King Richard should never have trusted. Created Warden of the East March and Middlemarch under the new regime; murdered near Thirsk in Yorkshire while trying to collect taxes.

Oxford, 13th Duke of - John de Vere (1443-1513) The de Vere family were staunch supporters of the House of Lancaster; always had been. He narrowly escaped the carnage at Barnet, and remained a thorn in the side of the Yorkist cause until he was finally capture in 1474. He was imprisoned in Hammes (near Calais) for the next ten years; he should have been executed. Worried that he would join Tudor and the other exiles in France, King Richard ordered his removal to an English prison but, deVere was warned just in time and was able to win over his jailer, James Blount, who arranged his escape to France. Blount brought many of his men over to the cause, providing the Tudor side with a core of professional fighting men. After the death of his first wife (Warwick's sister) in 1506, de Vere married the lady Elizabeth Scope. He lived to be an old man but, despite considerable wealth and prestige, he failed to produce an heir and the House of de Vere died with him.

Ratcliff, Sir Richard - longtime friend and supporter of Richard III. As a Northerner, it was probably Ratcliff who actively discouraged Richard from his plan to marry his niece, Elizabeth of York. Perished on Bosworth field. The 'rat' referred to in Colyngbourne's rhyme.

Richard III - Bastard Children Both Richard's bastard children were probably born before his marriage to Anne Neville. His daughter **Katharine** was old enough in 1484 to marry William Herbert, Earl of Huntingdon. 'Old enough' in those days can mean anything; even small children were forced to go through a betrothal ceremony so that ambitious parents could gain wealth, power and property. Katherine undoubtedly died young. Any children she may have had did not survive her. **John of Gloucester** was knighted by his father in 1483 and, although still a minor, he was appointed Captain of Calais. Executed by Henry VII. **Richard Plantagenet** apparently lived in obscurity as a stonemason until his death, age eighty-one. An entry in the Parish register of Eastwell in Kent records the following: - *Rychard Plantagenet was buryed the xxij daye of Desember, Anno ut supra - 1550*. If true, he would have been born in 1469 when Richard, then Duke of Gloucester, was 27 years of age. There is no firm proof however that King Richard did, in fact, have a second illegitimate son.

Richard III - Birth Place Richard was the only surviving son (three brothers died in infancy) born in England. Edward and Edmund were both born in France; George entered the world in Ireland. Richard may have made use of the fact that he was English-born to augment his claim to the throne.

Richard III - Elizabeth of York In the 17th Century Sir George Buke claimed to have seen a letter written by Elizabeth of York to the Duke of Norfolk urging him to intercede on her behalf with King Richard. Elizabeth speaks specifically of the marriage propounded with her uncle and then refers to him as *'her onely joy and maker in this world'* and that she was his in heart and thought. This letter was reputed to have been written **before** Queen Anne's death. It seems apparent that there was at least a close personal bond between Richard and his niece. If an incestuous relationship existed, no proof has been offered beyond court gossip, although Richard was finally forced into issuing a public statement, denying any intent on his part to marry her. Shortly afterwards however, she was sent north to Sheriff Hutton.

Richard III - Friendship Friendship did not seem to play a part in Richard's thinking. Both Hastings and Rivers had shared exile with him way back in 1470. Both men may have assumed that they were dealing with the same Richard - they weren't!

Richard III - Marriage Contract Richard had a clause inserted in the marriage contract which stated that he would continue to enjoy his wife's estates even if the marriage ended in divorce which was a distinct possibility since without the papal dispensation, the marriage was technically illegal.

Richard III - Physical Appearance & Tudor Propaganda
Anthony Cheetham in The Life and Times of Richard III suggested that he was - *"weak and sickly child, he struggled through his early years, causing an anonymous rhymester to comment, with a note of*

surprise, that 'Richard liveth yet'.''

John Rous (writing shortly after Bosworth) in his History of the Kings of England - describes Richard as having been born with teeth (it was believed that babies born with teeth would inevitably become murderers), and hair down to his shoulders and, that he remained in his mother's womb for two years before he was born!

Polydore Vergil (*Anglica Historia*) describes Richard as *"little of stature, deformed of body, the one shoulder higher than the right . . . a short and sour countenance."*

Thomas More's *History* describes Richard as *"little of stature, ill-featured of limbs, crook-backed ...hard favoured of visage."*

The hunchback idea may have come from the biblical reference to the laws of the priesthood given to Moses from God (Leviticus 21: 16-23). Any form of blemish excluded a man from the Holy of Holies so, by extension then, a hunchback could not rule as King.

Richard III - Political Expediency, Learning of The Earl of Warwick's execution without trial of the royalist leaders after the battle of Edgecote prompted historian Charles Ross to comment in his book RICHARD III - *'Here Gloucester's former guardian offered him a prime example of the ruthless and unlawful elimination of political opponents, who could not be regarded as traitors, for they had not been in arms against their king. Gloucester himself was to follow this precedent in 1483.''*

Richard III Society Aims:

a) To promote in every way historical research into the life and times of King Richard III.

b) To secure a reassessment of the historical material relating to this period and of the role in English history of this monarch.

c) To circulate all relevant historical information to members of the Society, the media and all educational organizations.

Wydville, Anthony - 2nd Earl Rivers (1442-83) Elizabeth Wydville's brother, Edward V's governor, responsible for the child's unbringing on the Wales border at Ludlow. An ideal choice, Mancini describes him as *"a kindly, serious and just man, and one tested in the vicissitudes of life."* Very religious, he was also charming, well-educated, elegant, cultivated and had travel extensively throughout Europe. While at Ludlow he translated from the Latin 'The Dictes and Sayings of the Philosophers'. This was one of the first books printed in England by William Caxton; Rivers was his patron. Executed by order of Richard III at Pontefact.

Shore, Jane (Elizabeth Lambert) - King Edward IV's favourite mistress "for many he had, but her he loved". She seems to have been quite an extraordinary woman described by More as: *"proper she was, and fair: nothing you would have changed, unless you would have wished her somewhat higher...yet men delighted not so much in her beauty as in her pleasant behaviour. For a proper wit had she and could both read well and write, merry in company, ready and quick of answer, neither mute nor full of babble ... she never abused to any man's hurt but to many a man's comfort and relief"*. After the King's death, she again became the mistress of Lord Hastings, then the Marquess of Dorset. When Richard, as Protector, had Hastings executed in 1483, Jane was accused of complicity in his treason and was arrested and imprisoned. She was made to do public penance as a whore through the London streets dressed only in her kirtle, carrying a candle. Richard's plan to discredit her backfired however since she bore herself with such dignity and grace that the public sympathized with her. Thomas More wrote that Richard *'spoiled her of all that ever she had ... and sent her body to prison'*. Married Thomas Lynom, Richard's solicitor.

Stafford, Henry - 2ⁿᵈ Duke of Buckingham (1454-1483) - Although a brief but major character in the story of Richard III, Buckingham remains an enigma; a man driven by ambition at cross-purposes with itself. Essentially a loner and unpopular, his exalted opinion of himself was to be his strength and ultimately, his undoing. He was approximately two years younger then Richard. According to Alison Weir in her excellent book *'The Princes in the Tower'*, Buckingham is described as a proud man, jealous of the power of others and ruthlessly ambitious. He lacked judgement and often acted on impulse. His friends found him to be bluff and hearty, witty and talkative - in fact he was gifted, says More, with marvellous eloquence and had a real talent for persuasive speaking and public oration. More also tells us that Buckingham was strikingly handsome and impressive in appearance. Executed for treason by order of King Richard III.

Stanley, Thomas Lord - Married Margaret Beaufort in 1472. Described beautifully in Charles Ross's book *Richard III* as *'shifty, self-seeking and unreliable'* it was this same Stanley who would play a major role in Richard's downfall. After Bosworth, Stanley became the Earl of Derby and served as Lord High Steward at Henry VII's coronation. Later, he stood godfather to Henry VII's first born son, Prince Arthur. Stanley died in his bed in 1504, presumably at his estate, Knowsley Hall in Lancashire. When the redoubtable Margaret Beaufort decided to seek inclusion in a religious life, Stanley was forced to sign away his conjugal rights. It is obvious that she had no further use for him.

Sir William Stanley - brother to Thomas, Lord Stanley. Sir William's treacherous nature would prove his undoing. Incriminated along with others in the plot to advance the pretender Perkin Warbeck, he was publicly executed by Henry VII as an example to others who might still harbour loyalties to the House of York.

Tiptoft, John - Earl of Worcester - "the Butcher of England", so called for his brutal execution of the Earl of Desmond in 1467. This execution warrent was issued illegally by Elizabeth Wydville (she stoled Edward IV's signet ring) in retaliation for disparaging remarks made by the Earl about her. Tiptoft exceeded his mandate however by murdering the Earl's two young sons as well. Served as Treasurer of England for three years under Henry VI, then Constable of England under Edward IV. A handsome man (see effigy along with his two wives at Ely Cathedral), he was also one of the greatest scholars of the 15th Century. He studied in Italy and had in his collection many precious classical manuscripts which he presented to Oxford University before his death. He was executed in 1470 by order of Warwick in retaliation for his brutal execution of captured sailors on board the *Trinity,* anchored in Southampton. He asked that his head be severed in three strokes 'in honour of the Trinity'! Whether he meant the Holy Trinity or the ship is unknown.

Tudor, Henry VII King (1457-1509) **Commoner Origins** - Beaufort: John of Gaunt (4th son of Edward III) and mistress, Catherine Swynford, a commoner, produced three sons who took the name Beaufort. Declared legitimate (obviously their parents did not marry), they were barred from right of succession. Tudor: Henry V's widow, Catherine Valois married Owen Tudor, a Welsh squire. Their eldest son, Edmund Tudor, was created Earl of Richmond, married Margaret Beaufort and was killed fighting for the Lancastrian cause at Carmarthen Castle prior to the birth of his son, Henry.

Warwick, Richard Neville, Earl of Warwick (1428-70) 'The Kingmaker' - Eldest son of the Earl of Salisbury, Richard's mother's brother. Warwick acquired the title and estates of through marriage. His father was executed by Queen Margaret after Wakefield, the head displayed at Micklegate along with the Duke of York and his son Edmund. His death made Warwick the foremost peer in the realm. Warwick's illegal execution of Elizabeth Wydville's father and brother (after Edgecote) was not only unwise but downright stupid. By doing so Warwick had effectively burned his bridges, putting any chance of a reconcilliation with King Edward out of the question. Slain at the battle of Barnet, he was buried with his brother at Bisham Abbey. When Henry VIII destroyed the abbeys, the tombs was obliterated.

Bibliography

Bennett, Michael - The Battle of Bosworth (Alan Sutton Publishing Ltd., UK)

Bartholomew, James - Inside the Tower, The Alternative Guide - Herbert Press in association with H.M. Tower of London

Boardman, A.W. - The Battle of Towton - Alan Sutton Publishing Ltd. (UK)

Cheetham, Anthony - The Life & Times of Richard III - General Editor - Antonia Fraser (Weidenfeld and Nicolson)

Cohn, Norman - Europe's Inner Demons: The Demonization of Christians in Medieval Christendom (Pimlico)

Dept of the Environment -Tower of London: Official Handbook - R. Allen Brown, P.E. Curnow

Dickinson, J.C. - Monastic Life in Medieval England (Adam & Charles Black, London, UK)

Dockray, Keith - Richard III: A Reader in History - (Alan Sutton Publishing, UK)

Drimmer, Frederick - The Body Snatchers: Stiffs and Other Ghoulish Delights, (Carol Publishing Group)

Radu R. Florescu & Raymond T. McNally - Dracula, Prince of Many Faces - His Life & Times (Little, Brown & Company)

Foss, Peter J. - The Field of Redemore: The Battle of Bosworth, 1485 (Rosalba Press)

Gies, Joseph & Frances - Life in a Medieval Castle / Life in a Medieval City (Harper & Row, New York)

Gillingham, John - The Wars of the Roses: Peace and Conflict in 15th Century England (Weidenfeld & Nicolson, London)

Girouard, Mark -Windsor, The Most Romantic Castle (Hodder & Stoughton)

Goodman, Anthony -The Wars of the Roses: Military Activity and English Society, 1452-97 (Routledge)

Green, V.H.H. - The Later Plantagenets (Edward Arnold Publishers, UK)

BIBLIOGRAPHY

Hallam, Elizabeth M. - The Chronicles of theWars of the Roses: Preface by Hugh Trevor-Roper (Viking Press)

Hammond, P.W. & Anne F. Sutton - Richard III: The Road to Bosworth Field (Guild Publishing, UK)

Hammond, Peter - Her Majesty's Royal Palace and Fortress of the Tower of London (Crown copyright 1987)

Hibbert, Christopher - Tower of London (Published in the UK by the Reader's Digest Assoc. Ltd., London in association with Newsweek, New York)

Hicks, Michael - Richard III, The Man Behind the Myth (Collins & Brown Ltd., 1991)

Horrox, Rosemary - Richard III, A Study in Service - Cambridge studies in medieval life and thought (4th Series) (Cambridge University Press)

Humble, Richard - English Castles (Artus Books, London)

Jacob, E.F. - The Fifeenth Century (1399-1485), Oxford University Press

Jenner, Michael - Journeys Into Medieval England (Penguin)

Kendall, Paul Murray -Richard the Third (W.W. Norton & Company)

Lamb, V.B. - The Betrayal of Richard III: An Introduction to the Controversy (Alan Sutton Publishing Ltd., UK)

Manchester, William - A World Lit Only by Fire: The Medieval Mind and the Renaissance: Portrait of an Age (Little, Brown & Company)

Mancini, Dominic - The Usurpation of Richard III - Translated/Introduction by C.A.J. Armstrong (Alan Sutton Publishing)

Myers, A.R. - England in the Late Middle Ages (Penguin)

Parnell, Geoffrey - The Tower of London (English Heritage, 1993)

Platt, Colin - Medieval England: A Social History and Archaeology from the Conquest to A.D. 1600 (Routledge)

Pollard, A.J. - Richard III and the Princes in the Tower (Alan Sutton Publishing)

Potter, Jeremy - Good King Richard? An Account of Richard III and His Reputation (Constable, London)

Richard III Society - Richard III: Crown and People. A selection of articles from the Ricardian, Journal of the Richard III Society, March 1975 to December 1981. Edited by J. Petre (Alan Sutton Publishing)

Rose, Tessa - The Coronation Ceremony of the Kings and Queens of England and the Crown Jewels, (London:HMSO Public.)

Ross, Charles -Richard III (Methuen) - The Wars of the Roses, A Concise History (Thames and Hudson)

Rowse, A.L. - Bosworth Field and the Wars of the Roses, (The History Book Club, London, 1967)

Ryder, Peter F. - Medieval Buildings of Yorkshire (Ash Grove Books)

Seward, Desmond - The Wars of the Roses: Through the Lives of Five Men and Women of the 15th Century (Penguin, 1995)

Shakespeare, William - The Complete Works of William Shakespeare (Parragon)

Turnbull, Stephen -The Book of the Medieval Knight, (Arms & Armour Press)

Ward, Jennifer C. - English Noblewomen in the Later Middle Ages (Longman)

Weir, Alison - Lancaster and York, The Wars of the Roses (Jonathan Cape, London) UK - The Princes in the Tower (Pimlico)

Williams, Neville - The Life & Times of Henry VII (General Editor - Antonia Fraser (Weidenfield and Nicholson)

Williamson, Andrey -The Mystery of the Princes: An Investigation into a Supposed Murder (Alan Sutton Publishing) UK

Williamson, David - Kings and Queens of Britain (Webb & Bower) UK